H_NGM_N

MURDER IS THE WORD

JC Gatlin

Milford House Press

Mechanicsburg, Pennsylvania

MILFORD HOUSE
an imprint of Sunbury Press, Inc.
Mechanicsburg, PA USA

For information about special discounts for bulk purchases, please contact Sunbury Press Orders Dept. at (855) 338-8359 or orders@sunburypress.com.

To request one of our authors for speaking engagements or book signings, please contact Sunbury Press Publicity Dept. at publicity@sunburypress.com.

ISBN: 978-1-62006-060-5 (Trade paperback)

Library of Congress Control Number: 2019938255

FIRST MILFORD HOUSE PRESS EDITION: April 2019

Product of the United States of America
0 1 1 2 3 5 8 13 21 34 55

Set in Bookman Old Style
Designed by Chris Fenwick
Cover by Ivan Zanchetta
Edited by Chris Fenwick

Continue the Enlightenment!

For my little brother, Mitch

Jan. 22, 1981–Dec. 17, 2012

CHAPTER ONE

_N E_RLY GR_VE

Saturday, June 23

Something—or someone—caught Brooke's eye, and she leaned over the kitchen sink. With her nose pressed to the window, she studied the woods beyond the gravel drive. The dark oaks loomed over the brambles, and a breeze rustled the branches of the trees and the bushes, but she saw no one there.

Brooke scolded herself and laughed at her overactive nerves. Obviously, she'd imagined the movement. It wasn't the first time. To be honest, she never wanted to live this far out in the Florida backwoods. It was too isolated. Too dark. Too quiet. And even more so tonight, it didn't feel safe.

She looked down at the coffeepot that'd been sitting in the sink since early that morning. Turning on the faucet, she ran a sponge under the water and then saw movement again from the corner of her eye. This time she knew she saw branches move. She turned off the tap. The running water gave way to the stillness of the kitchen, and she listened. Her eyes focused. She blinked and peered closer to the window-pane. Searched the tree line.

The branches brightened—a quick flash a few feet off the ground. What the heck was that? A flashlight? She focused on the trees. A light glowed and shined in her eyes.

Startled, she jumped back and bumped into her husband, who was suddenly standing behind her. She let out a short gasp.

Ash didn't seem to notice he startled her, or maybe he just didn't care. "You're home late."

He held an empty Jack Daniel's bottle in one hand and placed his free hand on her shoulder, moving it down to grip her upper arm. He towered over her. At six foot four, he had the body of an ex-athlete that showed surprisingly little evidence of the amount of alcohol he consumed.

She twisted her arm to break his grip. "Someone's out there." She turned and peered out the window. The woods looked dark again.

Ash shoved her aside and leaned over the sink. His breath fogged the glass. "I don't see no one."

"I saw a light—a flashlight or something."

He looked down at her. "Where you been all day?"

"You know. I was helping Winnie with the float. We lost track of time."

He chuckled as if he knew more than he was letting on. "You were there all day?"

"Of course." She almost spat the response, as if the faster she answered him the more likely he would believe her. "Like I said, we lost track of time."

"Winnie dropped by this afternoon." He removed a cell phone from his pocket and dropped it on the granite island in front of her. "She said you left it behind when you bailed on them."

Avoiding eye contact with Ash, Brooke picked up the phone and examined it. The screen was black, the battery dead. Her breath caught in her throat. How could she be so forgetful? So careless.

"Where'd you go?" He stepped closer, crowding her personal space.

She set the phone on the counter. The truth would instigate a bigger, angrier fight. Running a hand through her hair, she looked away. "I had errands to run."

"You were seeing *him* again. You were with that fake-tanned, pansy-ass principal again."

"Of course not." Sighing, she smoothed her red dress. The feel of the expensive fabric soothed her. "You're being paranoid."

"Am I?" He paused, as if giving it some thought, and stepped away from the sink. He slammed the empty bottle onto the island countertop. The glass reverberated against the hard granite and nearly fell as he walked to the fridge. He reached toward the upper cabinets and swung the doors open. He grabbed another bottle of Jack. The top popped with a quick thwap that made her cringe. She decided not to comment on it.

"I had work to finish." She faced the sink again, glanced out the window. It was the truth. Sort of. "At school."

"On a Saturday night?" Ash demanded, his words slurred.

She didn't answer. He stood behind her, and she could feel his breath on the back of her neck. She could smell the liquor. It made him sound raspier than normal.

"Kinda dressed up, huh?" he whispered in her ear. "For working on a Saturday … during summer."

She turned away. Yes, she was wearing her favorite red dress, but it was old, really. Nothing special. And it certainly didn't mean anything. "I wasn't with him."

"You're lying. Again." He paced the kitchen, raising his arms, spilling whiskey from the open bottle. Swinging around, he moved behind her. "You and him got somethin' planned, don't you? Whatever it is, you ain't takin' my daughter."

Not this again. She put her hands on the countertop and squeezed her eyes shut. "Ash, you always get like this when you've been drinking. Your imagination is—"

"Darla is my little girl. She's my daughter."

"I'm done."

She pushed past him, out of the kitchen. He followed her into the dining room.

"You're not taking her."

"Ash, please." She forced her voice to remain calm. If she got emotional, the argument would spiral out of control. Again. So, she inhaled before continuing. "I should've never told you. I knew it was a bad idea. I knew you wouldn't be able to handle it, but I didn't have a choice."

"You had a choice." He grabbed her arm, jerking her and sloshing more whiskey from the bottle. She turned to face him. He leaned down to meet her eye to eye. "You chose him over me."

"That's not what happened." She took the bottle from his hand. "I can't talk to you when you get like this."

"Don't turn this around on me." He grabbed the bottle and threw it at the wall. The glass shattered.

Brooke jumped at the sound, and it brought a heavy silence to the room.

"You an' that pretty boy," he said, his voice growing louder, "ain't takin' my daughter."

Brooke stared at the wall. Wet streaks ran down to the glass shards at the baseboard. She couldn't take her eyes off it. He stepped closer to her, opened his mouth as if to say something more, and waved an arm at her. He stumbled out of the dining room. She watched him a moment and considered leaving him alone. She could retreat to the kitchen. Avoid him. Let him sleep it off.

Then she thought of Darla—he was going after their daughter.

"Ash? Ash! What are you doing?" She followed him to the front entry and grabbed his arm to prevent him from heading up the staircase.

He yanked his arm free. "You ain't takin' Darla."

"Ash, stop it. This is all in your head."

"Get outta my way." A quick shove with his right hand to her upper chest pushed her downward.

With a loud crack, her right shoulder hit the narrow table beside the front door, knocking over the family photos and sending a vase of white lilies crashing to the tile floor. Glass shattered, spilling water and the large trumpet flowers across the floor. Brooke felt her dress fabric give and then rip along the seam. She got up onto her knees and thrust herself forward on shards of the shattered vase, to the bottom step of the staircase. She scrambled up after him, reached for his left leg, grabbed the bottom of his jeans. She pulled. He fell facedown, hitting the steps. She held tight to his leg. He mashed his boot heel into her face.

She grunted but held tight. She gripped his leg with both hands, struggled to pull him down as he inched upwards. He shook his leg. She let go and fell backward. He scrambled up another step. She regained her balance and launched after him. She grasped his foot. Tugged. Pulled his leg as hard as she could. Her right hand slipped. His foot sprang out of the boot, knocking them both off kilter. Gravity took over and they tumbled together to the floor.

Brooke wiped blood from her lip and stood up, now towering over him. "Just leave. Leave, if that's what you want, but you're not taking our daughter. She won't go with you."

"Why?" He got to his feet. He reached for her, wrapped his fists around both her arms and shook her. "Did you tell her? Did you?"

"No," she screamed, sobbing.

He released her.

She looked away. "No, I didn't say a word."

"You turn'n her against me?"

"No." She faced him, looked into his eyes. She clenched her jaw, swallowed her tears. "We're a family. You're my husband. Darla is our daughter. None of that has changed."

"We ain't a family." He raised an arm, causing her to flinch, but he pointed at her instead. "You broke this family."

"We can move past this." Her voice was a whisper, audible over her sobs. But she knew he heard.

"Can we?" he said, spitting a drop of blood as he spoke.

"Yes. I love you. You love me. Right?" She moved closer to him, waiting for an answer. "Right?"

"I don't know." He wiped his mouth with the back of his left hand but wouldn't look at her. "I don't know anymore."

She tried to process what he'd said. The words made her tremble.

"I don't know," he repeated.

After several moments of silence, he removed his wedding ring and flung it at her. It bounced off her chest and landed on the floor with a dull clink. His head turned, his eyes seemingly focused on the small gold band, and slowly, he looked back at her. Without another word, he brushed past her and opened the front door. It slammed shut behind him, followed by the sharp squeak and bang of the screen door.

She dropped to her knees, listening. His angry footsteps crunched the gravel in the drive. The truck door slammed. The engine started, followed by spinning tires and upended gravel. He sped away.

When all was quiet again—and dark—she looked up. Her little girl was watching her from the upstairs landing. Her face peeked out between the spindles of the staircase.

"Everything's okay, baby." Brooke got up and returned to the dining room. She didn't want Darla to see her cry. "I'll be up in a minute to tuck you in."

"But Mommy—"

"Bed. Now." She yelled louder than intended and caught herself. She took a quick breath. "I'll be up there in a couple minutes."

Standing in the dining room, she looked down at the front of her dress and studied the split seam running along her thigh. Maybe she could sew it, she thought as she noticed the broken glass on the floor. Picking up a couple of the larger pieces, she watched the drying amber streaks of whiskey run down the dining room wall and pool along the baseboard. She left the puddle and went into the kitchen. When she placed the glass in the sink, a nauseated churning in the pit of her stomach chilled her and the hairs on the back of her neck stood on end.

She became keenly aware of the silence. Like before. Turning her head, she listened, and glanced out the window over the sink.

Two eyes stared back at her.

Large and white, they widened, staring into the kitchen. They moved ever so slightly as if to get a better view. She could see no other features of the face, just the eyes. They blinked.

Brooke exhaled and stumbled backward, almost falling. She looked away. Her hands gripped the edge of the granite countertop and she steadied herself. She looked back at the window. Darkness.

Running to the entry hall, she locked the deadbolt on the front door. Her other hand flipped off the porch light. She leaned across the table and peeked out the front window. A moth fluttered in the upper corner of the porch. Wind scattered dead leaves across the weathered planks of the porch. The old swing swayed back and forth, its chain squeaking. Beyond it was blackness. It lay heavy over the drive, and the woods, and everything hiding within it.

She held her breath and concentrated. Her eyes squinted to find a body moving in the darkness. Some shape. Something. Anything to confirm that she had in fact seen someone out there. It couldn't just be her nerves. Not this time.

She let out a breath as a face popped up in the window. Their eyes locked, inches apart, separated by a single, thin pane of glass.

Her mind scrambled to process what she was seeing. A figure. Was it male? Female? Was it wearing a ski mask? She could see nothing but the eyes. They stared back at her. Studied her. She screamed. The eyes widened as if startled and vanished from the window.

Brooke looked to the front door. The screen door outside squeaked as it opened. The doorknob turned, twisted back and forth. It stopped, only to be followed by a knock.

At first, it sounded faint, almost polite, then intensified. Pound! Pound! Pound! Something outside wanted in.

She ran to the kitchen. Her cell phone lay on the island countertop. It wouldn't turn on. There was a landline phone hanging on the wall. She grabbed the receiver. The black coiled cord wrapped around her arm. The dial tone blared over the pounding on the front door. She stretched her neck to look behind her, into the entry hall, and a sideways glance out the window. The pounding on the front door grew louder. Turning back to the phone, she mashed the buttons. An operator came on the line.

"911. What's your emergency?"

"There's someone outside my house." Her voice wheezed. She could barely speak. She hyperventilated. "They—they're trying to break in."

The knocking stopped. The screen door slammed shut against the frame. The house turned quiet again. The operator on the phone asked another question, but Brooke wasn't listening. She stared out the kitchen window over the sink. A shadow moved across the porch. Something rustled along the side of the house ... a faint scuffle that started at the foundation and rattled up the wall.

She scanned the kitchen, listening. A paralyzing fear rippled through her body. Above her, the disturbing knocks turned to blunt footfalls along the upper edge of the ceiling. Someone was walking on the roof over the porch. The footsteps stopped as quickly as they began, replaced by an unnatural silence.

The operator on the phone spoke again.

Brooke dropped the handset, shrieking, "Darla!"

She ran out of the kitchen and stumbled back into the front entry. Taking the steps two at a time, she screamed for her daughter and scrambled onto the upper landing. She burst into Darla's room. Flipped on the light.

"Darla?"

The room was quiet, the window open. The bed empty.

The wooden rocking horse sat in a corner, with the purple plush elephant sitting atop it.

"Darla?" Brooke moved to the closet and flung open the bifold doors. No. She turned to the bed, dropped to her hands and knees, and looked under it. No. She sat up. The wind whistled through the open window, disturbing the curtains. She rushed to it and looked outside.

The bedroom overlooked the front porch, and she squinted, focused, tried to see her daughter in the yard. Brooke's eyes searched the yard and then the woods.

On the horizon, the silhouette of the water tower overshadowed the trees. Below it, the abandoned orange grove spread out like dead shrubbery. Wind weaved through the brittle branches. Even from the upper bedroom window, she could hear the ghostly whine.

She scrutinized the gravel drive beyond the front porch roof. Her minivan was barely visible, covered by the solid shadow of their old farmhouse. Ash's black truck was gone.

"Darla!" She leaned out of the window as far as she dared. Her voice echoed through the woods. It reverberated and then disintegrated into silence. Brooke pulled back into the bedroom, when a flash of light caught her eye.

Coming through the dead branches in the grove, it rippled like a strobe light. Like a flashlight. Bright, then dark, then bright again, moving toward the old water tower.

Brooke screamed for her daughter.

She pulled her head from the window and left Darla's room. Racing down the staircase, she slammed into the front door. Unlocked it. Swung it open. Burst onto the front porch.

"Darla!" Her voice rang out as she stumbled into the yard, to the edge of the driveway. No one was there. She looked back at the house, up at Darla's open window. The curtains moved. She turned her head. Branches snapped in the grove. Something, someone was running through the trees.

Brooke hollered, "Stop!"

Only the wind shrieked back.

"Darlaaaaaaa!" Brooke let loose till her throat burned. She ran into the dead grove. She plowed through the dry branches. Moss dangling like spider webs brushed her face and caught in her hair.

She pushed on. A few minutes later she felt winded and her calves burned, but she continued forward. The branches scratched her. Cut her. Slowed her down. The seam in her dress ripped higher, freeing her legs with a rush of cool air. She paused to catch her breath. Gulped air and called out for her daughter. A faint echo returned, but nothing else.

The water tower eclipsed part of the horizon. From the top of the structure, a line of light crossed the black sky. It waved and wagged as if someone was signaling to her. She didn't have time to think about it. She picked up speed, willing her legs to move faster. Pushing her way through the brittle branches and leaves, she came out the other side of the thicket.

Now the tower dominated the sky. Brooke raised her head to look at the rotting structure and yelled again. She heard a thud. ... Followed by another. Sounds of movement came from within the rusted drum. Something hid inside it. Darla.

Brooke called out to her as she paced around the rusted steel legs. Coming to the back, she looked at a graying wooden ladder rising high above her. She listened to the tinny bangs in the structure. Thud! Thud-thud-thud! Someone was stomping, trying to get her attention.

Inhaling deeply to calm her nerves, she gripped a rung and lifted herself up, thankful for the mobility her split dress provided. Each step took her higher. Flecks of paint splintered and showered like glitter beneath her feet. The wood felt soft and she prayed it would support her weight. Continuing upwards a good hundred feet, she willed herself not to look down. She climbed another fifty.

Reaching the top, she maneuvered off the ladder and onto the narrow, curved platform wrapping around the rusted drum. She touched the rough, orangey metal railing and inched around the ledge. She came to the spot where Ash had spray-painted her name so many years ago. The letters were fuzzy and faded. She paused next to the *B* and listened. More rustling. Another bang.

"Darla?" Brooke's fingers grazed the rounded wall as she stepped, looking for a way inside. Coming to a jagged rip in the shell barely large enough for her to squeeze through, she squatted and poked her head inside. She wished she had a flashlight.

"Darla?" she called out weakly, trying to see. She could sense movement in the blackness. Something solid slithered through the beams of moonlight shining down from rusted holes in the tin roof, making the white light quiver.

She held her breath and squeezed her right leg through the small opening, and then the rest of her body until she was crouched inside the dark drum. She called for her daughter as she stood. She stepped deeper into the hollow, her feet squishing on the muddy floor.

Another rustle of movement and a flash made her pause. "Darla?"

Completely still, she looked around. Particles floated in the moonbeams, disturbed by her movement through the shallow muck. Between the lines of light was utter blackness, so thick it could've been a wall. She inched forward, froze.

Eyes were staring at her from across the circular space. They blinked. Startled, Brooke fell backward but caught herself. And found she couldn't move.

Frozen with fear, she watched the eyes rise. Someone was standing, moving, cutting through the slivers of moonlight. Water squished with every footstep that brought the black mass closer to her.

"You ...." She saw clearly now as her eyes adjusted to the dark. "What are you doing?"

Her voice caught in her throat as the figure's arm shot forward, jabbing something into her neck. A pinprick. Sharp. Painless. Instant.

Brooke stood, stunned. For a moment, the only sound was her muffled breathing behind the stifling hand pressed over her lips. She wiggled, trying to free herself, but was held fast. She tried to speak, but the hand pressed harder, the thumb jamming against her nostrils, cutting off air. She knew she should be panicked. But she didn't feel anything. She could hear her own sluggish heartbeat in her ears as her pulse slowed as if it was a clock winding down, tick by tick. Her eyes felt heavy, her breathing labored.

She thought of her daughter and wanted to call out, but she could no longer feel her body. She was floating. Ash's smiling face—a memory from long ago, from when they were teenagers—was the last image to run through her mind before absolute darkness engulfed her.

CHAPTER TWO

NEW_ TRAVEL_ FA_T

Thursday, June 28

Tori Younger held her phone near her face, using the selfie mode as a mirror. She touched her hair, forcing a stray strand behind her ear, and ran a finger over her left eyebrow. Between the wind and the humidity, she would look terrible on the air. But what could she do?

The phone buzzed in her hand, startling her. The name "ASH MARTIN" flashed on the screen and, with it, a flood of memories rushed through her head. Ash. Brooke. The old gang. Home.

She hadn't spoken to him—or Brooke, or anyone back in Elroy Springs—in how long? It'd been a while.

The phone buzzed again as her cameraman waved. She didn't have time to catch up now. She swiped Ash's name with her thumb, ignoring the call, and dropped the phone in her purse.

The wind blew her bangs into her eyes again, and she whisked them back with one hand while gripping the microphone in the other. Wearing a white blazer, skirt, and uncomfortable high heels, she positioned herself in front of the camera. Viewers would have a clear shot of the Buckhorn High School entrance behind her and its red brick arch. Surrounding it were crimson and gold marigolds that looked desperately thirsty. For a late June morning, the air already felt hot and muggy as the strong breeze swirled around her.

She smoothed her skirt. "If it gets any windier, we'll have to do this take inside the building."

RJ stood across from her on the grass, close to the curb. He balanced there, holding his camera steady. He raised a hand, motioning to her. "Let's take it."

When she set her purse on the ground, she felt the cell phone inside vibrate with the voicemail alert. She wondered what Ash wanted. If it was bad news, Brooke would've called. Or maybe Ash was calling about Brooke.

She reflected with some bitterness and pushed the thoughts to the back of her mind. No time to dwell on that now. Focusing, she glanced at the three teenagers waiting on the sidewalk in front of her. Two boys and a girl wore sandals, shorts, and T-shirts bearing the school logo.

She looked back at RJ. Tall and lean, with a shaggy mop of brown hair and a solid three-day stubble across his jaw-line, he was only four or five years older than the high school kids. Dressed in baggy cargo shorts and a green T-shirt with a faded yellow smiley face emblazoned across his chest, he could've passed as a student himself. RJ smiled and held three fingers in the air. He counted down.

She cleared her throat and gulped a breath. When RJ signaled, she released it and launched into her perky, serious, on-camera voice.

"As visitors walk into the student exhibition at the Buckhorn High School's Summer Academy, they're greeted by Bolt Jr." She held the mic in her right hand and motioned with her left. "Bolt, decked out in full Buckhorn High regalia, is handsome, polite, and ...." She stepped aside, revealing Bolt Jr., a silver-and-gray metallic robot with frozen facial features. It cocked its head to one side, raised a stiff arm, and then spoke. "Hello. Welcome to Buckhorn High School."

Bolt looked like he'd stepped right out of a *Star Wars* movie.

"Why ... hello, Bolt." Tori chuckled and turned back to face the camera. "He's a robot made by three local high school students participating in a summer science program."

She motioned to the three teenagers. They smiled and waved at the camera. Tori inched toward them.

"Tell me, April. Where did you get the inspiration to build Bolt?" Tori held the microphone a few inches from the teenage girl's face.

Wearing a purple beret that allowed a river of long black hair to cascade down her shoulders, April leaned in and spoke into the mic. "I don't really know because, you know, it was kinda inspired by a lot of things." April talked with rapid-fire energy. "Obviously it's computer science because we built a robot and fed it commands. It's physics because we made him move, using actuators and electronics. It's engineering. It's art. It's many types of science in one project."

A lanky boy with glasses and a bad complexion nudged April out of the way and faced the camera. "We put our whole heart into this. At first, we thought it would be impossible, but we worked together as a team and made it happen."

"Thank you, Bobby." Tori turned back to the camera as the wind picked up. "Bobby, Craig, and April are just three of the thirty-six students attending a five-week summer enrichment program that includes a veteran science teacher and mentors from the University of South Florida."

The wind howled, nearly whipping the mic from her hand. April's purple beret lifted into the air, whirled, and blew into the street.

Tori yelled "Cut!" as Bobby darted off the curb.

"I got it." He flailed his arms, chasing the hat.

Tori watched him reaching for the hat. Grasping it. Not paying attention to anything else. She yelled a second too late.

Bobby ran into the path of an oncoming SUV.

The impact came with a violent punch. She watched in horror as Bobby bounced, as if in slow motion, off the black hood. He cartwheeled into the air. His arms and legs twirled like an acrobat, his head flung back. He landed on the pavement, face up.

Tori threw down the mic. She scrambled to the curb.

Behind her, RJ dropped his camera. She was vaguely aware of him and the other two teens as she bolted into the street.

The SUV halted. Tires smoked. The engine revved. The windows were tinted black. Tori couldn't see the driver and approached the car. It lunged forward, nearly hitting her. She stepped back as it rushed past and sped away.

RJ screamed something—she wasn't sure what—and he ran after the black SUV. She watched him disappear down the street and then turned to Bobby.

The boy lay still on the asphalt in the bus lane. She knelt beside him and placed two fingers on his neck. He stirred, groaned.

"Don't move," she said in a low, calm voice, unsure if he even heard her. April and Craig hovered over them, and Tori looked up. She covered her brow with a hand to shield her eyes from the bright morning sun. She looked at April. "Call 911."

April brought her hand to her mouth and turned away. Craig took out his phone. Students from every direction ran into the street. Cars honked. Others maneuvered around them.

"Call 911." Tori gestured to Craig as he aimed his cell phone.

Was he snapping a picture? Taking video?

A crowd gathered behind him. He stood there holding up his phone, pointing it at his friend lying by the curb. She called to him again, but he didn't respond.

Louder and in a firmer tone, she said, "Craig."

He finally looked at her.

She motioned to the phone in his hand. "Call 911."

Craig looked confused but turned his phone around. He dialed for help, and Tori turned back to Bobby. Blood oozed from his head and across his face. His right arm contorted away from his body in a disturbing position. She slipped off her blazer and placed it over Bobby's upper body like a blanket.

He groaned, coughed, and muttered incoherently.

"Your arm is broken," she said. "Try not to move."

His face scrunched with pain. He murmured a couple of words and stirred.

She thought he might try to sit up. She placed a hand on his chest. "Don't move." She raised her voice. "Bobby, can you hear me? Stay still. You've been hit by a car."

"We need to get him out of the street." April knelt beside them, her eyes wide, her mouth open. "We can't leave him here. We need to get him out of the street."

Bobby cried out. His torso wriggled under the jacket.

"No, we can't move him." Tori pushed the teenage girl back and then stood. She looked at the crowd of students, drivers, and teachers surrounding them. "Everybody, please back up and give him some room." She looked at April. "Find a blanket or something we can cover him with."

April inhaled and exhaled repeatedly as if she was on the verge of hyperventilating. She hovered over Bobby and cried in his face. "Oh my God, we've got to do something. He's going to die."

Tori grabbed April's arm and pulled her to her feet. "Bobby needs you to stay calm. He needs your help. Go find a blanket, okay? Can you do that for him?"

April nodded. She gulped another deep breath and made her way through the crowd. Craig rushed past her, running toward Tori.

He came up beside her. "The ambulance is on its way." He turned his head toward Bobby and froze. "Is he—is he going to be okay?"

"He'll be fine." Tori forced a smile. "Now, why don't you ask around to see if anyone recognized that car?"

Craig shook his head. "But what if—"

"There's nothing you can do." She squeezed his shoulder as she spoke. "But we need to track down that car. Ask the students and parents. Can you do that for me?"

Craig nodded, looked at his friend again, and turned to the crowd. He asked a couple of students if they knew anything. They shook their heads. He turned to a woman. Tori watched him a moment. She looked back at Bobby.

He mumbled through a gurgling in his throat. She couldn't understand what he was saying. Blood spatters dotted the white blazer covering his torso.

Moving to his other side, Tori sat on the grass and took his left hand in hers. She gently squeezed it. Bobby's face relaxed. He muttered something else under his breath. She thought he said "Mom."

"Hold on, Bobby," she whispered. "Help is on the way."

RJ returned, wheezing. She looked up at him. Their eyes locked, communicating without words. He bent at the waist, placing his hands on his knees. He gulped a lungful of air.

April returned and stood next to him. "This is all I could find."

She handed a small blanket to Tori. The powder-blue material, with dried spit crusted in the center, looked like a baby's blankie. Tori nodded, and April set the blanket near Bobby's feet.

"Speed racer got away," RJ said, wheezing. "I tr—I tried to get the plate numbers."

Tori turned her face toward the echo of screaming sirens. Two police cars approached, followed by an ambulance. The crowd parted, allowing the vehicles through. When the ambulance stopped, two EMTs jumped out of the cab and strode over to the victim.

"He got hit by a car," Tori said to them. She still held Bobby's hand.

"How long ago?" The tall man with dark hair, dressed in a short-sleeved white shirt, dark pants, and latex gloves, knelt beside her.

"Ten minutes, maybe." Tori remained focused on Bobby and squeezed his hand. "He's been slipping in and out of consciousness."

"What's his name?"

April said, "Bobby Greene." She sat and looked down at her friend, and then up at the EMT.

"Age?" The EMT removed the bloody white blazer and placed a stethoscope on Bobby's chest.

"Sixteen. He'll be seventeen in a couple a' months. Late August, I think." April rocked as she spoke, her arms wrapped around her knees. "Is he gonna be okay?"

The man ignored her and asked questions as he checked Bobby's vitals.

Tori listened to April answer the medic and turned her head to find RJ. He stood a few feet away, holding his camera, filming the EMTs. She watched him for several seconds before a persistent humming caught her attention. Her purse vibrated on the ground near the curb, and she found her buzzing phone inside it.

The name "ASH MARTIN" flashed across the screen.

She looked back at Bobby and the medics. The two men tended to the boy as another man wheeled a stretcher from the back of the ambulance. A few feet away, a police officer pushed RJ and his camera away from the action. She glanced at her phone again.

Now she knew it was bad news. But there wasn't time to deal with it. Whatever it was, it had to wait--maybe call him back later or talk to Brooke. Swiping Ash's name away with her thumb, she dropped the phone into her purse and focused on the chaos in the street.

The medics lifted the stretcher and carried Bobby into the ambulance. Amid the crowd standing near the ambulance, RJ filmed the scene. A police officer pushed him out of the street, back toward the curb.

Tori called out to him, "Let's get to the hospital."

He lowered his camera. "No can do. Pittman wants us back at the mother ship."

"What?" Tori watched the ambulance leave, sirens screaming. She had to yell. "We can go *live* at the hospital."

He pressed through the onlookers, approaching her. "It's a no-go." He held his camera facing the ground and stood beside her. "Pittman called us back. He's pissed."

"Why?" She shook her head. "We're on the story."

"Guess not." He shrugged and shook his head. "He's putting Simone Adams on it and wants our asses back at the station, pronto."

Now what? Could this day get any worse? She picked up her purse just as her cell phone dinged with Ash's second message.

CHAPTER THREE

IF IT BL_ _DS, IT L_ADS

Without so much as a knock, Tori swung open the glass door to news director Pittman's office on the eighth floor of the SEBC-TV News building. Pittman sat at his desk, the black phone receiver to his ear, and looked up. She marched straight to him and dropped a manila file folder onto the clutter of papers and folders.

His thick brows drew together in an agonized expression and he slammed down the phone. He opened his mouth. She cut him off.

"I know what you're gonna say." She leaned forward across his desk. "But you had no right to put Simone Adams on the story. I was already there."

"You know what I'm gonna say?" Pittman's voice rose in a falsetto, spraying her with tiny droplets of spittle.

She pulled away.

His eyes narrowed and his forehead rippled with deep crevices. He thumped his fingers on the desk. "You know what I'm gonna say about a reporter and a photographer on location at a hit-and-run and I get virtually no footage? You know what I'm gonna say about a reporter who should've gone live with a breaking story but—"

"That boy needed my help."

He huffed and moved back in his chair. Behind him, a large window looked out over downtown skyscrapers reflecting sunlight and the hustle of traffic running along Kennedy Boulevard far below. "You and RJ were right there. We should be airing footage of that kid bouncing off the hood of the car. At the very least, we should have exclusive footage of you tending to the kid as he lay in the street. Hell, you should've been interviewing the paramedics in the back of the ambulance."

"That kid needed my help, not my commentary." She looked down at the specks of blood on her skirt. She'd left her blazer in the street, in front of the school. Pittman's angry voice snapped her back to attention.

"I've got noth'n but nerdy high school geeks talking about robot physics and mechanics—nothing we can air." He waved at the monitors on the wall. "And a hit-and-run happens right in front of you, killing a high school kid, and we get no film. Nada. Zip."

"Bobby wasn't killed." She cleared her throat, straightening her back. She glanced at the monitors across the room. Each was broadcasting a different program, but all were soundless. Most had commercials running, except for one playing the footage of her interviewing Bolt Jr. and the teenagers in front of Buckhorn High School. Another was set to Simone Adams interviewing Bobby's family at the hospital.

She turned back to the news director. "We could've gone to the hospital. You shouldn't have pulled us."

"You blew your chance when I got no hit-and-run footage." He pointed at the televisions. The image of Tori yelling to Bobby as the camera fell and hit the ground scrambled across the screen. Pittman raised an arm, pointing a remote control. The TV went dark. "I can't sit through it again," he said.

"Just give us another chance. We'll head over to the hospital and interview—"

"I'm assigning you to a new story." He raised a hand, silencing her. "There's a new Chick-fil-A opening in South Tampa tomorrow."

"Chick-fil-A? I'm not covering another restaurant opening. That's the third one this year."

"Our morning viewership loves it. Besides, they're a sponsor."

To override him, Tori spoke louder. "The trial for that teacher who hired a student to murder her husband is coming up. Let me cover that."

"It's already being covered."

"Then let me do a follow-up on the body that washed ashore on Apollo Beach."

"You're covering the Chick-fil-A opening." Pittman crossed his arms.

She laughed to hide her annoyance. "It's not news."

"You want news? Get me another hit-and-run, but this time on film." He paused and looked around the office. "Where is your cameraman, anyway?"

"RJ's unloading his equipment," she said. "He didn't want to be here for this."

* * * *

Even in tennis shoes, RJ's footsteps echoed against the concrete walls of the dark parking garage for the SEBC-TV building. Red-and-white news vans, each plastered with a glittery yellow lightning bolt—the "dynamic logo" of SEBC-TV News—lined the parking spaces and surrounded a dirty blue Camry. He popped the trunk and grabbed the strap of his camera bag. Lifting the bag over his shoulder, he picked up an equipment case and lights, and carried them to his Jeep parked three slots over. He'd owned the vehicle, a 1979 CJ-5 with large tires and a faded red paint job, since he was fifteen years old.

As he placed the bags in the backseat, he noticed two teenagers emerge from the stairwell.

"Hey, camera guy!" The boy's voice rung out, reverberating off the walls, and RJ froze. The teenager waved. "You're the camera guy, right?"

"Oh. Craig, April." RJ stood beside the Jeep's rear bumper, facing them as they approached. He set the equipment case on the pavement. "How'd you get in here?"

"We slipped past the security guard," April said, leaning an arm against the news van parked next to his Jeep. She thumped her fingers against the back door. "And followed a pizza delivery guy to the stairs."

"Classic." RJ smiled, shaking his head as he lifted the equipment case into the backseat of his Jeep. "How's Bobby?"

Craig's face clouded with uneasiness. "They won't let us see him."

"Just family." April's eyes looked watery and she dabbed her cheeks with a tissue.

"And Simone Adams," Craig added, "she's at the hospital now."

"I heard. But I'm sure your friend will be okay." RJ turned his attention to strapping down the camera bag in the seat.

Craig reached for RJ's arm. "We need to talk to her." He tightened his grip. "Can you do that for us, camera guy? Can you put us in touch with that reporter lady?"

RJ placed a hand to his chest, tapping the yellow smiley face emblazoned on his t-shirt. "Call me RJ."

"It's urgent that we see her." Panic rose in April's voice. She looked at Craig and back at RJ. "I think she's the only one who can help us."

"You want me to put you in touch with Simone Adams?" The idea made him chuckle. Tori would love that. He grinned at the kids—then noticed the distress in their eyes. They weren't kidding. He placed a hand on April's shoulder. "You're serious. What's going on?"

April reached for RJ's hand. Her bottom lip trembled. "I don't think his accident was an accident."

"Come again?" His left eyebrow rose a fraction.

She looked up, her face pale. "I mean, what if he knew something?" she asked. "What if he saw something he shouldn't have seen, and they hit him—on purpose?"

"On purpose? You punk'n me?" RJ removed his hand from April's shoulder and took a step back. He watched April tremble, and glanced at Craig. The boy was staring at her. RJ squinted, studying them. "You are, aren't you? You're punk'n me."

"No. I don't know." April threw her hands in the air. "This whole thing is crazy, you know? That's why we want to talk to her."

"Okay." RJ looked at his camera equipment in the backseat. This was insane. He himself saw Bobby Greene run into the street. It was an accident. The kids couldn't be serious. But what if they were? Maybe there was something here. He turned back to them. "Of course, we'll help you. Have you talked to the police?"

"Sure," Craig said, "but they looked at us the same way you're looking at us."

"We didn't know who else to turn to," April said.

RJ gave them a reassuring smile. "You did the right thing."

"Thank you." A tentative smile curved her mouth. "So, you'll contact her for us?"

"You'll put us in touch with Simone Adams?" Craig's louder voice echoed through the parking garage.

"Let's just say you came to the right team." RJ maneuvered between them and stretched his arms across their shoulders. He lumbered forward, leading them away from the line of white vans and toward the stairwell on the other side of the garage.

"Let's start at the beginning," he said. "And please, tell me everything."

* * * *

Tori slammed Pittman's office door behind her and marched toward the elevators, fuming. She mashed the orange Up button on the wall panel, and exhaled, wanting to scream. She pressed the button again. Her phone buzzed, and she moved her finger. The phone buzzed again.

"Okay, okay. Keep your pants on." She fished the vibrating phone from her purse. The name "ASH MARTIN" flashed across the screen.

The elevator doors opened, and several people stepped off the carriage. They brushed past as she held her phone. It buzzed again. Whatever it was, whatever Ash wanted, she was in no mood to deal with it. While preventing the elevator doors from closing, she answered the call anyway.

Ash's deep voice blared in her ear: "I didn't think you'd pick up." She turned down the volume.

"Ash? It's good to hear from you." She stepped into the empty elevator. "How's everyone back—"

"Tori, something happened." He let out a long breath.

He sounded nervous.

"I gotta tell you something," he said.

"What is it? What's wrong?" She knew it: bad news. The elevator doors closed. She pressed the *11* button. It brightened and the elevator rumbled upwards.

"It's Brooke ..." His voice cracked.

Was he crying?

He slurred his words as he spoke. "Brooke died on Saturday night."

"What?" Tori thought she misheard him. "What's going on with Br—"

"She passed away," he said.

She gulped a breath and planted her free hand on the wall above the railing. The elevator carriage seemed to spin. She squeezed her eyes shut. The accident. The blood on her skirt, her arms, her fingers. Pittman's angry tirade. Now, Ash's call about Brooke. No, she misunderstood. It had to be a bad connection. "She what?"

"I'm sorry ...." Ash's voice trembled, and he cleared his throat. "It looks like she took her own life."

"Suicide?" She couldn't believe what she was hearing. Brooke committed suicide? How was that even possible? She'd known Brooke since they were eight years old. They grew up together. Went to school together. We're practically sisters. Tori had been the maid of honor at Brooke's wedding. And now he was telling her Brooke committed suicide? That made no sense. It wasn't possible. The elevator dinged as the carriage came to a stop. The doors opened. Two men in the hall looked at her. She focused on her phone.

It sounded like Ash cleared his throat as if he was trying to get his voice back. "She took her life. I hate being the one to tell you this."

"No... I-I don't believe it." She brought her free hand to her cheek, brushed her fingers through her hair, pulled it back from her face.

The men entered the elevator, staring at her. One of them punched a button. The doors shut. She missed her floor but didn't care. She could only think of Brooke—and her daughter. "How's your little girl?" Tori could barely get the words out. "Is she okay?"

"Darla's not doing so well. She won't eat. She's not sleeping. She won't speak."

"It's shock," Tori said slowly, digesting the words. She shook her head and forced an awkward laugh. "I don't know what to say. Oh my God, Ash. I can't believe this."

She'd talked to Brooke only a couple of weeks ago. Or was it a couple of months? She always got so busy and was horrible at returning phone calls. They didn't see each other or talk as often, since Tori left Elroy Springs and moved to Tampa. Brooke and Ash had visited her a few times and they brought Darla. But Tori never returned home to visit them. Once she left, she never looked back.

"How could this have happened?" she asked. "Brooke called me, but I didn't call her back. I just thought—"

"Brooke knew that. You were her best friend."

"That's what I'm saying. We were best friends. She was my best friend since—"

"Tori, it's okay. Really, it is. Brooke understood."

"I should've called her back right then. I should've come to see you guys—at least once. I should've come home, but I couldn't—didn't, you know—"

"I know." The line went silent. He drew a breath that whistled through the phone's speaker. "The funeral is on Friday."

"This Friday?"

"In three days." He paused again. Static rippled through the speaker. "I wanted you to know, in case you want to come back home for it."

"I want to be there. I need to be there. It's just—"

"What?"

She didn't answer. The elevator stopped and the doors opened. The two men stepped out of the carriage, into the lobby. More people stepped in. The doors moved, and she waved her hand between them to keep them from closing. As they pulled back into the wall, she rushed off the elevator.

The lobby was crowded, noisy. She looked for someplace quiet, private. The stairwell.

"It's what, Tori?" Ash sounded even more emotional than before. "You were Brooke's closest friend. She still talked about you, even after everything that happened. None of that mattered to her."

"It's just that—" She entered the stairwell and let the heavy door shut behind her. She sat on the first step. Inhaled, before blurting it out. "I can't go back."

"You gotta let it go. Please."

"I don't think—"

"We're all going to be there."

The thought of them *all* being there chilled her. That was the problem. Didn't he understand? She didn't want to face everyone. How could she? She rubbed her temples with her free hand, clearing away the soupy haze. She needed to process this. "I want to. I really do."

"Good. Then, I'll see you at the funeral?" He'd gained control, sort of. His voice still trembled. "You're coming home—"

"Let me think about it for a minute. Okay?"

"It's time to come back," he said. "Brooke would've wanted that."

"I know." She paused when the door opened.

A pizza delivery boy, wearing faded jeans and a sloppy "Pepperoni Does It Better" T-shirt, entered the stairwell. He stared at her a second and then maneuvered past her, up the stairs.

She turned her back to him and cupped a hand over her chin as she spoke into her phone. "Give me some time and I'll call you back ...." She let her voice trail off and ended the call.

How would she find the strength to go home again? Even for Brooke's funeral?

CHAPTER FOUR

_HE _RU_H IS OU_ _HERE

Tori brooded in her office with the blinds drawn. After the accident at the high school and her meeting with Pittman—and the phone call from Ash—she needed to be alone. Sitting at her desk in front of the monitor, she tried to focus. It was pointless, though. Her mind kept drifting back to childhood summer days. Days in Elroy Springs. Crushed dreams and humiliation. There was no way she could go back.

Instead, she ordered flowers to be sent to Ash's residence. She opened Facebook and found Brooke's profile. There were dozens of memorial messages and photos posted on Brooke's wall.

"We'll miss you!"

"You were loved!"

"You were the best teacher ever!"

There had to be a hundred messages from Brooke's students and fellow faculty. Many had uploaded pictures, such as Brooke wearing the school colors at a homecoming game, of her pushing her daughter on a swing set, and a family portrait of mother, father, and daughter.

One photo caught Tori's attention. She clicked to enlarge three girls on vacation at the beach. In the center was Brooke, as a beaming twelve-year-old, standing in the surf on Ormond Beach. Brooke always stood at the center of attention, with her ready smile, a head of unruly blonde-brown hair, and a curvy, athletic frame that had matured earlier than the other girls at school. She grew up so fast, Tori thought. Perhaps too fast.

Tori stood on Brooke's right. At twelve years old, she looked awkwardly tall, with a flat chest, braces, thick glasses, and auburn hair bundled up in a blue baseball cap.

On Brooke's left was the other member of their teenage trio, Winnie Bennett.

All freckled-faced, with white-blonde hair, Winnie held a Nestle Crunch ice cream bar in her right hand like she was showing off a trophy. She looked overdressed for a day at the beach. Where Brooke and Tori wore bikinis, showing off and enjoying the warm Florida sunshine, Winnie wore a baggy, gray T-shirt. She glared at Brooke, and anyone could read her jealous, judgmental expression. Tori laughed as she studied the old photograph.

The three of them held seashells for the camera. They looked so young and innocent. Could life ever be that happy again?

She flipped to another photo. This one posted by a student, it couldn't have been more than a year or two old. It was of Brooke, sitting beside Ash, on the bleachers. They could've been watching a track meet or a Friday night football game. Either way, they were having a good time. Her elbow rested on one knee, her chin in her palm, a wistful, reflective expression on her face. It was such an ordinary, average moment in her life. She looked so happy and content.

In fact, Brooke looked happy and content in every photo. No shadow of doubt. No dark countenance, curl of the lip, or hollowness in the eye that would betray inner turmoil or desperate sadness. Nothing to indicate the kind of end she ultimately met.

How could she not go to Brooke's funeral?

She was being crazy.

Selfish.

A coward.

A knock on the office door interrupted her growing list of self-deficiencies. As it opened, she caught RJ's reflection in the monitor, coming up behind her. She closed her internet browser and glanced at him. "Where you been?"

"Wouldn't you like to know." RJ grinned.

He could do this thing with his eyes that made them seem more intense as if he was squeezing more light into them. Never taking his gaze off her, he reached toward the bottom edge of the monitor. She swatted his hand. He pulled it back and leaned away from her.

"What's with you?"

She crossed her arms. "Pittman had no right to pull us off the hit-and-run."

"Preach'n to the choir." He leaned against the door and folded his arms, copying her.

She huffed. "He's got us covering some new Chick-fil-A opening tomorrow morning."

"A Chick-fil-A opening." He nodded as if taking a moment to absorb what she was saying. "That's a big deal."

"Yeah, big deal. Like last week, we covered South Tampa socialites with psychic pets and, remind me again, what'd we report on before that?"

"Bert and Ernie." His voice dropped, and he looked down at his feet.

"Exactly. Are Bert and Ernie gay? The definitive evidence." She snickered. "We're really setting the world on fire."

"I know. It was ridiculous. Like any self-respecting gay Muppet would sport a unibrow."

"That's not the point." She glared at him.

He came forward and sat on the edge of her desk. "What if I told you that an even bigger story just landed in our lap."

She swallowed, listening. Skeptical, but listening. "Bigger than a new Chick-fil-A opening?"

"Those two kids from the high school—April and Craig." He paused as if waiting for her to acknowledge the names. When she didn't, he continued. "They approached me in the garage. They claim Bobby Greene was mowed down on purpose."

"On purpose?" She thought about it a moment. "But he was chasing a hat and ran into the street. It was an accident."

"The kids don't seem to think so. That car had been hanging around campus and following the kid."

"You mean it was waiting for him?"

"And it got him." RJ whistled. "According to his friends, he may have seen something he shouldn't have."

"Like what?"

"Something at the textile company his father works at." RJ adjusted his position on the edge of her desk. "Bobby's father was supposedly going to blow the whistle on the company dumping phosphates into the bay. Now someone is sending him a message to keep him quiet."

She chewed her bottom lip. Were they on to something? "We need to confirm this. We need to get hold of the father right away."

"And find out what he knows."

Tori stood. "Does he have proof? We need to get down to the hospital and talk to that dad."

"Slow down, Nancy Drew. Let's talk to those kids first."

"You mean April and Craig? They want an interview?" She sat again, leaned back in her chair.

"Well, technically, they wanted to talk to Simone Adams, but I was thinking …." He waved a hand in front of her face, swiping it near her ear. He pulled back, holding a folded Post-it Note in his hand, like magic. "If *you* call them first …"

"What's that?" She grabbed the note and unfolded it. A phone number was printed in bold, black numbers.

"It's April's cell," he said. "She can get us in touch with Bobby's dad."

Tori paused and looked at her monitor again. She thought of Brooke. The funeral. Going home. She couldn't dwell on that now.

She shot RJ a determined look. "What are we waiting for?"

* * * *

Thirty minutes before the appointed hour of midnight, Tori shuffled along the dank, half-lit sewer tunnels beneath downtown Tampa. RJ held up his camera, following. Beside them, iron-rung ladders led to service traps in the ceiling. A five-foot-wide corridor extended ten feet or so, before dead-ending into a concrete wall.

"The Scooby Gang is really meeting us down here?" RJ had a backpack slung over his left shoulder. He took out a pair of compact LED flashlights, holding one and clipping the second to his belt.

"April and Craig said they wanted to show us live, as it was happening." Tori's voice echoed, making her pause for a second. Catching her breath, she listened to the echo fade. She flipped her backpack off her shoulder and swept the flashlight beam, so it intersected with his and pierced the empty blackness. A dark mass lay ahead of them, indefinable in the dim light.

"Don't their phones have cameras?" RJ moved his flashlight below his chin. It lit his face with odd shadows. "They could take a video and send it to us, you know."

"I want to catch these corporate polluters red-handed." Tori reached over to thump his flashlight away from his face, but it slipped in his hand and spilled light directly at her. She covered her eyes as RJ laughed. Her eyes adjusted after a couple of seconds and she returned his amusement with a light shove. "Stop it. Be serious. He said we'll catch the factory workers in the act when their shift ends at midnight, so we have to act like professionals."

"I don't know. ... You really think they're going to climb down here and dump phosphates out of a bucket like old mop water or something?"

"Listen." Tori turned to him. "Have you heard of the book, *An Unreasonable Woman*?"

"How many times are you gonna tell me about that today?" He rubbed the stubble on his chin. "Some chick takes on a corporation that's dumping chemicals into the Gulf of Mexico."

"That chick's name was Diane Wilson," Tori said. "And she changed environmental practices in an entire industry. She made a difference. She—"

"And you think we're on to something as big as that?"

"I don't know. After talking to Craig and April, then Bobby's father ... I think so."

Tori heard a sound and she glanced down the tunnel. A soft echo tumbled out of the darkness ahead of them and they both froze.

"What was that?" she whispered.

Their flashlights crisscrossed the mouths of smaller tributary pipes. The light pierced the blackness, but they didn't see or hear anything more. They seemed to be alone. RJ moved his light and shrugged.

"Sewer rats." He moved the light away and played it along the concrete walls.

The thought made her skin crawl, but she moved forward anyway. He followed behind her. "We should've started with an interview with Bobby's dad. Like in a dark parking garage or at a park bench," he said. "Or, even better, how about at The Florida Aquarium? Nothing says environmental protection like sea turtles and manatees."

"We can do that later," she said, and walked faster, traipsing along the muddy pathway. "Besides, we'll get all the footage we need, down here. The rest is superfluous."

"You can't use words like superfluous when you're sloshing through the sewer." RJ's light hit a clump of dirt, tree limbs, and a furry rodent's body. He shook his head. "We'll never get the smell of this place out of our clothes."

Tori turned toward the clump along the wall and then looked away. She nudged him. "Stay positive. This will be a good career move in the long run."

"I am positive. You know my motto: Stay positive, test negative."

After a moment's quiet, he continued. "Did you ever see that episode of *The X-Files* where Mulder and Scully pursue that creature through the sewers? It was like half human and half fluke worm."

"No."

"It's a classic."

"I'm sure it is." Tori looked around. Maintenance walkways framed both walls. She climbed onto one.

"This reminds me of that episode." RJ came up alongside her.

"Would you shut up?" She waved a free hand at him. "You talk too much." She continued along the narrow maintenance walkway.

"If we have to cover that Chick-fil-A opening in the morning, we can't be out all night," he said.

"Stop complaining." She suddenly halted, and he bumped into her. She turned and shined the light in his face. "Did you hear that?"

He paused, narrowing his eyes. "More rats?"

"No. Voices."

"You're imagining things." He clipped the flashlight to his belt and let his backpack stuffed with camera equipment slip off his shoulder. "I'm telling you, it's like an episode of *The X-Files* down here. Creepy."

"The textile workers. I think they're coming." She started to say more but the chirp of her phone interrupted her. The sound echoed around them and they both jumped. Tori glanced at the screen. The name "BROOKE MARTIN" flashed in blue letters. Tori's mouth opened in shock.

"Who is it, April or Craig?" RJ moved next to her. "Bobby's father?"

She didn't answer. Her thumb pressed the Text icon and she read the message.

"Whatever I am, you made me."

Tori gasped and dropped the phone into the murky puddle beneath the maintenance walkway. It made a small splash and shattered into pieces.

"What is it?" RJ placed a hand on her shoulder. "What'd it say?"

Tori jumped down from the walkway and landed in shallow, stagnant water pooling on the concrete floor. Using her fingertips, she picked up the top plastic half. The phone was ruined. She studied the cracked touch screen, wondering if she'd really seen what she thought she saw. Who would text her from Brooke's phone?

"You deaf or just ignoring me?" RJ jumped down beside her. The light splash of his feet and resounding echo gave way to another distant sound.

It grew louder. Distinct footfalls, along with a low mesh of indistinguishable voices, echoed up from a tunnel on their left.

He turned his head in that direction. "Someone's coming."

The voices grew louder.

He grabbed her arm. "If those people mowed down that high school kid, they aren't gonna be too keen on seeing us, either," he whispered.

Tori turned from the dripping fragments of her phone to the black tunnel ahead. Someone was coming.

CHAPTER FIVE

M_SSAG_S FROM TH_ GR_AT B_YOND

Tori held one fragment of her phone and studied it as the faint voices coming from the tributary tunnel ahead grew louder. Lifting the flashlight in her other hand, she lit the black passageway. In the pale beam, she could make out three figures. They carried camera equipment on their shoulders, like RJ's. She waved the light, lighting their faces. A woman raised her arms, covering her face.

"Simone Adams." Tori's voice echoed as they approached. "What the—?"

"Vicki." Simone motioned to her cameramen, halting them.

Tori stiffened and inhaled. "My name is Tori."

"That's right, sweetie. My bad." Simone flipped a hand through her puffy red hair and pushed it away from her face.

RJ shot her a guarded smirk. "Well, well, Ms. Adams." He winked at Tori as he recited the woman's signature sign-off. "And wherever there's news, you'll find my shoes."

"Oh, you're cute." Simone chuckled and extended a hand toward his mouth, running the tips of her fingers across his stubbly cheek. "Real cute."

Tori moved in front of RJ, blocking Simone. "What are you doing here?"

"Looks like I should be asking you the same question." Simone never took her eyes off RJ.

Tori lowered her flashlight. "We're following up on a tip."

"In the sewers?" Simone's eyes enlarged, as if she noticed the broken cell phone in Tori's hand, and then looked at the ground. She moved her foot to mash the remaining fragments into the mud. Looking up, she flashed a toothy smile. "You're kinda outside your element, wouldn't you say? I haven't seen many Chick-fil-A cows running around down here."

"That's not the kind of story we're covering." Tori stared at the crushed phone. She started to protest, but Simone cut her off.

"Well, Vicki, ..."

Tori cringed. "It's Tori."

"Of course." She paused and licked her lips. "I spoke to Bobby Greene's friends at the hospital. Apparently, they'd given you guys a message for me. Funny how I never received it."

"You had no right to talk to them." Tori stepped closer to her. "Stop horning in on my story."

"Let it go, already." Simone and her two cameramen pushed past Tori and stepped onto the service walkway. Turning, she shook her head and let out a long sigh. "There's no evidence of any dumping per se. The kids obviously just wanted attention." She winked at RJ again, and continued forward, catching up to her crew.

"We'll see about that." Tori's jaw clenched so tight the tension twisted into her neck. She watched Simone and her camera crew disappear into the tunnel.

"You think Bobby's dad was mistaken?" RJ sloshed toward her, holding his equipment bag. "Maybe he's not think'n straight with his kid in the hospital and all."

"I suppose." Tori glanced at the pieces of her phone lying in the muddy water. She picked up the other half of the plastic protector with her fingertips and looked back at the tunnel for Simone. "It doesn't matter," she mumbled. "Maybe this isn't another *Unreasonable Woman*."

"We can talk to him again." He put a hand on her shoulder. "Maybe he got his nights mixed up. Or maybe the guy who does the dumping called in sick or is on vacation or something."

She stood there motionless for several moments, holding the wet fragments of her smartphone. She couldn't get the weird text out of her mind. What'd it say? RJ shined his flashlight on her face, grabbing her attention.

"Let's get the hell outta here," he said. "We got an early morning tomorrow."

She looked at her ruined phone. Brooke's name *had* flashed across the screen; she was sure of it. That message—whatever it was—came from Brooke's number.

RJ nudged her. "The Chick-fil-A cows are party animals," he said. "I don't know if you're aware of that or not, but it's a fact."

"Then I guess we're covering the party." She dropped the pieces of her phone into her backpack and zipped it shut. Lifting the strap onto her shoulder, she paused as RJ let out a long, throaty "Moooooo."

She looked over at him.

He laughed and mooed louder.

"Stop it," she said and brushed past him. "It's not funny."

He chased after her. "Moo!"

"Stop it!"

"Moo!"

"Stop it!"

Their voices echoed in the dark tunnel behind them.

* * * *

It was well past one when Tori and RJ arrived back at her apartment. She unlocked and opened the door, and stopped him in the doorway, placing a hand on his chest. "You didn't need to walk me all the way up here to my door."

He hesitated, stretching out in the frame with his arms raised to grasp the casing above his head. He grinned. "I know. I'm just worried about you."

"Well, stop it. I'm fine."

"It's that hack harpy, isn't it?" Perhaps taking the hint, he stepped back and leaned against the door. "Did she really rattle your chain that much? She pulls this kind of crap all the time."

She shook her head. "It's not Simone. It's ...." She

hesitated, letting her voice trail off. Who would've sent her that text message from Brooke's number? She wished she could remember what it said.

"It's what?" He placed the palm of his left hand on the door and reached for her with his right. "Is this about that mysterious text?"

She pulled away. "No. It's nothing, really."

"Nothing. Really." He stiffened as though she had struck him. "I know you, Tori. You may think I don't, but I do."

"It's not important." She looked at him, into his eyes. He was clearly waiting for an answer. She stumbled to give him one. "An old friend passed away. We'd drifted apart over the last few years, but we were best friends growing up."

"I'm sorry. I didn't know." He reached for her, and she backed away.

"I'm trying to figure some things out, you know, on my own," she said.

He turned into the hallway, stopped, and whipped back around to face her. "I'm not trying to pry. God forbid you ever open up to me."

"RJ, please." She looked at her feet again. "It's not like that. I'm just not ready to talk about it." She reached for the door, slightly pulling it forward to indicate she was ready to close it.

"Fine." He stepped out of the way, giving her space. "I'll see you in the morning, bright and early. Like in four hours."

She watched him walk through the hallway and into the elevator. Finally, she shut and locked the door.

Tori's apartment looked like a library. Or maybe an old used bookstore. Mismatched bookshelves overflowing with stacked novels, biographies, encyclopedias, and self-help books lined every wall. She owned an enormous collection of true crime books and she'd read every one over the years. *An Unreasonable Woman* sat on the third shelf, between Ann Rule's *Dead by Sunset* and Norman Mailer's *The Executioner's Song*. Passing through the book-cluttered living room, she wandered into the kitchen and opened the fridge. Just two half-eaten containers of three-day-old, greasy

Chinese food. After a moment's consideration, she closed the door.

Instead of fixing a midnight snack, she took a shower and climbed into bed. She lay in the dark for twenty minutes, tossing from one side to the other, before sitting up and turning on the lamp. She picked up the framed photograph on the nightstand.

The picture seemed like a hundred years ago now. It was the same photo she'd seen on Facebook, of her and Brooke and Winnie as teenagers on Ormond Beach. She set the photograph down, slipped out of bed, and found her laptop.

Booting it up, she sat in the dark and surfed the internet. She searched for Brooke Martin's name and found an obituary. She read it, and tears formed in the corners of her eyes. There were a few scant details beyond stating that Brooke was a mother, wife, and teacher at the local high school.

Tori found an article from the *Elroy Springs Gazette*, dated several days earlier.

Local History Teacher Found Dead

The body of Brooke Martin, a history teacher at Elroy Springs High School, was found hanging from a water tower overlooking her family's property. Police have ruled it a suicide.

Hanging? Brooke hung herself? Tori couldn't believe it and reread the paragraph to make sure. She couldn't understand it. Brooke taking her own life was one thing—*one terrible thing*—but hanging herself? It didn't make sense.

Scrolling down, she continued to read.

Deputies responded to a 911 call from the victim's residence yesterday. Authorities confirm it was Martin who made the call, but she provided no information beyond her name and address. When deputies arrived on the scene, they found Martin's body hanging from the old structure. She had already taken her life.

"We believe the call to 911 was a cry for help," Sheriff Mike Bennett said today. "Unfortunately, we didn't arrive in time."

Deputies recovered the body and sent it for post-mortem ...

Tori stopped reading. She stared at Sheriff Mike Bennett's name on the screen and the very letters chilled her.

He was still pitching for the Tampa Yankees when she'd left Elroy Springs, still struggling to work his way up the minor leagues. She had no idea he'd given up on baseball. But elected sheriff? How strange was that? She hadn't seen or spoken to him in five years. It was enough time to be over him. Her life had moved on and she was living content and happy without him.

That wasn't true. She couldn't say a day went by she didn't relive their whole relationship. Thinking about what she should've said or done differently. She lost sleep and gained weight, thinking about their wedding day and that moment just before the ceremony when she learned he'd changed his mind. He stood her up. Humiliated, she left, took a job in Tampa, and never looked back.

How could she go home again and face everyone?

Face him.

She felt an impulse to reach out to him. They hadn't spoken in five long years. It was time he heard what she had to say. Problem was, depending on her mood, those words were honest, hostile, and full of truth. Other days, they were remorseful and teary-eyed. But she could still call him, see how he was handling this tragedy. If this wasn't a good excuse to make contact, what was?

Luckily, her phone still lay in pieces in her backpack. She shuddered and scolded herself. The thought was inappropriate and unforgivable. She knew that.

She hated herself for even thinking about her selfish, petty, broken heart when nothing, but Brooke's tragedy should matter. Her childhood friend was dead—took her own life. It was there in black-and-white on the laptop screen.

She reread his quote.

> "We believe the call to 911 was a cry for help,"
> Sheriff Mike Bennett said today. "Unfortunately, we
> didn't arrive in time."

He didn't arrive in time, and Brooke hung herself. *Hung herself?*

Brooke leaping to her death from the top of that old water tower was more believable than hanging herself. Of the hundreds of true crime paperbacks lining Tori's bookshelves, not a single one recounted the morbid details of a woman committing suicide by hanging. Overdose? Perhaps. Wrist cut? Most definitely. But hanging?

Well, there was one book—a best seller, in fact. *Her Last Breath.* Police found a CEO's wife swinging in the attic, but of course, she hadn't really hung herself. She hadn't even committed suicide. Her husband staged the suicide to cover up her murder.

A cover-up.

That made more sense, in fact. The Brooke she knew would never take her own life. No way would she leave her family—her daughter—like that.

The thought chilled Tori and she looked away for a moment, forcing back tears, and then returned her gaze to the screen. The article included more quotes from Sheriff Bennett, and she read each one a couple of times, before lifting a finger to touch the screen and cover his name. Another search found more articles, with more quotes from the sheriff, students, and the school principal.

She noticed Ash wasn't quoted in any of them.

Pushing the troubling thoughts from her mind, she folded her laptop and turned off the light.

* * * *

Friday, June 29

Four hours later, Tori stood near the entrance to the new Chick-fil-A restaurant, next to the costumed cows. She tried to focus on the broadcast and stifle an uncontainable yawn. Restless sleep plagued her all night as she wrestled with nightmares of Brooke. Her suicide, her pale face, her blue lips. They'd spoken a word, but Tori didn't remember what Brooke might have said. There wasn't time to think about that anyway. She had to maintain her energy and report on the absurdity parading around her.

The celebration was an outlandish spectacle, to say the least. She couldn't imagine any summer blockbuster premiere or presidential inauguration commanding so much commotion and exhilaration. Streamers and banners fluttered above the restaurant. Four American flags flapped in the wind near the street. Greeters in black-and-white cow aprons welcomed patrons, handing them menus, calendars, and coloring books. A line of cars thirty deep wrapped around the restaurant in the drive-through lane. She inter-viewed families emerging from tents, who'd camped out over the last few nights. RJ filmed the cows waving at passing cars and performing cartwheels and backflips.

Tori felt exhausted by late morning. Maybe from the lack of sleep. Probably from the unnerving thought of Brooke's death. She couldn't get it out of her mind.

To be honest, she and Brooke had drifted apart. Sure, there were phone calls at first, after Tori's humiliating wedding debacle. Brooke insisted it wasn't Tori's fault, and they commiserated about men, relationships, and unrealistic expectations. When Brooke announced her pregnancy, Tori sent a card and baby clothes but didn't return home to at-tend the baby shower. Brooke insisted Tori come back for Darla's birth. Tori sent a purple plush elephant instead. A year later, Brooke, Ash, and the baby visited Tori in Tampa, and the women caught up with each other's lives. But Tori could tell then—things had changed.

Brooke had changed.

What if Brooke wasn't the same person she knew growing up? What if this Brooke had the capacity to take her own life and leave her family and daughter behind? What if she didn't even know this Brooke?

RJ tapped her shoulder and let her know things were winding down. "You wanna grab lunch? I'm partial to the grilled chicken sandwich," he said. "I think it's the pickles."

She declined. Instead, she rushed from the crowded parking lot and drove to the nearby mall. Finding the Cell Horizons store, she bought a new smartphone. She also stopped at an engraver to have a locket made for Darla. She could put a photo of Brooke in it. Tori had it mailed to the Martin residence in Elroy Springs, along with a sympathy card. By lunch, she sat in the food court and picked at a salad. Her mind kept drifting.

Brooke had been her best friend since the third grade. They'd been friends for over twenty years. But that didn't mean they were still the same people they knew from the past. People grow. They change, for the good and the bad. The old Brooke would never check herself out like that. She would never leave her family or her daughter. Had Brooke changed into the type of person who could climb that water tower overlooking her place? Step by step, climbing higher and higher until she reached the top? Tie a rope to its rotted planks and a noose around her neck?

The thought made Tori want to hurl. Rising from the table, she grabbed her bags and left the uneaten salad behind. Almost running, she headed for the parking lot.

Slipping into her Camry, she sat behind the steering wheel and locked the doors. She glanced at the small blue bag containing her new smartphone. She decided to leave it turned off—there wasn't anyone she wanted to talk to, anyway. After a couple minutes, she backed out and headed downtown, to the aquarium.

Tori spent the rest of the afternoon sitting in front of the shark tank. The blue-green water, the darting fish, the dim light filtered from above should've soothed her. It didn't. Rippling shadows crossed her face, and she thought about Brooke. Truly, deeply thought about her. And it hit her—she would never see or speak to Brooke again.

She'd missed her chance to return calls.

To have long talks about their lives and loves, like they used to.

That connection to her childhood was gone.

Tori broke down and sobbed, sitting on the bench in front of two nurse sharks and a snaggletooth tiger shark, bathed in a blue-green shimmer. She put her face in her hands and cried, until she could cry no more. Some people stopped and asked if everything was okay. She shooed them away.

When she finally stopped crying, she sniffled and pulled a tissue from her purse. She watched the sharks for a moment, staring at their sleek, graceful movements through the water. Listless and drained, she considered leaving, but decided against it. She couldn't face her empty apartment yet.

Instead, she found the small blue bag from the Cell Horizons store and pulled out her new phone. She spent an hour programming it, disappointed the past text messages hadn't carried over to this new one. The old messages were lost.

Pulling up the contact list, she found Ash's number. He didn't answer. She left him a message: "Ash, this is Tori. Did you text me from Brooke's phone last night? Call me."

She disconnected. A funny thought popped into her mind as she sat there watching a school of angelfish change directions in a single, sweeping turn. RJ was right; they should've interviewed Bobby's dad here.

An hour later, Tori's dirty blue Camry pulled into the dark parking garage at the SEBC-TV News building. She parked next to the fleet of red-and-white news vans and stared at the glittery yellow lightning bolt logo on the side of the van next to her car. Her stomach growled. She hadn't eaten all day, but the thought of food repulsed her.

She entered the building and passed security. The elevator took her to the eleventh floor. Pulling her key card from her purse, she stopped.

Her office door was slightly open. She took a breath. Pushed the door.

A voice called her name from the hallway.

CHAPTER SIX

D_UBLE _R N_THING

Tori stopped at her office door and turned to see RJ in the hallway. He rushed toward her.

"Where you been all day?" he said, his voice rising as he approached.

She stared at him, debating how to answer. "I had some things to take care of."

"The police have been trying to reach you. They've got more questions about Bobby Greene and the hit-and-run. I told them you broke your phone."

"I got a new one at the mall."

"You missed the planning meeting." He stood beside her, in front of the office door. "Pittman has us scheduled to cover the boat show over the Fourth of July weekend."

"The boat show?" She shook her head. It might as well have been another restaurant opening.

RJ flashed a toothy grin, beaming. He looked like a kid who could barely contain his excitement. "We got an interview set up with Twiggy the Skiing Squirrel."

"No." She walked into her office and plopped down at the desk. This was even worse than a restaurant opening. She may as well write for a high school newspaper. "No more monster truck rallies. No more fast-food openings. No rodent interviews."

He followed her to the desk. "Technically, it's his handlers."

"I don't care—"

"Chill. I've got a surprise for you." Taking her hand, he pulled her to her feet.

She resisted. "I don't have time to—"

"Humor me, okay?"

He led her out of the office. They returned to the elevator and he pushed the Up button.

She pulled her hand from his and asked, "What are you doing?"

He raised an eyebrow. "You'll see."

The elevator arrived, and they took it to the roof. When the doors opened, RJ grinned and stepped onto the flat roof-top overlooking downtown Tampa. He motioned for her to join him.

Tori stepped out of the elevator. She regarded the setup before her: A white linen tablecloth covered a square card table, and two chairs faced each other, all beneath the black TV cable wires and antennas. Plates, a six-pack of Corona, and several brown paper bags sat on the table. A candle served as the lonely centerpiece.

RJ pulled two white cartons of Chinese food out of the bags. "I got you chicken lo mein and sweet 'n' sour chicken."

"I don't know what to say." She stepped beside him as he pulled a chair out from the table. She took the seat. Steam rose from the open cartons and he scooped lo mein noodles onto a plate.

"It's your favorite." He handed it to her and popped the cap on a Corona. "I know your childhood friend passing away and Simone Adams pulling another one of her bitch-of-the-universe stunts got you squirmier than a bucket of tad-poles. But I want you to know I'm here for you."

"Thanks." She took a bite of the noodles, and then looked around the rooftop. The Tampa skyline—with the curved Rivergate Towers, the sharp edges of the Bank of America Plaza, and the SunTrust Financial Centre—stretched out before them. Blue sky and white clouds re-flected in the mirrored glass of the Skypoint Condominiums across from her, and she was surprised by how stunning it all looked. "It's actually kind of nice up here. Very beautiful."

"Tell me about it." He chuckled. "You remember that old Superman movie where Lois Lane has dinner with Superman on that penthouse terrace, and she interviews him, and he tells her he has X-ray vision and she asks him what color underwear she's wearing?"

She stared at him, unsure how to answer.

He shrugged. "This place reminded me of that scene," he said, looking away. A moment later, he perked up. "Oh, and there's more ..."

He hit Play on a purple iPod sitting on top of the air-conditioning unit, and the opening beats of Justin Timberlake's *"Rock Your Body"* thumped through the speakers. It competed with the hustle of rush-hour traffic and honking horns some thirty stories below.

She laughed. "You know, you're about the last person on earth who even owns an iPod."

"It was my niece's. She gave it to me." He slipped into the chair across from her. "It's classic." Striking a match, he lit the candle in the center of the table. "So, are you gonna tell me where you been all afternoon?"

"I told you. I bought a new phone." She took a sip of beer, staring at the flickering candle. The flame was barely visible in the early evening sun. Neither said a word for a solid minute, until RJ cleared his throat.

"Like I mentioned, you missed the planning meeting," he said.

She interrupted him. "Did you tell them that we should cover that trial coming up for the teacher who hired her student to murder her husband?"

"No."

"What about the follow-up to the body that washed up on Apollo Beach?"

He scratched his head. "Pittman assigned us to cover the boat show over the Fourth of July weekend."

"I know. You told me."

"And ... we're interviewing Twiggy the Skiing Squirrel." He smiled as he told her. "We're going live for the next four mornings."

"Four mornings? Are you serious?" She twisted the noodles around the fork. "I can't do another boat show or hot dog stand or—"

"You got a better offer?" He hesitated, watching her eat. "We can get the Sunshine Sweeties to cover it."

"No, we're not handing over the story." Holding the small white carton, she stuffed the fork with the twisted noodles into her mouth. She chewed, and then wiped her lips with a paper napkin. "A stupid, pointless story is better than no story at all."

She stood and blew out the candle.

He scooted back in his seat. "Where you going?"

"Look, this was very thoughtful." She stepped away from the table and headed toward the elevator. "But I'm not hungry. I'm sorry."

He got up from the table. "Your friend's name was Brooke Martin, wasn't it?"

She stopped at the elevator and turned around. "What?"

"Brooke Martin. That was your childhood friend."

"How do you know about Brooke?"

He looked down at his feet. "You left Facebook open on your computer. I had to Google some stuff and you weren't in your office and I saw her pictures."

"Why? Why would you do that?"

"I'm really, really sorry." He stepped toward her. "I wasn't trying to snoop or anything, but it was there and once I saw it, I couldn't unsee it. And you said you'd just lost your friend and I was worried." He pointed back to the table. "I wanted to make you feel better, that's all. We've been partners for two years and I've never seen you like this, and I guess I ... wanted to help."

She willed herself to smile. "It's okay. It's ... this is something ... I can't talk about yet. I, um ... told you I needed time."

"What happened?"

The elevator bell dinged, and the doors opened. She shook her head. "Look, thank you for dinner, RJ. It was thoughtful."

She stepped into the elevator and let the doors close.

Returning to her office, she slammed the door and leaned against it. Brooke's memory had haunted her all day. But it wasn't only that.

It was Mike and their relationship.

And their whole humiliating wedding day. Everyone waiting. Staring at her. Knowing she'd been a fool, that he'd never loved her, and she'd been chasing him all that time. She could still feel everyone in the church laughing.

She ran away to Tampa. Vowed never to face him again. And now he was a sheriff and would be at Brooke's funeral. It was all too much. Tori knew she was being selfish and immature, and nothing should matter but Brooke's funeral.

With her eyes shut, Tori knew that. Dear Lord, she knew it.

When she opened them again, she noticed the photograph of Brooke on her monitor screen. It called to her with voices from the past.

Childhood voices.

Whispers from her teenage self, arm in arm with Brooke and Winnie. Those were happier days on Ormond Beach. She walked to her desk and stared at the photo. It made her smile.

Taking her new phone from her purse, she dialed Ash. It rang. Then rang again. His recorded voice came over the speaker: "You've reached Ash Martin. I'm tied up at the moment, but will call ..." She ended the call and set her new phone on the desk.

The door opened, and RJ popped his head into the office. "Look, I'm sorry if I overstepped some boundary. The Superman movie reference was probably too far."

She didn't look up. "No, it's me. I'm in a mood."

"If you want to talk about—"

"No, I don't." How many times did she have to say that?

"Okay." He stepped toward her with his arms raised. "No pressure."

Her phone buzzed and she answered it, turning her back to RJ.

"You called?" It was Ash.

"Yes," she said in a hushed tone. "I wanted to talk to you."

A long, awkward pause followed, and then he said, "Did you change your mind? You coming to the funeral?"

"No. I can't face everyone yet." She sat back in her chair, which creaked with the movement. The monitor lit up and the photo of teenage Brooke stared back at her. Tori cleared her throat. "I know it's horrible and I'm a horrible person, but—"

"None of that matters."

"I know. I know. You're right. It's just ..." She glanced at the photograph again, wondering if she really had the courage to say it. Letting out a breath, she blurted it out. "He'll be there, won't he?"

"Who?"

"You know who."

Ash cleared his throat again. "You're talking about Mikey B? Of course, he'll be there. We'll all be there."

The sound of his name rang in her ear. "And sh-she'll be there too, won't she? His wife."

"Yes, I'm sure Charlotte will be there."

Her heart sank. "Charlotte? Her name is Charlotte? I didn't know that."

Ash sighed. He sounded impatient.

"Is that why you wanted me to call? To talk about Mikey B. and his wife?"

"No," she said. The photograph of Brooke watched her, judged her. She turned off the monitor. "No, that's not why I called."

"Well?"

"I needed to know something. Did you send me a text, using Brooke's cell phone?"

"Come again?"

"I received a text last night from Brooke's cell phone. I don't remember what it said, but it was her number."

"That's absurd." Ash laughed and the sound crackled in the phone's speakers. "Why would I text you—from Brooke's phone?"

"Do you have it? Her phone."

"Do you know how this sounds? No one texted, called, or contacted you from my wife's phone." Ash's tone was sharp. "Look, I hope you change your mind about coming to the funeral, but I understand you got your reasons."

She forced a smile, hoping it reflected in her voice. "I'll be there in spirit. I'm sending flowers. And I mailed Darla a locket. She can put a photo of her mother in it. I wish I could do more."

"Good. It's appreciated," Ash said. "And I get it. You have to do what you think is best."

He hung up. Tori stared at her phone for several seconds and then noticed RJ watching her.

"You aren't going to the funeral?" he asked.

She didn't answer and instead thumbed through the contacts on her phone. She found Brooke's profile. That familiar number came up on the screen. If she dialed it, would Brooke pick up? Like normal? Like nothing had happened?

The phone lit up in her hands and dinged. Tori jumped, startled. Another text message came in and the phone dinged again. Then another. She pressed the Text icon. "BROOKE MARTIN" appeared on the screen. She opened the text messages.

"Whatever I am, you made me."

"Whatever I am, you made me."

"Whatever I am, you made me."

Tori shook her head. She rubbed her eyes. The text messages were still there. Her thumb clicked on the phone number. It dialed. She waited for the connection. There was no ring on the other end. It went straight to voicemail. Brooke's recorded voice echoed through the office: "Hi, this is Brooke. Don't hang up just 'cause I can't answer the phone right now. If you leave me a message, I'll call you back. I promise."

Tori ended the call.

RJ asked her again what was going on.

She didn't answer. Glancing at the clock on the wall, she considered it. A quarter past seven. She'd be there by ten.

She dialed Ash. Waited. His cell phone rang. She waited. It rang again. Voicemail picked up. "You've reached Ash Martin. I'm tied up at the moment, but will call—"

She ended the call. It dinged again with another text. She stared at the screen. Another message from Brooke's number.

"She needs you."

Was Ash sending her these messages?

Tori dropped the phone. It landed on the floor with a thud. Dinged again. She left it lying on the tile. It dinged with another message. Then another. She didn't need to read them to know what she had to do. She'd try Ash again on the road.

If this was some sick game he was playing, she'd find out why. If someone else was sending the messages, she'd find out who.

RJ picked the phone up from the floor. She took it from his hand.

"I'm headed home ... to Elroy Springs ... to the funeral," she said. "I'll be back in a couple of days."

"You're what?"

"I'm going home." Opening the door, she turned back to him. "We can reschedule the interview with the skiing cat—"

"Squirrel."

"Whatever. We can schedule it for the end of the weekend. I'll meet you at the boat show on Saturday."

"The hell you will." He followed her out the door. "I'm driving."

CHAPTER SEVEN

IN C_LD BL_ _D

Tori ran down the battery on her new smartphone as RJ drove west on I-4. The red CJ-5, overloaded with cameras and recording equipment, along with their overnight bags, bounced wildly on the interstate. Tori's black dress hung from a hanger attached to the roll bar behind her. Listening to it rattle, she stared at the text message reading "She needs you."

Who needed her?

Brooke?

Darla?

Ash had said his little girl was in shock. Wasn't talking to anyone. Withdrawn. Losing a mother at any age was unbearable. A girl Darla's age, losing her mother was something ... well, something she'd never get over. So, of course Darla would need her. Is that what the message meant? Tori mulled it over as she stared out the window, watching the dark landscape roll by.

RJ cranked up his purple iPod. Justin Timberlake's *"What Goes Around ... Comes Around"* blared through the speakers. Somehow it seemed fitting. She glanced at RJ as he motioned toward the front panel, probably explaining why Timberlake was the modern-day Elvis.

But she wasn't listening. She was thinking about Darla.

Brooke and Ash had visited Tampa about a year after Darla was born. Tori remembered how cute the baby looked. They'd even brought the purple plush elephant. Darla was such a happy baby, all gurgles and giggles. And Brooke seemed so happy too. Or did she?

RJ reached over and turned down Timberlake. "So, you're going home. How long has it been?"

"Quite a while." She didn't want to admit to the five years or provide any details that would lead to a conversation about why she left Elroy Springs and moved to Tampa. She didn't want to talk about exes or past relationships.

Unfortunately, if RJ picked up on any hint to drop the subject, he didn't let it slow him down. He kept probing.

"You never talk much about home," he said. "Or about your past."

"It's the past. Why dwell on it?" Tori said, but she didn't mean it. She couldn't help but dwell on Brooke.

If her best friend had symptoms of depression, Tori didn't notice. But, how could she?

Tori had a one-track mind back then and steered every conversation to—she wasn't even sure what to call him now. The ex-fiancée? The sheriff? Mike? That first year after he'd unceremoniously dumped her, right before their wedding, she struggled to understand what happened. Every conversation dwelled on why he'd run, what he could've been thinking, or the degree of his douche-baggery. Then it became a personal inquisition about what she could've done differently or what signs she missed that their relationship was crumbling. It got to the point that she and Brooke talked about nothing else, and every conversation brought back all the anger and hurt and embarrassment.

It wasn't Brooke's fault. She was merely the connective tissue to a painful past.

The blame lay at Tori's own two feet. She brought it all on herself. But to heal, to move beyond it—if that was even possible—she shied away from any connection to that past, including Brooke. It was the only way she knew how to avoid the mental anguish. After a while, Brooke didn't call as often. And Tori lost touch with everyone back in Elroy Springs.

"But aren't you excited?" RJ asked, still hammering her with questions. "Aren't you looking forward to seeing your family and old friends and all the places where you grew up?"

She glared at him. "We're going to the funeral of my childhood friend who committed suicide."

Tori had been a terrible, horrible friend. And she knew it.

Her temples pounding, she pressed her forehead against the plastic window and listened to the Jeep rattle. The flimsy doors vibrated in the wind, making a noise that sounded like *Awful person, selfish woman.* That's exactly what she was. Brooke tried to maintain the friendship back then, but Tori was stuck in her own oblivious black hole. *Awful person, selfish woman.* Now, Darla needed her, and she wasn't going to make the same mistake twice.

RJ turned toward her and back at the road. "And?"

"And what?" She'd tuned him out and wondered how long he'd been talking.

"You still gotta look for the positive in it all." He gripped the steering wheel. "Stay positive, test negative. That's what I always say."

He smiled at her, but she didn't acknowledge him. Letting out an irritated huff, she cranked up Timberlake. RJ's fingers tapped the steering wheel to the beat.

Neither said a word.

He turned onto a state road that swerved off the interstate and curved more sharply. They headed south, passing a sign notifying them of "FROSTPROOF 48 MILES" in reflective white letters. Elroy Springs was only a few miles from Frostproof.

After a wordless half hour amplified by the blaring music, he turned down the knob and broached the subject again.

"So how long has it been since you went home?"

Shaking her head, still feeling unsettled, she folded her arms and leaned back. It was going to be a long ride, no matter how fast he drove.

He kept one hand on the wheel and motioned to her with the other. "I don't know what's going on, but it's time to come clean. Something got under your skin and it's more than your friend passing away."

"You wouldn't understand." Her tone held a note of impatience.

"That does it." He turned the steering wheel, pulling the Jeep to the shoulder. The tires screeched, spitting gravel as they came to a stop. He turned toward her. "Sure, I would understand. We're friends, right? We can talk to each other."

She looked down at her phone. "You'll think I'm crazy."

"Maybe you haven't gone all Natalie Portman in *Black Swan* yet." He paused, staring.

Still, she refused to look at him.

He persisted. "But you're getting there ... ever since you broke your phone in the sewer."

"Okay. Okay." She threw up her arms, waving her phone. "I've been getting text messages from Brooke's cell number."

"Brooke?" RJ's head whipped toward her and his left brow rose high on his forehead. "You mean *the* Brooke Martin?"

"Yes, that Brooke Martin."

"You mean, like messages from the dead?"

"No, That's ridiculous." She forced a laugh. It wasn't that the thought hadn't crossed her mind; it was that she knew better. She looked down at her dark phone. "Either Ash or Darla is trying to tell me something. One of them must have Brooke's phone."

He took the phone from her hand and stared at it. "What do the messages say?"

"There have been a few. Most say, 'Whatever I am, you made me.' Then I received another text message, which I think is about Darla, that said, 'She needs you.'"

"She needs you." He repeated it as if clarifying that he'd heard her correctly.

She answered with a quiet, simple yes that appeared to exasperate him.

He leaned across the seat, his voice rising. "*Who* needs you?"

She could tell he was getting excited. "Darla, I think. Brooke's daughter. Brooke would email me pictures and they brought her to visit once. She was a cute kid."

"And you think the little rug rat is texting you?"

"Or her father."

He handed the phone back to her. "I don't get it. Why?"

"I don't know why." She shook her head.

He leaned back in the seat. "You know there are actual documented cases of ghosts contacting the living through their cell phones."

"Don't go there. ..."

"We're *there* already." He raised his hands and wiggled his fingers to make air quotes for the word *there*. "We arrived *there* when you got the first message. When was it?"

"In the sewer."

"That's why you dropped your phone." He grinned and nodded. "If this is a message from Brooke, a real, honest-to-god stretch from the other side, then she's trying to tell you something."

"It's Ash, or maybe someone in their family trying to—"

"I bet we'll find EVPs and—"

She talked over him. "I simply want to attend the funeral, see what possible motivation Brooke's family could have for texting me these messages, and then leave. We'll head out to the boat show immediately after."

"If Brooke is strong enough to send messages to your cell phone, we'll definitely get EVPs." He talked fast, as if he could hardly get the words out. "Where'd she die?"

"What?" She paused. "What are EVPs?"

"Electronic voice phenomena. You know, spirit voices. You see it in all the reality shows. Now the question becomes, where do we find her spirit?"

"I feel sorry for your mother." Tori rubbed her forehead. Why'd she ever worry that he, of all people, would think she's crazy, when he himself was clearly walking the edge. The thought brought on a headache. "It's no wonder you don't have a girlfriend."

"I've got you."

"I'm your co-worker." Her voice was sharp, final. He didn't respond, and she wondered if she'd been too harsh.

RJ shifted into gear and rolled off the shoulder, merging into traffic on the highway. After several seconds, he interrupted the silence. "So, can I ask you how it happened?"

She swallowed and focused on the windshield. The road ahead was dark, spotted with bright patches under the highway lights. It took a moment for her to acknowledge his question. "How what happened?"

"How'd your friend die? She jump in front a train? Drink the Drano? Listen to Mariah Carey music?"

"Can you be any more insensitive?" Anger rose in her voice.

"I'm just trying to lighten the mood. Things are getting too heavy." He frowned and shrank back in his seat, maybe realizing the jokes weren't appreciated right now.

Or maybe he was just being RJ.

His head turned back to the road. "It's a valid question."

"It's a morbid question."

"It's the first thing anybody asks." He sounded defensive. "I'm sure it was your first question too, you know, when you heard."

"Actually, it wasn't." Her voice grew faint, thinking about Ash's phone call. "It didn't even register with me until later, when I read her Facebook page."

He looked over at her. "And?"

"And she hung herself." Tori tried to sound matter-of-fact. She didn't want to get emotional.

RJ's face remained locked straight ahead, focused on the road, and she was surprised that he didn't have a follow-up question. Perhaps he sensed how painful this conversation was for her.

Half an hour outside of Frostproof, Tori felt a twisted knot of angst forming in her stomach. Mile by mile, they were getting closer to Elroy Springs. Closer to home.

They cruised along a narrow two-lane highway, a large lake appearing and disappearing through the cypress trees on their right. RJ drove and sang along to his iPod—now Justin Timberlake's *"Summer Love."*

RJ glanced at her. "So, how big is this lake?"

"I don't know," she said, looking out the window. "It's two lakes, actually. Like conjoined twins."

The road followed along Twin Lakes, coming to a fork. Blue signs for US-60 directed traffic to the right, toward Frostproof; the left led to a bridge. Tori motioned for RJ to turn left.

Headed toward the bridge, they passed a wooden billboard advertising Sneaky Pete's Bar & Grill – just 15 miles. The sign boasted: "Best Gator Tail in the County."

"How's the gator tail?" he asked.

"Best in the county," she replied. A memory flashed through her mind, of slipping out of her house while her mom slept. Mike—they were just teenagers then—waited at her dock, and they took his boat up the lake to Sneaky Pete's. They danced and laughed in that little bar. She drank her first beer and watched the sun rise over the lake. The fleeting memory evaporated into some sense of dread. A peculiar premonition, really, that if she returned, she might never leave this place.

"We'll have to check it out while we're here," RJ said.

She looked over at him. "Maybe. If we have time."

The bridge crossed a narrow channel that connected the northern lake with its southern twin. Lights reflecting in the water flashed between the gray metal posts. Coming out on the other side, she watched as RJ steered the Jeep onto a two-lane highway, Route 103 / Clay Pit Road. She'd forgotten about the potholes. No, make that craters, and he slowed the Jeep to drive around each one. She could tell he was nervous about getting stuck, and she reminded him the Jeep had four-wheel drive. It didn't help.

Past the railroad tracks, the Martin house was a solid twenty-minute, bumpy drive into a forest of shadowy, gnarled trees. Swampland—overrun with webs of moss and sharp palmettos and clouds of mosquitoes.

Home.

"I'm calling Ash to let him know we're almost there." Tori pulled up Ash's number on her phone. She dialed.

It rang and rang.

No voicemail. No answer.

CHAPTER EIGHT

HOM_ SW_ _T HOM_

Tori noticed Brooke's minivan parked on the gravel drive in front of the Martin farmhouse. The dark home looked lonely—maybe even abandoned—nestled between a wild thatch of woods and a diseased orange grove. An old water tower rose above the orange trees, as if standing watch. RJ parked the Jeep beside a minivan with peeling blue paint. It looked equally lonely, like a pet sitting there, waiting for its owner to return.

Ash's black Ford wasn't anywhere to be seen. He might not even own the giant truck any longer, but she couldn't imagine him parting with it. She took out her cell phone and dialed his number again. Still no answer.

"Ash, where are you?" she said under her breath, staring up at the black windows on the second story. For a second, she thought she saw a face in the glass.

Laughing at her overactive imagination, she slipped down from the passenger seat of the Jeep. RJ followed and they approached the front porch, shrouded in deep shadows. Wood creaked beneath their shoes. A wooden bench swing rocked back and forth; its rusted chain squeaked with the movement. Someone could've been sitting in it a minute ago, she thought, and she rang the doorbell. Chimes echoed inside. After a moment, she knocked.

The last time she'd been here, knocking on this door, Brooke had opened it all wide-eyed and smiling. But no one answered now. RJ placed a hand on the swing's wooden armrest, halting the rocking motion. Tori stepped off the porch. The grove of dead orange trees monopolized the area on her left. She looked at the rusting water tower in the distance. Faded letters spelling out "BROOKE WILL YOU MARRY ME?" defaced the curved drum, but there they were—reminding her.

It'd been a summer afternoon before they all left for college, when the grove was still green and adorned with oranges. She'd been swimming with Brooke and Winnie in Twin Lakes, until Brooke broke the news. She was pregnant and certain that Ash would be furious. No sooner had she gotten the words out, they heard music blasting from the orange grove. It was an old Tim McGraw record and Brooke's favorite song, "Red Ragtop." The music blared above the grove and across the property, echoing over the blue lake waters. The girls squealed and ran to the orange trees as Brooke's parents stepped out of the house, onto the porch.

Ash and Mike—tall, lanky teenagers with their whole lives ahead of them—stood at the top of the water tower, arms raised, holding up the black, vibrating speakers—like a scene from some '80s movie. Ash was already in college, on a wrestling scholarship. Mike was in town, pitching a stretch of home games with the Tampa Yankees, and Tori's heart raced seeing him.

Ash set down his speaker and motioned to Brooke. He held a can of red spray paint in his right hand, waving it. Behind him were the words "BROOKE WILL YOU MARRY ME?"

Brooke screamed "Yes," and ran through the grove toward the water tower, toward Ash. Brooke's father stomped off the porch and took off after her, mumbling something about his impetuous daughter and that good-for-nothing wrestler. Whatever he said made Tori chuckle because, to be honest, she felt a twinge of jealousy, wishing it was Mike proposing to her.

But that passed. Brooke and Ash lost the baby a few weeks later, before college started. Brooke still married him, though, before the semester ended.

It seemed like a lifetime ago.

"I think that's where it happened." She shuddered, pointing to a massive black shape blocking out the stars on the horizon.

"That's where she hung herself? From that tower?" RJ whistled.

He looked back at the farmhouse with a perplexed expression. She saw the wheels spinning in his head. Women don't hang themselves. A mother doesn't leave her family behind. None of this made sense. She headed toward the Jeep, and then paused. RJ took off into the dead orange trees.

"Where're you going?" she yelled.

He didn't answer.

She grabbed a flashlight from the Jeep and looked up at the immense structure on the horizon. Why did he always have to make everything so difficult? She shook her head and ran after him.

Racing into the grove, she rushed into a wall of gnarled branches. Sharp sticks scratched her arms like bony fingers stretched out to touch her. She pushed through. Coming out the other side, she saw the water tower soaring above her. She walked cautiously toward it. Looked up at the base. The drum spiked into the night sky.

RJ came up behind her. "The thing's a death trap."

"It hasn't held water in decades. It's just kind of a corpse now." Her head raised, she imagined Brooke climbing the rickety ladder and stepping onto the catwalk circling the drum. The thought made her stomach turn. "This is where it happened."

He carried a digital recorder in his right hand, holding it high above his head. "Brooke Martin. Are you here? If you can hear me, please answer. Speak into this audio recorder."

Tori turned to him. "Are you serious?"

He lowered his arm. "Our ears may not be able to pick up Brooke's voice, but if she's here, we'll capture it on the recorder."

"That's ridiculous."

"It's science." He raised the recorder again. "Brooke Martin. Are you here with us? If so, speak into the audio recorder."

Tori ignored him and talked to herself, although she spoke loud enough for him to hear. "Why would a healthy young mother and high school history teacher climb this old thing and jump?"

RJ repeated her question into the recorder.

She walked around the base, stopping at a sorry-looking ladder. Still, it appeared sturdy enough. Something compelled her to mount it. She lifted herself onto the first rung and climbed hand over fist upwards. Twenty feet. Forty feet. The wind grew stronger the higher she went.

"What are you doing?" RJ called up from the ground. He paced around the metal legs, but she didn't answer.

At the top, she hesitated and maneuvered along the catwalk circling the base of the drum, now little more than a rusted orange-and-gray barrel. She sat, clinging to the weak railing, her legs dangling. From this vantage point she could see the tops of the dead orange trees and the roof of the Martin farmhouse. Above her, the sky was lit brilliantly with stars. The moon hadn't risen yet.

RJ made his way up and held out his arms, balancing on the frail platform. "Man, we must be two hundred feet up," he said.

"More like a hundred and fifty to sixty," Tori said, gazing at the miles of countryside stretching in every direction. Twin Lakes loomed on the horizon. She could see the north lake now and make out the bridge over the channel that connected the two lakes. A lone car crossed over, its headlights shining bright as a flickering candle on the horizon. Then it vanished.

"The average water tower is about a hundred and sixty-five feet high to get the proper pressure per square inch," she said.

"Thank you, Wikipedia."

"I'm well read." She looked up at him and smiled. "You should pick up a book sometime. You might learn something."

"I didn't think you read anything but true crime books." He sat beside her. His long legs dangled next to hers and he leaned his head back, pointing to the faded letters spray-painted across the drum. "I'm guessing there's a story here. That was Ash's idea of a proposal or something?"

She cranked her head to look behind her. The red letters looked weathered and the paint was blistered and peeling. Still, she could still make out "BROOKE WILL YOU MARRY ME?"

"She said yes, in case you're wondering." Tori whispered. She didn't want to disturb the settled calm around them. "Maybe that's why she took her life here. Because this place had some significance. Some meaning."

"The EVPs should be off the chart. You get any more text messages?" He stretched an arm, raising the digital recorder over the railing. "I'm telling you, she's reaching out to you."

"Someone is ..." She gripped the railing and looked down. Flecks of rust fell like snow from the post. She shook her head. "But it's not Brooke."

"Check your phone. Maybe she sent you more messages."

She felt her pockets for her cell phone. "I left it in the Jeep."

Annoyance flashed in his eyes. "Brooke could be contacting you right now. Look, I know you think it's her husband or their little girl, but that takes as much a leap of faith as to believe it's Brooke."

She looked at him. "Why?"

"Because .... Do you think a kindergartener would type that message, even if she could text? And why would Ash send you mysterious text messages? You've already talked on the phone."

"Then it's someone else in the family. Either way, that's what I want to find out."

"I'm telling you, it's Brooke. She—"

"Kids are advanced nowadays," Tori said. "They have smartphones and use tablets and program televisions and who knows what else they can do. And if it's not her, then maybe it's Brooke's father and he wants me to be there for his granddaughter."

"Maybe." RJ paused a moment, as if considering her argument. "Or maybe you just refuse to believe."

He held the audio recorder between them and pressed Play. They listened to his voice asking questions. Tori's voice was on it too, slightly fainter than his, asking why a healthy young history teacher would do this. They both listened for a response. Tori held her breath. But the only response came from the rising chirp of crickets in the background.

"We should try the house." He clicked off the recorder. "If her spirit isn't here, then it's inside her home."

"We're not breaking and entering," she stated.

"It's not a B&E if he's expecting us."

"I didn't get hold of him," she said. "He never answered."

"Great. He never answered." RJ laughed as if she'd made a joke. When she didn't return the laugh, he changed the subject. "The sky is lighting up."

"The moon's rising." Tori watched the moon duck behind the clouds and peek out again. Its pale light blended with the night and turned the sky from a rich black into varying shades of deep blue.

Following the tree line running perpendicular with the north lake, she could make out the rooftop of another house in the distance. She could barely see it but knew exactly what it'd become. Alone in the woods. Lost in cavernous shadows, unkempt, probably not much more than a nest for rodents, insects, and squatters. The thought saddened her.

She'd grown up under that roof. She and her mother moved in after they'd escaped her father, his rages, and their excuse for a life in Tulsa, Oklahoma. Tori had just turned eight years old and, upon moving in, she and her mother planted a banana tree in the front yard to celebrate their independence. She had loved that place. Now her home was a dilapidated shack, sitting forgotten beneath a canopy of oak trees and Spanish moss.

"You okay?" RJ tapped her shoulder.

She glanced at him, sitting beside her. His eyes narrowed again, doing that thing where it looked like he was squeezing more light into them. Maybe he needed glasses.

"Fine. Just tired," she said. For emphasis, she tacked on a yawn that started forced, but wound up the real thing.

"Look at the moon reflected on the water." Now he whispered, as if he too had discovered the fragile calmness of the night and any sudden movement or noise could scare it away. "It's beautiful."

"Yes, it is." She gazed again at the rooftop of her child-hood home. It took a split second for the memory to resurface. She was eight and swimming in the lake with Brooke and Winnie.

Winnie's big brother would come with her sometimes. Those were the best days, when she, Brooke, and Winnie spent time with Mike and his friends from the baseball team. They were always coming up with something wild and fun and a little bit dangerous.

One day, Mike climbed the huge oak at the edge of Tori's property and tied a rope to one of its thickest branches that hung out over the water.

"You ever wish you could fly?" he asked her after he climbed down, holding the dangling end of the rope.

She shook her head.

"I'll show you." He took off toward the shore, swung out over the water, and launched himself high into the air. He hung there for a moment before splashing into the lake.

Tori couldn't believe it. He flew. He actually flew.

Mike resurfaced moments later, his head bobbing above the water, and waved from the center of the channel. "Now you try," he yelled to her. "Come on, trust me."

If she'd known then ....

Shaking her head, she pushed the memory aside.

Crickets grew louder, lower, louder, giving way to hidden bullfrogs in the marsh. Then another sound split the night— the faint crack of a branch.

Tori clutched RJ's arm. "Did you hear that?"

"Hear what?"

"I don't know." She held her breath, remained still. The crickets and bullfrogs went silent. She turned her head, looked at the dark ground and trees beneath them. "Some-thing. We're not alone."

She heard the movement again. It came from behind.

"It's a cat or a raccoon or something," he whispered in her ear.

She raised a hand to him. Without moving a muscle, afraid to breathe, she listened. They both did. A sudden gust stirred leaves on the catwalk, followed by a soft thud echoing inside the drum.

"Something's in there." She paused, straining to hear.

The thud came again, as if someone was walking.

She called out, her voice quivering: "Hello?"

Silence.

She imagined a raccoon rooting around inside and laughed at herself for being so jumpy. Then the footfalls pounded again: *Thump-thump-thump-thump.* Someone was walking inside the empty water tank. Not some little rodent, but a human being. Walking upright on two feet. *Thump-thump-thump-thump.*

"This water tower is haunted," RJ said.

Clearly, he'd heard it too.

He held up the recorder and pressed the Record button. "Brooke? Are you here? Are you with us?"

Tori rose from her perch on the catwalk and walked around the drum. A rip in the metal casing appeared just large enough to squeeze into. She bent over, close to it, and called out again, "Hello?" Her voice echoed inside it.

She shined the flashlight into the cavity. The beam of light bounced off the metal wall and lit sticks and rotting leaves, and clumps of red mud with the random dollar weed sprouting upwards.

"You see anything?" he asked, hunching over her.

"Not yet." She peered through the rip. Her eye caught a sudden flash of movement. Something, someone, moved through the beam into the blackness on the other side. *Thump-thump-thump-thump.*

"Hello?" Her voice echoed.

"What is it?" He grabbed her shoulder. "What'd you see?"

"I'm not sure." She leaned into the rip, and his grip tightened.

"Hold on, Dora the Explorer." He grabbed her arm now, holding her back. "You're not thinking about going in, are you?"

She gave him a serious, determined look. "Someone's in there."

He squeezed her arm tighter. "I'm not going to be able to go through that opening with you. It's too small."

"I'll be fine." She swatted his hand away. She climbed through the rip in the metal wall, putting one leg into the dark drum, followed by the other. Once inside, she crouched, and then stood.

"I know someone is in here," she said, holding the flashlight. She shined the light from one side of the dirty curved wall to the other, until stopping on a pair of untied tennis shoes ... red, with white laces.

Tori stopped breathing and peered at the little girl standing in the dark.

CHAPTER NINE

PU_HING UP DAL_IE_

Tori's flashlight shined on the red tennis shoes and moved up the thin legs of a girl. She wore blue shorts and a pink T-shirt with the picture of a bear holding a balloon.

"What's going on?" RJ's head poked through the rip, and then a shoulder. Not much more of him would fit. "Talk to me."

Tori remained focused on the child. "Darla?" Her voice echoed around them. "Are you Darla?"

She inched toward the little girl, careful not to frighten her. The girl took a step back. Tori hesitated and knelt. "My name is Tori. Do you remember me? You and your mom visited me in Tampa."

The girl shivered and kept her head down, her arms locked tight to her sides.

"You're Darla, aren't you?" Tori touched the girl's face and wiped dirt from her cheeks. "Where's your daddy?"

She didn't answer.

RJ yelled from outside. He sounded panicked, but she couldn't respond to that right now. She focused on Darla.

"Let's get you out of here."

She took the girl's hand, gripping it as she stood, and led her away from the curved metal wall. They stepped through rust-colored puddles as Tori led the way with the flashlight. RJ looked in and then backed out. Coming to the narrow gash in the wall, she set the light on the floor and helped Darla through. RJ's hands grasped the child and he lifted her out. Tori followed, slipping through the rip.

He shot her a puzzled glance. "Who is she?"

"I think it's Darla Martin," she said. "Brooke's daughter."

RJ handed his cell phone to Tori. "Do you know her

father's number?"

"Not by heart. I'll call him when we get to the Jeep."

Leaving the flashlight behind, they climbed down the tower. On the ground, Tori took Darla's hand and led her through the orange trees. RJ followed. Catching up to them, he lifted the little girl into his arms and carried her to the Jeep. When he put her down on the gravel drive, Darla turned her head toward the farmhouse.

"Do you know where your daddy is?" Tori leaned down to look Darla in the eyes. "No one's home right now."

Darla wouldn't look at her. Tori glanced up at RJ. He shrugged in return. She picked the girl up with one arm and opened the Jeep's passenger door with the other. She helped Darla into the backseat. Tori's cell phone lay on the console and she dialed Ash's number. Still no answer. Frustrated, she ended the call.

RJ started the engine. "Where do you think her dad is?" he asked. "How could he leave her home alone?"

"I don't think he did." Tori looked at the dark farmhouse and back at Darla. "If the house is locked, she couldn't have been home."

"Then how'd she get here?"

"I don't know."

RJ's eyes widened. "So, now what?"

* * * *

Tori stared at the dark storefronts, some with a light or two glowing inside, as RJ drove through downtown Elroy Springs. If there was one place, she didn't feel like going, one place she wanted to avoid, it was the Sheriff's Department. But what choice did she have?

She glanced at Darla in the backseat. The little girl sat quietly, unblinking, hands folded in her lap. Tori's gaze returned to the passing downtown storefronts.

Nothing had changed in the last five years. The stores faced a roundabout that made up the center of Main Street, a circle of old buildings that included the courthouse, the

Elroy Springs Gazette, and a few old boutiques that catered more to tourists than residents. A Waffle House, aglow in bright yellow lights, topped off the street. In the center of the roundabout stood a spot-lit statue of the town's founder.

RJ parked along the street, across from the courthouse. The large concrete columns and high steps climbing to four glass doors were well lit. Several sheriff's deputy cars were parked in front, on the street. He turned off the ignition.

Tori took a breath and held it. There was no avoiding it now. As her stomach fluttered, she slipped out of the Jeep and stood on the curb. The courthouse and the Sheriff's Department alongside it faced her, waiting for her. And he was going to be in there, inside, waiting too. She knew it. The sheriff. The ex. Mike. She straightened her back.

RJ tapped her shoulder. "You gonna get the girl?"

For a second, she wasn't sure what he'd said, and then saw Darla sitting in the back, scrunched between the luggage and the black dress hanging from the roll bar.

Tori pushed the passenger seat forward and stretched a hand into the backseat. She helped Darla to the pavement and took the girl's right hand. RJ took her left. Together they walked up the stone steps and RJ opened a glass door into the courthouse.

Tori's heart was racing. She knew this moment would come sooner or later. It was inevitable. She wished she'd had time to change, or brush her hair, or … maybe she should wait in the Jeep. Sweat dripped down the back of her neck as they entered the building.

A young female clerk with jet-black hair and a shiny diamond stud in her left nostril sat at an open desk, separated from the public by a counter. She turned as Tori, RJ, and Darla entered, hand in hand. Rising from the desk, the clerk approached them.

Tori looked past her. No sheriff—anywhere. She thanked God under her breath.

A deputy sitting at a desk in a glassed-in office at the rear jumped to his feet. He stepped into the hallway, approaching them. A slender, rumpled-looking man some-where in his late forties, he wore a tan uniform that had been washed one too many times.

"Darla Martin?" He dropped to his knees in front of the little girl. "Where you been? We got all four cars out look'n for you."

"She's alright." Tori noticed the deputy looking up at her with wide, inquisitive eyes.

"Tori Younger? Why, hell's bells, it is you!" He jumped to his feet, wrapped his arms around her, and squeezed. Tori stiffened. The uncomfortable hug lasted several seconds before he released her and took a step back. He turned to the clerk. "Zoe, let the patrols know we found Darla Martin."

"On it," she said, turning as if to head back to her desk, then paused. She turned to Tori. "Where was she? Miss..."

The deputy laughed. "This is Tori Younger, of *Wake Up, Tampa Bay.*"

"I'm sorry. Who?"

The clerk politely took Tori's hand, baring an arm of spiraled barbed wire and rose tattoos. The diamond nose stud sparkled. She looked young, still in high school, and her face lit up as she gripped Tori's hand.

"Oh, your aura—it's so gray and gloomy."

Tori took a step back. "Excuse me?"

"I've never even seen a gray aura before. It used to be green, but now it's lost. You must be way off your path." The young woman shivered and ran a hand through her hair. She turned to RJ. "Now, you—your aura is a bright, vibrant blue, almost blinding."

RJ smiled and winked at her. "Well, I try."

"Totally pure blue auras are extremely rare, but blues are highly intelligent and charismatic people," she said. "They motivate and inspire others."

The deputy interrupted her. "This is Zoe, our summer intern. She's a little bit psychic."

RJ shook her hand. "I'm sure you have a bright, vibrant aura too."

Zoe whipped her hand from his grip, as if he'd shocked her. "You're famous," she said. "Both of you—millions of people adore you."

RJ chuckled. "Well, hundreds, maybe."

"This is Tori Younger," the deputy said. He looked at Zoe. "She's the one I was telling you about. Grew up here. Went off to the big city and became a world-famous news reporter. You know, *Wake Up, Tampa Bay.* It comes on at 5:00 a.m. every morning."

"Oh, I'm sorry, my parents don't let me stay up that late." Zoe rushed back to her desk and clipped a headset over her ears as she spoke. "But I don't think it agrees with you. I've never seen an aura like yours. You're at odds with the world around you."

"Thanks. How creepy of you to notice." Tori shot her an uncomfortable grin, and then turned to RJ. "This is Deputy Torres. He's been serving and protecting Elroy Springs for as long as I can remember."

"What's going on?" Deputy Torres said, and knelt to look at Darla face-to-face. After giving her a once-over, he stood. "Why do you have her? Where's her daddy?"

"Ash wasn't home." She put a hand on Darla's shoulder. "We found her all alone. That's why we brought her here."

The deputy turned to Zoe and pointed. "Leonard just left. Call him and let him know we have his granddaughter."

Zoe looked up from her desk and shrugged. "I don't think he has a cell phone."

"His nurse left her number. It's on a sticky note on my desk." The deputy nodded toward his office. As Zoe got up and headed for the office, the deputy looked at Tori. "Darla's grandfather should be back in a minute or two. He's been watching the little girl since Ash hasn't been himself—since, well, you know."

"I know." Tori frowned. "It's just awful. I'm still in shock."

"We all are." The deputy shook his head. "I'm glad you made it back, though. How long has it been? Seven, eight years?"

"Just five. I haven't been gone that long. Though sometimes it feels like more." Tori forced a smile and looked around the lobby. "Where's the sheriff?"

"The chief?" The deputy shrugged. "He's out look'n for this runaway."

Tori let out an audible breath. She'd received a reprieve. The deputy turned his head toward the front doors, and she followed his gaze. One door opened and a man in his late sixties entered the building, his eyes hidden behind dark sunglasses. He used a walking stick in one hand, while the other gripped the arm of a much younger, blonde woman. She led the man into the lobby.

Tori recognized him immediately ... Brooke's father.

"Little girl! Little girl!" the blonde woman called out, waving her free arm. She helped the older gentleman step toward Darla. "Oh, little girl, we can't believe you ran away on, of all days, the night before your mother's funeral." She turned to the grandfather and gripped his arm. She leaned in close to his ear and yelled, "YOUR LITTLE GRANDDAUGHTER RAN AWAY ON, OF ALL DAYS, THE NIGHT BEFORE WE BURY—"

The old man shook free of her grip. "I got it, I got it."

"IT'S YOUR GRANDDAUGHTER. THEY FOUND YOUR GRANDDAUGHTER," she yelled, gripping his arm again. She looked at Tori and RJ. "He's blind." She had mouthed the words, more than whispered them as she pointed at the old man's face.

RJ nodded and held up his hand, motioning that he understood.

She held out her hand to Tori. "I'm Veronica with the Aging Angels Agency. I'm Leonard's companion, and we were watching Darla when she vanished."

Leonard shook his head and leaned in Darla's direction. "Are you okay?"

Darla didn't answer.

Deputy Torres cleared his throat. "She doesn't seem to be hurt, but she's still not speaking. I'll see if I can track down her father."

Veronica smiled at the deputy. She leaned in toward the grandfather.

"HE SAID THE LITTLE GIRL ISN'T HURT, BUT—"

"I heard him," Leonard said, and leaned away from her. He nodded in the deputy's direction. "Thank you for bringing her back."

"I'm not the one who found her." The deputy put a hand on Tori's shoulder.

"I found her," Tori said. "She was in the old water tower." Tori couldn't see the elderly man's eyes behind the black glasses, but he lifted his head in the general direction of her voice. She didn't remember him looking so frail. He appeared as fragile as Darla. Tori shook her head. "I think she's traumatized."

"Post-traumatic stress syndrome." Leonard turned his head from Tori's direction, back toward Darla. "Losing her mother is a lot for my granddaughter to go through."

"Let's walk across the street and see if the Waffle House has some coffee," Veronica said, taking Darla by the hand. "Do you drink coffee?"

Darla took the woman's hand without looking up or saying a word.

The blonde shrugged and grabbed the old man's hand. "WE'RE GOING ACROSS THE STREET TO SEE IF THE WAFFLE HOUSE HAS SOME COFFEE."

He waved her away. "Go on, I can manage."

Tori watched the blonde roll her eyes and twirl around with Darla. She led Darla out the large glass doors. Tori turned and looked at the grandfather. "You're Brooke's father. I don't know if you remember me, but—"

He nodded and smiled. "Tori Younger. Yes, I remember you. You're one of Brooke's friends. Mikey B.'s wife, right?"

"No," Tori said. "No, we didn't get married."

"Oh." He frowned. "I'm sorry. I didn't mean anything by that."

"Mi—er, the sheriff and I haven't spoken in a long time. Since, well …"

"My mistake. Thank you again for finding my grand-daughter." He tapped his walking stick on the floor as he spoke. "You found her in that old water tower?"

"I'm afraid so," Tori said, watching him. She hadn't seen him in years, and he'd aged since then. Since the accident that took his sight. She remembered consoling Brooke at the hospital when it happened. Now he was babysitting his troubled granddaughter? Tori thought about it a moment, then continued. "I don't know what she was doing out there. Or how she got there."

"That's where they found … her, you know. *My* daughter, *my* little girl—" He choked up, and then composed himself. "That's where they found her body."

Tori studied him as he spoke. He obviously lived nearby, in town. How did Darla sneak out and get all the way back home and into that water tower, though? It didn't make sense. Something was wrong here, very wrong. Her mind was sorting the possibilities when she realized he'd stopped speaking.

"I'm so sorry," she said. "I loved Brooke. She was a good friend."

He coughed, collecting himself. "Thank you. I'm going to go check on my granddaughter. Would you like to join us for coffee?"

"No. Thank you." Tori squeezed his hand. She could feel him trembling. "But there is something I need to ask you."

"Yes?" His grip tightened on her hand.

She leaned toward him. "Do you have Brooke's cell phone?"

He released her and took a step back, almost stumbling. "What?"

"Have you been texting me from Brooke's cell phone?"

"I-I don't even know what texting is," he said. "And I can't use a phone any more than I can drive a bus."

"What about your caregiver—Veronica? Is that her name?"

"No, she doesn't have my daughter's cell phone. And why would she be texting you? She doesn't even know you."

Using his walking stick, he turned from Tori and made his way to the glass doors. RJ held the door open. Tori watched him lead the grandfather outside and down the steps.

Deputy Torres gripped her arm. "What was that about?"

"I'm not sure. Possibly nothing."

Tori turned from the entry doors to watch the deputy walk to the watercooler in the lobby corner. He poured two cups.

"I've been getting text messages from Brooke's cell number," she said.

"Whadda they say?" He handed her a cup of water.

She grasped it and took a sip. It was very cold, and she had to hold it with her fingertips. "Just cryptic nonsense. I think they were trying to get me to come back here."

"I'm glad you did. I wish it was under better circumstances, though." The deputy drank his water in a single gulp and tossed the cup into a wastebasket near the cooler. He looked back at Tori. "You really found Darla at that water tower?"

"She'd climbed inside it. We had to get her down." She took another sip. "If she was staying with her grandfather, how'd she get all the way out there?"

The deputy shrugged. "Could Ash have picked her up?"

"I don't think so. The house was locked. And she was inside the water tower like she was hiding or something."

"That's disturbing," he said, glancing down for a moment and looking back at her. His face turned dark. "Darla witnessed it, you know."

"Witnessed what?" RJ said, joining them at the watercooler.

The deputy cleared his throat. "Darla was on the scene when I arrived." His voice lowered, almost trailing off. "I think she saw it happen. She witnessed her mother ..."

RJ whistled and poured himself some water. "That's messed up. No wonder she's not speaking."

Tori glared at him and then looked back at the deputy. "Do you think that's why she was up there? Because it's where she saw—"

Deputy Torres shrugged, saying, "I honestly don't know."

"So, you found Darla when you arrived on the scene?" Tori paused and placed a hand on the deputy's shoulder. "When you found Brooke."

"I got Darla out of there before I cut her mama down," the deputy said. "Brooke made a 911 call a half hour earlier."

"And *you* found her?" Tori couldn't believe what she was hearing. "Where was Ash? Why'd she call 911?"

"Brooke hung up the phone before telling the operator what was going on. She'd call us whenever Ash was too drunk, and they'd start fighting."

Tori looked at RJ. She knew what he was thinking without either of them saying it. "Did Brooke call you a lot?"

The deputy nodded. "I guess. More so recently."

"Where was Ash?"

"He was sleeping it off at the church. He'd shown up drunk at an AA meeting, and Pastor Fields wouldn't let him drive home." The deputy looked way, seemingly focused on the exterior windows and their reflections in the glass. "I found Brooke's body at the water tower. She hung herself from the guardrail along the upper platform."

"I-I don't know what to say," Tori said. She looked at RJ standing next to her.

He shook his head and said, "All the more reason Darla or her grandfather wouldn't be sending you text messages. I knew what you were getting at when you asked the old man about Brooke's phone." RJ waved his arm, spilling water on himself. He didn't seem to notice. "Those messages are coming from Brooke."

She shot him a dirty glare and then looked over at the deputy. "Could Brooke's father have her cell phone?"

The deputy's eyes narrowed. "He said he didn't, and I don't know why he'd lie about something like that. So … tell me what the texts said."

"The first one was something about how we made her."

"Made her what?" The deputy looked puzzled. "Commit suicide?"

"That's how I interpreted it. And earlier I received a different message. It said: 'She needs you.' I think it's refer-ring to Darla." Tori pulled out her phone and brought up the text messages on the screen. She handed the phone to the deputy. "All these messages came from Brooke's number."

The deputy stared at it a moment, expressionless. He read the message out loud: "Whatever I am, you made me." He looked up from the phone, his eyes enlarged. "Hell's bells. Someone's play'n a prank on you."

"What do you mean?"

"I mean, this ain't funny." He opened his mouth, as if about to say something, and changed his mind. He shook his head. "Someone's prank'n you."

"Does that message mean something?"

"Whatever I am, you made me," he said under his breath, his face turning pale. "I know what it means."

He motioned for her to follow, and then turned to Zoe behind the counter. "Hold my calls."

Tori and RJ slipped into the office behind the deputy as he shut the door.

CHAPTER TEN

B_OOD _UST

In the cramped office, Tori noticed the many photographs and certificates depicting Deputy Torres' twenty plus years of public service. On the wall, a faded poster read: YOU DON'T HAVE TO BE A COP TO TELL BULLIES TO STOP. Beside it, his tan hat hung on a hook. He almost bumped it, pulling up a chair and motioning for her to take a seat. She sat at the corner of his desk as he hurried to two gray file cabinets in the corner and grasped a box sitting on top. RJ grabbed the matching chair and pulled it to the desk. She shot him a glance.

"What?" Sitting beside her, he stretched his arm across the back of her chair. "I need a place to sit too."

The deputy returned and placed the box on the desk. "These are Brooke's personal effects that were on her body." Hovering over it, he pulled out a folded strip of paper. "The suicide note was pinned to her blouse."

He handed Tori the rectangular strip. It looked like a fate from a Chinese fortune cookie that had been cut along the top and the bottom. Inscribed in black cursive penmanship, a sentence read:

"Whatever I am, you made me."

Tori leaned forward, studying it. "Brooke wrote this?"

"Her dying words. Anything look familiar?" The deputy sat in his chair.

Tori looked up. "This is the text message I've been receiving."

"I know." The deputy shook his head. "It's a prank. Someone's gett'n a real good laugh out of this."

RJ shook his head. "I don't think it's a prank." He leaned over Tori's shoulder and grabbed the note. "This proves it. Grab a penny, 'cause I think Patrick Swayze here is communicating with you."

The deputy shrugged and scratched his head. "I don't know what that means."

"It means this message is important and Brooke is contacting us through her cell phone." RJ could barely get the words out through the rising excitement in his voice. "Brooke is trying to tell Tori something. Probably something about her death."

Tori let out a derisive laugh to cover her annoyance.

RJ turned to her. "I saw that," he said.

"I wasn't trying to hide it." She took the note from his hands and read it again. The deputy was wrong. He had to be. This wasn't a prank. And, as much as she hated to admit it, RJ was right—that message did have some importance. But what? She looked up from the paper. "You're telling me Brooke wrote this note?"

The deputy nodded. "Yeah, like I said. She pinned it to her blouse."

"Who else knows about the suicide note?" She studied the paper, never looking up as she spoke.

"I don't know." The deputy watched her. "The sheriff. Brooke's family."

"Ash?"

"Probably," he answered.

She held the paper strip by the edges and walked to a lamp sitting atop the file cabinet. The light accentuated the handwriting. She analyzed the curve of the w, the loop of the y, while ignoring RJ as he rummaged through the box on the desk.

"Her cell phone isn't here," he said.

"She didn't have it on her when she died." The deputy seemed more focused on Tori than RJ.

"But she had her purse with her." RJ removed a leather purse from the box. Reaching into it, he pulled out a handful of square packets of antidepressants. "Looks like she was suffering from depression." He let the packets fall between his fingers and spill across the desk. "Suffer'n real bad."

Tori turned away from the file cabinet and flattened the note on top of the file cabinet. She snapped a photo with her phone. RJ looked over at her as the deputy rose from his desk.

"Hell's bells, Tori! What're you doing?" The deputy marched toward her and took the note from her hands. "You can't be taking photos in here."

"Brooke didn't write it." Her voice rose as she pointed to the paper. "That isn't her handwriting."

The deputy seemed stumped for words. "Come again?"

"I've known Brooke for over twenty years. We grew up together. I know her handwriting and this isn't it."

The deputy shook his head. "That's crazy."

"Maybe. Maybe not." She looked back at the window and turned to him again. "I'm telling you, Brooke didn't write this."

RJ raised a hand. "So where is Brooke's cell phone? It's not in her purse or with her personal effects."

"I don't know. Maybe it's at her house." The deputy shrugged and picked up the scattered antidepressant packets from the desk. He dropped them into the purse. "Guess it could be anywhere."

The young tattooed clerk entered the office and interrupted him.

"Pardon me, sir, but I've gotten six calls from the women's club," she said. "They've found Ash. He's drunk, naked as a jaybird, and wizz'n on Charlotte's prized azaleas."

"Thanks, Zoe. I'll take it from here." The deputy grabbed his hat off the wall, rattling the loose hook. "Looks like I better go get him before the chief gets wind of it."

The thought of seeing the chief—the sheriff—Mike—made Tori shudder. She took a breath and held it as the deputy flipped his hat atop his head and rushed past Zoe. Exhaling, Tori followed, with RJ tagging behind. They left the building and walked down the stone steps leading to the sidewalk.

"Ash is drinking again?" Tori asked.

Deputy Torres placed a hand on her back. "He's had a rough time."

"That's an understatement."

The deputy stopped. "Look, someone thinks they're being awful smart, sending you those text messages. Don't go making a big deal out of it and telling everyone. This funeral is gonna be tough enough to get through without adding more fuel to the fire."

"What do you mean?"

"I mean, there's enough gossip without this kind of stuff stirring up the church ladies," he said.

"It's not gossip. Brooke didn't write that note."

"Maybe she did, maybe she didn't." The deputy looked away and turned back to Tori. "Either way—put a pin in it for now. Let's get through tomorrow. This funeral is going to be rough."

* * * *

Tori ended the call and dropped her cell phone into her purse. Sitting in the front passenger seat next to RJ, she thought about Ash drinking again and Darla running away from her grandfather and returning to the old water tower. Brooke's suicide note she didn't write. The text messages. Coming home.

Mike.

RJ asked her again, a little louder this time. "Hell's bells? Did he really say that?"

"Deputy Torres is a good man."

"He's classic." RJ pulled away from the courthouse and maneuvered through the roundabout in the center of town. He glanced over when she turned up the music. Justin Timberlake blared through the speakers again. He turned it down. "Guess there's no point goin' back to the Martin house ... since he never answered and all."

"Nope." She twisted the volume knob, cranking up the music.

He turned down the volume. "Your parents—we stay'n with them?"

"My mom moved to Fort Worth. I called a friend." Tori stared out the window as RJ headed down Main Street, passing a Starbucks and a Dunkin' Donuts. She didn't bother with the music. For a few blocks she had a lump in her throat. She hadn't talked to Winnie since leaving Elroy Springs. Her old friend sounded friendly on the phone, excited, even. Still, Tori wasn't sure what to say about Brooke's death, the past, or anything else. Maybe she'd let Winnie do all the talking.

Tori gave RJ directions into a neighborhood of old houses with way too many American flags still waving after dark. Pink plastic flamingoes stood watch in the flower bed of every front yard. Winnie's house appeared on the lake side of the road, and neither flag nor flamingo was to be found.

Winnie still lived in the home her grandparents had built, and Tori remembered it precisely. She'd spent many afternoons there, completing school projects at the kitchen table, gossiping in Winnie's bedroom, birthday parties in the backyard. It was like a second home. Not just because she felt a deep kinship to Winnie, which she did, but because she wanted to be near Winnie's older brother.

She'd had it bad for him as long as she could remember. And the memory of the exact moment she first laid eyes on him still burned hot, as blistering as that summer afternoon when they met in the barn next to the house. A tall, hand-some sixth grader, Mike leaned over his dirt bike, fixing the broken chain, with two other boys on the baseball team. He wore a backwards baseball cap ... black grease smudged his right cheek and covered his T-shirt. When he looked up, he gave her a smirky, lopsided grin.

He tossed a greasy rag at Winnie and told her to get lost. Springing up from his bike, he rushed to the entrance and rolled the barn doors shut. Ever since that day, Tori had looked for any excuse to hang out there.

The barn still stood to the side of Winnie's house, and Tori noticed it as they pulled up.

RJ parked in the dirt driveway, behind a tan-and-green station wagon. Across from it, a heavyset woman with curly blonde hair sat in a porch swing, eating a bowl of ice cream. She set down the bowl, hopped up, and waved as Tori slipped out of the Jeep.

"Winnie," Tori called out. She could hear dogs barking in the house.

Leaping off the porch, Winnie shrieked and rushed into the yard. She wrapped her arms around Tori and gave her a hug. Then she turned to RJ. He leaned forward and shook her hand. Tori introduced them, and Winnie hugged him with the same enthusiasm she'd showered on Tori.

"Come in. Come in." Winnie led them along a walkway between flickering solar lights, to the covered porch. From the eaves, bristly fronds of hanging ferns rustled in the warm night breeze. She held the front door open and waved Tori and RJ inside. "Now, you two make yourself right at home."

Carrying overnight bags, Tori and RJ stepped inside. Three dogs—a Chihuahua, a cocker spaniel, and a pug—barked and jumped on their hind legs. Tori knelt and held out her hand. The pug sniffed it and resumed barking.

"They're not mine," Winnie said, holding the melting bowl of ice cream. She yelled at the dogs to hush up and put down the bowl. Grabbing a bag of bacon-flavored *Beggin' Strips* from a side table along the wall and shaking it to get their attention, she led the dogs to a room off to the side. "It's the Cavanaughs' cocker spaniel, old man Herman's Chihuahua, and, remember Jennifer Davis? It's her pug." Winnie corralled the dogs into the room and shut the door. "I'm boarding dogs while the owners are, uh, out of town for the Fourth of July holiday."

Tori listened to them yap and bark and scratch at the door as she looked around the living room. Blue and silver balloons bobbed and floated in every corner, on the couch, the end tables, and everywhere else she looked.

"They're for Brooke, you know, her memorial," Winnie said. "We're releasing them over the lake."

Tori set down her suitcase and draped her black dress over the sofa. She looked around. "Everything looks exactly the same. You haven't changed a bit, Winnie Bennett."

"It's Daniels now. I got married, um, last summer." Winnie picked up a framed photo from the end table. "His name is Howard and he's a widower. He was lonely. I was lonely. So, we, um, made it legal."

Tori squealed and hugged Winnie again. "You got married? When? How'd you meet him?"

"Would you believe Brooke introduced us?" Winnie handed the framed photo to Tori.

"I can't believe it." Tori stared at the photo of Winnie standing next to a smiling older gentleman with a shock of white hair. She looked up and glanced around the room. "Where is he? I want to meet him."

"He's away on a sales trip. Pharmaceutical sales, you know." Winnie laughed as if she'd told a joke. "He's gone so much I call him my part-time husband. But he knows every-thing that happened, and he'll be back in time for the funeral."

"That's good. I'm sure you could use his support with everything that's going on."

"Lemme tell you, if it wasn't for those pictures, I wouldn't even remember what he looks like." Winnie waved a hand at the picture frames on the fireplace mantle and then gestured to Tori's black dress folded over the back of the sofa. "That's a beautiful dress."

"It was hanging in the closet," Tori said. "I didn't have time to shop for something new."

"I hate buying clothes for any kind of formal event," Winnie said, running her hands down her sides. "The sales-lady talked me into a dress that's too tight. She said I needed to lose only a pound or two. Now I've been, you know, dieting like a mad woman the last week."

Tori looked over at the bowl of ice cream. "What are you talking about? You look great," she said as Winnie disappeared into the kitchen. Tori glanced at RJ and looked around the living room. Despite the balloons, the house looked every inch as she remembered.

Above the fireplace mantle hung a wedding portrait of Winnie and Howard, and framed photos of her grandparents were on either side. A family portrait stood like a proud trophy on the mantle, and on the wall hung many more photos. Tori noticed one of Mike, a faded Polaroid taken on the lake when they were teenagers. And then there was another, a recent photo of him and his wife—What's her face—Scarlett? There were twin boys in the photo with them.

RJ moved balloons off the couch and plopped down on the worn cushions. He put his feet up on the coffee table, kicking balloons out of the way. Winnie came out of the kitchen, carrying three Corona bottles. RJ took one and flipped on the television.

"You got ESPN?" he asked.

"Ummmm, channel thirty-nine, I think," Winnie said, and turned to Tori. "How about some iced tea? Let's get caught up. You know I haven't seen you in years."

Tori looked at the Coronas. "What about the beers?"

"Those are for your, um, friend." Winnie laughed out loud. "You know, to keep him entertained while we catch up."

RJ winked at her. "I like the way you think," he said, taking the beers and setting them on the coffee table, among a group of balloons. He popped the cap off one and leaned back into the couch, before aiming the remote at the TV.

"Alright then," Tori said, turning to Winnie. "We need to talk."

CHAPTER ELEVEN

TI_E BO_B

Tori followed her old friend into the cluttered yet familiar kitchen. Nothing had changed since Winnie's grandparents owned the place. Orange curtains framed the windows that matched a wallpaper border of citrus trees running along the top of the walls and under a clock was a calendar with a picture of kittens. The only new addition seemed to be the silver balloons—*even more, if that was possible*—floating over the kitchen table, their strings stretched taut to bricks on the tabletop.

"I was nervous about calling you." Tori plucked the string attached to a balloon. "I wasn't sure if you'd want to hear from me."

"No, I should be the one, you know, apologizing." Winnie shook her head. "Sorry I went all radio silent on you. I didn't mean to shut you out."

"Forget it. You had to stick with your brother."

"There were a lot of time I wanted to call you." Winnie directed Tori to take a seat at the table, among dozens of Tupperware dishes and all those balloons. She cleared a space next to a stack of newspapers. "This place is such a mess."

"It's fine." Tori sat at the table. The stack of newspapers caught her attention and she noticed the headline: "High School Teacher Found Dead." She tried to ignore it.

"I've been so busy getting everything ready for the, um, you know, funeral and memorial." Winnie opened the refrigerator and took out a pitcher of iced tea. "You wouldn't believe everything going on. It's been a hurricane around here."

Tori watched her, listening. She looked around the kitchen, remembering the years she'd spent in this house with Winnie and her grandparents, and, of course, Mike. She focused on the empty chair across from her.

Not that long ago, a teenage Mike sat there. He'd painted the inside of a cardboard box all black with suspended colored Styrofoam balls hanging in a row from one side to the other.

"It's the solar system," he had said. "And it's gonna win the science fair."

Tori had looked in the box and counted the balls. "The sun should be, like, ten times bigger and you've got nine planets, not eight."

"I'm counting Pluto as a planet."

"But it's not." Tori reached into the box and plucked the little white ball off the string. She held it up. "Pluto is smaller than our moon and it's on a whole different orbital plane than the rest of the planets."

"Hmmm," he said. "I guess once you've been up there you know you been some place." He laughed and grabbed the Styrofoam ball from her hand. He placed it back inside the box.

She snatched it again. "What does that even mean?"

"You know … the planetarium. James Dean plays a kid with his high school class at the planetarium. He says, 'Once you've been up there you know you been some place.'"

Speechless, Tori stared at him.

He squinted and cocked his head. "C'mon, haven't you ever seen *Rebel Without a Cause*?"

She stared at him, blank eyed.

He took the little Styrofoam Pluto from her hand. "James Dean. Natalie Wood." He waited for her to respond. When she didn't, he shook his head. "We've gotta watch it sometime."

Winnie's voice swept the memory away.

"I hope you don't want sugar in your tea." Winnie poured two tall glasses and brought them to the table. "Howard doesn't allow sugar or snacks within a five-mile radius of this house. But the jokes on him. Every time he leaves town, I stock the fridge with Häagen-Daz."

"Didn't you say you were on a diet?"

"I am. That's why I bought the kind with 'no added sugar' on the carton."

"Okay and no, I don't need sugar in my tea." Tori took the glass from Winnie's hand. She noticed three water bowls on the floor in the corner and she could still hear the dogs barking from the other room.

Winnie grinned and sat next to her. "So? Have you, er, talked to him?"

Tori pretended she didn't know who Winnie was referring to. "What? Who?"

"You know ... my brother. At the Sheriff's Department. Was he there?"

"No, he wasn't there." Tori paused. "I haven't seen him since before the, well .... So, how is he? How does he look?"

Winnie laughed. "You looking for honesty? Or you just want me to make you feel superior?"

"The truth, I guess." Tori broke into a wide, open smile. "As long as you're telling me he got fat ... or bald ... or homeless. I'll take anything you got."

Winnie smiled. "Mike's fine. You know, I'm sure he'll be glad to see you." The conversation lulled for a few awkward seconds, then Winnie perked up. "Enough about my stupid ol' brother. Tell me everything about, uh, RJ." Winnie moved the balloons out of the way and grasped Tori's hands in hers. "Who is he? Where'd you meet him? Is it serious?"

Tori shrugged. "RJ is just, well, RJ."

"And that means what, exactly?"

"He's my cameraman."

Winnie grimaced and made a tsk sound that was almost scolding. "He's more than that. What's going on between you two?"

"Nothing. He's a few years younger."

"Who cares? He's a cutie."

"We're friends. Co-workers." She noticed the volume of the television in the other room. It sounded like RJ had turned it up over the barking dogs. She looked back at Winnie. "We're work friends."

"I don't believe that for a second." Winnie raised her voice. The television volume got louder. It seemed like the dogs were getting louder too. "He's, you know, attending the funeral with you."

"We're covering an important story together. We're headed out right after the funeral."

"He's still supporting you." Winnie turned her head to look back into the living room.

Tori heard it too. The dogs' barking grew louder, and she tried to ignore it. "We're leaving for the Tampa Bay Boat Show immediately afterwards. I have to interview a skiing hamster or something."

"It doesn't matter." Winnie smiled at her. "I'm just glad you have someone in your life, you know, after everything that happened with my brother."

Tori forced a laugh. "Are you kidding? That was a million years ago."

"It was five years ago." Winnie shook her head. "And you'd been pining after him for decades before that."

"Winnie ... I'm now officially changing the subject. Again." Tori could tell the combined dog barking and TV volume were grating Winnie's nerves.

"Ummm," she said, "let's go outside. I got something to show you." Winnie got up from the table and made her way to the back door.

Tori followed, noticing the wooden key hook on the wall beside the door jamb. Several rings hung from the hooks with dangling keys. One set had a large pewter *B* attached to a thin chain and three keys hanging from the ring. Brooke's spare house keys. Tori had a set like it. They all did, back then. And for a second, she wondered if Winnie still had the keys to her old house too.

Outside, the barking dogs and loud TV gave way to the rising drone of crickets and bullfrogs near the lake. Winnie led Tori to the old barn on the side of the house and rolled the large doors open. She flipped on a light, revealing a large trailer dripping in silver-and-blue festooning garland and fringe. A cardboard castle sat on the flatbed, with painted bricks that looked like gray Legos snapped together. Turrets and towers with peaked blue roofs jutted from the base and the front boasted a meticulously created drawbridge of rope and plywood.

"It's Snow White's castle," Winnie said, rushing to it. She turned back to Tori. "It's our float for, you know, the Fourth of July parade through downtown."

Torri stepped into the barn and cautiously approached the majestic spectacle. "This is a Fourth of July float? It doesn't seem very patriotic."

"It was, um, my sister-in-law's idea. She's going to be Snow White, Mike's Prince Charming, and the twins are the dwarves—I mean, little people. She's made costumes and everything."

"What about you?" Tori looked over at Winnie.

Winnie shook her head. "Oh, uh, I'm the Wicked Witch. She's made me a costume too, with, you know, poison apples and everything."

Tori laughed and touched the float. There must've been eight rolls of silver fringe along the base, and the entire back side of the castle was still raw cardboard, lacking the intricate detail of the bricks and glitter.

Winnie came up beside her. "We're not finished yet," she said, pointing to the unpainted cardboard. "Brooke and Ash were going to join us, and she was working on that part of the float the morning she ..." Her voice trailed off.

Tori looked down at the worn barn floor. Her voice catching in her throat, she said, "What time is the funeral tomorrow?"

"Ten o'clock. We're having the services at the First Baptist Church and then a memorial dinner at Skeeter Park." Winnie turned and stepped out of the barn. She faced the lake, and Tori could only see the black outline of her body as she continued. "I, um, I still can't believe it. I can't believe Brooke ... her accident."

Tori walked out of the barn and stepped beside her. "She committed suicide."

Winnie sniffled and wiped her nose with the back of her arm. "That's what they say."

"You don't believe it?"

"I-I don't know." Winnie kept her eyes down. "Brooke was, you know, unhappy and all. I know that."

"She was obviously taking antidepressants. At the Sheriff's Office, her purse was full of sample packets. Was she clinically depressed?"

"I don't think so. Um, I mean I had no idea she was *that* level of unhappy." Winnie crossed the yard to the dock, where waves lapped against the shore. She stared, head down, at the water as she spoke. "But even if she was depressed, how could she leave her daughter like that? How could she do that to Darla?"

Tori stepped onto the dock. A small runabout, tied to a post, rose and fell with the incoming waves. Winnie seemed hypnotized by the movement, and Tori wondered what she was thinking.

"You don't think Brooke took her own life, do you?" Tori touched her arm.

Winnie shook her away, saying, "No. Yes. I don't know." Winnie looked at Tori with teary eyes. "What kind of question is that, anyway?"

Tori gulped. "Maybe we're both thinking the same thing."

"I don't know what to think." Winnie wiped her eyes. "I don't know what to think about any of this."

"I need to tell you something," Tori said. She watched the small boat tied to the post, and then turned to her friend. "I've been getting text messages over the past couple of days." She paused, listening to hidden frogs in the reeds. They sounded spooky, unnatural. And it made what she had to say all the more startling. "From Brooke's number."

"From her cell phone?" Winnie repeated it as if slowly digesting its meaning. "Someone's texting you from her phone? Who, Ash?"

"I don't know. If not Ash, then maybe Brooke's father. Or Darla." Tori stood beside Winnie and stared at the dark waves. "Deputy Torres thinks it's a practical joke. Someone is pulling a prank."

"Why?"

"The text message matches, word for word, the note Brooke left behind."

"The note? You mean, um, her suicide note? What'd it say?"

"Whatever I am, you made me." Tori watched Winnie's reaction. There wasn't one, as far as she could tell. "Any idea what that means?"

Winnie shook her head, and Tori could see the wheels turning.

Slowly, Winnie said, "I think it's something Brooke said once. Or maybe Ash. It sounds familiar and all, but I'm not sure."

"Why would they say it? What does it mean?"

"I don't know. Brooke was clearly unhappy, um, you know. She was in an unhappy marriage."

"Yeah, you said that." Tori pressed the issue. "So, who has Brooke's cell phone?"

Winnie shrugged. "Search me."

"You don't have it, do you?"

"No." Winnie thought about it a moment. "Uhhh—I'd imagine it's at her house."

"That's what I'm thinking too." Tori stared at the lake for several moments and turned back to Winnie. "I want to talk to Ash. See if he sent me the text messages. Or maybe Darla."

Winnie started to say something and then stopped herself.

Tori gripped her shoulder. "What is it?"

"Well." Winnie's face darkened with an unreadable expression. She clenched her hands, rubbing them together, and seemed to focus on the water, unable—or unwilling—to look Tori square in the eyes. "I can't say where the cell phone is now, but, um, the day she died, she left her phone in my barn. We'd been working on the float for the Fourth of July parade, and I ran it over to her house that evening and, you know, that was the last I saw it, I suppose."

"Was she home when you dropped it off? How'd she look?"

"She wasn't there." Winnie's eyes enlarged. "I gave the phone to Ash."

"Brooke wasn't there? Where was she?"

"She was ..." Winnie was clearly holding something back. "She was, um, out."

"But you don't know where she was?" Tori looked Winnie in the eyes. "Where was she?"

Winnie broke the gaze. Her hands trembled and she clasped them behind her back.

Tori continued pressing. "You're not telling me something."

Winnie shook her head. "I don't know. Ash was agitated, I guess, that Brooke wasn't home, and you know how he gets. I didn't stay long."

"Ash was agitated?" Tori stepped back. This was what she'd feared all along, and Winnie's demeanor all but confirmed it. "I don't think Brooke wrote the note and I need to find her handwriting to confirm it. Do you have anything that Brooke wrote?"

"Maybe. I think I can find something." The breeze off the lake picked up as Winnie turned back toward the house. Tori followed.

Inside, Tori noticed the dogs had stopped barking, although the TV volume still blared. She returned to the living room and found all three—the cocker spaniel, the Chihuahua, and the pug—sitting on the couch with RJ. Their heads turned and followed her every movement as she plopped down on the couch beside them. Winnie made her way upstairs, causing the dogs to leap off the couch with the synchronization of an Olympic swim team and race up the stairs after her.

Balloons floated everywhere in the room, surrounding the couch and both sides of the TV. Tori picked up the remote and muted the volume. RJ flipped his feet off the coffee table and sat up.

"Hey, I was watching that."

"You had it turned up so loud the whole neighborhood coulda been watching it."

"I couldn't hear it over the pooches howling," he said.

She looked back at the staircase. Somewhere upstairs, Winnie was opening and shutting drawers. She wondered what Winnie would find. RJ snapped his fingers and pointed at the TV.

Simone Adams was on the screen. Looking somber, the redheaded newscaster stood in front of the hospital ER entrance, holding a mic to her face.

Tori shook her head. "Is she still on this?"

"Turn the sound up," RJ said, reaching for the remote.

She held it away from him. "I don't want to listen to her," she said, gripping the remote.

"Something's going on. We need to hear this." He lunged forward, snatched the control from her hand, and turned up the volume.

Simone's face filled the screen. "… has taken a tragic turn. Bobby Greene succumbed to his injuries at four thirty this afternoon."

Tori leaned forward. "What!"

"The kid died?" RJ turned up the volume another couple bars. The camera followed Simone to an approaching ambulance, its lights flashing.

"Police are continuing their search for the hit-and-run driver and are following up on every incoming lead. We'll bring you updates as we receive them." Simone gripped the mic with both hands. "This is Simone Adams and wherever there's news, you'll find my shoes."

RJ turned off the TV and looked at Tori. "I can't believe the kid didn't make it."

"I don't know what to say." She sat back on the couch. "Should we send something to his parents? Flowers, maybe? A casserole?"

Winnie came down the stairs, followed by the three dogs. They barked and jumped at her feet as she waved a red-and-green envelope in her hand. She maneuvered around the balloons and made her way to the couch. The dogs jumped onto the cushion beside her and the cocker spaniel nestled on her lap. The Chihuahua sat beside RJ.

"Found it. It's, you know, a Christmas card from Brooke and Ash." Winnie panted as she spoke, as if the jog up the stairs and back down had knocked the wind out of her. She slipped the card from the envelope and handed it to Tori. "It's from them both, but Brooke wrote the note and signed both their names."

Tori opened the card and compared the handwriting to the photo of the suicide note on her phone. The pug sniffed the paper and gave it a lick. She pushed the dog away and studied the handwriting, noticing the letters in the pic looked straight and square, drawn tightly together in a masculine sort of way. The letters written on the card were large and loopy, more feminine. She handed the card and phone to Winnie.

Winnie glanced at the phone, then at the note, back at the phone. She leaned deep into the couch and stated, "They don't match."

Tori nodded. "Not even close."

Winnie handed the phone back to Tori. "What does it mean?"

Tori took a breath. The pug sniffed the phone and gave it a lick. She pushed him away. They were all quiet for several seconds.

Tori turned to RJ and then to Winnie. "Did you ever read *Her Last Breath*?"

He shook his head. "That's a new one."

"Lynda Leon, the wife of a CEO and mother of four, was found dead, hanging from the attic ceiling. She'd tied a belt around her neck and apparently committed suicide."

Winnie cupped a hand to her mouth. "That's awful."

"When police investigated, they found that her husband had staged the suicide. They'd been fighting, and she accidentally fell down the stairs and broke her neck. He panicked and was afraid the police would think he pushed her, so he made it look like she took her life."

"Oh, come on," Winnie said. "Surely you aren't implying what I think you're implying."

Tori stared at the suicide note on her phone, scrutinizing the handwriting. *Whatever I am, you made me.* "I don't know yet," she said in a low tone. "Now I want to see something Ash wrote. I want to compare his handwriting."

RJ stood, upending the Chihuahua. "Whoa—back that truck up." The little dog yelped at him as he paced the room. "We've gotta get back to Tampa tomorrow after the funeral. We've got a boat show to cover."

Tori lifted the Chihuahua into her arms, quieting it. The pug sniffed the little dog and gave it a lick. She stared at RJ, unblinking. "We've got some serious questions to answer, regarding Brooke's death."

"We're hitting the road." RJ shook his head and raised his hands. "Funeral's over and we're leaving."

"We can't. What about the text messages? And this suicide note Brooke obviously didn't write," Tori said. "And what about your VIPs?"

"EVPs. And Tori," he said, "we can come back. We'll cover the boat show and we'll come right back."

Tori took a deep breath. "Okay," she said. "I guess you're right."

That night, Tori stayed in Winnie's childhood bedroom upstairs, thankful that Mike's old bedroom across the hall had been converted into a home office. RJ slept on the couch downstairs, in the living room, amid balloons and dogs. Tori could hear the ramblings of Sports Center all the way to her room, even with the door shut. She did her best to ignore it.

The window offered a view of the backyard and the dock. She watched the lake sparkle in the moonlight.

Not so long ago, teenage Mike would've snuck out of this old house, his grandparents none the wiser. She could imagine him tiptoeing down to that dock and the small motorboat.

She would've been waiting for him a few miles up the lake, back then, in her own yard, beneath the giant oak by the water's edge, a rope still tied to its overhanging branch. He'd float to the little dock on her property and tie off. A small boathouse, not much more than a treehouse on stilts, looked over the dock, and it gave them privacy when he arrived, her mother oblivious to the rendezvous.

One September night, they climbed onto the tin roof of the boathouse to watch the Leonid meteor shower. Dozens of "shooting stars" streaked across the sky, and Tori lay beside Mike, face up with her head leaning on his shoulder, watching in awe.

She leaned over to kiss him, but he pushed her away.

"I don't know if I can be with someone who's never seen *Rebel Without a Cause*," he whispered to her, grinning.

She pointed at the stars as another streaked across the sky in a flash.

"Once you've been there," she whispered in his ear, "you know you been some place."

She gripped his chin and kissed him.

They made love for the first time that night on the roof of the boathouse, beneath the meteor shower. Afterwards, she knew he was the man she'd marry. Sure, she'd dreamed about it since the day she first saw him fixing his bike in the barn, surrounded by his buddies from the baseball team, and yelling at Winnie. Tori had harbored a schoolgirl crush for as long as she could remember, yet in that moment she realized he felt the same way.

She felt so happy in his arms.

She still missed that feeling.

Taking the spare pillow on the bed, she fluffed it and placed it beside her. She wrapped an arm around it and hugged it. At some point, she drifted to sleep while listening to the muffled highlights of the Rays versus the Rangers game.

The house was quiet when her eyes suddenly opened. She wasn't sure what time it was or what woke her ... until her cell phone dinged. Again.

She sat up in bed and glanced at her phone. Two new text messages. Both from Brooke's number. Clicking on the icon, she brought up the message.

"I' m glad ur here."

"R U there?"

Tori stared at it a moment and shook her head to clear her eyes. Was she dreaming? She read it again. Pressed Reply. Typed "Who is this?" and hit Send. She waited several seconds. The cell phone dinged. She jumped. Her thumb clicked the new message.

"Whatever I am, you made me."

CHAPTER TWELVE

R_ST IN P_AC_

Saturday, June 30

Tori listened to the church bells ring. Beside her, RJ steered the Jeep into the gravel parking lot, where a crowd gathered at the First Baptist Church of Elroy Springs. He parked, and she let herself out, smiling at a lot of familiar faces—people she hadn't seen in years.

Her simple, sleeveless black dress wasn't making the impression she wanted, and she wished she'd had more time to iron out the wrinkles. Plus, the new shoes were uncomfortably tight. RJ wore a dark blue suit. He'd left the top button of his shirt open.

Together, they walked toward the front of the church.

"You should've shaved," she said under her breath to him. "This is a funeral, not a fishing trip."

"I didn't bring a razor." He rubbed the stubble on his chin.

"And where's your tie?"

"Back off, Smother. I didn't bring one." His hand dropped to the top button on his shirt. "We left in a hurry, remember?"

As groups huddled on the front steps and people shuffled inside, Tori saw Pastor Fields. Deputy Torres was there too, dressed in his tan uniform, with his family. Then she saw him.

The sheriff.

The ex.

Mike.

Embarrassed, she bowed her head. But he'd already spotted her. Their eyes connected for the briefest second before she looked away. Logically, she knew he would be here. She knew she'd have to talk to him about Brooke and her tragic death and, possibly, the past. But emotionally, Tori had hoped he'd be out of town or something.

Wearing a crisp, tan uniform and a dark brown felt Stratton hat, Mike left the crowd and walked toward them with a woman by his side. Probably his wife, what's her name. Harlot? It was the inevitable moment Tori had been dreading for the last five years.

In her peripheral vision, she watched them walk hand in hand, husband and wife. Lovers. Partners. Together, they moved in excruciatingly slow motion. She tried not to look at him, pretended not to see him. She felt him, though. Sensed his presence, like gravity tugging on her body. With each step, the force between them grew stronger.

It was like an electrifying tether extending from his swaying hands, his biceps, his chest, from his warm, handsome face and piercing blue eyes that stretched out to grip her very core. Powerless against it, she felt oppressed under the weight of his stare. She couldn't help herself and she looked up. Their eyes met. Locked.

He was only feet away.

It had been five long years since she last gazed into those cruel, sensitive eyes. Five years since he disappeared. No explanation. No phone call. No goodbye. Five long years.

She couldn't just stand there. Should she pretend to be busy? She was mourning, that's what she was doing. She was busy mourning. Her hand found RJ's and clenched it. He moved his arm and turned his head toward her.

"What is it?" he whispered, and hesitated.

He was looking at Mike, and she knew he understood even without knowing the whole story. She could feel RJ's silent acknowledgment of the man standing a couple of feet away from them, who was pulling at her body and her heart with some magnetic force from the past. It made her knees weak. She wanted to run. But she didn't. She wanted to vomit. But she didn't. She could only stand there, in silence, gripping RJ's left hand in a vise.

No one spoke for several moments.

Finally, Mike cleared his throat. "It's been a while," he said, pushing the brim of his hat back farther on his head.

That was it. After five torturous years, the stalemate was over. He'd spoken first.

Tori's eyes glistened. She didn't blink. Her hand squeezed RJ's again, pressing his fingers till he cringed and tried to pull his hand away. She released him but remained focused on Mike. He looked taller than she remembered. The badge on his shirt pocket glinted in the sun.

She said, "You were elected sheriff?"

"Yep." He trembled. Was he nervous? He was still holding his wife's hand. It almost seemed like he was standing behind her.

He was nervous. Really nervous. He had left her at the altar for this woman. He unceremoniously dumped her for this woman. This was the woman he married. The cad broke Tori's heart and probably had no idea what to say.

Then he spoke. "I wasn't sure if you'd be here."

"Ash called me."

"Good. I'm glad. He's been having a rough time of ...." Mike didn't finish the sentence. His feet shuffled slightly across the gravel, displacing a couple of rocks, but he never broke his gaze.

"You look good," he continued. "Have you been okay? I mean, how've you been?"

"Fine." Tori's voice was stiff, formal, and she reached for RJ's left hand again. She felt his body tense next to hers, surprised, and she interrupted him before he could protest. "Thank you for asking."

There was another awkward pause, but it was Charlotte who broke the silence this time. Stepping in front of Mike, she wore a conservative, off-the-shoulder black dress with light gray watermelons printed on the fabric.

She extended her hand and smiled. "You must be Tori Younger. My husband has told me so much about you."

"He did?" Tori tried to control the muscles in her face. She didn't want to glare. Or seem angry. Or emotional. "Sheriff Bennett has told you about me?"

Charlotte kept her hand extended, weirdly unaware of the awkwardness. "My husband told me you two grew up together. You and Brooke were close friends with his sister, Winnie. I'm so sorry for your loss."

"Thank you." Tori glanced at the woman's hand but made no offer to accept it. She couldn't help but notice the little gray watermelons on her dress. Watermelons? Really?

Charlotte withdrew her hand and folded her arms across her chest. "Did my husband tell you we have children?" she asked.

The words stung. Tori's eyes watered. She would not cry, she told herself. She would not show anger or surprise or any emotion at all. Her lips twisted into a forced smile as she squeezed RJ's hand again, even tighter. "You have … kids?"

"Two boys," Mike clarified.

"Twins." Charlotte unfolded her arms and reached for Mike's arm, bringing him closer. "We're deliriously happy."

She was showing off, marking her territory. Tori could see that, even if the men couldn't. She pulled RJ closer in response, knocking him off balance. She kept her face frozen in the forced smile. "Well … good. Good for you both."

Mike nodded, as if signaling he understood information about his marriage and children was the last thing on earth she wanted to hear about right now. He turned toward RJ and extended his hand. "And you are?"

"I'm RJ, a friend of Tori's."

"A close, personal friend," Tori added. She shivered and released his hand but grabbed his upper arm.

"Yes," RJ repeated, flexing his bicep clenched in Tori's grip. "A close, personal friend of Tori's. I'm also her cameraman."

"You work together?" Mike said, emphasizing each syllable as if he'd picked up on some subtext.

She thought she detected a twinge of judgment in his tone.

As if confirming it, Mike winked at her and continued. "Well, I'm pleased to meet your close, personal friend, RJ. How long have you two known each other?"

Tori stared at him for a second. She wanted to ask, *How long have you known Charlotte?*—but the gray Velcro cuff on Mike's left wrist attached to an LCD screen distracted her. "That's some watch," she said, pointing to it.

Charlotte spoke up. "It's a blood pressure monitor. We're making sure he stays healthy."

Tori looked at Mike.

He nodded. "It's a heart palpitation. My father had it. I have it."

Tori was speechless. She remembered when his and Winnie's father passed away, and they moved in with their grandparents.

No one spoke for several seconds.

After the silence became awkward, Charlotte tugged Mike's arm. "The funeral is about to start. We should find seats."

"Wait." Tori's fingers dug deep into RJ's bicep. She couldn't believe Mike was wearing a blood pressure monitor for a watch. That scared her. "Are you okay?"

"He's fine," Charlotte said quickly, before Mike could respond. She flashed Tori a smile and turned to her husband. "Come on, Michael, darling, let's go."

Tori watched them a moment and then forced a smile. "You're right. We should find our seats."

Mike shot her a direct, reassuring smirk. "I'm fine, Tori. I really am ... and it's good to see you again." He tipped his hat to her.

His wife nudged him again and they headed toward the church. Tori watched him as RJ flapped his left arm, forcing her to release him and allowing the blood flow to return.

He leaned in toward her. "What was that all about?"

"Long, painful story." She walked toward the church.

"Is there any other kind?" He followed her. "So, your ex is the sheriff? You dated the town sheriff?"

"Dated? You could say we dated."

"You could say you kickboxed." He laughed. "Spill it."

Tori stopped. "I wouldn't say I was left at the altar, but a dress was bought. Vows were written. A honeymoon in Cancun was booked."

"Tori Younger has a past. Who knew? You got jilted by the town sheriff."

"He wasn't the sheriff then." Tori moved faster, a couple steps ahead of RJ. "Now let's go find our seats."

Inside the church, large colorful floral arrangements lined the walls beneath stained-glass windows that let in a rosy and pea-green light. Tori stared at the flowers as she and RJ joined the line in the sanctuary. Brooke's open casket lay front and center.

Winnie, wearing a tight black dress that looked stretched to capacity at the seams, greeted each incoming guest, shook their hands at the top of the aisle, and solemnly said, "Glad you could come. Take a seat. Glad you could come."

She handed Tori and RJ folded pamphlets with Brooke's picture on the cover and a poem typed inside. She gasped and adjusted her waistline. "I can't breathe in this thing," she whispered to Tori. "I could just kill that saleslady."

RJ cringed. "Did you really just say that at a funeral?"

Tori ignored the remarks, scanning the pamphlet and remembering the photo from Brooke's Facebook page. They approached the casket. Encircled by flower arrangements and next to an easel holding a poster-sized senior class photo, Brooke lay in a mahogany casket, her hands clasped, a calm shadow across her face. She looked so serene. The funeral parlor had clothed her in a white turtleneck that covered the bruises to her neck. It chilled Tori and brought a rush of tears to her eyes.

She could still see that vivacious, eight-year-old girl in Brooke's face. The one who strolled up on her bicycle fifteen years ago and let it fall on Tori's front yard like she owned the place.

Tori and her mother had moved into the small, white house on the lake. They'd escaped Tulsa and other troubles.

Tori was helping her mom plant a banana tree in the front yard.

Brooke interrupted them, standing there in pigtails, a T-shirt, and shorts. "We had a banana tree," she said. "Three of them. But the bananas were really little. Not like the ones you buy in the store."

Tori looked at the newly planted tree. "We prolly won't get any bananas till next year." She dropped her shovel and brushed a dirty arm across her forehead. She approached the strange girl, studying her.

Brooke stepped away from her bike and tilted her toward the tree. "You'll have ten trees by this time next year. Banana trees have a lot of shoots."

"What does that mean?"

"It means they make baby trees. Lots of them." Brooke laughed.

Tori laughed too. "You live 'round here?"

"On the other side of those woods." Brooke pointed west. "We have a whole yard of noth'n but orange trees."

"We just moved here." Tori looked back at her mom. "From Oklahoma."

"I never been there." Brooke turned her head and smiled. She was missing a front tooth. "My name's Brooke."

Tori looked away. It seemed like yesterday. And now that little girl was lying here in the casket, dressed in a white turtleneck to cover the bruises on her neck. Brooke would never have worn a turtleneck.

RJ gripped her upper arm and led her back into the aisle. They slipped into the farthest pew at the back of the church. Teenagers and their parents sat around them. Many were Brooke's students. Some dabbed at tears in their eyes.

Tori studied the faces of the mourners. Most wore black, and some of the older women paraded down the aisles in designer dresses and extravagant hats. A lot of men wore jeans and boots, and surprisingly colorful button-down shirts. She recognized a short, balding man in a black pinstriped suit standing in the back corner, jotting notes in a small spiral notebook. He had a Canon long lens camera hanging from his neck. She used to work with him at the *Gazette*. The summer intern from the Sheriff's Department waited in the viewing line with a group of high school girls. They wore shockingly short and inappropriate skirts—Zoe, especially, dressed in a black slip of a dress that exposed the barbed wire and rose tattoos on her right arm and a Chinese dragon slithering around her left. Tori looked for Mike and found him sitting between Winnie and his wife, What's her face. Starlet?

He removed his hat when Ash Martin entered through the front doors, with Darla, the grandfather, and the care-giver in tow. Every head in the church turned to watch them. Ash, wearing a dark brown blazer, looked ragged and thin, as if he hadn't eaten in days. His eyes were red-rimmed and glassy. He wiped them with his sleeve as he stepped toward the casket. His brown suit looked wrinkled. His hair uncombed. His face prickly with a couple days' stubble.

RJ nudged her. "See, he didn't shave either."

"He's grieving," she whispered. "He has an excuse."

She watched Ash take a seat next to Darla and her grandfather, at the front of the church.

Darla, somber, emotionless, silent, sat with her hands folded in her lap. She wore a blue dress with a yellow-and-green flower stitched on the front, and dirty white tennis shoes. The laces drooped down on either side like long skinny rabbit ears. Her face showed no evidence of tears, or even sorrow. She looked like some kind of expressionless doll. She sat there, head down, next to her father. The blonde companion and the grandfather sat beside them. From all the way in the back, Tori could hear her yelling.

"YOUR SON-IN-LAW JUST SAT DOWN NEXT TO YOU," Veronica screamed into Leonard's right ear. He leaned away from her as she grabbed his hand and planted it on Ash's face. "IT'S YOUR SON-IN-LAW, ASH MARTIN."

Tori shook her head and turned away.

The service began with the high school choir singing, "O, Faithfully Yours, Lord." When they finished, Pastor Fields called for prayer.

"Friends and family," he said in a booming voice. There was no mic or speakers. Just him. "We are gathered here today for a sad occasion—to mourn the passing of a wife, mother, teacher, and a friend, Brooke Martin."

After reading 1 Corinthians 15, he called up Brooke's father. Veronica helped Leonard to the front and positioned him behind the podium.

"YOU'RE AT THE FRONT OF THE CHURCH," she yelled from beside him, and then turned to the crowd. She cupped a hand to the left side of her mouth as if to keep the elderly man from hearing her. "He's blind," she said to the mourners.

Tori shut her eyes and shook her head, cringing.

Leonard told a heartwarming story about Brooke when she was growing up. Fifteen minutes later, Winnie gave the eulogy, an impassioned reminder that "Brooke will always be with us in spirit." Later, the pastor introduced Brooke's school principal to say a few words.

Principal Kyle Quinn rose. A somewhat short man, somewhere between five-seven and five-eight, he wore a Navy-blue suit that darkened his deeply tan face. He fumbled past Tori and RJ, into the aisle, and walked to the front of the church. He stood next to the casket, and Tori noticed how fidgety Ash suddenly looked.

"I've only known Brooke for a few years, but she was, without a doubt, one of the kindest, most intelligent people I've ever met." Principal Quinn sounded choked up. His eyes were kind and his voice soothing. The principal remarked how Brooke had been selfless and giving, working tirelessly to raise her family and her students alike. "We were truly good friends."

"Friends!" Ash screamed as he launched from his seat, bringing down a wreath and knocking over Brooke's father sitting next to him. He stormed to the podium, directly toward the principal. "You've got a lot of nerve showing your face here," he spat, shaking a fist.

The principal stepped back. "Excuse me?"

"She didn't love you."

"Mr. Martin, I know you're hurting—" The principal looked concerned about not only Ash leaning toward him and poking him in the chest, but of backing him into the open casket.

"You don't deserve to be here. You shouldn't be here." Ash kept pressing him backwards.

The principal raised his arms. "Mr. Martin. Ash. Please—"

"This is all your fault. She didn't love you. You should've stayed away from her."

"You're drunk."

"Did you think you could take my wife and daughter away from me? You think they would ever love you?"

"Mr. Martin, you're drunk and you're going to regret someth—"

"No, *you're* gonna regret something." Ash towered over the shorter man, leaning into his face. "Get away from my wife. I ought to knock your teeth down your throat. I ought to kill you for what you did."

Grabbing the principal by the lapels of his jacket, Ash pushed him into a line of flower arrangements. White Peace Lilies and purple orchids tumbled, upsetting the easel. The giant photo of Brooke clattered to the floor.

Principal Quinn got back to his feet just as Ash swung again. He blocked Ash's fist, and both men fell into the crowd. The principal toppled into a sobbing woman sitting in the front row, knocking her flat on her back.

In the confusion, people moved into the aisles. Some headed for the door. Others ran toward the front. The balding man in black pinstripes sprinted to the front, his camera swinging wildly from his neck. He snapped pictures of Ash and the toppled flowers. Mike and Deputy Torres, along with several other men, rushed toward Ash and Principal Quinn. Darla stood alone in the aisle as people hurried past. Tori pushed through the confused crowd and into the aisle. She ran to the front and scooped Darla into her arms. She covered the little girl's eyes so she wouldn't see what was going on next to her mother's casket.

Ash had hold of the principal's jacket again and swung the man forward. The principal stumbled and then hauled off and hit Ash square in the jaw. A large class ring sparkled before it connected with Ash's chin.

Ash tumbled back into Brooke's casket, hitting hard against the side. He fell to the floor beneath it. Rising, his mouth bleeding, he knelt in front of the casket. He stared at his wife's body and crumbled. "Brooke," he cried. "Why?"

He brought his head down to his knees and sobbed.

Tori held Darla tight, protecting her, as RJ came up beside her. She shot him a troubled look and glanced back at Mike and Deputy Torres as they lifted Ash to his feet. She looked for Winnie or Leonard but didn't see them. Around her, people scrambled in different directions. She did her best to stay out of their way and shield Darla as Ash was escorted out of the church. The crowd followed into the parking lot.

The service was over.

Tori glanced at RJ. "You asked why I never talk about home?"

Tori and RJ hurried across the parking lot, toward the Jeep. She still carried Darla, who remained stoic amid the chaos. Unlike Winnie, who stood alone by the rose garden, eating a Snickers bar. Tori told RJ to give her a minute.

"I've got Darla," she called out, setting Darla on her feet. Holding her hand, Tori walked over to Winnie. "I couldn't find Leonard or that blonde woman, his caregiver."

Winnie smiled and snapped her candy bar in half. She handed it to Darla. "Are you okay?"

When Darla didn't respond, Tori answered for her. "She's fine. But I didn't want her getting lost in the shuffle."

"As if," Winnie said, "this day wasn't bad enough." She popped the chocolate in her mouth and chewed as she talked. "I wish Howard could've been here."

Tori placed a hand on Winnie's shoulder. "It must be hard having your husband out of town so much."

"He and Brooke were friends." Winnie's gray eyes darkened as she held Tori's gaze. "I told you she introduced us, didn't I? He's going to hate himself for missing the funeral. They were good friends."

Tori didn't want to pry. However, a nagging in the back of her mind refused to be stilled. "Why did Ash fly off the handle like that? He attacked that man, the high school principal."

"Principal Quinn's a controversial figure in this town," Winnie said. "Brooke's death, then the school gets vandalized, and now the whole scene at the funeral."

"But why?"

"Gossip." Winnie shook her head. "Nasty, vicious gossip."

"And?" She waited for Winnie to continue. "Don't leave me hanging."

"There are people"—Winnie lowered her voice to keep Darla from hearing— "who are under the impression Brooke and her principal were, um, reviewing more than lesson plans after class."

"Who says that?" Tori looked back at the church and wondered if that was what Winnie didn't want to tell her last night. "Surely, no one believes that's true."

Winnie chuckled. "It's hard not to, when, you know, her own husband crashed a PTA meeting and accused her of sneaking around with Principal Quinn—right in front of the faculty and parents."

"Brooke and Principal Quinn? I …. No. I don't believe it."

"I didn't want to believe it either, but …." Winnie reached for Tori, as if wanting her full attention, and dropped her voice even lower. "I think she snuck off with him the night she died. When Brooke left her cell phone in my barn and I drove it back to her house, she hadn't gotten home yet. She'd left my place hours earlier, but wherever she went, she didn't go home."

"That doesn't mean she was sneaking around with the principal."

"No," Winnie said, "I guess not. But don't tell Ash that."

As Tori returned to the Jeep, her mind spun. Gradually, the crowd dissipated. Tori drifted over to the curb, beneath the moss-draped branches of an ancient oak tree and paused a moment to watch the family, minus Ash, as they walked across the street together, arm in arm. The funeral procession pulled forward, headlights on, headed to the cemetery where Brooke's remains would be laid to rest.

RJ tapped her shoulder. "You ready? We gotta stop by Winnie's, grab our bags, and hit the road."

"I can't stop thinking about *Her Last Breath*. What if, like in the book, Brooke and Ash were fighting, things got out of control, and she fell down the stairs? Or hit her head? Or something else equally horrible happened?"

"And her husband panicked and staged a suicide." He shook his head. "You don't have any facts to back that up."

"Not yet," she whispered, watching Mike position Ash into the back of his squad car. "Not yet."

CHAPTER THIRTEEN

_EA_ EN_

Tori trudged up the front steps of the courthouse and entered the lobby of the Sheriff's Department. Deputy Torres greeted her and hugged her, before leading her to the drunk tank in back. Ash lay on a cot in a small cell, facing the wall.

The deputy unlocked and opened the cell door. Tori stepped inside, approaching her old friend.

"Ash?" she said.

He didn't move. She sat next to his feet, which hung over the cot's edge. The box springs squeaked with her weight and she placed a hand on his shoulder.

"How are you? I'm so sorry for everything."

Turning his upper body, he twisted his neck to see who was beside him. The face that looked up at her was familiar, darker and wearier than she remembered it, framed with unruly hair and an unshaven face. But the eyes were the same.

She'd looked up into those eyes five years ago, in the church on her wedding day. Pastor Fields was trying to calm her, saying it's normal for the groom to arrive a little late to the ceremony. He'd seen it a hundred times.

Winnie stood behind her, holding the hem of the white gown and keeping pace as Tori walked from one side of the room to the other. Brooke raised a hand, halting them.

"Ash is out looking for Mikey B. right now," Brooke said with a fake smile. "Who knows? Maybe he's been in a horrific accident or something."

Tori wasn't sure if Brooke was joking.

When the door opened, and Ash entered the room— alone—Tori knew. She looked into his large apologetic eyes and she knew.

He shook his head and mumbled, "He's not coming."

She hated Ash in that moment, as if this was all his fault, somehow. It wasn't. And as wrong as it was, she never forgave him. It wasn't right. It wasn't logical. It was—

Ash grunted and turned back toward the block wall. Tori removed her hand from his shoulder.

"How you holding up?" She waited for a response. She didn't receive one and looked back at the deputy.

He shrugged, and Tori turned to look at the back of Ash's head again.

She stuttered, trying to make conversation. "Me? Not so well. I can't believe any of this. How's Darla? I saw her at the service."

The deputy interrupted her from the cell door. "She's staying with her grandfather."

Tori glanced over her shoulder at him. "Darla seems like a brave little girl. She's very pretty. Looks just like her—"

Ash stirred and moved his legs, forcing Tori off the cot.

She stood and took a step back. "Okay, I get it. You don't want to speak to me," she said. "But I wanted to see you before I left."

This triggered a response she was hoping for. He got up from the cot and stood to his full height. Ash was a big man, six-three or -four, with the musculature of an ex-athlete. The left side of his mouth was swollen, and his lip was crusted with dried blood where Principal Quinn had clocked him with the class ring. Ash neared Tori and she barely came up to his shoulder. He turned to the deputy.

"I need to see her." Ash's voice rose with fear. "I need to see my little girl."

The deputy shook his head and raised a hand, palm out. "I already told you. She's with Brooke's parents. You can see her in the morning."

"She's safe," Tori said, and touched Ash's arm. She looked at his bloody lip. "You need to focus on you. Get better."

He turned to her and his eyes enlarged. His mouth opened, as if in surprise, as if he had just noticed her.

"Tori, I'm glad you came for Brooke's funeral. She would've wanted you to be here."

He stared at her with bloodshot eyes. Maybe from the alcohol. Maybe he'd been crying.

"It's the least I could do." Tori squeezed his arm. "Do you need anything? Is there anything I can do for you and Darla?"

He laughed, then cringed and reached up to touch his lip. Turning away from her, he returned to the cot. He sat on the edge and placed his head in his hands. "You can get me a drink."

"That's not funny."

"I know." He sounded clearer now, more like his old self. "I'm going back to rehab. I can check myself in tomorrow."

"Good." She sat next to him. "You and Darla can start picking up the pieces."

"That's right," the deputy added. "And it sounds like Principal Quinn isn't pressing charges."

"The principal." He huffed. "Yeah, good for him."

Tori paused, considering what he'd said. "That was quite a performance back there at the church. I take it you're not a fan of Principal Quinn."

He looked at her. "You could say that."

"Why'd you attack him?" She spoke slowly. "Because of the rumors circulating about him and Brooke?"

"You heard them too?"

"Sounds like you believe them. Is that what you and Brooke had been fighting about?"

"Who says we've been fighting?" he asked, raising his voice.

She didn't let it intimidate her. "She called 911 the night she died."

"I wasn't there."

"But you were fighting earlier that night, right? About the principal?"

"Look, Tori. I'm glad you made it. Now have a safe trip back to Tampa."

"Ash, what does Brooke's suicide note mean? Whatever I am, you made me."

"What?"

"The note Brooke left behind. What does it mean? Someone has been texting it to me."

"Not this again."

"Where is Brooke's phone?"

"I don't know."

"If you don't have it, does Darla? Or Brooke's father?"

"How many times do I have to tell you? No one has Brooke's phone. No one's texting you."

He stared at her for several seconds, as if there was something he wanted to say but couldn't get the words out.

He wanted her to understand something—she was sure of it.

As if giving up, he stretched out on the cot, again letting his feet hang over the edge and pushing Tori away.

She stood as he said, "I'm in no mood."

"But Ash, listen. Please." She touched his shoulder again, and he shook her hand away.

Without turning around, he muttered, "Look, it's not that I'm not glad to see you, but my wife is dead. I haven't slept in four days. And I've been ..."—he slurred his words now, turning to face the wall, his head on the pillow— "taking the edge off ...."

Tori knelt beside the cot and leaned toward him.

He turned around to glare at her. His eyes were bright red and watery. After a moment, he flipped back to face the wall. "Now go home. Leave."

The deputy tapped her shoulder. "Let's give him some time to rest."

"Okay. Again, I'm sorry. For everything." She wanted to say more. There were so many unanswered questions, but he wasn't in the right frame of mind.

Tori followed the deputy out of the jail cells and back into the lobby. Mike stood by the reception desk, his arms folded across his chest, waiting for them.

"Sheriff—" Tori said, surprised to see him.

He squinted and curled his lip. "You can still call me Mike."

"I thought you'd be at the cemetery."

"Charlotte is attending the burial. I need to be here. I'm keeping Ash overnight. Let him sober up and cool down." He reached for her but pulled his hand away. "It was good seeing you … at the funeral, I mean."

"I liked seeing you, er, it was good seeing you too." To her annoyance, she felt flushed.

He seemed to be searching for something to say. "I heard you stayed over at my sister's place."

"We caught up," she said. "And she's married now."

"To a pharmaceutical salesman." He chuckled and the conversation lulled again.

She glanced at his wrist monitor. "How serious is it?"

He paused and turned toward Deputy Torres. She stared at him as well.

"You know, I'll …." The deputy turned his head from Tori, to Mike, and back to Tori. "I've got rounds to make."

Tori watched him stride past the glass doors and disappear outside.

Mike cleared his throat, getting her attention. "I told you I was fine," he said. "I have to cut back on the Sausage Egg McMuffins."

"What happened to baseball?"

He looked down at the floor. "They cut me. My heart condition was an issue."

"So, what? You take the most stressful job you can find?"

"This isn't an exciting town." He chuckled as if he'd told a joke. "Besides some teenagers vandalizing the high school, nothing happens 'round here."

"But town sheriff? You've got to be the youngest elected sheriff in history."

"Naw," he said, shaking his head. "Sarasota elected a twenty-nine-year-old back in the day. And Rush County, Kansas, elected a kid who was just twenty-two."

"But, sheriff?" she asked. "They actually elected you?"

"I know, right? I'm still a minor celebrity 'round here, so people voted for me. People still talk about my no-hitter." He gazed at her a few moments, as if studying her. "But look at you. You're on the news. You made it. To be honest, I was nervous about seeing you after, what, four years?"

"Five." She corrected him a little faster than intended and didn't want to sound like she'd been counting the days. She walked to the large glass doors. Outside, RJ stood at the curb beside his Jeep, holding his cell phone to his ear. He rested an arm on top of the meter as he spoke. She watched him put down his phone and look over. He pointed at his wrist.

She touched the glass. "Looks like RJ is ready to head back to Tampa."

"You're not leaving yet, are you?" Mike raised a hand as if stopping traffic at an intersection.

Tori froze.

He took a breath and continued. "We're having Brooke's memorial tonight at the lake. My sister organized every-thing."

"We've got another story to cover. Deadlines, you know." She turned away from the door. "It was good seeing you again and meeting your wife. I hope you have a good life together. I really do."

"Wait. Hold on a sec." He stepped toward her. He seemed nervous, unsettled, though it didn't reflect in his voice. "I think we've got some things to talk over."

"No, we don't." She looked away.

He took a step closer and touched her arm. "Let's talk a minute. Clear the air."

"Okay. If you want to talk, let's talk." She stepped away from him and paced in front of the receptionist desk. "Brooke and Principal Quinn. How long has that been going on?"

"You mean the gossip?"

"It's obviously more than gossip to Ash." She watched Mike, studying his posture, his face, the age lines at the corners of his eyes. "And now Brooke is dead. Do you think there's a connection?"

"Probably." He looked down at his boots, as if he was considering her words. After a moment of an uneasy silence, he cleared his throat. "I think Brooke had been unhappy with Ash and her life for quite a while. Unhappier than any of us realized."

Tori watched him. "She was fighting depression?"

"She committed suicide," he said. "She was taking anti-depressants."

"Since when? Who was treating her? Who prescribed those antidepressants?"

"This is what you want to talk about?" He walked into his office and plopped down in the rolling chair behind his desk.

She followed him. Cluttered with fishing equipment and bowling trophies, the small room bore his personality in every corner. Even a framed James Dean poster hung on the wall. She couldn't help but wonder if his wife had made him move all this crap out of their home.

Glancing around, she approached the desk. "There's something weird going on. Someone is trying to tell me something. Someone's making a point."

"About what?"

"I don't know. ... Th-that's the problem," Tori stammered. She noticed his dark brown Stratton resting on top of the desk. "Someone is texting me messages from Brooke's phone."

"From her phone?"

"Yes. Do you know who has it?"

"It's probably with her personal effects. Ash hasn't picked them up yet."

"It's not. We already checked."

Mike got up and walked out of the office. "We who?"

"Deputy Torres." She followed Mike into the lobby. "And what's more is that whoever has her cell phone is texting me that suicide note."

"You're not making any sense."

She pulled her phone from her purse and handed it to him. Mike entered the deputy's empty office and headed for the file cabinets in the corner. He grabbed the box containing Brooke's belongings and removed the suicide note. Holding it up, he compared the note to the message on the phone. When he set the phone back on the desk, he shot her an irritated glare.

"You had no right going through Brooke's belongings," he said. The shiny gold badge on his chest loomed large between them. "That suicide note was private."

"It's not a suicide note."

"What?"

"I mean, maybe it's supposed to be, but Brooke didn't write it. That's not her handwriting. Compare her *w*'s with the *w*'s on the note. Look at the *y*'s ...." From her purse, Tori fished out the Christmas card and handed it to him.

He looked at it and back at the suicide note. He didn't respond.

Tori looked away and said, "I know she called 911 the night she died."

"What of it? So, she called 911 ... again. She dialed 911 every time Ash got drunk and they got into a fight. Which, by the way, was happening more and more frequently."

"And that doesn't raise a red flag? I mean, do you really believe Brooke would end it all and abandon her daughter like that? Where's the coroner's report?"

"Why? You won't find anything different in it." Mike folded his arms across his chest.

"What if she died—in an accident—and then her death was staged to look like she hung herself."

"The coroner's report confirms she died of strangulation, consistent with a hanging. She was alive when she hung herself." He walked to the file cabinet and pulled a folder from the drawer. He set the folder on the desk. "Here. Read it for yourself."

Tori flipped through the report. "There was bruising on the neck. She also had a high concentration of Deletycide in her system?"

"It's the antidepressants. There were samples in her purse and a dozen, or more empty sample packets scattered on the ground where the deputy found her body. Deletycide can be a powerful sedative, and she took enough to put a rhinoceros to bed. She didn't want to feel anything when she jumped."

"She took twelve packets?"

"The irony is—she didn't need to hang herself. She had enough of that drug in her system to end her life all by itself."

"But the coroner didn't find any tablets in her stomach."

"Her body had absorbed them already. Listen, Tori ... no one wants to believe Brooke ended her life, but it happened. She was an unhappy woman in an unhappy marriage."

"Sheriff, please." Tori leaned toward him. "There's something seriously wrong here."

A high-pitched beep went off on his wrist monitor that sounded like a truck backing up. Mike paused. His eyes grew wide. He looked at the wrist monitor and sat in his chair. Tori reached for his arm. He raised his hand, holding her back. He took a deep breath and shut his eyes.

"Dazzy Vance, 2,045 strikeouts, 3.24 ERA. Walter Johnson, 3,508 strikeouts, 2.17 ERA," he muttered. "Jim Palmer, 2,212 strikeouts, 2.86 ERA."

"What should I do?" Her voice trembled. "Should I call 911?"

"Give me a sec," he said, and continued reciting. "Pedro Martinez, 3,154 strikeouts, 2.93 ERA. Kid Nichols, 1,873 strikeouts, 2.95 ERA. Greg Maddux, 3,371 strikeouts, 3.16 ERA." The beeping stopped, and he lifted his arm, checking the monitor. Taking another deep breath, he turned to her.

She was about to ask him what happened when he continued, picking up where he'd left off. "I think your imagination is running in overdrive."

"Sheriff," she said.

He cleared his throat. "It's tough when a friend dies. Even more so when that friend takes her own life. Those left behind have trouble accepting it."

"Sheriff—"

"I don't know what to tell you. It was an unhappy marriage and she was an unhappy wife. That's why there's rumors circulating about her and the principal." Mike leaned back in the chair.

"Sheriff—"

"None of us want to believe Brooke took her own life. It's natural for those who loved her to look for other answers, look for a reason, but—"

"Sheriff—"

"It happened. It's horrible and it's not fair, but it happened. We have to pick up the pieces and move on."

Tori screamed, "Stop!" and then regained her composure. She spoke as calmly as she could. "Would you just stop? You had an episode, an attack, a heart palpitation."

"It was only a blood pressure spike," he said. "And you're gonna give me another one if you don't chill."

"You're too young to have a heart *anything*. You're thirty-two. You shouldn't even be worried about cholesterol yet, much less blood pressure."

"It's never too early to take care of your cholesterol, and if you wanna help me, then tell Brooke goodbye." He put the note back in the box. He handed her the phone and the Christmas card. "Come to Brooke's memorial. It's at Skeeter Park. Starts at four."

"Brooke's memorial?" She recalled seeing balloons in Winnie's house. Dozens of them. "Winnie's got something planned for it, doesn't she?"

"Everyone's written farewell notes to Brooke, and Winnie tied them to balloons," he said. "We're releasing them over the lake."

"Farewell notes." Tori thought about it. They would hold handwriting samples and Ash's would be one.

"It'd be good to see you there," Mike said. "I know a lot of people would like to catch up with you." He stepped beside her and placed a hand on her shoulder.

She took a breath, looking up into his eyes. His touch felt electric, and his fingers lingered there too long to be an accident.

"I'm sorry for everything," he whispered. "I hope you know that."

Tori stared at him. She wasn't sure if he meant everything with Brooke or everything between them. Maybe he meant both. She withdrew and turned away. "Sheriff—"

"Mike."

"Sheriff, excuse me. I need to make a phone call."

With her cell phone to her ear, Tori left the Sheriff's Department. She ran down the front steps, toward RJ's Jeep parked by the meter on the curb. He greeted her and ran around the front to the driver's side. Sitting behind the steering wheel, he turned off the iPod as Tori jumped into the passenger seat. She ended the call and set her phone on the center console.

"So, what happened?" he asked. "Who has Brooke's phone?"

"Ash doesn't have it and doesn't know who does," she said. "Or if he does know, he's not saying."

"We've done everything we can for now." He put the key in the ignition. "We'll grab our bags from Winnie's, get on the road—"

"RJ—"

"Be back in Tampa before dinner, get to bed early, then cover the boat show bright and early."

"RJ—"

"We can come back after the holiday, find out what's going on here—"

"RJ." She yelled his name. "I got another text message last night."

He stopped talking. She picked up her phone from the center console and handed it to him.

He took it, but his eyes remained fixed on her. "Yeah? And ...."

"Something's wrong here," she said. "Someone is trying to tell me something."

"It's Brooke—"

The corner of her mouth twisted with exasperation. "No, it's not a ghost."

"Then you're getting punk'd." He reached toward her and placed a hand on her shoulder. "That deputy friend of yours is right. It's a prank."

"It's not a prank."

"Those are your only choices. It's one or the other."

"Or ..."—Tori paused and licked her lips— "it's *Her Last Breath* all over again."

"It's not *Her Last Breath*." He turned his head, still holding her phone but not looking at it.

"It could be. The coroner's report confirmed Brooke died of strangulation and the bruising on her neck confirms she was alive when she hung herself."

"Then your theory she died someplace else and her suicide was staged doesn't hold up. It's not *Her Last Breath*."

"But something still bugs me. She had a high dosage of Deletycide in her system and there were at least twelve empty sample packets on the ground where they found her body. But the coroner didn't find any tablets in her stomach."

"Okay, CSI. What's your point?"

"Something just doesn't add up here." Tori took a breath. "But between the text messages and the purported suicide note ... whatever happened, Ash is at the center of it. He's involved in her death and I can prove it. We need to find something with his handwriting."

RJ threw up his arms and brought them back down hard on the steering wheel. He still held her phone and almost dropped it. "There isn't time."

"We can call Pittman. Reschedule the interview with that skiing raccoon."

"Squirrel. And we're not doing that."

"I already have," she said. "Pittman moved the interview back twenty-four hours. I told him we were on to something here."

RJ tossed her phone back on the center console. "I don't believe it."

"Everyone who knew Brooke has written farewell messages and attached them to balloons," she said in an even tone. "We need to look at them before they release them over the lake. One of them will have Ash's handwriting. Either prove he did or didn't write the note."

"Then what?"

She looked at him. "What do you mean?"

"Let's say you find he wrote the suicide note," he said. "Or you find that he didn't. Then what?"

"I don't know. I haven't thought that far ahead yet," she said. "Just drive."

He paused, staring at her. She looked over at him.

"What?" she asked.

He nodded, indicating her seat belt. "They save lives, you know."

Tori shook her head. "Go. Brooke's memorial starts at four."

CHAPTER FOURTEEN

_ISSED THE _ARK

Tori watched the lake appear and disappear between the trees as RJ drove along Route 103 / Clay Pit Road. Holding her phone to her ear with her left shoulder, she clutched the dashboard for support. The Jeep hit another pothole, jolting its passengers.

"That's right. A suicide note was found, but it's not her handwriting." She looked over at RJ gripping the steering wheel with both hands, his knuckles white, and mouthed the words "News director Pittman." RJ didn't acknowledge her, keeping his head straight and eyes focused on the road. He hit another bump and bolted forward in his seat. She bounced too, hitting the side door and nearly dropping the phone.

"I sent you photos and we can get video footage too," she said, recovering. "Maybe a few interviews, get hold of the coroner's report. ...... Yes, we know the boat show is this weekend. We'll be there. Tomorrow. I promise."

She ended the call, shut her eyes, and bit down hard on her lower lip. "Pittman reviewed my notes. The Sunshine Sweeties are covering the opening for the boat show, but he wants us to handle the interview with that skiing monkey."

When RJ didn't correct her, she looked over at him. The Jeep bounced as it hit another pothole.

They continued along until reaching a wooden sign welcoming them to Skeeter Park. Branches brushed both sides of the Jeep and a heron jutted across the road in front of them. As they waited for it to cross, Tori watched the late-afternoon sun glimmer off the water. Ahead, by the boat docks, a clearing emerged with picnic tables and grills. A large open pavilion housed a gathering of townspeople. It looked like there were more people here than at the church that morning.

RJ parked. Tori hopped out among an armada of pickup trucks and duallies. Families carried casserole pots and bowls of mac and cheese to picnic tables set under sprawling oaks and skinny pine trees. Gator tail, freshwater catfish, and corn on the cob cooked on four smoking grills. An assortment of key lime pies and peach cobblers lined the top of one picnic table, next to pitchers of sweet tea and two ice chests filled with cold Coronas and Bud Light.

A balding man wearing Bermuda shorts, leather sandals, and white socks greeted them. The black Canon camera with a long lens hung from a strap around his neck, like it did at the church a few hours earlier.

"Tori," he said, all bright eyes and wide smile. "I don't know if you remember me. I'm Edison Beyer. We worked together at the *Elroy Springs Gazette* a few years back."

Tori shook his hand. "Of course, I remember you. I recognized you at Brooke's service earlier. How've you been?"

"Just fine, just fine." He leaned back as if to admire her and smacked his lips. "I thought I saw you at Brooke's service. Wasn't that a spectacle, what with the grieving Ash Martin attacking the high school principal in front of the casket? Drama, drama, drama."

"At least it gives you something to write about." She turned to RJ. "Edison and I worked together at the *Gazette* before I moved to Tampa."

RJ extended a hand. "Pleased to meet you."

Edison gave him a hearty handshake and then slipped a small American flag pendant into his palm. RJ held it up.

"It's in memory of Brooke, being an American history teacher and all." Edison turned to Tori and pinned a pendant to her lapel. "And the Fourth is right around the corner."

Tori looked down at the shiny flag on her lapel. "Thank you."

"It's good to see you again," he said, and waved at another couple getting out of a truck in the parking lot. "If you'll excuse me, it looks like Mayor Winslow has arrived. I'm hoping he'll give me a quote about the whole funeral service fiasco."

He headed off toward the parking lot. Tori glanced at RJ, rolling her eyes. He shook his head.

Nearing the center of the festivities, she saw Winnie running toward them with open arms. She'd changed out of the tight black dress and was now wearing shorts and a large white tee, her blonde hair pulled back behind a visor. A small American flag pendant was pinned below the neckline. Tori felt overdressed, still wearing her sleeveless black dress and heels.

"What are you doing here?" Winnie shouted as she wrapped her arms around them both and squeezed them close. "I thought you left already."

"We're staying another night." Tori broke out of the embrace. "If that's okay."

"Okay?" Winnie hugged Tori again and squeezed her even tighter than before. "Are you kidding? I'm, you know, so glad you're back."

Tori listened to Winnie ramble while leading them to a foldout table covered with cards and pens. All the silver and blue balloons that filled Winnie's house a few hours earlier now floated around the table. Tori had no idea how Winnie transported them here. They covered the table and surrounding area so thoroughly, Winnie barely had enough room to sit.

She picked up a plate of half-eaten pie and shot Tori a sly grin. "My brother. He said he talked to you."

"He said hello."

"Good. I'm glad." Winnie paused, and then motioned with her fork to the crowd around the picnic tables. "Are you hungry? We have enough food to feed all of Elroy Springs and half of Frostproof."

"I can see that," Tori said, looking at the enormous spread.

"Good. I'm famished." RJ laughed and rubbed his belly.

Tori playfully poked him in the stomach and turned to the table, examining the small post cards. Some were blank.

Others had handwritten messages stating, "We'll miss you" and "Rest in peace."

"These are the cards everyone in town wrote to Brooke?" Tori asked, reading some of the messages. She noticed the variations of the handwriting, some printed, some cursive, most illegible.

Winnie finished the pie and pointed to the blank cards. "I hope you'll take a moment to write a farewell note to Brooke." Winnie held up a strand of blue and silver balloons. "We're, um, attaching the notes to helium balloons and releasing them at sunset. They'll float up and over the lake like a thousand little stars soaring to heaven."

"All her friends and family have written notes?" Tori counted the stacks of cards and looked for some organizing pattern to the piles. Surely there was one written by Ash.

"You bet." Winnie handed her a pen.

She took it and scribbled a message on a blank card. She set the card in the pile with the other notes, wondering how she could get hold of the one Ash wrote. Winnie took her card and pointed her toward the smoking grills.

Realizing she'd have to comb through the cards later, Tori made her way to the grills and joined the crowd with a plate of grilled bass and vegetable skewers. Neighbors greeted her and bombarded her with questions.

Pastor Fields flipped gator tail and catfish on a large gas grill. Mayor Winslow visited with a group circled around him. Edison Beyer stood beside him, writing in a spiral notebook. A few feet away, under a whitewashed pavilion, the high school band played Warren Zevon's *"Keep Me in Your Heart."* That summer intern from the Sheriff's Department danced alone on the grass, swaying to the music. She waved her tattooed arms and the jewelry in her face glinted sunlight. Her girlfriends joined her in front of the pavilion, clasping hands and slow dancing to the somber song.

The sheriff sat at a picnic table with his wife—What's her face. Hamlett? She'd changed, too, and was wearing a white dress with little red cherries printed on it. They were visiting with Principal Quinn, who held a frozen steak against his face, covering his left eye.

Darla sat at a picnic table with her grandfather and his blonde caregiver. Veronica tried to spoon-feed him a green-and-yellow mush. He kept pushing her hand away.

"I BROUGHT YOUR PEAS AND APPLESAUCE," she yelled in his ear.

He turned his head to the side and scrunched his face, knocking the spoon to the ground. She picked it up, wiped it clean on her skirt, and tried to feed him again.

"DO YOU WANT PEAS AND APPLESAUCE?"

"No." He folded his arms across his chest, pouting. "I want a hot dog."

Tori approached the table with her plate. When Leonard and Veronica greeted her, Tori noticed they both had shiny American flag pendants pinned to their shirts.

"Please sit down." Veronica patted a spot on the bench beside her. Her flag pendant jiggled like an actual waving flag as she spoke. "I'm feeding Leonard, but he refuses to eat anything. And he was just as stubborn about his insulin shot this morning."

Tori sat beside Darla, but the little girl didn't look up. She remained focused on the page she was coloring.

"Watcha drawing?" Tori looked down at the picture. Darla had sketched the old water tower in dark brown crayon. A stick figure woman hung from it with a rope around her neck. Two more stick figures watched in the distance, on the horizon. One pointed to the hung woman. Tori studied it for several seconds.

Veronica shook her head. "She's been coloring the same horrid thing for a week now."

Tori wondered who the two stick figures in the distance were. Policemen? Maybe the deputies who arrived on the scene? She was about to ask, when Veronica slammed her hands on the table.

"He's got a lot of nerve showing up here." Droplets of spittle shot from Veronica's mouth.

"Who?" Tori looked around.

"The home-wrecking playboy principal." Veronica pointed to Principal Quinn sitting at the table with the sheriff and his wife.

Strutting in her black slip of a dress, the sheriff's intern approached the principal. Tori hadn't noticed that the Chinese dragon tattoo on the girl's left arm coiled around an attacking tiger. It seemed appropriate, somehow, and Tori chuckled as the girl grasped the principal's arm. She tugged him to his feet as he dropped the frozen steak. His eye still looked swollen and angry, but he followed the girl to the pavilion, anyway. The band now played Jamey Johnson's *"Lead Me Home,"* and the principal took several students' hands. They stood in a circle, hand in hand, heads bowed.

Veronica slapped the table again, knocking the little flag from her lapel. It hit her plate with a little ping. "He's got a lot of nerve, after the uproar he created at poor Brooke's funeral. He ruined the service."

Tori said, "He's gonna have one helluva shiner. Ash has a mean right hook." She watched the principal lead a prayer with the intern and the high school girls under the pavilion.

"Look at him, carrying on with those girls." Veronica folded her arms and huffed. "Ash had every right to clock him at the church. Everyone hates him. Even some of his students vandalized the school."

"I heard about that."

"The sooner that man leaves town, the better. He's done enough damage as it is."

"He's leaving town? Where's he going?"

"He got a fancy-schmanzy job in Tallahassee." Veronica huffed and turned to Leonard.

Tori saw RJ standing next to Pastor Fields at the food table. His paper plate looked overloaded with catfish, watermelon, and corn on the cob. He held up his plate as if asking her if she wanted some too. She shook her head and turned back to Veronica.

Tori turned back to Veronica. "I can't picture Brooke having an affair."

"Well, believe it. You know Ash crashed a PTA meeting, all slobbering drunk, and accused the principal of sleeping with his wife?" Veronica laughed, recalling the event. "He caused quite a show, turning over desks and throwing office supplies and threatening to kill Principal Quinn if he ever came near her again—all in front of the entire PTA. Brooke was so embarrassed she ran right out of the school and over to the nearest divorce attorney."

"But they weren't getting a divorce, were they?" Tori couldn't believe what she was hearing.

Veronica leaned in closer to Tori's ear. "Word on the street … she and Principal Quinn conspired to run away together. She aimed to leave Ash and go off to Tallahassee to be with that freaky geek. You know that's a fake tan, right?"

Tori shook her head. "How could you know that?"

"Look at the man's face. Skin isn't naturally that orange."

"No," Tori said. "I mean, how could you know Brooke planned to run off to Tallahassee with him?"

"Hey, don't kill the messenger." Veronica turned to Leonard again and screamed in his ear: "YOU NEED TO EAT YOUR PEAS AND APPLESAUCE."

Tori took a deep breath and adjusted her smile. The corner of her mouth twisted with exasperation. and she looked away, catching Winnie jump from the foldout table amid the cards and balloons. Waving her arms, Winnie called out for the crowd's attention after the band stopped playing. She cleared her throat and asked if everyone had signed a card. Apparently satisfied, she launched into a funny story about Brooke, when they were growing up. The crowd laughed. Finally, she motioned to a group of Brooke's students to come forward and read a poem.

As the kids recited, Tori turned to RJ, who'd sat down with his plate, and she whispered in his ear, "I want to look through those cards."

"What for?" he whispered back.

Tori motioned to the table of cards and balloons. "I can match the handwriting on one of those notes." She held up her phone and brought up the photo of the suicide note.

"Are you serious?"

"Like a heart attack."

Tori rose from the picnic table and made her way to the little foldout table under the oak trees. RJ followed. Holding up her phone, she compared the handwriting on the first card. She grabbed the next one, looked it over, and then pushed it aside and reached for another. The balloons swayed with the movement.

Frustrated, she looked at RJ. "Find the one Ash wrote."

"Ash is still in jail." He held up a card, glanced at it, put it down. "How could he have a note here?"

"He's her husband. He's got a note here." Tori held up another card. The balloon attached to it bobbed above her head.

A voice behind them asked what they were doing.

Tori jumped and looked up at Mike. The brim of his hat shaded his face. She dropped the card in her hand. "I-I'm checking something out."

"You can't be tampering with people's personal notes to Brooke." Mike took the cards and balloons from her and set them on the table. He turned to RJ, who was setting the note in his hands back on the table.

Tori said, "I have to. Brooke didn't write that suicide note. Someone else did." She grabbed another card from the table and Mike slapped it out of her hand.

"You're gonna set my blood pressure to spiking. You know that? You're gonna send it right through the roof." He gripped her upper arm. "These are private messages to Brooke. You have no business reading them."

"I'm not reading them. I'm comparing handwriting samples." She held her breath, expecting the monitor to start beeping again. It didn't.

His grip tightened on her arm and he pulled her away from the table. "This is over," he said. "It ends. Now."

"You're not listening." She tried to free her arm, but his hand held her tight with gentle authority.

They walked to the lake and onto the pier, side by side and a little too close. Neither said a word as his boots and her heels struck the wooden planks. Several boats tied to the posts jounced in the water on either side, and she noticed Winnie's runabout on her right. They stopped at the edge.

Tori wondered if he intended to toss her in the water, and broke free of his grip. She ran her hands over her black dress, smoothing the wrinkles. She looked up at him. He was staring at her, unblinking.

"What do you think you're doing?" he asked.

Tori's eyes glistened. She cleared her throat. "Did you ever read *Her Last Breath?*"

"There it is. It's goin' up." He looked at the monitor on his wrist. "Yes, ma'am, it's goin' up."

"I know that Brooke didn't write that note. I know you said they'd been fighting. I know he's drinking again. He not only attacked Principal Quinn at Brooke's funeral, but at a PTA meeting too."

"Look at that spike." He turned his arm so she could see the monitor on his wrist. "I'll be dogged, those numbers are going right on up."

Tori forced a reserved smile. "I don't want to give you a heart attack," she said, "I only want answers to a few questions."

"Okay." He dropped his arm and looked down at her. "Ask away."

"Was Brooke going to run away to Tallahassee with that school principal? Is there any truth to those rumors?" She turned and looked at the horizon. The sun blazed over the lake, and she could feel its heat on her face. "That's a motive."

"A motive for what?"

"A motive for something more happening that night, other than Brooke ending her life." She paused before continuing. She wasn't sure she wanted to say it out loud. But it needed to be said. "It's a motive for murder."

"Murder?" He huffed, almost laughing. "I feel it going up. It's going up and it's all you."

"Okay. Maybe murder is ... I don't know ...." She stammered, searching for the right words. "But it's motive for something. What if Ash and Brooke were fighting about the principal or about her taking Darla and leaving? What if things got out of control? Maybe Ash is covering up an accident."

"You're lashing out." Mike touched her shoulder. "I get it. You don't want to believe that Brooke could take her own life and leave behind a little girl and a husband."

Tori exhaled and looked away. "I don't want to believe Ash wrote the note and staged a suicide, either."

"Would you stop it?" His face darkened. "Would you think about what you're saying?"

"I know exactly what I'm saying." She paced along the pier, coming to the edge. Winnie's small motorboat rose and fell with the waves beside the dock. Tori turned back to him. "I'm saying ... what I'm saying is there are some questions that need to be answered."

"I get it. I really do. You're mad at me and you have every right. But don't take it out on Ash and his family. You deal with me, if you want. But you leave them out of it."

She clenched her hands into tight fists. She could feel her blood pressure rising too. "Would you stop bringing this back to you?"

"This is not about *me*," he shot back, "this is about *us*. Our past. Our relationship. Our problems. And if you're not going to say it, I will."

She held a hand to his chest, stopping him. "You lost your right to say anything when you ran out, when you left me and ran off with ... with What's her face. Varmint?"

"Charlotte." He raised his hand to meet hers, still planted firmly against his chest. His fingers touched hers and she had the wildest urge to jump back.

"Charlotte—yes, whatever." She withdrew her hand and turned away. "You left me for her. And Ash had to tell me you didn't love me anymore."

"So, there it is. You want to kill the messenger."

"Don't be ridiculous." She looked away again.

"No, I think I see what's going on here. Ash had to tell you the wedding was off, and now you're ready to spit nails and get even with him."

Tori paused. Sunlight sparkled red on the water. Gray rain clouds gathered in the west. "That's not true."

"It is, or you wouldn't be trying to spin this tragedy into something it's not." He came up beside her. They both stared at the shimmering water. "You're throwing Ash under the bus."

"I'm not throwing anyone under the bus. I just want to find out who wrote the suicide note and who is texting me that note. And why."

Neither spoke for several seconds; they stood there, side by side, staring at the lake.

He broke the silence. "Have you talked to Ash since that day he told you?"

"What?" She didn't look at him.

He cleared his throat, spoke louder. "Have you talked to Ash? I mean, besides at the jail this morning. Have you talked to him?"

"We've ...." She recalled Ash and Brooke's brief trip to Tampa with Darla. His phone call in the elevator at the SEBC-TV News building. Seeing him at the church and in jail earlier that day. She replied, "We've visited."

"You talked about the day I left? About him having to tell you what happened?"

"What's your point?"

He took a breath and licked his lips, as if taking a moment to gather his thoughts. "My point is you're carrying a lot of anger. I did you wrong. I'm guilty as sin and can never make it up to you. But you took it out on your friends. You turned your back on Ash. On Winnie. On Brooke."

"Stop it."

"You didn't come to see Brooke when Darla was born."

"I said, stop it." Tears flooded her eyes.

"You weren't here when Ash went to rehab, and Brooke needed you most."

"Yes, I was mad at them. They knew you were leaving me. They knew I was in love with you—I always have been—and you never loved me. They knew our whole engagement was a joke and that I was a joke for believing it."

"That's not true."

"It is. I was a stupid kid with a childish crush I shoulda grown out of."

"We were both stupid kids with childish crushes." His voice was crisp, emotionless.

She could've slapped him, but she held back. They stared at each other, unblinking.

Something shiny caught Tori's eye. Looking up, she saw dozens of silver and blue balloons rise into the blue part of the sky. They floated above the lake.

"We need to talk about what happened," he said. "Between us."

"I don't want to talk about it." Tori watched another group of balloons rise into the sky. There had to be at least a hundred. They floated east, away from the storm clouds, reflecting the bright sunlight. She looked back at him. "We're not discussing the past. We're not discussing the wedding—"

"You were engaged?" a feminine voice interjected.

Mike and Tori turned to see Charlotte standing at the pier entrance by the shoreline. She was shaking, her eyes so wide the whites competed with her pale face. Her white cherry-print dress rippled in the breeze.

"You never told me you were going to ...." Charlotte couldn't even say it. "H-how could you have been engaged and not tell me that? How could you?" She turned and ran off the pier.

Mike opened his mouth. Looked at Tori. Looked back at the shore.

Tori stared at him and into the blue eyes that knew her so well. Those eyes had seen her through so many adventures growing up—birthday parties and church picnics and football games, and the night they watched the Leonid meteor shower and he took her virginity under the shooting stars.

And the wedding that never happened—those eyes were pleading with her now.

She nodded, releasing him, and watched him turn. He ran after his wife, leaving Tori alone on the pier. She looked at the sky. The balloons were faint shimmers now, as the last glint of sunlight hit them, and they disappeared into the atmosphere.

She looked back at the gathering in the park. The card table was empty. Still, she had to find something with Ash's handwriting. It was more important now than ever. And she wouldn't leave without it.

CHAPTER FIFTEEN

D_RKNESS F_LLS

As soon as she sat in the Jeep, Tori slipped off her heels and wiggled her toes. The memorial picnic had lasted several more hours, and after countless "Good to see you's" and "How long has it been's," she couldn't wait to get out of that black dress and into some jeans and tennis shoes.

RJ pulled out of Skeeter Park and rolled onto the dirt path. "So, back to Winnie's?"

Tori shook her head as she massaged her soles. "Remember last night at the water tower, you talked about finding EVPs in the Martin house?"

The Jeep bounced, and he turned the wheel, avoiding another deep rut in the road. "You aren't starting to believe me, are you?"

"I believe I can find something with Ash's handwriting at the Martin home."

"You're suggesting we break into his house?"

"It's not breaking in when you're practically family. Besides, it's now or never. We have to be back on the road first thing in the morning, right?"

"You're serious?"

"Yes, I'm serious." She paused, wondering if she needed to explain herself. Wasn't it obvious? "I need to know if Ash wrote that note and we have an opportunity that won't come again. Ash is still in jail. Darla is staying with her grandfather. We can slip in and slip out."

"You're serious?"

"We already covered that. Yes, I'm serious." She turned to him and touched his shoulder. "Look, do you want to get your stupid EVPs or not?"

"Okay, you're serious," he said as they passed the welcome sign and came to the two-lane highway, Clay Pit Road.

He flipped on the blinker and turned east, toward the Martin house.

Neither spoke for several minutes, until RJ said, "So, you and Sheriff Bennett. Sounds like there's a lot of water under that bridge."

Tori sank deeper in the seat. "I don't want to talk about it."

"You still have some unresolved issues."

"I said I don't want to talk about it."

For the next twenty minutes, neither said a word. They passed by the bridge that crossed over Twin Lakes and rolled over the bumpy railroad tracks. RJ pulled up the gravel drive to the Martin house and parked next to Brooke's minivan. He turned off the ignition.

"The sheriff seems like a nice enough guy. I don't know why you'd even break up with a man like that. He's tall, handsome, and wears a uniform—"

"I didn't break up with him," she snapped at him, wishing he'd drop it already. "He broke up with me."

"Okay, now I get it. All the pieces are coming together. Ken dumped Barbie."

"No—"

"Yes—"

"No." She paused. "If there are unresolved feelings—and I'm not saying there are—it's not because he dumped me."

RJ looked at her, waiting for her to continue. "And?"

"And if there are any unresolved issues, it's because he never told me why. It was just over."

To her right, she could make out the orange grove. The water tower stood above the gray tree carcasses like some kind of rusty robot from a 1950s sci-fi movie. She could imagine it coming to life and stomping its way through the dead trees. She looked away.

They walked around the house to the back, where a tool shed stood, and a few feet away was a laundry line with a sheet and several shirts still hanging from it. She wondered if they'd been hanging there since Brooke died. The house itself was dark. Empty.

She glanced at her watch. It was almost nine o'clock. She gave RJ a fleeting glance and switched on her flashlight. Crossing the yard, they stepped onto the back porch and approached the door. She shined the dim beam at the knob and gave it a futile turn.

RJ whispered, "It's locked."

Tori nodded. There didn't appear to be a deadbolt, just the lock in the door handle. She wished she'd grabbed those keys hanging by the back door at Winnie's house. Brooke's spare house key would've come in handy right now.

"Maybe there's an open window or something." RJ walked toward the windows overlooking the porch.

Tori called out to him, "You got a credit card on you?"

He looked puzzled. "Yeah. Why?"

"I left my purse in the Jeep." She held out her hand, palm up. "Give me your card."

He pulled his wallet from his back pocket.

She shook her head, taking the card from his hands. Inserting it into the crack between the door and the frame, she felt for the bolt. The plastic card pressed hard against it. Nothing happened.

"It's a debit card," RJ said, leaning over her. "Maybe it doesn't take debit."

She pushed him back a little and pressed the card harder through the space. The bolt slipped back. The door creaked open an inch.

Tori pushed it open and handed the debit card to RJ. She smiled. "Bet you didn't think I could do that."

"Good job, MacGyver." He returned the card to his wallet and stepped forward.

Tori placed a hand on his chest, stopping him. "Wipe your feet." She pointed at the doormat. "We've been walking through mud and weeds. Who knows what we might track in?"

RJ wiped his feet, and together they entered the dark house.

In the living room, she went to a wall covered with family pictures and played her light over them.

He whispered, "Maybe that's a good thing."

"What is?"

"Not knowing the real reason he left you," he said. "Sometimes, not knowing is kinder than the truth. You know what they say, ignorance is bliss."

"But there's no closure."

She looked back at him. He held a voice recorder in his left hand.

"Closure is overrated." He raised the recorder. "Brooke Martin, can you hear me?" He peered in the darkness at the ceiling. "Speak into the recorder."

Tori turned the flashlight on him and then shined the thin beam around the room. A large couch and recliner sat angled in front of a fifty-five-inch television. Hunting rifles hung from a rack on the wall. Nothing out of place. Her heels struck the hardwood planks of the floor with a hollow sound that echoed around them, making the home seem lonelier.

RJ wandered around the room, holding up the recorder. "Brooke Martin ..."—he raised the recorder above his head— "are you here with us?"

Tori played the light on the ceiling. "Why do you keep looking up? You think she's floating around up there like Casper the Ghost?"

RJ raised his arm higher, holding up the recorder. "Brooke Martin, if you're here, give us a sign."

The back door slammed shut with a loud, hard bang. Tori jumped. RJ dropped the recorder.

"What was that?" She threw the dim beam of the flashlight on the door.

RJ picked up the recorder and shook it. He turned it back on and held it up in the air. "She's here," he said.

Tori cringed. "It was the wind. It pushed the door shut."

He tried one more time. "Brooke, did you slam the door? Were you trying to get our attention?"

They waited, frozen, listening. The house was silent. The wind kicked up again and whistled through a window.

Tori shook her head. "Come on, let's find something with Ash's handwriting," she said, taking RJ's arm.

He looked across the living room one last time, and then followed.

As they crept through the house, she said, "And closure is not overrated. It's necessary."

"If you say so."

She stopped. "Everything was going great. We were planning the wedding and our life together. Then, out of nowhere, he vanishes. It's our wedding day and he up and disappears. Ash had to tell me the wedding was off. And it makes no sense, you know, because we were so happy."

"Guess *he* wasn't."

"What do you know?" She shot him a dirty look and resumed walking.

They made their way to the front entry and shined their light on the small table next to the front door. A broken vase lay beneath it with wilted lilies scattered on the tile. Tori lifted a framed photo from the floor. A spider web of cracked glass cut through Brooke, Ash, and Darla's faces. "Wonder how long that's been lying there?"

RJ shrugged.

She set the picture frame back on the table and aimed her flashlight past the staircase and into the adjacent dining room. Dark streaks ran down the wall to the baseboard. Tori shined her light on broken glass scattered on the floor. She looked at RJ.

"You think it's connected to the dead flowers by the door?" she asked.

He leaned closer to the wall and ran a finger across the stain. "Someone threw something at the wall."

"I think it was a liquor bottle," she said, moving the light from the floor to the dining room table. "Watch your step."

Construction paper cluttered the table. Tori looked at the drawings and picked one up. A stick figure woman hung from a water tower by a rope around her neck. Two stick figures—*policemen?*—stood on the horizon. One was pointing to the hanging figure. Tori handed the drawing to RJ.

He made a face. "She's kinda liberal with the black crayon."

"It's her mother."

"Yeah, I got that. That girl's got years of therapy ahead of her."

Tori took the picture and studied it again. She folded it and put it in her back pocket.

"What're you doing?" he asked.

"There's like a dozen identical drawings here. Ash'll never miss it. Now we gotta find something with his hand-writing on it in all this mess."

"Tori, look." He reached for her, but she was shining the light beyond the dining room and into the kitchen. She didn't go into it. Instead, she made her way back to the front entry and the staircase.

She stopped on the middle step. "You know, if he wasn't happy, then he needed to tell me that." She turned to RJ. "But I never heard from him again. Not a single word. Nothing. Nada. One day he's the love of my life and the next day he's not a part of my life in any way, shape, or form. How do you deal with something like that?"

"I don't know." He shot her a quick apologetic smile.

She scrunched her face and shook her head and continued up the staircase. "Then stop bringing it up. I don't want to talk about it."

"Clearly." He followed her upstairs.

Three bedrooms branched off the upstairs landing. She looked in the first bedroom, a little girl's room with a frilly bed, scattered clothes and dolls on the floor, and a wooden rocking horse in the corner. She recognized the purple plush elephant sitting on the horse and it brought a smile to her lips.

The door across the hall opened into the master bed-room. Tori shined her flashlight across the unmade queen-sized bed. She was about to comment on the sheets when something caught her eye. She walked into the bathroom and found one of Brooke's dresses hanging on the shower rod in front of the curtain. The medicine cabinet door swung ajar above the vanity. She pulled the mirrored door open as RJ came up behind her.

"What'cha looking for?"

"Something to confirm she was depressed. There should be antidepressant prescription bottles in her medicine cabinet. But there's nothing here. Not even St. John's wort."

"Maybe she wasn't taking anything prescribed for the depression. Maybe she was managing it with exercise and diet and stuff."

"I don't know. If she was as depressed as everyone says, you'd think she would have something for it. She must've talked to a doctor about the antidepressants. She got those sample packets we found in her purse from someone."

"Lemme ask her." He raised his arm again, holding up the recorder. "Brooke Martin, were you taking antidepressants or any kind of prescription for your depression?"

"RJ, it's not funny. The coroner's report showed that she had Deletycide in her system, and the deputy found twelve empty sample packets on the ground near her body. But there were no tablets in her stomach. Doesn't that bother you?"

"It bothers me she's not responding to my questions. We should be getting some strong EVPs here."

"Forget the EVPS. If she took that many tablets, there'd be a few left in her stomach. She drank something with the drug in it."

RJ turned to her. "So, what are you saying?"

"I don't know." She thought about it a moment before answering. "I have this funny feeling … like we're playing a game of Hangman, but the letters on the board aren't forming a word."

"Or maybe you don't know what the word is yet."

Stepping out of the bathroom, Tori moved past the bed. She found a cubby with a desk. A monitor, along with papers and cards, cluttered the top.

"Have at it," RJ said. "I'm going to keep checking the house."

RJ left as she made her way to the desk. She opened the center drawer, rifled through it, shut it. She opened a side drawer and pulled out several envelopes. By the time she'd gone through all the drawers on the right-hand side of the desk, her excitement was turning into exasperation. There was nothing here but old light bills, old tax receipts, old everything. She opened the bottom drawer and started on that.

"Bingo," she said. "Birthday cards."

RJ returned to the room, stepping beside her as she searched through the cards and envelopes. She flipped through them and stopped. One had her name written on it—in Mike's handwriting: "For Tori".

She glanced at RJ. He nodded toward the envelope in her hands. "You going to open it?"

She tore open the envelope and pulled out two folded notebook pages. A scribbled message in the top margin caught her attention.

> Mikey B. asked me to give this to you, but I chickened out. I couldn't give it to you on your wedding day and then you left town before I had the chance later. Sorry. I know this hurt you. — Ash

She scanned the first page and flipped to the second. The handwriting haunted her, as did the memory, and she didn't need a date to know it'd been written five years ago.

> Dear Tori,
> I know I owe you an explanation. I'm not even sure where to begin, but I'm guessing that doesn't matter anymore. It's how a thing ends that counts, right? Not how it begins.
> I never wanted to hurt you and I didn't mean for this to happen, but we can't get married. It's not that I don't care about you or I don't love you. You've been like a kid sister for as long as I can remember. And I will always love you, but not in the way you deserve.
> You deserve so much more than I can ever give you. You're smart. You know stuff. Get out of this town. Go to New York. Travel the world. Write a book.

I'm just a dumb pitcher who'll probably never make it
to the majors. I'll never get out of this town, but you
can. You can go see the stars. And once you've been
up there you know you been some place.

She put down the letter as her eyes teared. She couldn't
read any more, even though it all came rushing back.

A night some sixteen years ago.

She'd turned fifteen. With her mother out of town, she
had the whole house to herself for the weekend. Brooke and
Winnie came over and Tori couldn't believe it when Mike
showed up with them. He brought beer and taught the girls
drinking games. When Brooke and Winnie drifted to sleep,
Mike and Tori sat up late into the night, side by side on the
couch with a bowl of popcorn between them. *Rebel Without a
Cause* played on a cable station. James Dean sat next to Sal
Mineo at the planetarium and looked up, awed by the stars
above them. "Once you've been up there you know you been
some place," he said.

Mike looked down at Tori and awkwardly put his arm
around her. He displayed all the restless allure of James
Dean, with his face lighting up and darkening with the old
movie on the TV screen.

When it ended, they slipped outside into the backyard
and sat on the dock. They watched the stars, and Mike
pointed. "Once you've been up there you know you been
some place," he whispered to her.

She could still feel his breath on her ear. It burned hot,
even to this day.

RJ reached for the note in her hands, startling her. She
pulled it away.

"What's wrong?" he asked. "What does it say?"

"Nothing," Tori said, collecting herself. "It doesn't matter
anymore."

"Well, it's got to be something. You look like you're cutting onions." He reached for it again and she pulled away.

"No, it's private." She stiffened and looked down at the note. "We've got Ash's handwriting. Now we need to see if it matches Brooke's note."

Tori grabbed her phone and pulled up the suicide note. She enlarged the photo to zoom in on the lines Ash had written in the margin and compared it to the handwritten note. The same slanted *w*'s and *y*'s appeared in both notes. In fact, the handwriting was identical, or near enough.

"It matches," she whispered. "The handwriting matches. Ash wrote the suicide note."

"Let me see it." RJ grabbed the pages from her hand. She reached for it, but he turned away from her.

"Look at the part Ash wrote. Don't read the letter, okay?" She considered the ribbing RJ would give her over the mushy Dear John letter and held the phone back a moment before begrudgingly handing it to him.

He took it and held it next to the note. "I just want to compare the handwriting." His head bobbed from the letter to her phone and back to the letter. After a moment he glanced up, his eyes large. "Do you know what this means?"

"No, tell me ..." came a deep voice behind them.

Tori and RJ turned and shined their flashlights on a man standing in the doorway.

Tori gasped and said, "Ash ... you're home."

CHAPTER SIXTEEN

_OLD _ASE

Tori and RJ stood, trapped, in the dark master bedroom. Ash framed the doorway.

"What are you doing in my home?" Ash flipped a switch on the wall; light flooded the room. "What are you doing in my bedroom?"

Tori squinted in the sudden brightness and said, "I could ask you the same question." She looked over at RJ. He still held the letter and cell phone. She took a step toward Ash. "I thought you were in jail."

"Mikey B. released me. That scumbag principal ain't pressing charges." He pointed at the letter and cell phone in RJ's hands. "What's that? You goin' through my desk?"

Ash reached for the letter. RJ waved his hand, closing his fist over the paper. When he opened it, palm out, fingers spread, the letter had vanished. Ash shook his head.

Tori felt RJ's hand brush hers, quickly, quietly, practically imperceptible. She slipped the letter into her back pocket.

"I received another text message." She touched Ash's arm, grabbing his attention. "From Brooke's cell phone."

"Not this again." Ash sounded curt and distracted. An eyebrow rose in amused contempt. "I already told you I don't have her phone. Is that why you broke into my home? To find a cell phone?"

Laughing, RJ shook his head. "Naaaww. Don't be silly. We were hoping to get EVPs from your wife."

Ash looked perplexed. "What?"

Tori put a hand on RJ's back as she addressed Ash. "Okay ... stop it. Just stop it. Ash, we're here because I was looking for something with your handwriting on it."

"Why?"

"I know you wrote the suicide note, *Whatever I am, you made me.* I know that's your handwriting and I was looking to prove it."

"You're right." Ash paused, as if his mind was spinning. He shook his head. "I wrote it."

A long silence followed. She knew it. She'd been right all along, and no one believed her. But he wrote the suicide note. Only, that meant ....

She shuddered, realizing what that meant. Anger welled inside her, which turned to a deep sadness. Her stomach churned and her legs felt wobbly.

Looking at RJ, she said, "Can you give us a minute?"

He turned to Ash and back to Tori. "Are you sure?"

"Please."

"I'll be outside. Call if you need me." RJ shrugged and left the bedroom.

Tori watched him disappear into the hallway and heard his footsteps on the stairs. When they were alone, she turned to Ash. "Did you stage Brooke's suicide?"

"What?" He seemed genuinely surprised.

"Did you stage Brooke's suicide?" She tried to keep her voice calm. She wasn't sure if she wanted to know the answer, but she asked anyway. "Were you involved in her death."

"No." He stepped past her and went to the window beside the rolltop desk. He stared out the window for several seconds and placed a hand on the glass. "No, of course not."

"Then tell me what happened." She wondered what he was looking at so intently. "Why did you write a suicide note for Brooke?"

"Look, it's not a suicide note. It's a letter—" He shook his head and shut his eyes. He leaned forward and pressed his forehead against the glass. "Or part of a letter I wrote a few years ago when I was in rehab."

"What does it mean?" She stepped closer to the window, closer to him, but didn't touch him. "Why'd you pin it to her body?"

Ash turned, upsetting the curtains, and yelled, "I didn't pin it to her body. I wasn't even there. Brooke and I had a fight that night. I left. Then the next morning, I get a call from Mikey B. telling me Brooke was dead. But we've fought before, you know. I never expected ... you know ...."

"Okay, so you weren't here." She studied him. His face contorted in pain. He seemed sincere, grief stricken. But could she trust him? Did she believe him? "Where were you that night?"

"At the church. Pastor Fields said I showed up drunk to the AA meeting and I passed out on a pew in the sanctuary."

"What were you and Brooke fighting about?"

He flipped back around and faced the window, placing his forearm against the glass as if holding back the intruding night. He spoke quietly again, almost whispering. "She'd been out all evening seeing that pansy-ass principal. She lied. Said she was helping Winnie with the Fourth of July float. But she was with him."

"Do you think something happened with the principal?"

"She wanted to run away with him. She wanted to take Darla and run away to Tallahassee. But I guess something happened—maybe he turned her down."

Tori looked at her feet. Her hand grazed the letter folded in her back pocket and she thought of the note Brooke had left behind. "And she was fighting depression? She had anti-depressants in her purse."

He turned from the window. "She'd been unhappy for a long time. Depressed."

Tori's fingers felt the rough paper in her back pocket, and she shook her head. Something still didn't add up. Even if Brooke was depressed and having an affair with the principal and he broke it off, it still didn't explain that message.

"Whatever I am, you made me," Tori said. "What does it mean?"

"That note, that message, it's from an amends letter I wrote when I was in rehab."

She looked up, her eyes enlarged. "That's why it looks ripped along the edges."

He nodded. "She ripped it from my original letter."

"Why? What does it mean?"

"It was just a line, taken out of context."

"But what does it mean?"

He looked at her, his bottom lip trembling. "I think ... she was telling me something. Telling me I ... I drove her to this. To this decision ..."

"No, Ash." She stepped toward him, feeling great sympathy for him, and she touched his shoulder. "You don't know that."

"Yes, I do." He turned, forcing her hand away. "We weren't happy anymore. She didn't love me. And it was my fault."

"Because you're drinking again?"

"And fighting. And the accusations. I never believed he could make her happy, so I never believed she'd run away with him. I couldn't accept ...." He stopped talking.

The room turned quiet, and cold.

"Accept what?"

"I don't accept it ... that she could do it." He leaned forward against the window, burying his face against his arm. "She killed herself, Tori. She killed herself over him."

Tori left the farmhouse with RJ and they paused at the Jeep. She put a hand on the door but didn't open it. Turning, she watched him step past Brooke's minivan. "I guess you heard all that."

"He sounded like a disgraced televangelist," RJ said. "So, Brooke really committed suicide."

"That's what he says." She turned to face the spindly orange grove. The water tower was nothing more than a black mass against a starry sky. The sight chilled her. "Could she walk out her house, through those trees, to that water tower? It's just not her. It's not the Brooke I knew."

"People change," he said. He stepped past her, to the driver's side of the Jeep. "C'mon, let's head back to Winnie's and get some shut-eye. We gotta be on the road first thing in the morning."

She ignored him, staring at the silhouette of the old water tower. It called to her. She headed toward the grove.

RJ shut the driver's-side door and yelled, "Where you going?"

Thinking through the events again, Tori quickened her pace around the dead trees. Whatever happened that night, Tori had to know how it would've driven Brooke to take her own life. She had a heated argument with Ash. A fight. A liquor bottle shattered against the wall. He left. She ran.

She would've felt heartbroken. In despair. He was explosive, enraged. She was lost. And Tori imagined how that felt.

Now running among the trees, Tori couldn't avoid the limbs that scratched her arms, ripped her flesh. Just as they had scratched Brooke's arms as she pushed through the brittle branches. Coming out on the other side of the grove, Tori looked up at the rusted water tower.

It dominated the sky.

She stepped to the weathered ladder and climbed. Reaching the top, she stopped. Brooke would've stopped here too. And walked around the catwalk circling the tower's hull. Her marriage to Ash would've been racing through her mind. Maybe she fought with the principal, too. He was moving to Tallahassee without her. She was alone. Found a spot. Tied one end of the rope to the railing. Draped the noose around her neck. And jumped.

Except Darla was there. The deputy said Darla witnessed the whole thing.

Brooke wasn't alone.

RJ came up beside Tori, startling her. She hadn't heard him climb up after her.

"Ash believes"—her voice caught in her throat— "Brooke committed suicide."

"And you don't buy it?"

"I don't know. I was so sure he did something, but

now. . ." She perched on the edge of the catwalk and leaned against the rickety railing. Tori felt Brooke's presence all around her, causing a deep sadness. It overwhelmed her. Fighting back tears, she removed Mike's letter from her back pocket and unfolded it.

RJ sat beside her.

She ignored him and focused on the letter. She knew heartache too. What if Brooke had been in love with the principal and he rejected her. Could that have sent her spiraling into a depression? Mike's rejection sent Tori into one. But suicide? Tori never contemplated suicide. No matter how bad she felt, no matter how much she hurt, she never thought about ending it all. Could Brooke have felt that way?

Tori imagined her own self tying one end of a rope to the railing and the other end around her neck. Would she jump? Mike's letter echoed in her head. *I will always love you, but not in the way you deserve.* She put down the letter and looked out at the expanse of treetops stretched out below her.

The dark woods haunted her.

The line from Mike's letter haunted her too. *I will always love you, but not in the way you deserve.* She shook her head to force it from her thoughts. RJ stared at her. He must've been rambling about something because he stopped talking, and she noticed the awkwardness between them.

After a moment, he broke the silence. "Why do you keep reading that old letter?"

"The handwriting matches—"

"Don't give me that. It's about Sheriff Bennett."

Tori watched him a moment. "Ash was telling me he should've told me sooner—the sheriff—that he didn't feel the same way about me as I did about him."

"You need to get past that."

"You don't understand."

"I understand."

"No, you don't," she snapped at him, though she didn't mean to. "He dumped me like radioactive waste, without so much as saying 'You suck' or 'Go to hell' or 'I hate you.' No reason. No explanation. You don't just get over that. Not something like that."

She glanced back at the lake and remembered when teenage Mike would sneak over to her house in the middle of the night. She'd wait for him on the dock in her backyard, and they'd climb to the small boathouse that overlooked the water. They'd sit on that slanted tin roof, far away from prying eyes, and stare at the moon and the stars. How many summer nights did they spend lying there, side by side? Conversations drifted from school to parents, from baseball to books, from life to life after death. What started as a friendship developed into a deep understanding of each other. They were James Dean and Natalie Wood, together and inseparable. Sometimes, while lying there on that boathouse roof, they loved each other so much they wanted to leap off it together, holding hands, into the black abyss.

RJ stared at her for several seconds without moving, and then threw his head back and waved his arms. His voice took on a mocking tone. "Oh my God! What is this world coming to? Right is left. Up is down. Marvel is DC. Cats are dogs. A guy dumps you without telling you why." He laughed as she looked away.

They were quiet for several moments. The chirping crickets grew louder.

RJ broke the silence. "You know we're gonna have to sneak back into Winnie's."

"No," she said under her breath. Following the tree line running perpendicular with the north lake, she could make out the rooftop a couple miles in the distance. "I know where we can go."

CHAPTER SEVENTEEN

SHAD_W _F D_UBT

Nestled on a wooded lot, an abandoned lake house sat rotting along a winding, unpaved path that disappeared into the lake. Plywood covered the windows, two-by-fours crossed the doors, and dirt daubers' and wasps' nests blotched the front port. A FORECLOSURE sign wobbled in the breeze. The whole scene demoralized Tori as she stepped out of the Jeep.

"Whose house is this?" RJ asked then whistled as he came up beside her. "This place has got to be haunted."

"Only by the past," Tori said. For a moment the moon slid behind the clouds, and water, sky, and air darkened. "It's been vacant for a few years."

The full moon broke free, lighting her path. She crossed the dirt driveway, to the front of the house, and stepped onto the filthy porch. The windows were boarded tight, the front door padlocked shut. A neglected banana tree stood lopsided in the front yard, as if years of wind and weather were slowly pushing it over. She remembered when she and her mother had planted it.

"This is your place?" RJ placed a hand on her shoulder.

"I grew up here." Tori left the porch and went around the side of the house. The lake came right up to the backyard.

At the steep overhang along the bank, Tori looked down at the channel that stretched out to the lake. A covered deck rose above the boat dock, like a treehouse on stilts, overlooking the lake. Wooden steps climbed to it. A few feet away, a rope hung from a large branch of a majestic oak tree. The only sound came from the gentle waves slapping against the shore, and the rising and falling chirp of bullfrogs. It all brought back memories.

"Brooke, Winnie, and I used to go swimming over there." She pointed at the large oak and the rope swing swaying in the breeze. "It feels like yesterday and a million years ago at the same time." She looked up at the enclosed deck. "When I was a kid, I'd sit up there and read. I spent summer afternoons reading and writing in that little hideaway, watching the lake and listening to the birds."

"Sounds like you miss it." RJ's voice turned quiet, as if he realized her fleeting memory and didn't want to disturb it.

She didn't answer. Mike's folded letter weighed down her back pocket. Why he never mailed it didn't matter; his voice ringing in her ears did. *I will always love you, but not in the way you deserve.*

Ash knew that all along. They all did. And she'd been a fool for years. *I will always love you, but not in the way you deserve.* That admission revealed an ugly truth: Mike didn't fear committing; he feared committing to her.

She removed the letter and held it with both hands. Pausing, she listened to the night wind over the lake.

RJ jumped up and said, "We're getting too serious. Let's go for a swim."

Tori peered into the channel. She hadn't swum in that lake for twenty years. "You think there's gators?"

"Probably," he said, over his shoulder.

RJ ran down the flagstone steps to the dock, leaving his dress shirt, slacks, and shoes in a trail behind him. Grabbing the rope, he swung out over the channel and launched himself into the water. He came back up, splashing, his head bobbing above the waves.

"Come on in," he called out, raising an arm and waving. "The water feels good."

"I don't have a swimsuit," she yelled back, now standing at the shore edge of the dock.

"Me neither." He laughed, splashing water with a circular motion. The gothic cross tattoo on his arm expanded with his bicep as he waved. "You worry too much," he called out. "Let go."

Tori watched RJ for several moments and then let the letter fall to the dock. She slipped off her heels and the sleeveless black dress. As naked as the day she was born, she swung on the rope over the water, let go, and dove in.

She splashed deep into the dark water, dropping fast and sinking to the muddy bed. Arms of soft hydrilla brushed her legs. She looked up at the surface, bubbles rising around her face with the swat of her arms. The moonlight, a fuzzy white smudge above her, quivered. It was moving away from her, growing fainter.

She mashed her feet into the mud, squishing the thick hydrillas. A rock pressed against her left sole. She pushed up, forcing her body through the water, toward the faint, murky light above, but her body dropped again, and she fell back to the muddy bottom.

Alarmed, she exhaled, and bubbles rushed from her nose and mouth. She kicked her legs, flapped her arms, forced herself to rise again. Coming up a few feet, she wasn't rising fast enough. Her heart thumped. Her lungs ached. A sharp pain split through her forehead. She needed air. The smudgy white light above her looked miles away. She wouldn't make it.

She kicked harder. Again, in a wild panic.

Drowning.

Something gripped her right arm, locked tight on her bicep. Bubbles exploded around her as she struggled to free herself and get to the surface. The strong hand tightened around her and she kicked harder, panicked. She thrashed upwards. Her head cut the water's surface and she gasped for air, coughing.

"Breathe." The deep voice beside her sounded muffled, almost dreamlike, barely heard through the water in her ears. She rubbed her eyes and gulped another breath. Her pulse raced.

For a second, she was sixteen years old again, cradled in Mike's embrace as they watched the streaming flashes of the Leonid meteor shower. He held her tight, comforting her.

Until she felt the arm wrapped around her waist and the warm body pressed against her. She turned to RJ and looked into his wet face.

"I thought you could swim." His breath was hot in her ear.

She pushed him back, splashing out of his arms. "I can swim. It's just been a few years."

He reached for her again, and again she splashed water at him. He relented.

"You sank like a rock."

"I was coming up." She coughed again, expelling lake water. Her ears felt clogged and her eyes burned.

He splashed water at her. "You don't know how to swim."

"I said it's been a long time." She splashed back at him. He splashed at her again, which she returned. A moment later, he had one arm around her while the other wiped lake water from her eyes. Their legs kicked together, in sync, keeping them afloat.

"You shouldn't go skinny-dipping if you can't swim," he said. "It kills your street cred."

"I can swim. The cold water shocked my system." Ducking underwater, she swam around him and a few feet away. When she came up for air at the surface, she ran her hands through her hair, smoothing it away from her face.

She glanced over at RJ. His laugh echoed across the lake.

"I was kidding," he called over to her.

She turned away. "It's not funny." She focused on the rippling waves.

He yelled out, "Okay, I'm sorry. I didn't mean anything by it. You're a great swimmer. Michael Phelps would be jealous."

She turned her head, glancing at him again. "You ruined the romantic moment."

"Is that what this is? Romantic?"

She didn't answer. She focused on the moonlight reflected on the water and looked back at the old house on the shore. RJ called out to her. The tat on his arm caught her
attention again.

Turning, she swam back to him. He seemed surprised when she put her arms around his neck and kissed him. When their lips parted, their eyes locked.

"I think you're sharing something with me," he said to her. "Something important."

She stared at him, pleading with her eyes. "It's getting late," she said, changing the subject. "We'd better go."

"Yeah, 'cause it's getting romantic, right?" RJ returned.

She kissed him again and then, together, they swam back to the dock.

Coming out of the water, she picked up her clothes and noticed Mike's letter on the planks. She reached for it, when a reflection in the water caught her eye. A bluish, wavy image of RJ grinned and bobbed a suggestive eyebrow at her. She dropped her clothes, picked up the letter from the dock, and walked up the steps to the covered deck.

It seemed pitch-black for a moment, and then her eyes became accustomed to it and she discovered that the moonlight lit the deck quite well. The noisy chatter of crickets and bullfrogs grew louder.

RJ came up behind her. "There's no furniture?" he asked. "We sleeping on the floor?"

Tori had a better idea. She climbed out the side of the enclosure and up to the roof. RJ followed. She lay down, face up, with her hands behind her head. RJ lay beside her. They remained there, like that, for several minutes, not saying a word, simply observing the moon and the stars.

Tori broke the quiet. "Brooke's gone. She's really gone."

"I know."

There was a long silence between them. RJ whistled and the sound echoed over the water. It broke the tension. "So whaddya want to do when we get back?"

"Film the boat show," she said. "Interview that skiing squirrel."

"Classic." He laughed. "But what about after that? I mean, where do you see yourself in five years? You know, when you grow up."

"I don't know. I'd like to humiliate Simone Adams on air."

"Get in line." He chuckled and turned quiet again. She listened to him breathe. After a moment, he said, "I see you writing true crime books."

Tori entertained the idea. "I can see that, too. I'd kill it—no pun intended."

"You could write a book about that Tampa teacher who paid her student to kill her husband. You'd be the next Ann Rule or Priscilla Prescott."

"Hell, I'd be the next Truman Capote." She snickered at the thought and turned her head to look at him. "How about you?"

"I see myself as this famous paranormal investigator."

"No, seriously." She leaned up on her elbow. "What do you see yourself doing?'"

"Seriously. I'd investigate crazy, out-there cases and post the videos on my YouTube channel. It'd get millions of hits because, you know, I got actual proof of ghosts or Bigfoot and I'd be exposing hoaxes. I was born to be a YouTube celebrity."

She laid her head back down. "You're strange, you know that? But it works for you."

"You laughing at me?"

"No. I hope you become a famous paranormal investigator and find proof of aliens and Bigfoot and ghosts. Maybe they'll make movies about your scariest cases."

"You are! You're laughing at me." He wrapped his arms around her, tackling her. She laughed and pushed him away. They wrestled for a moment, and she screamed and kicked her legs. He kissed her neck. Just as quickly, they stopped. She could hear, no—feel—him breathing beside her. Falling back against the roof, held tight in his embrace, she put all thoughts of Ash and Brooke and their terrible secrets right out of her head. And even Mike seemed like someone she used to know. She felt good—healed.

At least for the time being.

Opening her eyes, the next morning, Tori looked down over a breathtaking lake bathed in golden light.

Her lips curved into a smile as she realized where she was.

Turning her head, she saw RJ lying beside her, sound asleep. She waited for the inevitable morning-after pang of regret … but it didn't come. Everything about last night felt right.

It would be short-lived, though, she knew. Climbing down from the roof and returning to the dock, she found her clothes. She stared at her phone for several seconds and pulled up Brooke's contact. Tori typed: "Brooke?" She sent the text and waited. After several minutes, her phone dinged.

"Yes"

Tori stared at it. She recalled what Ash said and the gossip of Brooke having an affair with the principal. Could a broken heart have led her to kill herself? Her fingers shaking, Tori typed: "Did you end your life?" The reply was instantaneous.

"No"

Tori read it. She typed: "Were you murdered?" She waited for the answer.

"Yes"

She repeated the response, and typed: "Who murdered you?" No answer returned. After a long minute, she looked back at the lake and at her phone. She typed it again: "Who murdered you?" She waited. Her phone dinged with the incoming response.

"You already know that answer."

Tori shook her head. She didn't know how to respond. Her phone dinged again. She read the message.

"Whatever I am, you made me."

Her hand trembling, she put down the phone.

CHAPTER EIGHTEEN

_N_MI_S

Sunday, July 1

Early morning and it was already, as expected, scorching hot. Tori and RJ returned downtown and parked in front of the Waffle House, the Jeep packed with their suitcases and bags and Tori's black dress hanging from the roll beam. They had just enough time for a quick breakfast before heading back to Tampa.

Inside, Tori slipped into a booth near the large front windows. RJ sat across from her and spread his recorder, laptop, headphones, and notepads across the table.

"How do you feel about driving?" He booted up the laptop. "I've got several hours of recordings at the Martin house and that water tower to go through."

"You're going to listen to all that?" She shook her head. "There's nothing on there but you, me, and the crickets."

His brows shot up. "I know. You're a skeptic."

"I'm not a skeptic. I just don't believe in ghosts."

She ordered scrambled eggs and orange juice when the server arrived. RJ, with his headphones on and scribbling numbers and notes in his notepad, seemed oblivious, so she ordered a stack of waffles with maple syrup for him. When the server left, Tori noticed the morning edition of the *Elroy Springs Gazette* on the table. The front-page headline screamed: "Angry Husband, Doting Principal Disrupt Funeral Service."

"Looks like Edison got his story," she said, unfolding the paper and scanning the article. She wondered if he got a quote from Mayor Winslow. When the food arrived, she moved the paper out of the way. RJ lowered the headphones to his neck and did a double take at the large front window. He dropped his pencil.

"Uh-oh—" His eyes got big.

Tori sipped her juice. "What is it?"

"Your Kryptonite."

"My what?" She turned to look out the window. A bright red-and-white SEBC-TV News van, with the glittery yellow lightning bolt logo emblazoned on its side, sat parked in front of the courthouse.

Storming out of the Waffle House, Tori raced outside and crossed the street, headed for the courthouse. She pushed open the glass doors and entered the Sheriff's Department. Mike paced back and forth in his office, punching his right fist repeatedly into his open left hand. A redheaded woman sat in front of his desk. Her voice stopped Tori cold. For a long moment, she stood frozen, caught and held, unmoving. Simone Adams turned her head toward the office door and smiled.

"What's going on here?" Tori said and stepped into the office.

Simone put a hand over her heart and scowled. "Why, Vicki Younger," Simone said, mocking shock. "Whatever are you doing here?"

"It's Tori."

"Of course, it is. My bad." Simone made a tsk-tsk sound and gave her a tight, thin-lipped smile. "Now, if you don't mind, we're trying to hold a meeting here."

"Why don't you try holding your breath instead." Tori placed her hands on the desk and addressed Mike. "What is *she* doing here?"

Simone answered instead. "I read the notes you emailed to Pittman. Very interesting." She straightened her back and folded her arms. "He assigned the story to me."

"There is no story. I'm dropping it."

"Oh, there's a story here, alright." Simone laughed and shook her head. "Popular high school history teacher is murdered by her husband, who tries to cover it up by making it look like she committed suicide. I'll get national exposure breaking this."

"My initial investigation was wrong." Tori glanced around the office at the bowling and fishing trophies displayed on the bookshelves. A rod and reel leaned against the wall in the corner, next to the framed photo of James Dean. She looked back at Mike and held his gaze. "Ash has an alibi. He didn't murder Brooke."

"That's what I was telling her," he said. Mike slapped open the file with the palm of his hand. "Ash wasn't home that night. He was at an AA meeting."

Simone shook her head. "Actually, he wasn't." She got up and leafed through the papers in the file, picked up one sheet, and studied it a moment. "If you'd bothered to check, you would've found that meeting had been cancelled."

"Pastor Fields led the meeting." Mike leaned back in his chair. "Ash was there ... all night long."

"Pastor Fields is lying," Simone said. "And so is Ash. His alibi just fell apart."

A sudden flush of red colored Mike's face. "What? Why? Why would the pastor lie?"

"He's covering for the husband." Simone took the file from Mike's hand. "And I hate to say it, but Vickie dug up some interesting facts about the schoolteacher's murder."

"Again, with the murder? This is getting out of hand." Mike threw an accusing glance at Tori, as if she had stirred up a hornets' nest after he told her to leave it be. "We investigated Brooke's death and found no evidence of foul play."

Simone leaned forward and pointed a finger. "The husband was drunk that night. He had a fight with the misses over her fling with the hottie principal. Things escalated, and he killed her and panicked." She paused for dramatic effect. "Backed against a wall, he wrote a suicide note and made it look like she hung herself over the soured affair."

"You can't be serious." Mike jumped from his desk, sending his chair teetering. "This is crazy."

"It's not crazy, sheriff." Tori raised her hands to calm him. "There are hundreds of cases out there, where what *appeared* to happen isn't what *actually* happened. Take *Unnatural Causes*, for example, by Priscilla Prescott. A caregiver is found to have murdered her elderly patient, even though it appeared the old lady had died of natural causes."

Mike opened his mouth. Tori shushed him.

"Or *Death in the Deep End*," she continued. "A high-society wife appears to have drowned in her pool. Turns out the neighbor murdered her over an ongoing argument about the property line. I could go on."

Mike shook his head and folded his arms across his chest. "What are those? Mystery novels?"

"True crime books," Simone said. "And Vickie is making a valid point."

"*And Then She Was Gone*, another book by Priscilla Prescott, and a perfect example of what's going on here." Tori beamed as she spoke, becoming more animated. "A pregnant wife disappears, and it looks like the cheating husband has murdered her. Turns out it was the other woman's boyfriend who was framing the husband. It's never the most obvious suspect."

"Dramatic true crime books aside, look at your coroner's report," Simone said to Mike. "The schoolteacher had Deletycide in her system, but no tablets in her stomach."

"Which implies she drank something with the drug in it." Tori nodded toward Simone and turned to Mike. "But why were there all those sample packets around her and in her purse when the deputy found her body?"

A cold, congested expression settled on his face. "We've already been over this. Her body digested the tablets."

Tori started to answer, but Simone beat her to it. "Twelve tablets? Her body wouldn't have had time to absorb that many tablets that close to death."

"And your point is?"

"My point is," Tori said, talking over Simone and placing a hand on her shoulder. "My point is that you need to examine her body for a needle puncture. I think she was injected with a high-dose Deletycide and the open sample packets were scattered around the crime scene to suggest a suicide. I suspect that if we examine the body, we'll find a needle puncture."

Simone winked at Tori and leaned across the desk. She raised her thumb and index finger, indicating a miniscule amount. "Extremely tiny and easy to miss. It was meant to be overlooked."

"A needle puncture?" Mike considered this a moment, and then shook his head. "We can't examine the body. Brooke's already been laid to rest."

"Exhume her body," Simone and Tori said in unison.

As if responding to their request, the monitor on Mike's wrist beeped. He hesitated before looking at his arm. The beeping intensified. He raised a finger, motioning them to give him a moment. Shutting his eyes, he took a deep breath and exhaled. "Tom Seaver, 3,640 strikeouts, 2.86 ERA. Lefty Grove, 2,266 strikeouts, 3.06 ERA."

Simone turned to Tori. "Is he okay? What's he doing?"

"His blood pressure is going up." Tori turned and walked out of the office.

She could still hear Mike's voice from the lobby. "Nolan Ryan, 5,714 strikeouts, 3.19 ERA." He recited the stats with rapid-fire passion. "Randy Johnson, 4,875 strikeouts, 4.875 ERA."

"This is ridiculous." Simone's voice carried into the lobby, and Tori cringed as she poured a cup of water from the cooler. Simone sounded confused. "Sheriff Bennett, what are you doing?"

"He recites baseball stats when his blood pressure rises," Tori said, returning to the office with a cup of water. She set it on the desk. "It helps him relax."

"Roger Clemens, 4,672 strikeouts, 3.12 ERA. Cy Young, 2,803 strikeouts, 2.63 ERA." The beeping stopped. Mike opened his eyes. His breathing returned to normal. "Sorry, you were saying?"

Simone looked perplexed. "What just happened?"

"The sheriff has a congenital heart disease. It runs in his family," Tori said, returning to her seat. "He has to relax to lower his blood pressure."

"I'm good. I just needed a minute." Mike picked up the cup of water and took a sip. He turned his head toward Tori and then Simone. "Look, ladies. This is a small Christian town, and Brooke Martin was a well-loved, respected citizen. No one will stand for us exhuming her body. Do you know what kind of controversy that'll create?"

Simone leaned back in her chair. A knowing smirk crept across her face. "What kind of controversy will be created if she was murdered and the town sheriff ignored it and let the murderer go scot free? Or worse, is found to be covering it up."

Mike sank back in his seat.

Tori glanced at Simone's folder. "You got all that from my notes?"

Simone hesitated, and then answered. "Well, when you look at the evidence—"

"My evidence," Tori interjected.

"*The* evidence." Simone's nostrils constricted, and she shook her head, clearly not in answer to Tori's question but in dismissal, as if Tori were a fly buzzing around her head. "Whether it was an accident or intentional, I think the husband did something to that schoolteacher and covered his tracks by trying to make it look like she committed suicide."

"That's what I was thinking too," Tori said, as if considering what she was saying. To be honest, agreeing with Simone spooked her. "Granted, it is conjecture. But when you add the text messages from Brooke's phone, the evidence of stalking, the volatile nature of the Martins' relationship, and the fact that the suicide note is in the husband's handwriting .... And if Ash was lying about being at the church AA meeting that night ...."

Simone grabbed hold of Mike's arm. "I'd say it justifies opening a murder investigation."

He stood again and swatted her grip away. "Now, wait one minute."

"I'd like to run the story tonight and end it with you

saying something like, 'In light of the evidence that investigative reporter Simone Adams has brought to our attention, we have decided to open a murder investigation.'"

Tori leaned toward Simone and stated, "This is not your story."

"Pittman assigned it to me."

"I gave it to Pittman," Tori said in a raised tone.

Mike slammed his hands on the desk, making a loud thwap that got their attention. When it was quiet again, he spoke. "There is no murder investigation."

Simone sighed, losing her patience. "We have Ash. We have the facts. And we have the story. I'm going on air with it. It can end with the town sheriff thanking me for the questions I've brought to light and opening a murder investigation, or it can end with me asking my viewers why the Elroy Springs Sheriff's Department is sweeping this under the rug. What are you hiding, sheriff? Are you covering up a murder?"

Tori interrupted before Mike could answer. "But there are other people with equal motive and opportunity." She shook her head. "You can't spin this to make Ash look like he murdered his wife. We need to look at Principal Quinn's involvement too."

Mike went to the window and stared outside. "Principal Quinn is a respected member of this community," he said.

"The teacher's illicit lover?" Simone laughed and turned to Tori. "Oh, Vickie, this gets more and more salacious."

"*Carnage in the Classroom*, by Eleanor DeWitt," Tori said. "Did you ever read that book?" She waited for an answer.

Simone and Mike both stared at her.

After a moment, she continued. "Brenda Hillfigger, an elementary school teacher in Albuquerque, New Mexico, was found dead at her desk when students arrived for class one morning. It appeared she'd been stabbed, and the school janitor was the last person to see her the night before. He was the obvious suspect—until the teacher's relationship with the school principal came to light."

Simone let out a long, drawn-out huff. A shadow of annoyance crossed her face. "And your point is?"

"My point is, even though the janitor was the primary suspect, he wasn't the murderer. Brenda Hillfigger had been having an affair with her principal and threatened to expose the relationship if he didn't leave his wife, so he killed her."

Simone shut her eyes and swallowed. "In this case, it's the husband. It's an open-and-shut case. There are no other viable suspects here."

"This isn't a murder case," Mike yelled, returning to the desk.

"Yes, it is," Tori and Simone said simultaneously. Simone stood, put her hands on her hips, and looked down at Tori.

"Look, Vickie. It's my story and I will follow whatever direction the leads take me in, including convicting that no-good, piece-of-human-waste of a husband in the court of public opinion. Now you need to get out my way and head to your little coverage of the boat show back in Tampa."

"We're not leaving."

"Fine. But stay out of my way," Simone said, and turned to Mike, all but dismissing Tori. "I'd like to interview you about the night the schoolteacher's body was found. Do you think we could conduct it at the high school? I'd like all the students' cards and wreaths in the background."

Wide-eyed, mouth open, Mike looked befuddled. He closed his eyes and rubbed his temples.

Simone continued for several moments, hardly taking a breath, until she suddenly stopped and looked over at Tori. "What are you still doing here?" she asked. "Don't you have a boat show in Tampa to cover?"

"I'm not surrendering the story to you."

Simone's face relaxed, and a faint smile crossed her lips. "You're too close to this, Vickie."

Tori nodded in defeat and got up, upending the chair she'd been sitting in. "Fine, Simone, but this isn't over."

She left the cluttered office, slamming the door behind her, and stormed back into the lobby. How was this happening—again? Simone swooped in and stole another story. Hesitating at the glass entry doors, she couldn't help but wonder if Simone was right. Maybe it was time to head back to Tampa, cover the boat show, and just move on.

Her phone dinged with an incoming text. It was from Brooke.

"Don' t give up on me. "

Tori stared at the message, and looked back at Mike in his office, talking to Simone. Tori turned toward Deputy Torres. He sat in his office, typing on his computer as a man in overalls sat across from him, waving his hands. They seemed unaware she was even there. A different girl sat behind the reception desk, directing an incoming call. She looked as young as Zoe, probably another high school or college student interning for the summer.

Out the front door, Tori could see RJ still sitting at the window booth in the Waffle House across the street. He was talking to a woman in the booth across from him. It looked like Winnie Daniels.

Leaving the Sheriff's Department, Tori pushed open the glass doors and nearly plowed into a woman entering the building.

Thin, with shoulder-length black hair, and wearing a green pleated skirt decorated with triangular bunches of purple grapes, the woman gasped, coming face-to-face with Tori. It was What's her face. Garlic?

Charlotte squealed, "Tori? You're still here?"

"I-I was just leaving," Tori said, noting the judgmental expression on Charlotte's face.

"You were seeing my husband?" Charlotte blocked her exit. "I'm glad I caught you, then, before you left. I have some things I need to say to you."

CHAPTER NINETEEN

WAR_I_G SIG_S

Tori backstepped into the lobby as Charlotte pushed through the front doors.

"I was just bringing my husband his lunch." Charlotte held up a brown paper sack. Tori could smell the egg salad and pickles on the sandwich inside as Charlotte waved the bag. "He'd forget his head if it wasn't screwed on."

"Guess that's part of his charm," Tori said, and looked past the woman, through the glass doors. She could see the Waffle House across the street and RJ talking to Winnie in the booth in the front windows. Tori didn't have time for an exit interview with her ex's new wife. "I've got to be going now."

"Hold on," Charlotte returned. "Hold one second. There's something I need to say to you."

Tori clamped her jaw tight and stared. How the woman could wear that green pleated skirt with a swirling swash of purple grapes was anyone's guess. She certainly couldn't take her seriously. Anyhow, it looked like there was no way out of it. She looked at Charlotte, waiting.

Charlotte smiled. "I wanted to apologize for getting so upset yesterday at Brooke's memorial dinner."

Tori nodded and started to say, "It's okay," but Charlotte interrupted.

"So, you were talking to my husband again, alone?"

Tori looked around the lobby. The new girl sat at the reception desk, talking on the phone. Deputy Torres typed away at the computer in his office. The man in the overalls still sat at the desk across from him, waving his arms as he spoke. Mike and Simone still strategized in his office. "We weren't alone, Mrs. Bennett."

"Michael told you we have a family, didn't he? Twin boys." She set the lunch sack on the receptionist's counter. The receptionist looked up at them as Charlotte opened her purse. "Now, let me see. Where are those pictures?"

"Mrs. Bennett, I—"

Charlotte didn't let her finish. "Call me Charlotte. I mean, we're practically family, right? I mean, with you being engaged to my husband all those years ago."

"It was a long time ago, and I have to hit the—"

"You've known my husband for a long time, I hear." Charlotte held several photographs in her hands.

"Since we were kids."

"How special." Charlotte handed the photos to Tori. "And you two dated in high school?"

"We were good friends." Tori glanced at the pictures. Twin boys in diapers, wearing cowboy boots. Twin boys pointing to the monkeys at the zoo. Twin boys blowing out the candles on a birthday cake. "We knew each other as kids."

"Friends? You were engaged." She laughed. "But I don't need to be worried about you two, do I?"

Tori handed the photos back to her. "No, that's ancient history. And, if you must know, he broke up with me."

"But here you are again, talking to my husband."

Tori forced a smile. "We were discussing Brooke."

"We have twin boys, you know."

"I know. I saw the pictures," Tori said, losing patience. "They're adorable."

"I have more pictures." Charlotte opened her purse and then hesitated. She looked back at Tori and smiled. "You and RJ? You two are too cute for words."

"We're just friends. He's my cameraman."

"There's that word again … friends," Charlotte said. "You're so pretty and successful. I bet you've got someone waiting for you back home."

"Not at the moment, no."

"You're a career woman. On the news, on television." She smacked her lips and whistled. "I bet you're raring to get back to your life in Tampa as soon as possible."

Tori looked out the front doors again. RJ was still in the booth at the window, talking to Winnie. Tori looked back at Charlotte.

"And you are going back, right?" Charlotte stepped in front of her, blocking her view.

Tori shifted her head to look outside, only half listening to Charlotte. "Going back? Oh, yeah."

"When?"

"I'm sorry. What?"

"I asked"—Charlotte enunciated precisely— "when are you leaving?"

"As soon as possible." Tori moved past her and opened the glass doors. "I apologize, but I have to go."

Not daring to look back, Tori left Charlotte and that ugly-ass green skirt behind. She bound down the stone steps outside the Sheriff's Department and bolted across the street. The Waffle House looked crowded with the morning rush, but RJ still sat in the booth, with Winnie across from him. She was wearing his headphones as he played something from his laptop. Tori slipped into the booth next to Winnie and looked intensely at RJ.

Winnie removed the headphones. "RJ, um, he found something on his recordings," she said. "It sounds like a voice."

Tori wasn't listening. "Simone Adams is interviewing the sheriff." She raised her voice, her agitation growing. "That woman is convincing him to open a murder investigation."

RJ's face brightened. "That's what you wanted, isn't it?"

Winnie turned to Tori, and then back to RJ. "Who is Simone Adams?"

"Yes, but ..." Tori folded her arms. "But the bitch keeps calling me Vickie."

"Why do you even care?" He looked back at his laptop and struck a few keys. "She pulls this crap all the time."

"Who is Simone Adams?" Winnie asked again.

RJ answered her without looking up from the screen. "It's this other newscaster Tori competes with."

Tori opened her mouth and let out an indignant oomph. "I don't compete with her. I'm just better than her."

Winnie's eyebrows rose like two exclamation marks. "I still don't know who she is."

"Thank you for saying that." Tori smiled at Winnie and squeezed her hand, then noticed she had finished the plate of eggs and the juice glass was empty. It didn't matter. Tori was too fired up to eat, anyway. "I'm not putting up with Simone's crap."

RJ stopped typing and looked up from his laptop. "Let it go, already. Besides, I've got big news."

Winnie nodded. "He found a voice. We think it's Brooke."

"What?" Tori glanced over at the laptop screen and at the black and green boxes of jagged lines. They looked like an EKG reading.

RJ took the headphones from Winnie and placed them over her head. "Just listen."

He tapped a key on his laptop. A second later, Tori heard white noise filtering through the speakers. He turned up the volume. She heard her own voice, faint and far off, as if she'd yelled something to him from another room. They must've been in the Martin house and she was in the master bedroom rifling through Ash's desk.

RJ's voice came in loud and clear. Then there was something else. A faint, fading, faraway noise ... she almost wanted to call it a voice.

She looked at Winnie, then over at RJ. "Play it again," she said. "Can you rewind it?"

His fingers worked the keys, and she listened to the recording again. RJ's voice asked the question, *Brooke Martin. Can you tell me what happened? Did you commit suicide?* Something answered. Maybe. It sure sounded like it. She shook her head in disbelief.

"It's electronic voice phenomena," he said. "I told you we'd get something."

Winnie nodded. "It's Brooke."

"I wouldn't go that far," Tori said. "I'm not even sure that's a voice. Maybe it's something from outside. A bird or a bat or something."

"Speaking?" RJ leaned forward, over the table. "A bird or a bat is answering my question?"

"Um, she's saying 'mother,'" Winnie said. "Plain as day. That's Brooke's voice."

"Mother? Why would she say 'mother'?" Tori removed the headphones. "That's not answering his question."

RJ shook his head. "Not mother. Murder. She's saying 'murder.'"

They were silent for a moment.

Winnie let out a nervous chuckle. "This is too much." She nudged Tori out of the way and slipped out of the booth. "Could Brooke really be communicating with us?"

"No," Tori said.

"Yes," RJ said, speaking over her.

"No," she said again.

"Yes," he said. "It's empirical evidence that can't be refuted. That's Brooke's voice on there, and I've still got hours of recordings to listen to. Who knows what else I picked up."

Winnie grabbed her purse from the table. "Well, speaking of pick up, I'm picking Howard up at the airport and I've got a freezer full of Haagen-Daz to dispose of."

RJ looked up at her. "Howard? Your husband?"

"You mean, we're finally going to meet him?" Tori asked, looking down at her empty plate.

"Correction," RJ said. "You mean, you *wish* you had time to meet him. We're about to hit the road."

"Oh, I wish you did have time. You'd love him," she said, and smiled at Tori. "Everyone does. My brother and his wife. Ash. Even Brooke. She adored him."

Tori nodded. "I'm sorry he missed her funeral."

"It's just as well," Winnie said. "He's a widower and, um, still doesn't do well with funerals."

"The poor man. I'm glad you two found each other." Tori rose from the booth and hugged her, and RJ reached out to shake her hand.

"I'll send you the audio clippings if I get more EVPs," he said.

"As long as Brooke's not saying anything scary. I can't handle scary." Winnie shuddered and headed for the door. Stopping, she turned and said, "Have a safe drive home, and call me when you get back to Tampa."

She disappeared out the door as RJ dropped his keys on the table. "I'm giving you the keys to the Jeep. I wanna keep going through these recordings on the way back."

"We're not going back," Tori said. "At least not yet."

"Don't go there," he said. "I'm warning you, don't go there."

Tori sat back in the bench seat. "We've been working this angle. It's our story. And you said it yourself, you've got this empirical evidence from Brooke herself. I don't know if empirical is the right word or not, but that's not the point right now."

"No, Tori." RJ put down the headphones. "We have another assignment to get to. And you wanted Sheriff Bennett to look into this, to consider Brooke was murdered. You did it. You've done right by your friend."

"Brooke doesn't deserve to have her story told by *that* woman."

"You're right. She doesn't." RJ took a deep breath and exhaled loudly. "But there's nothing you can do about it. We have to hit the road."

"We're not leaving. Not yet."

"You promised."

She shook her head. "No, I didn't."

"Yes, you did."

"No."

"Yes." RJ raised his voice. "You did."

"I'm not letting this go," she said. "Have I ever told you about the book, *Carnage in the Classroom*?"

"Lemme guess. Another true crime book."

"Listen," Tori said. "Brenda Hillfigger, an elementary school teacher in Albuquerque, New Mexico, was found dead at her desk when students arrived for class one morning. It appeared she'd been stabbed, and the school janitor was the last person to see her the night before. He was the obvious suspect—until the teacher's relationship with her principal came to light."

"Annnnnd?" He stretched the word out so long it bordered on mocking her.

"The principal, RJ," she said. "The principal."

He laughed. "Great sleuthing, *Murder, She Wrote.* Now we're back to the principal as a murder suspect."

"That's not all. Pastor Fields lied about Ash crashing at the church the night Brooke died. That means Ash doesn't have an alibi anymore."

RJ hesitated. "I don't even want to ask this, but ... where was he the night his wife died?"

"He *wasn't* at an AA meeting."

"Why would the pastor lie about that? What's in it for him?"

"I don't know yet, but we need to talk to him and find out why." Tori leaned forward and lowered her voice. "Ash didn't murder Brooke. I know it. I feel it. He wasn't there. He may have been lying about his whereabouts that night, but he wasn't at the house when Brooke died. Someone else is behind th—"

"Stop," RJ said. "Just stop."

Tori snapped back, surprised. "What?"

"We've got to leave," he said. "If we're not back in Tampa to cover the boat show, we'll lose our jobs."

"I don't care."

"I do." He closed his laptop and set the headphones on the table. "Now, I'm going to hit the head. Then we're going to get in my Jeep that's packed with all our stuff and drive back to Tampa in record time. Our next assignment is waiting." He got up from the booth. "And if I gotta tie you up and strap you into that passenger seat, then so be it. We're leaving. So ... do you need to go before we hit the road?"

"I'm fine." She looked down at her empty plate. Her stomach growled.

"Okay. Suit yourself." He headed for the restrooms.

Tori stared out the window, focused on the stupid red-and-white SEBC-TV news van parked across the street. Her stomach growled again. Looking at her empty plate, she noticed the headphones beside it.

She had heard something. Some kind of sound ... but was it a voice? Or even—and she laughed at herself for even thinking it—Brooke's voice? She slipped the headphones on her head and turned the laptop around. Opening it back up, she replayed the recording.

RJ's voice boomed and she turned down the volume. *Brooke Martin. Can you tell me what happened? Did you commit suicide?* Something answered. Or at least it sure sounded that way. She hit replay and turned the volume up. A faint voice spoke. Replay. Again. It sounded like Brooke, as if her voice was coming through some child's string-and-tin-can phone. Did it sound like Brooke, saying "mother?" No. She said "murder." Tori pressed replay once more. She listened, closed her eyes, strained to hear.

"Murder."

She heard it plain as day now: "Murder."

Tori removed the headphones and tossed them onto the table. Her eyes teared up. Glancing at her phone, she thought about the text messages. Darla. Ash. Pastor Fields. Principal Quinn. She looked out the window. Across the street, Simone and her cronies were packing equipment into the van. RJ's Jeep, parked in front of the restaurant, sat there.

She looked back at the table. His keys just lay there, waiting.

* * * *

Tori's cell phone buzzed, with RJ's name and number appearing on the screen. She sent him to voicemail with one hand as she steered the Jeep with the other. Pulling into the parking lot of the First Baptist Church of Elroy Springs, she heard the gravel crunch under the tires. A lone black-and-white bus sat parked under a sprawling magnolia, and she rolled to a stop beside it. Behind her, next to the road, Pastor Fields balanced atop a ladder as he changed the letters on a white message board.

So far, the message read: "Thank you Lord for all who," and the pastor was positioning the black *s* as Tori approached.

He turned his head and smiled, looking down at her. "It's my Independence Day message," he said.

"It's simple and to the point," Looking up, she placed a hand to her brow to block the sun from her eyes. "I like it."

The pastor placed the *s* on the board and then dug through a carton of letters in his free hand. He held up a black *e*.

Tori watched him for a moment. "Pastor Fields, do you have a minute?"

He put the *e* in place and glanced down at her, saying, "I thought you were leaving right after the memorial."

"That was the plan," she said. "But then something strange happened. We need to talk."

He looked into the plastic container and fished a hand through the letters. He held up a capital *R* and threw it back. A moment later he had a lowercase *r* in his hand and affixed it to the board.

Tori continued. "It's important."

"Is this about Ash?" He remained focused on the sign, placing a *v* on the board.

"Yes," Tori said, looking up. She expected him to stop and climb down from the ladder. When he didn't, she said, "You told the sheriff that Ash showed up here drunk to an AA meeting on the night Brooke died. You said Ash crashed here all night."

"Yes." He was fishing through the container again.

"Why'd you lie to him?"

The pastor stopped, as if caught off guard by Tori's question. Then he resumed his work, placing an *i* and a *c* on the board. "I don't know what you mean."

"The sheriff knows you lied. The AA meeting was cancelled that night." She watched the pastor place the final letter, a lowercase *e*, on the board. He leaned back on the ladder as if to admire his work. She wondered if he was even listening.

He climbed down the ladder and set the large container of plastic letters on the ground. He stood in front of her. "Maybe we'd better talk inside."

Tori read the message: *Thank you Lord for all who served.*

Tori looked back at the pastor. Finally, she was getting somewhere. She picked up the tote box and followed the pastor to the front of the church. They walked up the steps and paused at the front doors.

He reached for the knob and hesitated. "How did the sheriff find out?" he asked.

"Simone Adams."

"Oh, that she-devil." He shook his head. "I should've known she was trouble when she came to talk. She's a lost lamb, that one."

"She's more like a wolf."

The pastor opened the door and entered the church. Tori followed him inside.

"She didn't buy your story and did some digging. She let the sheriff know that, as an alibi, you're less than reliable."

"The meeting wasn't cancelled." He sat down in a pew and looked down at his feet. "We held it at a group member's home whose back had gone out and couldn't make it to the church. I can't say any more than that."

"Then you and Ash were at a meeting that night?"

"No." He raised his head and met her gaze. "Miss Younger, can I be honest with you?"

"I don't know. Can you?"

He didn't smile at her joke. "Ash was drunk that night and I found him vandalizing the high school," he said. "He was smashing the trophy case and spray-painting derogatory words about the principal across the walls."

"That's where he was that night? He left Brooke and his daughter home alone to go raze the high school?"

"I found him there, intoxicated, and got him out as quickly and quietly as possible. I brought him back to the church, where he passed out. He didn't move a muscle till the next morning, when Sheriff Bennett arrived and told us of Brooke's tragic demise."

"So, he was here, passed out all night long?"

"I couldn't let him take the rap for defacing the school property," he said. "Not after everything he and Brooke had already been through."

"What exactly had they been through?"

"You understand, he's fighting demons …"

"I know. He's a lost lamb too," she said.

He shot her a disapproving glare, and said, "After storming the PTA meeting, drunk, and wrecking the cafeteria, accusing Principal Quinn of sleeping with his wife, he was already violating a restraining order by stepping foot on the school property. Then, most recently he caused a scene at a bar in Frostproof."

"You're talking about Sneaky Pete's."

"He caught Brooke there with another man and again tore the place apart. Sheriff Bennett was called to break up the fight. After all that, Ash would've been looking at jail time if what he'd done at the school came to light."

"And court-appointed rehab," she said. "Maybe that would've been best for him."

"Maybe."

"Pastor, who did Ash find Brooke with that night at Sneaky Pete's? Was it Principal Quinn?"

"I don't know."

"Do you believe the rumors that Brooke and the principal were having an affair?"

"Only two people know the answer to that—and one of them is dead now."

CHAPTER TWENTY

F_ _L ME _NCE

Thunder rumbled in the distance and rain clouds followed Tori from the church to the high school. She parked just as her cell phone buzzed. RJ's name popped up on the screen, but she didn't have time to talk. Besides, what could she say to him?

Swiping the call to voicemail, she noticed the hundreds of cards, posters, and wreaths lining the chain-link fence surrounding the campus. She stared at them, thinking about Brooke, when a balding head popped up in the door window, startling her. It was the reporter from the *Gazette*.

Edison Beyer poked his head into the Jeep. A Canon camera hung from a strap around his neck and bumped the door. "Looks like the afternoon rains are coming early today."

"What are you doing here?" She noticed the camera bumping the door as he spoke.

"I could ask you the same thing," he said, extending a hand into the Jeep. They shook as he continued, "There's an SEBC-TV news van outside the courthouse." He pointed to the street behind him. "You got a few questions for Principal Quinn about the whole Brooke Martin affair?"

Tori shook her head, being vague. "I'm just looking into something."

"Great. Spill it," he said. "We're both members of the press."

Tori nodded. "Yeah, I read your article in the morning paper. Putting Ash and the principal's fight during the service on the front page makes the *Gazette* look like a tabloid."

"Glad you liked it." He jaunted in front of the Jeep and over to the passenger side, the camera swinging back and forth along his chest. Opening the door, he slid into the seat next to her. "That means a lot. We never partnered on any articles back when you worked there."

"No, we didn't." She sized him up, wondering how such a meek and mild man could be so brazen. "Look, Edison, I don't have time—"

"Word on the street is that Brooke may not have committed suicide." He stared at her, wide-eyed and excited. "That the whole suicide was in fact staged."

"Where did you hear that?"

"Is that what you're investigating?" He grinned.

She paused, studying his face. "I asked you first."

"C'mon, you know you can't keep something like that under wraps." He toyed with his camera as he spoke. "Okay. You wanna know how I know about it? I'll tell you. I was having breakfast at the Waffle House and overheard you and your boyfriend talking."

"You were eavesdropping on us?"

"No, I call it attentive," he said. "And besides, this is huge. Nothing like this has ever happened in Elroy Springs before."

"Until now," Tori said. "That's what makes it so shocking."

"Yeah, it's shocking." He swallowed and sat back in the seat. "Is that what brought her here?"

Tori looked over at him. "Brought who here?"

"Simone Adams," he said. "I told you I saw her news van outside the courthouse."

"What does she have to do with anything?" Tori saw the front doors open in the school and leaned forward. She was no longer listening.

Edison continued. "Are you kidding?" He sounded surprised. "She's Simone Adams."

"So?" Tori shifted in her seat and unbuckled the seat belt. She remained focused on the school building. Principal Quinn stepped through the double glass doors and down the front steps, carrying a bucket. Water splashed over the sides.

"I was going to ask you, since we have a history working together and all," he said, and looked over at her. "Can you introduce me to her?"

"No." She turned the key in the ignition to Off.

"As a favor?" he pleaded. "Because of our history. We worked together all those years ago."

"No." Tori opened the door as she spoke. Thirty yards ahead of her, the principal dumped the bucket of water on the grass. She wondered what he was doing and glanced back at Edison. "I'm not introducing you to that woman and we're not partnering on this."

"But it's Simone Adams." He sounded hurt. "She's a living legend, and it's always been a professional ambition of mine to meet her. She accepted my friend request on Facebook, and I hear she's single."

"There's a reason she's single. The woman reads Stephen King to cancer patients in the children's ward and microwaves butterflies in her spare time. I'm not introducing you." She left him sitting in the Jeep and ran across the campus, toward the principal. He was moving back up the front steps, carrying the empty bucket. She raced after him, taking the steps two at a time.

Flinging open the double glass doors, she entered the high school and paused in the front hallway. Her eyes adjusted to the dim light. A smell of fresh paint assaulted her nostrils. Principal Quinn and several students held brushes and buckets, scrubbing graffiti from the painted block walls.

Tori approached them and asked, "What happened here?"

Four smashed trophy cases lined the wall, the shelves littered with splintered wood, glass shards, and broken awards. She could still make out some of the letters spray-painted on the walls: H-O-M-E-W-R-E–The rest were hidden beneath a fresh coat of paint.

Principal Quinn put down his paintbrush and turned to Tori. "May I help you, Miss ..."

"Younger," a girl said, stepping out of the group of students and moving beside the principal. "That's Tori

Younger." The girl smiled, and Tori recognized her as the intern from the Sheriff's Department. Her jet-black hair pulled back in a ponytail, she wore a dark orange T-shirt that still revealed the bright tattoos on her arms. "It's me, Zoe. You met me yesterday with Deputy Torres."

"I remember you," Tori said. "You make quite a first impression."

Zoe frowned. "Oh, Miss Younger. Your aura—it's so dark and gray. It's the residue of fear and has the potential of serious health problems if you're not careful."

"I'll work on that," Tori said to brush her off, and turned to Principal Quinn. "I'm one of Brooke Martin's friends. We attended high school here together."

"That's right." The principal nodded. "The newscasters for *Wake Up, Tampa Bay*. Is there something I can do for you, Miss Younger?"

Tori stepped closer and focused on his black eye. "How's your eye? Looks like you've got quite a shiner."

"It's healing." He backed away from her.

She smiled. "I wanted to talk to you about Brooke. She was certainly loved by her students. The campus is overflowing with cards and wreaths."

"We're still mourning her." The principal nodded. "Some of the students are collecting money to commission a statue in her honor."

"That'll be nice." Tori waved a hand at the graffiti on the wall. It may have read: 'LEAVE US ALONE' or 'LIES ALL DONE.' She wasn't sure which, but it was clearly Ash's handiwork. "What a mess," Tori said.

Zoe walked to the wall and placed a hand on the spray-painted ALONE across the brick. "I feel a troubled peer—a boy. Several boys, actually."

"You know who did this?" Tori looked at the principal, wondering if he suspected Ash. To Zoe, she said, "Does the sheriff know?"

She closed her eyes and shook her head. "I wish I knew, but I can't see their faces. I just feel their emotions. Troubled. Angry. A deep, muddled red."

"Some student's idea of a prank," the principal said. "We're cleaning it up."

Tori studied the graffiti. Another phrase might be STAY AWAY FROM HER, scribbled in large black letters that were bleeding through the fresh coat of paint. The trophy case could be mistaken for a pile of rubble. Ash's wrestling trophies lay mangled and broken in the heap. He'd been here. His alibi still stood, though, even if it had changed slightly.

She wondered what the principal knew. "So, no idea who did this this? Besides someone with a deep, muddled red aura?"

"Miss Younger." Principal Quinn paused and cleared his throat. "I'm very busy. Let's stop beating around the bush. You're here because you're wondering why Brooke's husband attacked me at the funeral."

"Oh, that man has a red aura so dark it's almost brown," Zoe said, wiping a smudge of paint from her cheek.

Tori glanced at her and back at the principal. "He believes you were having an affair with his wife. There's gossip—"

"Let's talk in private," he said, touching Tori's arm and leading her away from the group of students. "I've heard the gossip. I know what he believes. He's been quite vocal. Mr. Martin has been prone to drinking, and, like so many alcoholics, he lashes out at people."

"What're you saying?" she asked as they walked down the hall. "It's all in his head?"

The glass doors to the offices on the right opened and an elderly woman stepped out, holding a clipboard in her arms, her white hair pulled into a tight bun. She called out for the principal.

"The superintendent is on line one," the woman said.

She looked like she could've been the school librarian with the severe bun and a Number 2 pencil behind her right ear but was probably his assistant.

Principal Quinn waved at her and turned back to Tori. "Excuse me. I need to take this call."

"Please," Tori said.

As the principal turned to go, she followed. "Let me ask you another question, real quick, while we're walking. Did you see any signs of depression or anything that would've—"

"Miss Younger, she was in an unhappy marriage with a husband who drank and abused her." He passed the elderly woman and headed through the doorway. The woman pulled the glass door behind them, but Tori grabbed it.

Raising her voice, she said, "You're leaving Elroy Springs, right? You've accepted a position with the school board in Tallahassee." She remained in the doorway. "Did you plan to take Brooke and Darla with you?"

"Excuse me?" The principal turned around, his voice echoing in the empty hallway.

Tori approached him. "Were you planning to take Brooke and Darla to Tallahassee with you?" she asked. "Were you going to run away together?"

"That's an absurd question." He paused at his assistant's desk outside his office.

She picked up the phone and told the superintendent he'd be right there. Putting the receiver to her shoulder, she looked at the principal. "Sir, the superintendent is waiting."

He acknowledged her and turned to Tori. "I know what that drunk says about me—that Brooke and I were indulging in a relationship beyond that of the typical principal-teacher dynamic. But that was a rumor. And that's all it was, a rumor. Now, if you'll excuse me."

He entered his office and shut the door.

From the hallway, Tori stared at his closed door a moment. In a few strides she went back and opened it. She entered his office and closed the door behind her, glancing around: no books, no pictures. All those lay packed in boxes. A television set sat alone on the bookshelves. Packed boxes lined the walls. "I have to ask—"

The principal stood at his desk. "Miss Younger, I have a call waiting."

He waved her away and reached for his phone. Tori approached the desk. She placed her hand over his to prevent him from picking up the phone.

"One more question," she said again. She glanced down at his cluttered desk. Papers, file folders, and boxes covered the shiny top, and several orange and white prescription bottles stood next to the phone.

"Look," he said, "I knew Brooke well. We were close, but I will not acknowledge baseless gossip."

"Is it baseless?"

"You're referring to Brooke's husband crashing a PTA meeting, drunk and angry. He accused me, in front of every teacher and parent in attendance—said he knew I was sleeping with his wife. Ever since that afternoon, the tongues in this town haven't stopped wagging about it."

"I've heard about that incident."

"You see?" His voice rose. Thunder rumbled outside, as if punctuating his argument. "Gossip."

"But I was talking about Ash finding you and Brooke at a bar in Frostproof." Tori noticed there were three prescription bottles and she could make out the shape of the pills inside them.

"I've never even been to a bar in Frostproof, much less be in a position to meet one of my teachers at one." He picked up the handset and pressed a red blinking light as Tori spoke.

"But the sheriff broke up a fight between you and her husband."

"No. Why would I be fighting with her husband?"

"I don't know. How's your eye again?"

His coolness was evidence that he was not amused. "Listen, Brooke married a drunk with anger management issues. Why they're bringing my name into their sordid insanity is beyond me."

"He seems pretty convinced. Could Brooke have thought something was there, or misinterpreted something between you?"

"Never." His eyes enlarged and his lips pursed back as if he'd smelled something rotten. He shook his head at her. "There was never anything like that between us, and Ash didn't catch us at Sneaky Pete's or anywhere else, for that matter. I've never even been there."

"But there was a fight. The sheriff--"

"Maybe Ash caught Brooke with someone, but it wasn't me. As I said, I've never been to Sneaky Pete's." The principal paused then added, "Even if I was the type of principal—the kind of man—who would even entertain an inappropriate relationship with one of his teachers, Brooke was not the kind of woman to cheat on her husband. She loved him, despite … despite his demons."

Tori paused, thinking. She focused on the three orange prescription bottles next to the phone. One of the labels read "Deletycide." She looked up at him. "You take antidepressants?"

He scrunched his face and wrinkled his nose. "Pardon me?"

"I noticed the prescription on your desk. It's Deletycide."

The office door opened, interrupting them, and Zoe poked her head in the room. "Principal Quinn, you've got to see this."

"What is it, Zoe?" He motioned her in as she bound into the office, her black ponytail whipping behind her head. She picked up the remote control from his desk and aimed it at the television.

The principal froze. He placed the headset of the phone against his chest and turned his head toward the TV. A black-and-white image of Andy Griffith filled the screen, followed by a laugh track responding to something Barney Fife had said. The principal looked back at Zoe. "I don't have time for this."

She waved a tattooed arm, hushing him, and aimed the remote. The channel changed and Simone Adams' face appeared on the screen. Zoe turned up the volume.

"…has opened a murder investigation into the death of local schoolteacher and mother of one. Authorities are searching the Martin house for evidence," Simone said on screen. Behind her, several squad cars were parked in front of the Martin farmhouse. Brooke's minivan was visible next to them. "Brooke's husband is a person of interest in his wife's death, as the police investigation has revealed that her suicide was staged."

Tori looked at Principal Quinn and said, "They're searching the Martin house."

"I'll call you back," he said into the receiver, and hung up the phone.

On screen, Simone walked across the driveway, toward Mike. She held her microphone near his face. "Sheriff! Sheriff! Can you tell us what evidence led you to open a murder investigation?"

"Not at this time," he said. "We're not prepared to make any statements to the press."

Simone whipped her arm back toward her chest so she could speak into the mic. "What do you expect to find in the Martin house?"

The camera zoomed in on Mike as he shook his head. "I can't speak to that at this time."

She brought the mic back to her mouth. "Can you tell us where the victim's husband is during this investigation?" She moved it to Mike's face.

"Mr. Martin is inside and cooperating with the investigation," he said.

Simone turned to the camera, her face filling the screen. "Tomorrow morning, the investigation continues as Brooke's body is exhumed from Sunset Hills Cemetery ..."

A loud clap of thunder rattled the windows.

Zoe eyed Tori and Principal Quinn. "I guess I'd better get back to the Sheriff's Department," she said.

Outside the high school, Tori settled into the tan leather seat, flipped on the headlights and wipers, and threw the Jeep into gear. Leaving the premises, she pulled onto Dune Road. The rain came down in sheets.

Tori drove through the driving rain and dialed Mike's number. It was the first time she'd called him in five years. The line rang, and she held her breath. It rang again. He picked up.

"You're exhuming Brooke's body in the morning?" she asked without introducing herself.

"You saw the newscast." He recognized her voice. Or still had her number programmed in his phone. "You wanted a murder investigation. Now you got one."

"Did you find anything incriminating in Ash's house?" She checked the rearview mirror. Lights from a vehicle behind her were coming up fast.

Mike's voice crackled through the speakers on Tori's phone. "You know I can't discuss that."

Tori glanced at the rearview mirror again. The lights looked even brighter, closer. She sank back in the seat. When she turned off Dune Road, the car behind her turned.

It wasn't a sheriff's squad car, she decided, squinting into the mirror. Though she could hardly make it out in the rain.

"I left the high school," she told the sheriff. "I talked to Principal Quinn and noticed a prescription for Deletycide."

"And?"

"Doesn't that seem like a coincidence? Brooke has Deletycide in her system, and he has a prescription."

"You need to stay out of this, Tori. I'm not telling you again."

"Wait, there's more," she said. She thought about the graffiti on the school walls and the smashed trophy case. 'Leave her alone' had been spray-painted on the wall. Or was it 'Lies all done?' "You need to talk to Pastor Fields. He lied about Ash attending the AA meeting because he was covering up Ash's vandalism at the high school. But Ash still spent the night at the church."

"Tori," Mike said, "thank you, but I've got it covered. Now, I want you to stay out of this. Are you listening? Stay out."

She agreed and ended the call.

The lights grew brighter in her rearview mirror. She sped up. Maybe it was a truck. It kept pace with her and turned on its brights, blinding her. Tori flipped her rearview mirror to deflect the light.

The headlights rushed up behind her. She eased off the gas to see if the truck would pass. The Jeep slowed. The truck did the same.

Tori mashed her foot on the gas pedal. Accelerating, she skidded on the wet pavement and sped along the narrow two-lane road. The truck kept up with her. Glancing in the mirror as she drove, she knew someone was toying with her—the truck would fall behind whenever she accelerated but never far enough to lose sight.

Tori slowed, watching the truck lights grow. She waited until the last second and then wrenched the Jeep's wheel to the right. Screeching, the Jeep's tires left black streaks on the pavement as it slid sideways. Shifting, Tori slammed on the brakes, spraying a column of dirt and gravel. The truck swerved, its headlights blinding, knocking the Jeep off the road in a skid. The front tires hit a fallen tree branch and the Jeep launched into the air. It landed with a hard crash that sent it sliding downhill into a ditch and slamming sideways into a substantial tree. The passenger door crunched against it and the airbags deployed.

CHAPTER TWENTY-ONE

RO_D R_GE

Tori caught her breath. Dazed but otherwise feeling okay, she looked around. The airbags had deployed and surrounded her in a smoky haze. The Jeep fumed, lodged against a tree.

She straightened in the seat and shifted into reverse. Her foot mashed the gas pedal. The engine revved. Back tires spun. Mud exploded like shrapnel behind her. She slapped the steering wheel and sighed.

For the first time, she got a good look at the vehicle that had run her off the road.

It wasn't a truck, it was a minivan. Like Brooke's old van.

But how? She rubbed her eyes. Squinted in the rain. She must be seeing things.

It was Brooke's minivan; Tori was sure of it.

The van waited at the top of the ditch, engine revving. Tori watched it through the rain. The headlights flipped on again, blinding her. The minivan engine revved louder, and the vehicle took off, disappearing around a bend. Its loud screeching tires died away.

Tori turned off the Jeep's engine and eased herself out the door. She plodded through the mud and rain to inspect the back end. The right tire was half buried in mud, the passenger side smashed against a gnarled cypress tree.

Catching her breath, she paced alongside the vehicle. An unseen animal screeched in the dark woods She jumped back in the Jeep and slammed the door shut and locked it. Her annoyance increased when her hands wouldn't stop shaking. She couldn't believe she hadn't seen another car pass by on this road.

With no other option, she called RJ. "Let me start by saying I'm sorry."

"What happened!" RJ's voice blared loud through the phone's speakers. "Where are you? Where's my Jeep?"

"Again, keeping in mind that I'm okay—your Jeep is at the bottom of a ditch. It's stuck and I can't get it out."

"You wrecked my Jeep?"

"Someone ran me off the road."

"You wrecked my Jeep."

"No, it wasn't me. Someone ran me off the road. And RJ, they were driving Brooke's minivan."

"You wrecked my Jeep."

"Did you hear me? Someone driving Brooke's minivan ran me off the road."

"Where are you? Where's my Jeep?"

"I'm off Dune Road about a half mile or so, on some little turnoff. I'm by the high school."

"Look, I'm at the Sheriff's Office with Winnie," he said. "We'll find you."

Tori ended the call and waited. She killed the headlights and shrank back in the driver's seat. Trembling, she couldn't take her eyes off the empty highway and jumped when her phone beeped with an incoming text. It was from Brooke's number.

"Are you okay?"

Tori stared at the message. A moment later, another text came in.

"Are you hurt?"

Tori typed "No," but didn't send the message. She stared at her phone, when a third message popped up.

"Just glad ur ok."

Tori read it and tossed her phone down in the seat beside her. She wished RJ would get there soon.

It took half an hour before two headlights came down the highway. The deputy's squad car pulled up, and RJ jumped out, not bothering to shut the passenger door. He rushed into the ditch and planted his hands on the Jeep's chrome bumper. "My girl. My beautiful girl!"

She followed him into the ditch and said, "It's not as bad as it looks."

"What have you done?"

"It wasn't me. I was run off the road."

"My poor girl. Just look at it. Look at it!"

She grabbed his arm, trying to get his attention. "Did you hear me? Someone tried to kill me."

He walked away from her, circling the Jeep and pausing at the tree. "We'll get you fixed, don't worry. I promise. Everything'll be okay."

"Did you hear me? Someone tried to kill me."

He straightened up and faced her. "Then they need to get in line. I could kill you myself right now. Look what you did to my girl."

"It's not my fault. Someone ran me off the road—on purpose. And RJ, whoever it was, they were driving Brooke's minivan."

She waited for him to respond. He continued pacing around the Jeep, petting the scratched metal.

After a few moments, she said, "We're getting too close to the truth about what happened to Brooke and someone is sending me a message."

"I don't want to hear it. You took my Jeep. You left me at the Waffle House, took my Jeep, and smashed her into a tree. So, unless someone is texting you about a mechanic and a good body shop, I don't want to hear it."

"I'm sorry, RJ. I don't know what else to say."

"Calm down, Mr. Barringer," Deputy Torres said as he slid into the muddy ditch beside them. "I've called a tow truck. It'll be here shortly."

"She crashed my Jeep. She took it and crashed it. I should press charges, you know that? I should sue you. I should ... I should ... I should tell Simone Adams your real age."

Tori stared at him a moment, speechless. Finally, she threw her arms in the air and turned. "You're right. I messed up. I took your Jeep without your permission and I wrecked it. I'm sorry."

He laid his head against the hood and pet the grill. "Look what you did to my Jeep. My poor girl. You wrecked her."

Deputy Torres tapped Tori's shoulder. "Let's give him some space. The tow truck will be here in a minute."

She turned to him. "I didn't mean to wreck it. Someone ran me off the road."

"I know." He shot her a sympathetic smile. The radio from his squad car crackled and a female voice reported that the burglar alarms were going off at Ash Martin's tree trimming business. Another deputy's voice responded to the call and the deputy listened to it for a couple seconds before turning back to Tori. "Brooke's minivan ran you off the road?"

"I'm sure of it."

"You think Ash was driving it?" He pulled a notebook from his shirt pocket and started scribbling.

"No." She hesitated. "I don't know. I—they ran me off the road."

"Okay, take a deep breath and start from the beginning. Tell me what happened."

Tori paused and looked back at the Jeep. "I was leaving the high school on my way back from talking to Principal Quinn. It was raining, and these headlights came barreling down on me from behind."

The deputy stopped writing and held up his pen. "You were talking to Principal Quinn? About what?"

"About the rumors of him and Brooke having an affair."

"I bet he loved that."

"He denied it, of course, and I left. And then, out of nowhere these lights came up behind me. They had their brights on and the light was reflecting in my rearview and side mirrors."

"What'd you do?"

"I slowed down to let them pass me, but they stayed on my tail, so I sped up. They kept up and flashed their lights. Then they pulled up alongside and swerved into me, ran me off the road, into the ditch."

"You okay?"

"Yeah, I guess. I got out and looked up. They were there at the edge of the road, revving the engine, watching me. That's when I saw it was Brooke's minivan."

"Are you sure?"

"I'm positive."

"But you—" he started when the voice on the radio blared again, reporting that a group of students with candles was congregating outside the high school. He leaned into the squad car through the window and reached for the radio. "Thanks, Zoe," he said, and slipped out and turned to Tori. "But you didn't see the driver?"

"No. It was too dark. Raining. I couldn't see anything. Then it took off."

"Okay. At least you're safe now. I want to take you to the hospital and get you checked out."

"No, I'm fine. We need to go to the Martin house. We need to check out Brooke's minivan," Tori said as the tow truck arrived. "I want to see for myself ...."

They watched the tow truck for half an hour as it pulled the Jeep out of the ditch. Without saying a word, RJ hopped in the cab of the tow truck, and Tori rode with the deputy.

Twenty minutes later, the deputy pulled up to the Martin house and parked beside Brooke's blue minivan. Tori got out of the squad car and stepped to the van. She placed a hand on the hood.

"It's warm," she said. "It's been driven recently."

He caught up to her and knelt beside the front tire. "Looks like paint from RJ's Jeep."

"That's where it hit me. This proves it. Someone was driving it and ran me off the road." Tori looked around. Ash's truck was absent, the house was dark. "Doesn't look like anyone is home."

They walked to the front porch. Someone had spray-painted "MURDERER" across the front door.

"It doesn't look like Ash is home," he said.

Tori pressed her lips together in anger. "Can you blame him? I'd get as far away from here as possible, too."

"The whole town's gone crazy since the story broke," the deputy said, stepping beside her. "Even more so now, with Brooke's body being exhumed in the morning."

"I know," she whispered.

He placed a hand on her shoulder. "I'm just glad you're okay."

She froze. "What?"

"I'm just glad you're okay." He'd said it slowly, as if surprised by her reaction. "What is it?"

"Deputy, I want you to be honest with me. Do you have Brooke's cell phone?"

"Excuse me?"

"The last message from Brooke's phone. It said, 'Just glad you're okay'."

"Yeah, so?" He paused, staring at her as if waiting for a further answer.

She searched his face. Neither spoke for several seconds, until he laughed and looked away.

"Hell's bells! You think I sent you that message, don't you?"

Tori chewed her bottom lip, her eyes never blinking. "Did you?"

"That's crazy." He let out a throaty laugh, but it sounded forced.

"RJ said he was at the Sheriff's Office when I called. You were with him, weren't you?"

"He and Winnie were at the station. We were about to start looking for you when he got your phone call."

"You knew about the accident."

"Yes." A shadow of annoyance crossed his face. "But how does that equate to me sending you text messages from Brooke's phone? Connect the dots for me."

"Only minutes after I hung up with RJ, I got another text from Brooke's cell. Brooke—or someone—knew I'd been run off the road and was in an accident. It had just happened."

"And you think I sent the text?"

"It makes sense. You were there with RJ. You were the first to know. The only one to know."

"Maybe RJ texted you."

"Maybe." She flashed the deputy a knowing smile. "But that night we arrived in town and brought Darla to the station, you said you knew I wasn't coming to the funeral and hoped I would change my mind. You had access to Brooke's phone and could've taken it from her personal effects. You'd seen the suicide message. You could've text it to me."

"Why? Why would I do that?"

"You knew it would get me here. A puzzle—a mystery—I couldn't pass up."

"If I wanted you to come, wouldn't I have picked up a phone and called you?"

She didn't answer. Zoe's voice crackled over the squad car radio, reporting that Brooke's father and his caregiver were in the Sheriff's Department, demanding that the sheriff find and arrest Ash.

Mike's voice came over the radio, telling Zoe that he'd handle it.

"But he won't leave." Zoe responded, sounding frustrated.

The deputy leaned forward, closer to Tori. "Like I said, everyone's on edge with that newscast about the sheriff opening the murder investigation and Brooke's body being exhumed in the morning. It's made the whole town a little crazy."

"I suppose. . ."

"And it's only going to get worse, till we know what happened to Brooke. But there's nothing more we can do tonight." He walked over to the passenger side of his squad car, opened the door, and waved her over. "C'mon, I'm gonna drive you back to Winnie's."

CHAPTER TWENTY-TWO

BIT_ TH_ BULL_T

When they pulled into Winnie's driveway, Tori turned to the deputy. "There's something I keep thinking about. Something that keeps bothering me."

Deputy Torres parked the squad car and faced her. "What's that?"

"Have you seen the pictures Darla keeps drawing?"

"I don't think so. Why?"

"She keeps drawing two people at the water tower the night her mother died. You and another figure. Who is that other person she keeps drawing?"

"There wasn't another person there. I was alone."

"Then why does she draw two people?"

"I don't know." His eyes narrowed, becoming serious. "Why don't you ask her?"

The condescension of his remark grated her. "She isn't talking," she said. He already knew that. Still, she wasn't ready to resume the line of questioning and changed her approach. Her voice softened. "Deputy, did you see something that night at the water tower? Something you couldn't write up in an official report?"

He looked as if he were weighing the questions. "Look, this has gotta stop," he said after a moment of silence. "I wanted you to attend Brooke's funeral because she was your best friend. When I heard you weren't coming, I knew it wasn't right. Knew it'd be something you'd regret. And maybe I shoulda reached out to you, but I didn't. I didn't call you or text you … from my phone or Brooke's."

A tap on the window interrupted them and Tori turned to see Winnie waving. Tori opened the door and got out of the squad car. Winnie gave her a halfhearted hug with her free arm while wrangling four leashed dogs.

Tori looked surprised. The pug, the cocker spaniel, and the Chihuahua jumped and barked and struggled against the leashes, along with a Jack Russell terrier that ran circles around Winnie, wrapping its leash across her legs.

"You got another dog?" Tori asked.

"It's, um, it's the Petersons' Jack Russell. They'll be back on Monday." Winnie lifted her leg, stepping out of the snare. She looked at Tori and her face turned dark. "Did you see the news? Mike's opened a murder investigation and they're exhuming Brooke's body tomorrow morning."

"I heard."

"RJ was right. Brooke was saying 'murder' on that recording. That's Brooke, you know, saying 'murder.'"

Deputy Torres slammed his car door shut. "What's this about Brooke saying 'murder'?"

Tori watched him go around the front of his car. He approached Winnie, and the dogs lunged at him, barking and wagging their tails. He took a step back, looking down at them and back at Winnie. "What do you mean, Brooke was saying 'murder'?"

Winnie pulled back on the leashes. "RJ has a recording he took at Ash's house. It's got, um, Brooke's voice on it, saying 'murder.'" Winnie glanced at the squad car. "Where's RJ, anyway?"

The deputy turned to Tori. "What's she talking about?"

"It's a long story," she said to him. Addressing Winnie, Tori said, "RJ's riding in the tow truck. They're taking the Jeep to the mechanic."

The deputy nodded. "Tori crashed the Jeep."

"Someone ran me off the road," she added.

"Good Lord! Are you okay?" Winnie touched Tori's shoulder. The dogs surrounded Tori, sniffing her ankles and pawing her legs.

She took a step back. "I'm fine," she said. "His Jeep has seen better days, though."

"Well, come on inside. Let me fix you some dinner."

Winnie motioned to the deputy. "Do you have time to eat with us?"

Zoe's voice crackled again over the radio. "A fight's broken out between Ash Martin and a couple of men at the Beef 'O' Brady's. The owner is requesting someone to go out there and break it up."

Deputy Torres shook his head and returned to his squad car. "Whole town's gone crazy. Ash's house and business got vandalized. Students are congregating outside the high school. Brooke's father won't leave the Sheriff's Department. It's gonna be a long night."

After they watched the deputy leave, Tori followed Winnie as she tugged the dogs toward the house. They entered the kitchen through the back door.

"Where's Howard?" Tori asked. "Did you pick him up at the airport?"

"He, um, he got a call from another doctor's office and set an appointment to introduce a new blood pressure medication," Winnie said. "Guess he's spending the night in Atlanta and will catch a flight back tomorrow."

"Maybe I'll have the opportunity to meet him."

"Oh, I hope so. You'll love him." Winnie unsnapped the leashes from the collars and all four dogs ran to the water bowls on the floor next to the cabinet. She paused, and then scrunched her eyes. "Sorry about the mess. It's parade stuff."

The balloons for Brooke's memorial had been replaced with boxes of red plastic apples piled up on the kitchen table and stacked against the walls. Tori wasn't even sure what to say about it. "What is all this?"

"Apples," Winnie said, taking a plastic apple from a box. "We're filling them with candy and will, you know, throw them to the kids during the parade."

Tori picked one up. The apple felt light and hollow. A large bag of Tootsie Rolls lay on the table next to the box. "Why?"

"The Snow White theme," Winnie said. She tossed the apple back into the box and said, "It looked like you and the deputy were having some intense conversation out there. What was that all about?"

"We were." Tori pulled out a chair from the table and pushed the boxes of apples out of the way.

Winnie took the chair across from her. She opened the bag of Tootsie Rolls and popped one into her mouth. "About what?"

"Oh, Brooke's cell phone. He has it and he's been texting me those cryptic messages."

"Deputy Torres?" Winnie laughed. The cocker spaniel approached her and shook his wet muzzle, splashing water droplets across the room and covering the table legs, chairs, and her jeans. She reached down and petted the top of the dog's head as she spoke. "No, he can't be."

"'Fraid so. He saw something that night, when he found Brooke's body at the water tower."

Tori shook her head when Winnie offered her a Tootsie Roll. A bag of Jolly Ranchers sat on the table too. Tori looked from the candy to Winnie, and said, "And whatever that was, or for whatever reason, he can't come forward. So, he's been texting me, trying to lead me to the truth behind Brooke's murder."

"And he told you that?"

"No. He still claims he doesn't have her phone. Says he isn't the one texting me. But who else could it be?"

"I don't know." Winnie bent down to address the dogs. The Chihuahua and the Jack Russell terrier pawed her legs, nipping at each other and pushing the cocker spaniel away. She lifted the Chihuahua to her lap. The Jack Russell's body went stiff, his ears flattened, his eyes grew wide. She leaned over and petted him as she spoke. "Why are you so sure it's him?"

"Tonight, I was run off the road and crashed into a tree." She paused and looked down at her leg. The pug was licking her calf area. She pushed it away. "Just minutes after I call RJ, I get another text from Brooke's cell, asking me if I'm alright. Minutes. He was with RJ when I called. He knew about the accident before anyone else."

"I was there too, you know, when you called RJ. We were at the Sheriff's Department and I didn't see him pick up his phone or send any text messages."

"Maybe he did it when you weren't paying attention. It only takes a few seconds."

"Maybe." She set the Chihuahua on the floor. "But you know there's someone else who, um, knew about the accident before we did ... before you called RJ and told us."

"I'm listening. Go on."

"The driver who ran you off the road."

Tori noticed the wooden key hook by the back door. The key chain with the large pewter *B* dangling from a chain was missing. "Where's Brooke's keys?"

Winnie turned to the door. "What?"

"Brooke's keys to her house." Tori got up from the table and approached the door. All four dogs followed her across the room, watching her inspect the key hook. She asked, "Weren't her minivan keys on that ring too? Where are they?"

Winnie twisted her torso to face Tori. "Um, I don't know."

"How long have they been missing?"

"I-I don't know."

"When did they disappear?"

"I haven't paid any attention."

"Who had access to them? Who was here today?"

"Lots of people, you know. We've been working on the Fourth of July float all day."

"Who?" Tori asked again. She returned to the table, the dogs on her heels.

"Lots of people. My, um, brother and his family. The mayor and his wife. Um, Brooke's father and that loud blonde lady." She paused. "What's her name? Leonard's caregiver."

Tori glanced at the door and the wooden key hook, and then down at her phone.

That night, Tori shifted onto her left side and back to her right. She couldn't sleep and looked at the clock on the nightstand. The glowing numbers read 2:25 AM. RJ still hadn't returned, and he wasn't answering his phone. He'd turned it off, for all she knew.

Somewhere downstairs, a cacophony of barks—a tinny yip of the Chihuahua, a deeper holler of the cocker spaniel, a hiccupping yelp of the pug—further fueled her insomnia. She covered her head with a pillow, trying to drown out the ruckus. The barking grew louder. Flinging back the sheets, she sat up in bed and stepped to the bedroom window.

Moonlight reflected on the lake. The pier looked quiet, almost lonely, with Winnie's little runabout bobbing beside it. Moss dripping from the cypress branches rippled in the breeze. And beneath one tree, something—*someone*—caught her eye.

For a second, she thought it might be RJ.

Whoever it was, he must've riled the dogs.

She pressed her nose to the glass and analyzed the twisted shadows crisscrossing the ground. A gust rustled the moss, but she spotted no person moving. Had she imagined the figure in the shadows?

The night seemed quiet, despite the noisy barking coming from downstairs.

She scolded herself and laughed at her overactive nerves. Obviously, she'd imagined it—whatever *it* was.

She needed sleep and looked at the bed. The clock on the nightstand flashed to 2:34, and then she saw *it* again in her peripheral vision—something moved behind the trees. The shape was there for a second and melted into the black cover of a cypress tree. Her eyes focused. She blinked and pressed her face against the windowpane. She searched the lakeshore and pier.

The shadow stepped out from behind the tree.

A ghostly figure.

Human.

Tori stopped breathing and her eyes widened. Was she seeing what she thought she was seeing?

The figure stopped and turned.

She could feel it looking up, staring at her.

Transfixed, she couldn't look away. The barking stopped. The room turned silent. Dark.

A sharp ding startled her. She jumped and craned her neck to look back at the nightstand. Her cell phone lit up and flashed.

She rushed to it and read the message.

"Are you there?"

It was Brooke. Tori typed: "What do you want?" and waited. She returned to the window. Her eyes searched the shadows … the dark trees … the pier … the lake. The figure was gone. Her phone dinged again, and she glanced down at the screen.

"Tomorrow morning. Be there."

She stared at the message, and typed: "At the cemetery?" She waited. No response. She stared at the phone, back out the window, at the phone. It dinged in her hand.

"Be there."

A sudden chill ran up the back of her neck, and her fingers tingled as she typed: "Who are you?" The reply came almost instantaneously.

"You know who I am."

She blinked. She didn't believe it. Gripping the phone, her fingers pounded out: "You're not Brooke. Who are you?" She waited for the response, but none came. She looked out the window. The yard stood empty, and she wondered if she'd imagined the figure moving between the trees. Watching her. Maybe it had been a trick of moonlight and twisting shadows. But the dogs had responded. They'd been barking at *something*. After several minutes, she typed it again: "Who are you?" She waited. Her phone dinged with the response.

"Whatever I am, you made me"

She bit down hard on her lip as her fingers pounded out another message: "Whoever you are, I'll find you." She pressed Send and waited. The clock flashed 2:40. A branch scratched at the window pane.

No other reply came. The conversation was over. Putting down her phone, she left the bedroom. The staircase creaked as she bound down the steps, rushed through the living room, and entered the kitchen. She flipped on the light and found Winnie hunched over the dogs.

"What are you doing?" Tori asked.

Winnie rose, holding a large bag of Kibbles. She filled three bowls on the countertop. "Something stirred up the doggies. I was just, um, quieting them down."

Tori walked over to the back door and checked the lock. "I saw someone outside."

"In the backyard?" Winnie put down the bag of dog food.

"Yes, in the backyard. Someone was out there." She looked down at the cocker spaniel, Chihuahua, pug, and Jack Russell terrier. All four pranced around the food bowls, their heads turning in unison with Winnie's every move. "I think the dogs saw him too."

"Probably just teenagers." Winnie picked up a small bottle and turned it over the dog bowls, dripping a thick liquid over the top of the food. She placed the bowls on the floor in front of the dogs. "High school kids hang out by the lake at night, drinking and making out. Doing things teenagers do."

Tori watched the dogs gulp down the food. Winnie placed the bottle back on the counter.

"What is that?" Tori asked. "What'd you give the dogs?"

"Valerian root oil." She picked up the bottle. "It's a natural herb to calm the dogs. They'll sleep like puppies."

"It's a sedative?"

"Just a few drops." Winnie set the bottle on the counter. "I'm sorry they woke you. They should sleep all night now."

Tori watched the dogs another moment, then turned to look at the empty living room. Winnie must've noticed her staring at the lonely couch.

"He didn't come back?" she asked, touching Tori's arm.

"I guess not." Tori returned her gaze and noticed a cell phone on the table. She asked Winnie, "Were you on the phone?"

"I was talking to Howard." Winnie picked up the phone from the table. Her brows drew downward in a frown. "Looks like his appointment at the Atlanta doctor's office was a slam dunk. He's staying over another night."

Without another word about it, she turned off the kitchen light.

CHAPTER TWENTY-THREE

A_HE_ TO A_HE_

Monday, July 2

Before sunrise, Tori watched the crowd gather outside Sunset Hills Cemetery. Winnie, who'd driven her there that morning, left the parked station wagon and headed toward her brother, Mike. Mayor Winslow spoke to a crowd of townspeople. Edison Beyer stood next to him, scribbling in a spiral notebook. Brooke's father held Pastor Fields' hand, along with that of his caregiver. They looked like they were praying. Zoe and a group of high school students congregated at the entrance. Family and supporters waited for the gates to open. Ash and Darla, understandably, were not
present.

Tori couldn't help but stare at each of them, wondering where RJ was. He still hadn't called. She couldn't think about that now, she told herself, and concentrated on the faces in the crowd. Most likely, one of them was standing outside Winnie's house last night and texting her from Brooke's phone.

The black iron entrance to this quiet resting ground opened daily at seven. On this morning, however, Mike, along with several other police officers, had parked on the sidewalks and blocked traffic with red and blue emergency lights flickering. Deputy Torres stood in the middle of the street, waving at the cars lining up along the curbs. Mike strolled about, nodding at a few people as he moved. She could almost hear his wrist monitor beeping and see his mouth move as he recited baseball stats.

Her mind flash backed to a windy day some twenty years ago. Tori had never been to a funeral before, nor had she ever seen a dead body. Mike and Winnie stood in this cemetery, over an open grave, holding hands. Their father had passed away, and the funeral was long and upsetting. Tori had never seen Mike cry before.

When the service was over, Brooke wrapped her arms around both Mike and Winnie, hugging them. Tori rushed to them and hugged them too. They stood there like that for several minutes, arms intertwined, just outside those black iron gates, until Mike and Winnie had to leave with their grandparents.

Now it was Simone Adams and her camera crew outside the gates.

Tori approached the woman as she stood next to the news van, holding a compact to her face and patting her poufy red hair. She wore a bright green dress that contrasted with her hair color and clashed with the red-and-white van behind her.

"You went on air accusing Ash of murder." Tori placed a hand on the side of the van. "Now the whole town is in an uproar."

"I did no such thing," Simone said, checking her reflection in the compact. "I simply pointed out that he's a person of interest in this murder investigation, and maybe, possibly implied that he's Sheriff Bennett's prime suspect."

"Someone who witnessed the murder keeps texting me," Tori said, "and I think that person is pointing the blame to someone else."

"Give it up. I already know all about your Deep Throat and I'm not buying it."

"But there's more going on here than—"

"Exactly. And I'm on it." She closed the compact and dropped it in her purse. "Go back to Tampa and cover the holiday boat show. The professionals are working."

"And you're pushing the story in the wrong direction. If Ash gets proven innocent, he can sue you for defamation of character."

Simone laughed and looked at Tori. "Look, sweetie. You're not scaring me off, and I'm not sharing the spotlight with you."

Tori started to respond, when Edison Beyer interrupted her. He approached them, the Canon camera swinging from the strap around his neck. "Hello, ladies," he said, and extended a hand.

Tori and Simone stared at him, unblinking. Neither said a word.

Edison withdrew his hand. He looked over at Tori. "You want to introduce me?" He wagged his head in Simone's direction.

She grinned, betraying nothing of her annoyance. "Simone, Edison ... Edison, Simone."

"Edison Beyer with the *Elroy Springs Gazette*." He turned to Simone and extended his hand again.

Simone looked at him, her expression vaguely disapproving. With a flip of her red hair, she turned and walked away. A moment later she was motioning to her cameramen to start filming.

After a solid twenty minutes passed, the gates to the cemetery opened and people flooded onto the grounds. The size of the crowd took Tori by surprise, and again she studied the faces, wondering. Zoe and her high school friends rushed ahead of everyone.

Veronica led Leonard by the hand, following the kids. "WE'RE WALKING NOW," she yelled at him. "I'M LEADING YOU TO YOUR DAUGHTER'S GRAVE."

Pastor Fields guided them through the gates. Mayor Winslow and his entourage followed.

Then RJ emerged from the group.

He nodded at her, and she ran to him. She smiled, and neither said a word for several moments.

"Hi," she said.

"Hi." He cleared his throat. "I guess a lot of people turned out. Kinda morbid, if you ask me."

Tori nodded. "It sure looks that way."

They walked side by side, following the crowd to Brooke's grave.

"You want me to film this?" He nodded toward Simone and her camera crew. "Looks like Maleficent and her flying monkeys are already on the job."

She ignored his joke. "Look, I'm sorry. I shouldn't have taken your Jeep and I'll pay for the damage."

"You bet you're paying for it," he said. "And I stayed in a motel by the garage last night. You're paying for that too."

"I know. It's my fault. It's all my fault. And you have every right to be mad."

"Look, I'm not mad. It's..." He hesitated and swallowed, as if he tasted something nasty. "You lock on to things and you don't let go. You need to let go."

"You're right. I need to let go." She squeezed his arm. "I'm just glad you're still speaking to me."

They stopped near the grave site and blended into the crowd. A backhoe was already there, digging. Brooke's coffin hadn't been in the ground long enough for the dirt to turn hard or for grass to grow over the mound.

RJ didn't look at Tori, and she wondered how she would make this up to him.

"You are still speaking to me, right?" she asked.

He didn't answer. After a few moments of uncomfortable silence, he unfolded his arms and nodded to the active backhoe.

"Wouldn't it be crazy if they lifted that coffin out of the grave and a snap broke and the coffin tumbled open and an alien body rolled out?" he asked.

"What?" She wasn't sure she'd heard him correctly.

"It was a scene in *The X-Files*," he said. "What if an alien body tumbled out of the coffin?"

"If I remember," she said, thinking about it a second, "Scully debunks the alien body and reveals it to be the decaying corpse of an orangutan."

"Very good." He shot her a surprised grin. "I've never been more impressed with you. That almost makes up for wrecking my Jeep."

She watched the backhoe dump the final pile of dirt to the left of the now open grave and move to the side. A crane lifted the coffin from the hole. RJ placed a hand on her shoulder. It felt warm and friendly, and she knew then he'd forgiven her.

Winnie approached and waved to them. "C'mon. I'll take you to pick up the Jeep."

Tori turned to her and called out, "We can't leave. Not yet."

RJ's voice rose as he shot her an impatient glare. "You've said goodbye already. Two or three times now."

"I want to talk to Pastor Fields."

RJ threw his arms up in the air. "Ten seconds ago, you agreed with me. I heard you. You agreed that you need to let this go."

"I know, I know. I need another minute." She touched his hand on her shoulder and examined the crowd again. Brooke's father and members of her family huddled together under the magnolia tree. Pastor Fields stood over Brooke's grave, with his head bowed and his Bible open. Mayor Winslow joined Zoe and the group of students, their heads following the coroner's team as they moved the coffin toward a black van.

For the first time that morning, Tori realized that the principal wasn't anywhere to be seen. She wondered where he was and wanted to talk to Pastor Fields. "I want to follow-up with the pastor," she said to RJ. "It'll just take a minute."

He frowned, his eyes level under drawing brows. "There isn't time."

"A minute. That's all." She left RJ and Winnie and walked over to Pastor Fields. "Did you talk to the sheriff?"

"About Ash Martin?"

She nodded and looked down at the fresh grave. "I told the sheriff about Ash vandalizing the school. You need to explain what happened."

He nodded. She heard Simone Adams' voice a few feet behind her and saw the newscaster and her crew standing near the gates. They were filming the sheriff's wife, What's her face. Snarl It?

Charlotte leaned into the mic Simone was holding. "I'm not surprised," she said. "I've suspected her husband was involved in this whole sordid mess all along."

RJ nudged Tori. He'd come up behind her without her noticing it. "It's over," he said. "Simone Adams has the story. She's got it covered. There's nothing left for us to do but go pick up my Jeep and get the hell out of Dodge."

* * * *

Early that afternoon, RJ talked to a mechanic, who may or may not have been Sam of Sam's Body Shop, in a garage with three bays, scattered tools, and the Jeep raised on a hydraulic platform. Tori could see them from the waiting room as she sat next to Winnie, on an uncomfortable vinyl bench next to a vending machine.

"So, Howard should, you know, be back later today," Winnie was saying as Tori stared out the large window that looked down the street. There was a Church's Fried Chicken, a Pizza Hut, an old-fashioned barber shop next door, and Charlotte's florist shop across the street. They were a few blocks south of Main Street. Tori half listened to Winnie as she rattled on. "He missed his flight but he's, um, catching another one."

Tori observed the cozy little building with colorful planters in the windows. A U-Haul trailer hitched to a large black F-150 truck sat parked along the curb.

"That's Ash," Tori said, cutting Winnie off in mid-sentence and pointing out the window.

Winnie turned. "He's got a U-Haul." She placed a hand against the glass. "Is he leaving?"

"That's a good question." Tori grabbed Winnie's hand and pulled her to her feet. They rushed out of the mechanic's shop and headed across the street to the florist.

Bells on the shop door dinged as Tori and Winnie stepped inside. Ash and Charlotte were talking at the register and paid no attention to the newcomers.

"I need to get paid," Ash said. He looked ragged and tired, even more so than Tori had seen him before. Unshaven, in a dirty gray T-shirt and jeans and muddy boots, he'd been drinking. "You still owe me for trimming the trees in the back."

"I don't owe you for anything, you murderer." Charlotte turned away from him. Her black hair was pulled back in a ponytail and she wore tan capris with a peach-colored blouse decorated with yellow pineapples of varying sizes. "Now, leave. Get out before I call my husband."

"Not without my money."

Tori cleared her throat and said, "Excuse me."

Charlotte and Ash turned toward Tori and Winnie, standing inside the doorway. Tori noticed Darla sitting on the floor, coloring. It was the same drawing: black scribbled sky, a stick figure of her mother hanging by the neck from the water tower, two policemen watching from a distance, on the horizon.

Tori said to Ash, "We need to talk. You and me. Now."

A chill, black silence lay heavy over the room, until Winnie let out a nervous chuckle and reached for Charlotte. "C'mon, Char, let's take Darla outside."

Charlotte gave them an exasperated sigh and took Darla by the hand. "You want to see the greenhouse?" she asked the little girl. "It's got lots of pretty flowers and plants."

Winnie turned the deadbolt to the back door behind the counter and held the door open, allowing them through. "I love your top," she said to Charlotte. "Are those pineapples?"

Tori watched them disappear out back. When the door shut behind them, she turned to Ash.

He shrugged his shoulders. "Look, I don't want to talk about Simone's news story," he said. "I don't have nothin' to say."

"I'm not here about that." She glanced out the front windows at his black truck and the U-Haul behind it. "You're leaving?"

"I'm checking back into rehab," he said. "I've got Mikey B. breathing down my back. Brooke's family wants to take Darla away from me. I'm losing jobs left and right. Since that news story ran, the whole town thinks I murdered my wife. Who can blame me for taking a drink?"

"You know what they say. The first step to recovery is admitting everyone else is to blame."

"You're not funny, Tori." He glared at her. "What do you want?"

"Where's Darla going to stay?"

"With my parents, back in Michigan. As soon as I'm released, I'm joining them. I'm getting the hell outta here."

"You can't leave. We need to find—"

He cut her off. "Have you seen my house since that bitch all but called me a wife beater and murderer on air? The windows got egged. Someone spray-painted 'murderer' across the front door. It's not safe."

"Brooke was murdered, and the crime scene was staged to look like a suicide."

"I didn't have nothing to do with that."

"I believe you." Tori tried to keep her voice steady. She didn't want to yell at him. "But Simone Adams told the sheriff you lied about your alibi that night. That you weren't at an AA meeting."

"I got wasted that night and woke up at the church."

"You don't even remember what happened that night?" Tori said, noting his body language. He kept his arms folded tight across his chest, his head tilted down, avoiding eye contact and focused on Darla's drawing and crayons scattered on the floor.

"I remember fighting with Brooke, leaving, and going to..."

"To the high school?"

He didn't answer.

After a brief pause, she continued. "What were you and Brooke fighting about?"

"I told you already. She planned to take Darla and leave me."

"And she said that? Those exact words?"

"No." He moved away from her and put his hands on the glass countertop. "Not exactly."

"Because you caught her with another man at Sneaky Pete's?"

"I caught her..." He turned and met her gaze. "She was waiting for the Beef Jerky Poser. Yes."

"But Principal Quinn wasn't there."

"Not yet. If I showed up five minutes later, I woulda caught them making out in a private booth in the back."

"How do you know that?" She took a step toward him and reached out but stopped short of touching him. Her voice pleaded. "How do you know that Brooke and Principal Quinn were having an affair? That she was going to leave with him and take Darla?"

He looked away again. "Drop it, Tori. It's none of your business."

"Why do you believe Brooke and Principal Quinn were having an affair?"

"Brooke told me Darla isn't mine." He spit the words as if the first time he'd ever said it out loud.

Her breath caught in her throat. "Say, what?"

He turned away from her, ran his hands through his hair, and whirled back. "Darla isn't my child. Brooke told me a few months ago and she wanted to tell Darla the truth. We'd been arguing about that ever since."

"And Principal Quinn is the father?"

"Yes."

Tori shook her head. "I just ... I can't believe that. She told you that?"

"She didn't have to. Just do the math, Tori. Darla's five years old. Principal Quinn moved here five years ago. He and Brooke have been—"

A loud blast of shattering glass rang through the shop. Ash flinched. Tori gasped as screams from outside stopped her cold. They raced to the window in the back of the store. Their ears buzzed as they looked out.

A giant tree limb protruded from the greenhouse roof. The glass walls, reduced to shards of sharp edges and jagged points, had collapsed, shredding the potted plants inside. Merely feet from the front perimeter, Winnie held Darla in her arms. Charlotte sat behind them on the ground, in the grass. It looked like the crash had thrown her backwards.

"Darla!" Ash cried and pushed past Tori to the back door. He bolted outside to his little girl and scooped her up in his arms.

Tori followed and ran to Winnie and Charlotte. She knelt beside them, checking for cuts and scratches. Winne had a gash on her forehead, above her left eye. A stream of blood ran down the side of her face. She didn't seem to notice—speechless and wide-eyed—her face pale as she stared at the damaged greenhouse. Tori looked up at it too.

"The greenhouse," Winnie said, raising a shaky hand and pointing to the structure. "A branch...it cracked. We heard it and ran."

"You saved her," Ash said to Winnie. "You saved my daughter."

"You saved both of us," Charlotte said, raising her arms in praise and prayer. Potting soil stained her blouse, smudging the pineapples. Dropping her hands back to her lap, she broke down, crying. "Dear God, you saved both of us."

Tori found a cloth in the rubble and held it to Winnie's head. "You're cut. We need to get you cleaned up."

"I'm okay," Charlotte interrupted, sputtering through her tears. Winnie glanced at her, taking the cloth from Tori's hand and holding it to her forehead.

RJ and the mechanic came running from across the street. Other people came out of stores and crowded into the backyard of the florist's shop. They murmured and gasped, pointing and shaking their heads.

RJ came up beside Tori and asked, "What happened?"

"I don't know." She looked from him to the greenhouse. "I was talking to Ash inside the flower shop when we heard the crash. Looks like a limb came down."

RJ turned as Winnie, running, held the bloody cloth to her head and disappeared into the flower shop. "They could've been killed," he said.

"Winnie got them out just in time." Tori watched several people crowd around Charlotte and help her to her feet. She cried hysterically and struggled to stand. A woman brought her a bottled water. She raised a hand, declining it, and marched over to Ash.

"You did this," Charlotte screamed through her tears. "Were you trying to kill me, like you killed your wife? Were you trying to kill me too?"

Ash didn't answer. He shielded Darla with his arms and moved her away from the crowd.

Tori watched him carry the little girl to the truck. He secured her inside as Charlotte shook a fist at him and screamed, "You're a murderer, Ash Martin! What's wrong with you?"

He got in his truck and pulled out of the parking lot, the tires spitting gravel, and towing the U-Haul.

"Simone is going to love this," RJ said. "You think she'll interview Charlotte again?"

"Without a doubt," Tori said. She looked at the branch jutting out the greenhouse roof. Large and heavy, the end looked smooth, as if it had been partially sawed.

The intense sound of shattering glass still echoed through the area as Charlotte's screams calmed. A crowd formed around her, muttering "Glad you're okay" and "Do you need anything?" They led her back to the side of the building, where she sat on a bench next to a trellis of purple morning glories.

Tori went to Charlotte, pushing through the crowd, and tried to comfort her. She waved Tori away, leaning against the trellis and catching her breath.

Two squad cars pulled up. Mike bolted out of his car, not even bothering to shut the door, and rushed to his wife. The crowd parted, giving him a clear path, and his hat flew off as he ran. Dropping to his knees, he wrapped his arms around her and held her. Tori got up and stepped away, back toward the shattered greenhouse.

Deputy Torres approached her. "Hell's bells. What a mess. Are you okay?"

Tori nodded. "Winnie's cut. She may need a doctor. Charlotte and Darla seem fine."

"How about you?"

"Never better." She shook her head, staring at the green-house. Winnie stepped out of the flower shop holding a brown paper towel to her head. Mike ran to her as Charlotte yelled for him to come back.

"You're cut," he said, checking the gash above Winnie's eye. "We need to get you to the hospital."

"It's nothing," Winnie said, returning the bloody paper towel to her forehead. "Just a scratch."

He talked to his sister for several minutes as Charlotte continued to call for him.

The SEBC-TV news van screeched to the curb, and Simone Adams filed out with her camera crew. They approached Charlotte, who once again shuddered with sobs, and setup lights and a tripod. Charlotte could barely speak when Simone pushed the mic in her face. Mike returned to his wife's side, telling Simone they had no comment and pushed the cameras away.

He motioned to his sister. "Can you take Charlotte home? She needs to rest."

"Wait," Charlotte said. "Michael, darling. Don't get excited, okay?"

He kissed her on the forehead. "I'm fine, dear."

"Please," she said. "Let your deputies handle this if you feel stressed."

With one hand pressing the paper towel to her forehead, Winnie put her free arm around Charlotte and led her across the street. She helped Charlotte into the station wagon parked in front of Sam's Body Shop and shut the passenger door.

As Winnie drove away, Mike approached Tori and

Deputy Torres. He tapped the deputy's arm. Together, they stretched yellow tape around the perimeter and roped off the grounds. Simone filmed them for a few minutes, before whistling to her crew and packing up the lights and cameras.

Tori watched in silence. Mike looked over at her but said nothing. She picked up his hat from the ground and handed it to him.

"Looks like the limb was cut," he said, assessing the damage to the greenhouse. Without saying another word, he ran a hand over the top of his head, smoothing back his hair, and put on his hat.

She was waiting for his wrist monitor to start beeping. She said, "Maybe you should find a quieter profession, like a librarian. Or caretaker at Sunset Hills."

"You're not funny." He stepped toward the ruined building and paused at the corner. "What happened?"

"I'm not sure." She stood beside him, looking into the cracked windowpanes. Jagged shards of glass covered the floor, the upturned shelves, and broken plants. She looked back at the florist shop behind them. "I was inside, talking to Ash, when the branch fell."

"Where's Ash now?"

"He and Darla left just before you got here."

Mike placed a hand over his brow as he looked up at the large oak tree. "He was trimming the trees here."

Tori noticed the crowd of onlookers crowding the parking lot and standing along the edge of the property. More people were crossing the street, coming toward them. She took Mike by the arm. "Can I talk to you? In private."

Mike's eyes scanned the tree branch above the greenhouse and back again. He seemed to consider it. He nodded. They walked across the yard, past the murmuring crowd, and through the back door of the flower shop.

Once inside, Tori turned to Mike. "Look, Sheriff. We don't know that this is in any way connected to Brooke's murder investigation."

"I don't know about that." He removed his hat and set it on the glass counter, next to the register. "It seems like an awful big coincidence, if you ask me."

"Anyone could've cut that branch."

"True. But not just anyone has my wife all riled up like Ash does."

Her brow furrowed. "Look, sheriff—"

"Mike."

"Sheriff, whatever." She paced in front of the freestanding shelves of flowering plants and greenery. "Did you talk to Pastor Fields?"

"I did."

"Then you know Ash's alibi still stands. He was drunk and vandalizing the high school hallways when the pastor found him, but he still spent the night at the church."

"So, it seems."

"And Brooke had been with Principal Quinn earlier on the day she died, and he has a prescription for Deletycide— the same medication found in Brooke's system."

"Go on." He folded his arms across his chest and leaned back against the counter. The register, candy jar, and penny dish sat on the glass top behind him. Two framed photos of his family stood on his left, and he nearly bumped them with his elbow.

She met his gaze. "Then someone driving Brooke's minivan runs me off the road."

"What does this have to do with that branch crashing through the greenhouse?" He glanced at his watch and turned his head to look out the window at the crowd outside.

She didn't answer right away. Instead, she walked over to Darla's drawing on the floor and picked it up. She looked at it a moment and then handed it to him, careful not to let her fingers touch his. "Darla keeps drawing the same picture."

He glanced at the drawing. "I've seen it. What's your point?"

"She's drawing what she saw on the night her mother died."

"It's called working through the trauma."

"Darla is drawing the deputy and a second person on the scene. I don't know why, for what purpose. But I think Deputy Torres has Brooke's cell phone and has been texting me from it."

"I don't believ—"

"Listen, please." Her voice sounded panicked, and she took a breath to calm herself. "Deputy Torres was the one who found Brooke's body. He says he was alone, but Darla keeps drawing two figures there. He had access to Brooke's personal effects and is the most likely suspect to have taken her cell phone."

"My deputy wouldn't do that." Mike glanced at his wrist monitor, likely out of habit more than concern. "I've known him for—"

"We've both known him for years—decades. But as I sat at the bottom of that ditch and called RJ, the mysterious texter contacted me out of the blue, up to speed on everything going on. When RJ showed up, he was—low and behold—with Deputy Torres."

"That still doesn't mean—"

"It's the only line of thinking that makes sense. He saw something that night at the water tower. He knows who murdered Brooke and, for some reason, can't come forward."

Mike opened his mouth. Tori raised a hand.

She continued. "He knew I wasn't coming to the funeral and he hoped I would change my mind. Said it himself when I first ran into him at your office. He knew those cryptic text messages would get me here. Knew I would look into Brooke's death and he's been trying to lead me to the truth ... the only way he could."

"Okay, okay. I don't believe it, but I'll talk to him." He grabbed his hat from the counter and placed it on his head. "I'll see if, by any crazy stretch of the imagination, he's got Brooke's phone and is texting you from it."

"Thank you, sheriff."

"Mike. You can call me Mike," he said, his voice hard and disapproving as he slammed the door shut behind him.

M_AN STR_AK

That afternoon, Tori and RJ entered the car rental shop, and Tori signed a rental agreement for a basic white Toyota Corolla. "If the Jeep doesn't get fixed today, you can take a rental back to Tampa," she told him.

"Don't tell me you're not coming back with me."

"I want to wait for the autopsy results."

"Tori, you promised."

"This is too important."

"I'm your cameraman," he said. "What's the point of my going back without you?"

"I don't want you to lose your job. This is something I have to do," she said. "You don't have to get caught up in it."

"I'm already caught up in it."

"If your Jeep's not ready, take the rental back. I'll wait for your Jeep and when it's ready, I can drive it home."

They drove back to Sam's Body Shop in the Corolla. RJ called Pittman to let them know they were still in Elroy Springs and would leave soon. Tori could hear Pittman yelling his response.

They found the mechanic was still working on the Jeep when they entered the garage. He straightened his back, smiled, and wiped his hands on a dirty rag. "Give me another hour."

RJ looked at Tori. "Looks like we're waiting. I'm not leaving without you."

He went to the vending machine in the corner of the waiting room as Tori's phone dinged with a new text. She looked at it. It was from Mike.

"Can you meet me?"

Tori typed back: "Did you talk to Deputy Torres?" A moment later, his response came in.

"Meet me at your old lake house. Alone. We need to talk."

Tori yelled to RJ, "I left something at Winnie's. Go get lunch, and I'll be right back."

"You better be right back," he said.

"I'll be right back. Now go grab lunch and pick me up a big salad." She jumped into the rental car and pulled out of the garage parking lot.

Mike was waiting for her.

* * * *

With nothing left to do, RJ ambled over to the Waffle House on Main Street. As he entered, he bumped into Principal Quinn rushing out of the double doors. The darkly-tanned man looked flustered.

"Excuse me," RJ said as the principal rushed past him and took off down the sidewalk. RJ watched him go, then entered the diner.

Despite the counter section being almost deserted, he selected a booth and ordered a water while perusing the menu. As the server moved about, bringing water and napkins, RJ took out his recorder and hit Play. He listened to the white noise, pausing and rewinding the playback.

When the server returned, RJ handed the menu back to her and ordered a tuna on rye with a Mountain Dew. She took his order, and he returned his focus to the recorder. He listened to one section, hitting Pause and Playback over and over. He swore he could hear Brooke's voice.

A young woman slid into the booth, sitting across from him. He looked up into the pale face surrounded by a river of jet-black hair and a sparkling diamond stud on her left nostril.

"You have a beautiful aura," Zoe said, smiling at him. "A pure blue aura is incredibly rare."

RJ shut off the recorder and stared at her. "What are you doing here?" he asked.

"Same as you. Having lunch."

"I already ordered."

"Me too. Tuna on rye." She licked her lips. "The waitress is bringing it over."

"That's what I ordered."

"I know," she said, her eyes widening. She leaned over the table and whispered, "So tell me, what'cha listening to?"

He noticed the tattoo on her left arm, a Chinese dragon coiled around an attacking tiger, and he wondered about the meaning behind it. Did it have some deep spiritual significance, or did she simply feel it looked cool on her arm? He gave her question a fleeting thought and decided to answer her. "Do you know what EVPs are?"

She shot him a coy look. "Electronic voice phenomena."

"I recorded spirit voices at the Martin house." RJ held up his recorder and brought it closer to her face. "I think I got Brooke's voice."

"Let me hear." She leaned farther over the table, pressing her ear to the recorder's small round speaker. He hit Play, and her eyes locked with his as she listened.

"Play it again," she said.

He played it again.

"I can hear her," she said. "That is Brooke's voice."

The two stopped talking and Zoe fell back into her seat while the server unloaded a tray of drinks and two tuna sandwiches. RJ opened his sandwich, poured mustard on the tuna, and stirred it with a fork.

"That's Brooke." Zoe stared at the recorder, not touching her sandwich. "There's no doubt."

RJ nodded. "I want to get more recordings. Maybe Brooke can tell us something."

"I believe I can reach her," she whispered. She stared at him, and with more confidence, stated, "I think I've been in contact with her."

RJ dropped the recorder. His left brow rose a fraction. "Come again?"

* * * *

Driving the rental car, Tori headed along Route 103 / Clay Pit Road, passing the narrow bridge that stretched over Twin Lakes, and waited at the railroad tracks for a train to pass. She drove by the old Martin house. Pulling over onto the shoulder near the house, she gazed through the car window at the gray, twisted orange trees in the abandoned grove. The water tower rose above it. Even from this distance, the faded letters of Ash's spray-painted proposal were still visible. She took a deep breath, hoping to dissolve the knot that grew tighter in her chest. The sky had been clouding up all afternoon, and the rain came down in heavy sheets as she continued along the two-lane highway.

Her cell phone buzzed ... RJ again. She sent him to voicemail.

By the time she reached the dusty drive with a mailbox marked YOUNGER, the rain had stopped, and she could see patches of blue between the scudding clouds. She turned onto the path that wound through oaks and pines until dissolving into the lake.

Tori parked in the yard beside a weathered foreclosure sign bound in knots of stinkweed vines. Behind it, the sickly banana tree she and her mother had planted all those years ago drooped from neglect. Rainwater dripped from its brown-and-yellow leaves.

At the side of the house, she found a window that had two boards nailed across the dirty glass. After she pulled them from the window frame, she raised the window and climbed through, into a dusty, dark kitchen. She entered the vacant house. It took a moment for her eyes to adjust, and she pulled open a drawer by the sink. Tattered twist ties. Scissors. A rusty can opener. A matchbook. She struck one, and her mother's familiar kitchen flickered to life. Memories swarmed like ghosts in the match light, until the flame went out.

Holding the matchbook, she stepped through the

measured silence. Floorboards creaked under her sandals. Each step had a different voice and she knew them all. Their faint echoes plodded ahead of her, into a long hallway where a sideboard once stood, filled with her mother's plates and good silver. Tori halted at the dining room entrance, hearing faint scraping noises around her. Something scurried in the walls. Squirrels? Maybe a family of hungry rats?

She'd forgotten how dark this house could get. Even more so, now that the overgrown jasmine covered the eastern exterior wall. Vines and leaves pressed against most of the windows, blocking incoming sunlight like heavy drapes drawn tight. It made the whole house feel cool and damp.

At the end of the hallway, stairs rose to the utter blackness of the second floor. An upstairs hall seemed foreboding, and she paused again, letting her eyes adjust. She trailed a hand along the wall as she crossed the hallway and slipped into her old bedroom. A sliver of afternoon light filtered in through the open door.

Her room looked smaller than she remembered, but it was brightly lit compared to the rest of the house. The window faced the western sky and brightened the spongy green carpet. Her white vanity still stood in the corner, as if waiting for her to return after all these years. Tears came to her eyes. The mirror was dusty, and her image looked distorted in it. She pulled out the flimsy center drawer. It was empty, but she pulled it all the way out and squatted to peer in the hole. She struck a match—something flickered in the dim light, stuck in the back.

Before the flame went out, she had a photo in her hand. A young Mike Bennett—fifteen or sixteen years old—stood proud on a pitcher's mound, wearing a muddy baseball uniform and lopsided ball cap. He was grinning ear to ear, holding up a trophy. She remembered every detail of that day. She put the photo into her pocket. The scent of the burnt match hung in the afternoon air.

She noticed the silence. Like before. Turning her head, she listened and glanced out the bedroom window.

The late afternoon sun shined brilliant, blinding her, and she brought an arm up to her face to shield her eyes. She looked down at the front yard, the drive, the scrawny banana tree.

Someone stood beside it, unmoving.

A man? A woman? She couldn't tell. Sunlight blared behind the figure, obstructing her view.

She stepped away from the window and rubbed her eyes. Her phone felt heavy in her pocket, and she fished it from her jeans. Glanced at it. No messages. She turned back to the window.

The figure just stood there, staring up at the house. Into the bedroom window. Watching her.

Or was it even a figure at all? Was it a tree stalk? A shoot from the banana plant? Weeds? The figure turned and moved. It was a person. Someone was actually out there. He … she … it walked across the yard and disappeared around the side of the house.

Tori leaned against the glass. She couldn't see where the figure went. Turning, she raced out of the room and down the stairs. She scrambled into the kitchen and hoisted herself onto the counter. A second later, she was out the window, back outside and headed for the side of the house.

Sherriff Bennett came around the corner, startling her. He laughed and said, "You made it."

* * * *

RJ sat in the passenger seat as Zoe drove her yellow Volkswagen Beetle up Clay Pit Road, to the Martins' driveway. She pulled onto the gravel drive and parked next to the old blue minivan. Hopping out of her car, she paused. He came up beside her and looked at the house.

"WIFE KILLER" was spray-painted across the front windows and "MURDERER" on the front door.

Zoe placed a hand over her brow as if to shield her eyes from the sun. "Do you think Ash is home?"

RJ looked down the driveway and at the orange trees in the neglected grove. "I don't see his truck."

"I can feel her presence." She raced up the driveway, gravel crunching beneath her shoes, to the front porch. "Brooke is here," she yelled back to him. "I can feel her presence. She's calling to me."

"Follow me," RJ called to her, and waved her over.

He led her to the back of the house. After using the same credit card trick Tori had shown him the other night, he jimmied the back door. They entered the house. He retrieved his recorder from his pocket and held it above his head.

He stepped into the living room. "Brooke Martin? Are you here?"

They wandered into the dark hallway. He wondered if he should grab his camera, and then remembered he'd left it at Winnie's. He kept the recorder raised as they came to the front entry hall.

"Brooke Martin? Are you here?" he called out.

They made their way upstairs, walked through the upper landing. They entered the master bedroom. A crash coming from downstairs, like something fell, shattered the silence and made them both jump. The two looked at each other. RJ ran to the window and scanned the area outside. Ash's truck wasn't out there. He exhaled in relief.

Zoe raised a hand and told RJ to stop. "Quiet," she said.

"What is it?" he whispered.

"Quiet," she said again. Her head turned toward the hallway, and then she looked at RJ. "Brooke is here."

CHAPTER TWENTY-FIVE

CR_EL S_MMER

Tori looked into Mike's face. "Were you just standing in the front yard? By that old banana tree?"

"I parked and came back here." Standing tall in his tan uniform, he looked down at her. The badge on his chest reflected the sunlight.

She looked past him, at the dock and the little boat-house, and the lake beyond it. A bass boat sped along in the distance and she could hear the loud engine rise and fade. "Did you see anyone else?"

"Anyone else? What are you talking about? We're alone."

"No, we're not. I saw someone standing in the front yard, watching the house. Wait here."

She jogged around the perimeter of the house. When she got to the back porch, she sat on the pavers, as did Mike, next to her. She stared at the lake. It seemed a full minute before either of them spoke.

"Are you okay?" He reached for her arm. His fingers wrapped around the dark fabric of her sleeve.

His grip felt strong, protective. Gooseflesh rose on her skin. She avoided his eyes, turning away so fast that his face blurred. "Did the autopsy results come back? What'd they find?"

"Nothing yet." He released her and stood. "It'll be a few hours."

"Deputy Torres knows what happened." She stood and stepped past him, walking toward the dock as she spoke. "He saw something or knows something and he's hiding it."

"He knows you think he has Brooke's cell phone. But he assured me he doesn't." Mike strode beside her.

"I don't believe him." Tori stepped onto the wood planks and looked out at the lake. Sunlight sparkled on the water with brilliant white flashes. She looked up at Mike. "He's been sending me the text messages."

"We already been down this road." His voice seemed to soften, as if he was telling her something, she didn't only need to hear but absorb. "He doesn't have Brooke's cell and, even if he did, he wouldn't send you text messages from it. I don't know what else to tell you."

"Then we need to talk to him again. Together."

"Tori, listen—"

"Oh, wait a second—wait one second." Raising an arm, she took a step back toward the edge of the dock. The logic started to click. It all became clear and she couldn't believe she didn't see it before. "Maybe you're right. Maybe it isn't Deputy Torres. He's not the only one who had access to Brooke's belongings."

"Hey." He took a step toward her. "I asked you here because I need to talk to—"

She spoke over him, the words coming out with an unbridled intensity. "Your high school intern—tattoo girl, Zoe what's her name—she had access to Brooke's stuff too. She could have Brooke's phone."

"—you in private. It's time we talk about what happened."

"To Brooke?"

"To us."

"No," she said. She waved her hands for emphasis. "Here me out. Things are starting to make sense. It's not Deputy Torres. It's Zoe—"

Mike shook his head. "I wanted to tell you I'm sorry. I know I hurt you and I never meant to."

"You're sorry?" Tori stared at him and forgot what she was going to say. She looked away. Her eyes glistened with tears and she blinked them back. She tried not to look at him and focused on the lake. The water flashed moments of silver as the afternoon sun struck its surface. The light warmed on her face.

Breaking the silence, Mike said, "I guess you and RJ are getting pretty serious."

"I guess."

"How old is he, anyway? He looks like he's still in high school."

"He's graduated from college."

Mike laughed. "You're a cougar. You know that, right?"

"Sheriff—"

"Tori, please. It's Mike."

"I can't call you—that. I can't stand to even say your name."

"Man, I did a number on you."

"No. Yes. I don't know. Maybe," she said, looking away. "I do know I can't get it out of my head that you made the wrong choice."

"What?"

She turned to him. "What's her face. You made the wrong choice with her. I've been in love with you since the first day I saw you fixing your bike in your grandparents' barn." Her voice choked as she struggled to get the words out. "We could've been very happy together. But you made the wrong choice."

"I know." Now his voice choked.

"But you never loved me?"

"I always loved you," he said.

The alarm on his wrist monitor beeped.

Tori jumped when she heard it, not expecting the interruption. The beeping continued. He raised his arm and ripped the cuff from his wrist. The beeping grew louder in his hand.

"I've had it with this thing," he yelled, swinging his arm back and launching the monitor high into the air. It swooshed past the end of the dock and plopped with a loud splash into the lake.

Tori couldn't believe what she saw. "Why'd you do that!"

"I might as well be wearing handcuffs," he said. "I can't do my job with that thing beeping at me all the time."

"But ..."—she searched for the words— "what about your heart? The palpitations?"

"Does it matter?" he said, giving her a sideways glance. "It ended my baseball career. My whole life has been retrofitted around some defect and I'm sick of it."

"But your dad. He might've lived longer if—"

He didn't let her finish. "If I'm supposed to die young, then some beeping wristwatch isn't gonna prevent that. Fate is fate. You can't escape it."

* * * *

RJ followed Zoe down the staircase. She stopped on the bottom step and he pressed against her back, listening. He kept his recorder going, hoping to catch evidence of Brooke's spirit. Would she speak to them? What would she say?

"There was an argument here," Zoe whispered. She tiptoed into the dining room and touched the stained wall. RJ could still see where the liquor made several running lines down the drywall. Shards of glass still sparkled on the floor.

She looked up at him. "Ash and Brooke. They fought. Struggled."

"What about?"

"I can't tell," Zoe said. Her head turned toward a narrow table by the front door. A broken vase and brown wilted lilies lay scattered on the floor near it. Something sparkled among the glass fragments of the vase. She rushed to it and picked up gold ring. It looked like a wedding band.

RJ whistled. "That's some finger shackle."

Zoe closed her hand around the ring and shuddered. "The fight turned nasty. He said hurtful things. She said things she didn't mean."

"You're getting all that from Brooke?"

She didn't answer and opened the front door. Stepped onto the porch. "Brooke tried to run. She fled into the yard. He followed."

Zoe ran into the yard, past the gravel drive and her VW Beetle parked next to the old minivan. She rushed into the orange grove. RJ ran after her.

"Brooke was running through here, her red dress ripped by the branches. She was out of breath. Stumbled. Looked back. Ash was coming." Zoe ran faster, crashing through the dead branches. She came to the clearing. "Brooke stopped here. She looked up, saw the water tower. She ran to it."

Zoe ran to the base of the old tower. RJ ran after her. She came to the weathered ladder and stopped. RJ bumped into her and realized they weren't alone. A man was standing at the base, beside one of the metal legs.

Principal Quinn held up an arm, motioning for them to stop. "Whoa!" he said.

RJ took a step back, saying, "What are you doing here?"

"I'm not sure." The principal looked dazed. "I got a text message ... from Brooke's cell number."

"What?" RJ said.

The principal held up his phone and shook his head, puzzled. "It said to meet her here."

* * * *

Tori still couldn't believe he'd tossed his wrist monitor into the lake, though the athlete still inside him impressed her. "What's your wife going to say when she finds out?"

Mike laughed. "Oh, she can still nag me about what I eat and how much I don't exercise."

Tori thought about that a moment. "Were you seeing her when we were engaged?" she asked. She didn't want to know the truth.

"No." His voice was soft, as if he was reflecting on some distant memory. "I met Charlotte in Cancun."

"At our honeymoon destination?" She chuckled and looked away. "I suppose there's irony in that, somewhere. You met the love of your life on our honeymoon."

"I think you two would like each other, you know, if you'd met under different circumstances."

She shuddered. "Don't push it."

"Okay." He raised his hands, surrendering. "Enough said."

"Is that all you had to say? If so, then apology accepted. Let's move past it."

He paused, watching her. "That, and I wanted to say I was wrong. I was wrong for what I did and how I treated you."

A slight smile crossed her lips. "Thank you."

"Then you forgive me?" He stretched out a hand, brushing her fingers.

"I—" She lost her train of thought. An electrical current rippled from his hand into hers. "I ... don't know," she whispered. "How about, I'll try."

"I'll take it."

They were silent for several seconds. He stepped closer to her, their eyes locking. She trembled. Her hand pressed against his chest. His face leaned close to hers, so close his hot breath blew a strand of hair from her forehead. Her heartbeat quickened, and she swore she could feel his damaged heart beating rapidly in his chest. A ding from his waist broke the spell.

It was a bell calling them to their corners.

He turned from Tori and looked down at his phone.

Her phone chirped too. She glanced at the incoming text, from Brooke's number.

"I'm waiting for you. At the water tower."

* * * *

Winnie Daniels stood at the kitchen sink, a bandage fixed to cut above her eye. She poured a cup of tea for Charlotte, who was lying on the living room couch with a damp washcloth covering her eyes and forehead. The dogs followed Winnie as she carried the tea out of the kitchen. They barked and jumped onto the couch, causing Charlotte to cry out. Winnie set the tea on the coffee table and apologized.

She scolded the cocker spaniel and Jack Russell terrier and picked up the Chihuahua and pug, holding one in each arm. She set them down on the floor when her cell phone dinged with an incoming message. Brooke's name flashed across the screen.

Winnie's face turned white.

"What's wrong?" Charlotte asked, sitting up. The washcloth fell from her face, and she glanced at her cell phone resting on the coffee table as it lit up and buzzed. She reached for it, read the message, and looked at Winnie with wide, surprised eyes.

* * * *

Pastor Fields stood outside the First Baptist Church watering the plants when he heard his phone chirp. Putting down the garden hose, he tugged his phone out of his pants pocket.

A message from Brooke Martin caught him off guard.

"I' m waiting for you. At the water tower. "

* * * *

Veronica stood at the kitchen sink, preparing an insulin shot, when she heard her cell phone vibrate on the counter. Putting down the hypodermic needle and insulin bottle, she picked up the device and dropped it. It clattered onto the tile at her feet.

"What is it?" Leonard asked, sitting at the kitchen table and holding a tissue over his index finger. His arm knocked the blood glucose monitor off the table and onto the floor. "What's wrong?"

"THAT—THAT WAS MY CELL PHONE," she yelled to him.

"I heard *that*." He turned his head toward her voice. "What'd you drop? What's wrong?"

She picked up the phone and ran a thumb over the screen. Gasping, she sat at the table across from him.

"What is it?" he asked again, removing the tissue from his bleeding finger.

"YOUR DAUGHTER!" She stared at the phone, reading the message.

"My daughter? What?"

"I got a text message from Brooke." Veronica's voice had turned quiet, almost speaking to herself. "She wants us to meet her at the old water tower."

* * * *

Tori stared at Mike. He put down his phone.

"I have a message from Brooke's cell number," he said. "Brooke Martin just sent me a text."

"She's waiting for you at the water tower?"

"You were serious." His eyes enlarged and the color drained from his face. "Someone is sending text messages from Brooke's phone."

"I told you," she said. She laughed and shook her head. "I told you I was getting messages from Brooke's cell."

"Yeah, but you were serious. Someone really is sending messages from Brooke's cell phone."

"It all makes sense now." Tori stepped away, waving her hands as she spoke. "Darla keeps drawing two people—two *officers*—at the water tower the night her mother died. Deputy Torres and Zoe. She was there that night."

"You're basing that off a picture a traumatized kid keeps drawing?"

"I'm basing it on the testimony of the only known witness to Brooke's murder. Plus, Zoe had access to Brooke's belongings at the Sheriff's Department. She could've taken the cell phone and she could've been texting me all this time. Hell, she was probably at the station with Deputy Torres and RJ when I called about getting run off the road and crashing the Jeep."

"Why?" He looked down at his phone and back at her.

"Why would she impersonate Brooke and text you all these messages?"

"I don't know," Tori said, "but maybe it's time to find out."

CHAPTER TWENTY-SIX

TH_ KILL_R IN M_

From the top of the water tower, RJ could see cars, trucks, and a black-and-white church bus pulling into the unpaved drive in front of the Martin house.

Mayor Winslow arrived, parking his white Cadillac on the other side of Brooke's minivan.

Veronica parked on the grass approaching the groves, and assisted Leonard. "I'M HELPING YOU OUT OF THE CAR," she yelled at him, and then waved at the mayor. He waved back as she turned to Leonard and said, "WE'RE AT YOUR DAUGHTER'S HOME."

Charlotte swung open the passenger door of Winnie's station wagon and joined Deputy Torres, Pastor Fields, and some other townspeople. Winnie caught up to them as the group disappeared into the grove.

RJ climbed down the tower ladder and hollered at Zoe. "There's a whole mess of people head'n our way."

Zoe turned away from Principal Quinn at the tower base and motioned as Leonard and Veronica emerged from the orange trees. Charlotte, Winnie, Deputy Torres, and the mayor followed behind them.

"Welcome," Zoe called out. "Did you receive a message from Brooke too?"

Principal Quinn held up his cell phone. "I got a text from Brooke."

Veronica led Leonard by his hand to the water tower and stood beside Zoe and the principal. She scratched her head. "Do you think it's really from her?"

"That's what I'd like to know," Deputy Torres said, stepping up behind them. "I got a text from Brooke to meet here, too."

"We, um, looks like we all got a text from Brooke." Winnie walked over to RJ and hugged him as he asked about the cut on her forehead. Greeting Leonard and Veronica, she hugged them too and they wanted the details about her bandaged eye.

"This is crazy," Leonard said. "My granddaughter is almost killed in that greenhouse accident and now some fool sends text messages from my daughter's phone."

"YOU'RE ON YOUR DAUGHTER'S PROPERTY," Veronica yelled in his ear, and he shrank back from her. She gripped his shoulder as if to hold him steady. Looking back at RJ and Winnie, she shook her head. "He forgets where he's at," she said.

"Everyone, please." Zoe stood and raised her tattooed arms, addressing the crowd as more people arrived. They wandered around the base of the water tower. "Brooke is reaching out to us. Her presence is here with us this after-noon."

"She's here?" Charlotte's eyes widened and she gripped Winnie's hand.

RJ noticed the various small, medium, and large pineapples printed on her blouse, and wondered what the woman's weird fascination with fruit was about. He put the thought out of his mind when Zoe spoke up again.

"I can sense her." Zoe lifted her head and shut her eyes. "I can feel her essence reaching out to me."

The anxious crows gathered around her. They murmured all at once, and Zoe quieted them down.

"Listen, everybody. Brooke contacted me earlier. She showed me things, snippets of her final moments before she slipped from this mortal coil. RJ can vouch for that."

She opened her eyes and glanced at him. He nodded, recorder in hand.

She smiled and turned back to the crowd. "Brooke wants to tell us something. That's why she called all of us here. This is where she died, and this is where her energy is the strongest. Now, everyone, form a circle and join hands."

RJ held up his recorder, wondering if Brooke was

communicating with them now. He again wished he had his good camera and wondered how Brooke's spirit would appear. He hoped for a full-body apparition floating above them as the group formed a circle beneath the water tower. Flipping on the cell phone camera, he hit Record.

The short, balding man who'd talked to Tori at Brooke's memorial tapped him on the shoulder. "I remember you," he said to RJ, and lifted his Canon camera with its extended lens. He snapped a picture and let the camera hang from his neck. "You're Tori's boyfriend."

RJ nodded. "And you're Peter Parker."

"Edison Beyer, with the *Elroy Springs Gazette*." He shook RJ's hand. "This is going to make a great story. I'm gonna take pictures."

Zoe hushed them and turned to the small gathering. "Everyone, join hands and form a circle." She stretched out a hand to RJ. "We need an unbroken circle."

He looked at her and shook his head. "Consider me a spectator," he said. "I wanna get this on film."

He took a few steps back to get everyone in the frame. The crowd sat Indian style on the grass. Winnie squeezed Charlotte's hand and took hold of Deputy Torres' hand with her other. Veronica led Leonard to the circle and helped him to the ground beside Mayor Winslow and Pastor Fields. She sat between them and took their hands.

Once everyone sat, Zoe nodded. "We're about to find out, once and for all, what happened to Brooke. Are you ready?"

"Guess she stopped texting," Principal Quinn said, and squeezed Zoe's hand.

She shut her eyes. "I think I can reach out to her. I can communicate with Brooke."

Charlotte let out a nervous chuckle. "Like a séance?"

"This isn't in God's order," Pastor Fields said to her. "We shouldn't be doing this."

"Please," Zoe said, "we must concentrate. Focus all your internal thoughts on extending your aura beyond your body and connecting with those around you. If Brooke called you here, she needs your energy to communicate."

"She didn't call us, she texted us," Veronica said to Zoe, and then leaned into Leonard's ear: "THE GIRL FROM THE SHERIFF'S DEPARTMENT THINKS YOUR DAUGHTER CALLED US."

Leonard cussed under his breath and waved his hand free.

Veronica grabbed it. "SHE WANTS AN UNBROKEN CIRCLE," she yelled at him. "WE HAVE TO HOLD HANDS."

Charlotte shuddered. "Do you think she'll materialize?"

"Not without a, um, Ouija board," Winnie said. She looked over at Zoe. "Do you have one of those? You know, a Ouija board?"

"We don't need a Ouija board." Zoe shook her head and brought a hand up to her brow. "I don't know if she'll materialize. She may. Hopefully."

"This is unnatural and we're playing with spiritual forces best left alone," the pastor stood. The mayor, gripping his hand, pulled him back down.

"I thought this had to happen at night," Charlotte said to the group. "It's the middle of the afternoon."

"The light is better for the, you know, cameras," Winnie said, looking over at RJ and Edison.

RJ held up his cell phone, recording the proceedings. Edison snapped pictures with his Canon.

Winnie turned to Zoe. "What if I, um, I have a question I want to ask Brooke?"

Charlotte laughed and squeezed her hand. "We all have the same questions. What happened to her and did Ash murder her?"

"No," Winnie said. "I-I have another question."

Zoe scrunched her nose. Her eyes narrowed. "What do you want to ask her?"

"I want to know..." Winnie touched the bandage above her eye. "—if she ever liked me."

Zoe stared at her for several moments, her mouth open. RJ lowered his camera phone. Charlotte huffed.

"Of course, she liked you," Charlotte said. "What kind of question is that?"

Zoe hushed everyone again, and Veronica yelled into Leonard's ear: "THE GIRL FROM THE SHERIFF'S DEPARTMENT NEEDS ABSOLUTE QUIET!"

Leonard cussed under his breath. He pulled his hand away. She grabbed it again.

"I'm going to try to ask Brooke a question," Zoe said. Bowing her head and shutting her eyes, she chanted under her breath. As her chanting grew louder, the diamond stud in her left nostril glinted, reflecting sunlight.

RJ raised his phone and resumed filming. Edison snapped more pictures.

"Brooke is here," she said, throwing her head back. "She's showing me that night. That night when she was running through this old orchard, calling for Darla. She came to the water tower, looked up and cried out for her little girl. She climbed the tower. A man was there, waiting for her."

"Who?" Leonard said, and leaned forward. Veronica gripped his hand. "Who was waiting for her?"

"I can't tell." Zoe thrashed her head back and forth, as if trying to clear away a falling haze. "The face is cloudy, like it's hidden in a fog. There's a struggle. A fight. He overpowered her. Brooke was defenseless as the man dragged her to the railing. He pulled something from his pocket. It's a piece of paper. A note. He pinned it to her blouse. He tied a noose around her neck and then ... oh, no! Dear God, no! He tossed her body over the railing."

"Who? Who did?" Leonard's voice cracked and he sounded on the verge of tears.

Veronica held him back. "We need to know who," she said, turning back to Zoe.

RJ turned the camera from Zoe to the people in the circle.

"Leonard's caregiver is correct. We need to know who," Mayor Winslow said, and Charlotte agreed. Winnie stuttered, struggling to speak.

Principal Quinn turned to Deputy Torres, and then to Zoe. "We need to stop this," he said.

"Not yet!" Zoe's voice cracked, as if she was straining to get the words out. "Keep the circle intact. I can still see her. Brooke's arms are thrashing. She's kicking, gasping for air. She claws at the rope, but it's useless. Her world turns black. A calmness overtakes her." Zoe opened her eyes and looked at RJ. "He hung her."

"She's dead?" he whispered. He zoomed the camera on his phone toward Zoe's head.

A melancholy frown flittered across her face and she shut her eyes again. Her head flung back and whipped forward. "A man climbs down the tower. He doesn't realize Darla is up there. He doesn't see her along the railing, above her mother's body."

"Who is he?" Charlotte asked, and leaned forward, squeezing Winnie's hand.

"It's someone she knew. Someone she loved. A family member." Zoe was crying now, tears streaming down her cheeks. A breeze rippled through her black hair. Her voice strained. "He's moving under the cover of darkness. Returns to the dead orchard. Disappears into the trees. Gone. He left her there. Oh, dear God. He just left her there."

"Brooke's gone?" RJ looked around. He wanted to see her, or some form of apparition, a misty figure, or at least an orb.

"She's gone," Zoe repeated. "She was murdered, in cold blood. I can feel her. I can feel the noose tighten around her neck, her lungs straining for air." She opened her eyes and pulled her hands free. "Oh, God, RJ." She stood and covered her mouth, sobbing. "Oh, God. She was murdered by her husband. Murdered!"

Pastor Fields stood, releasing the Mayor's hand and breaking the circle. "Ash did not murder his wife."

Edison tapped RJ on the shoulder again. RJ, with his phone in his right hand and his arms around Zoe, turned to him. Edison pointed to the grove. Branches were moving.

"Are you seeing"—Edison said, his voice trembling—"what I'm seeing?"

RJ stared at the waving branches of the dead trees.

He saw ... something.

A woman.

CHAPTER TWENTY-SEVEN

PLAY_NG W_TH F_RE

Tori pushed through the dead trees and stepped into the clearing. "RJ?"

He stood beneath the water tower, holding Zoe as she sobbed in his arms. Edison paced beside him, snapping photos of the group of people sitting in a circle on the ground, holding hands.

Zoe was screaming through her tears, "Oh, God. Her death was so violent. She struggled with that monster. Fought for air."

"What's going on here?" Mike stepped out of the grove, behind Tori, and his voice echoed through the clearing.

Zoe sniffled and wiped her eyes. Her head whipped around, and she gazed at Mike with wide, frightened eyes. "She's gone. I've lost her."

"I received a text from Brooke's cell phone," Charlotte said, waving to her husband. Breaking from the circle, she got to her feet and ran to him.

Mike embraced her as Tori stepped forward. "Your performance is over, Zoe. We know you contacted everyone here. We know you have Brooke's phone."

"No." Zoe shook her head, still wiping her eyes. "Brooke was here. We all felt her presence."

Winnie and Veronica agreed, and Mayor Winslow spoke up. "Zoe contacted Brooke."

"She recounted her murder," Zoe said. "She reached out to us, to me."

Mayor Winslow turned to Mike. "Sheriff, the town's getting a bad rap." He stood and wiped the dirt and grass from the seat of his pants.

"My kids are scared about all this talk of murder,"

Edison said as he stepped alongside the mayor. "They knew Mrs. Martin, and this is upsetting them."

"Yeah, what are you going to do about it, Sheriff?" Veronica stood now too and helped Leonard to his feet. "THE SHERIFF IS HERE."

Leonard pushed her back. "I can hear him."

Mike raised his hands. "I know everybody is worried about this. But nobody is more concerned than me and my men. They're working twenty-four hours a day on this matter. We want things to get back to normal in this town."

"How?" The mayor approached Mike, rubbing his hands together to remove the dirt. "If there's been a murder, we need to know now. We need to know our town is safe for our children."

Charlotte touched Mike's arm. "And why haven't you arrested Ash?"

"Ash is innocent." Pastor Fields addressed the group. "And this is nothing more than a witch hunt."

Mike looked over at Zoe. "Despite our intern's performance, we still don't know what happened."

"She's duping all of us," Tori said, pointing at Zoe. "She sent the text messages from Brooke's phone, and I want to know why."

Zoe shot her a brutal glare and bent down to pick up RJ's voice recorder. "You may not believe me, but Brooke had a message for us. All of us." She paused, and then pointed at the twisted, gray trees. "She wanted us to know that she was murdered—by him."

Tori turned her head. Ash and Darla stood at the edge of the grove, in front of a gnarled wall of dead orange trees. She wasn't sure how long he'd been standing there or how much he'd heard.

"Hey, hold it. Hold it right there!" Ash yelled. "Do you people believe her? Do you honestly believe she's communicating with Brooke?"

He turned his head, to look at each person there. The crowd stood still and silent.

After a moment, Veronica waved at Darla. "Little girl,

little girl! Your grandfather is over here." She turned to Leonard. "IT'S YOUR GRANDDAUGHTER. SHE'S HERE!"

Leonard eased himself to the ground.

Darla stepped behind her father, peeking out from behind his leg.

Ash took a deep breath, looking at Tori and back at the crowd. "You people beat everything, you know it?" he said. "I went to school with you, Mikey B. My Darla is in school with your twin boys. Mayor Winslow? Pastor Fields? What are you doing? I miss Brooke. Just like you, I miss her bad. But I can't help what happened. I can't bring her back. I wish I could. I wish I could trade places with her. Darla needs her mother. But that's out of my hands now. And so is what you think of me."

Tori walked over to Darla, who had a paper in her hand. Tori took it from her and stared at the drawing. The black scribbled sky. Her mother hanging from the water tower. The two police officers in the distance, on the horizon.

Tori looked at Zoe and her shiny diamond nose stud. "I'm done with this," Tori said under her breath.

She grabbed her cell phone and dialed Brooke's number. She watched Zoe, expecting her pocket to ring.

A buzzing sound came from the principal's pants pocket.

"Principal Quinn?" Tori said and pushed toward him while RJ stepped behind him. Tori held up her phone as it rang Brooke's number. "You've got the missing cell phone?"

He looked down at his pants. "What? No."

"You've got Brooke's cell phone." She stepped closer and held up her phone as it rang Brooke's number. "You've been sending me the text messages."

"No, it-it's not what you think ...." He pulled the ringing phone from his pocket and silenced it. He took a step backwards.

Tori pressed her index finger in his chest. "Why have you been texting me from Brooke's cell?"

Mike stepped beside her. "I'd like an answer to that question myself."

The crowd grumbled, asking "Why?" and "Did you really text all of us?" and "Was this all a show?"

"Wait! Wait a second!" Zoe raised her arms and moved to the principal's side. "Tori was right. I sent the text messages."

"I knew it!" Tori whistled and snapped her fingers, turning to Mike. "You see ... I told you. I told you she had Brooke's cell and was sending me all those messages." She paused, thinking about it a moment, and turned to Zoe and Principal Quinn. "Why'd you do that?"

"I had to get you all here," she said.

"But why?" Winnie brought a hand to the bandage above her eye as if it bothered her. A trickle of blood dripped down the side of her head and she wiped it away. "Why would you do that to us all?"

"I wanted you to know the truth," Zoe said. "I needed to tell you what happened."

"So, this whole séance was a farce?" Charlotte asked. She looked at Winnie. "You see, proper seances have to be done at night."

"Why?" Tori asked. "All the messages and the theatrics? Why pretend to be communicating with Brooke?"

Leonard got to his feet and said, "Did you see what happened to my daughter or didn't you?"

"Yes," Zoe replied, wiping her eyes. "I'm sorry ... I wasn't trying to deceive anyone, but it was the only way I could tell all of you what I saw." She looked over at the principal. He shook his head at her. She looked back at Tori. "I couldn't tell you myself. I was trying to tell you without ... without—"

"Without revealing our relationship" The principal placed a hand on Zoe's shoulder. "It's alright. Go ahead and tell them. I'm not letting you go through this alone."

"Your relationship?" Mike asked.

Edison snapped a picture and said, "Oh, this is good stuff!"

The principal raised an arm to hide his face.

"That makes sense. It makes sense now." Tori looked at Darla's drawing—the stick figures in the distance, on the horizon—and said to Zoe and the principal, "Darla hasn't been drawing two deputies. She was drawing the two of you. You were here that night. You saw Brooke's murder."

"I wanted to tell you what happened," Zoe said. She looked at Mike and Deputy Torres with teary eyes. "I wanted to tell all of you, but I couldn't explain what we were doing here that night."

The principal put an arm around her. "She was protecting me."

"She's your student," Mike said.

Zoe took the principal's hand. "I-I wanted to come forward with what we saw ... but if I did, I knew Principal Quinn would get in trouble. People wouldn't understand."

"In trouble?" Mike said. "You're underage. He's going to jail."

"It just happened." Principal Quinn withdrew his hand from Zoe's and raised both arms as if surrendering. "It was a one-time thing. A mistake."

"It wasn't a mistake," Zoe said, grasping for his arm again. He backed away from her, which brought her to tears again. "Please...you love me."

He looked down at her. "Zoe, you gotta understand."

She shook her head at him. "Say it! You love me."

Tori stepped between them. "Regardless of not wanting to expose your tryst, why the cryptic messages?" She put a hand on Zoe's shoulder, leading her away as Deputy Torres took hold of Principal Quinn and placed his arms behind his back. Tori walked Zoe toward Mike. "Why not give it to me straight in the text messages?"

"I-I didn't want you to trace it back to us," Zoe said, sniffling and wiping the back of her hand across her eyes. "If I said too much, I knew you'd know it was someone at the police station. You were already suspicious of Deputy Torres. But if I gave you a mystery, you'd figure it out."

Tori stopped. "But why did you keep texting me *Whatever I am, you made me*? What does it mean?"

"I don't know," Zoe said. "It looked like her suicide note. I found it in the box of Brooke's belongings."

"So, you don't know what it means?"

"Like I said, I knew it would get you here," she said. "Ash wrote it, not me. He pinned it on her shirt when he killed her."

"Maybe we'd better not stay for this," Veronica said, her voice quiet, her eyes lowered. She took Leonard's hand and pulled him forward.

The elderly man broke free of her grip. "No, I want hear what happened to my daughter."

"Oh, this is good," Edison said again, and snapped another photo. "Front-page headline in the morning!"

RJ grabbed the camera from his hands, breaking the snap. "That's enough photos. You got your story." He held the camera away from Edison and looked over at Tori.

She nodded and turned to Zoe. "Go on. Tell us what you saw."

Zoe pointed toward the lake in the distance. "We were lying on the bank, watching the stars ..." Her head turned toward the orange grove and then upwards. "We saw Brooke run out of the trees and climb up the water tower. She was screaming for Darla. Ash was waiting for her up there, and he flipped her over the railing. She had a noose tied around her neck and he hung her."

The principal, handcuffed and in the deputy's custody, called over to them. "We don't know that it was Ash."

Pastor Fields agreed. "That's right. Ash wasn't even here when Brooke died."

"Yes, we do," Zoe said, her voice raised, agitation building. "Ash murdered her."

The principal turned toward the deputy then over at Mike. "We couldn't get a good look."

"I did." Zoe pushed away from Tori and approached the principal. "I know what I saw."

"You know what you think you saw. But it was too dark."

"He killed her." Zoe was screaming now. She pointed at Ash. "He killed Brooke and strung her up in the water tower."

Leonard trembled and leaned on his cane. "Ash murdered my daughter..." he said, his voice choked. Veronica placed a hand on his back.

Ash shook his head. "No, I didn't."

Pastor Fields moved closer to Ash, as if ready to protect him from the mob. "He wasn't even here that night. I can vouch for his whereabouts."

Principal Quinn laughed. "Because you were with him when he spray-painted graffiti all over the school halls."

"And he cut the limb that crashed into my greenhouse," Charlotte said. "You almost killed me."

"Ash didn't cut that limb. It came a lot closer to falling on Darla than you," Winnie yelled back at her. "And Ash wouldn't have done anything to hurt his own daughter."

Mike waved his arms to silence the crowd and then turned to Ash. "I'm gonna have to ask you to come with me."

"I'm not going nowhere."

Mike took a step toward him, reaching for the handcuffs clipped to his belt. "Under the circumstances, I'm afraid you don't have a choice."

Deputy Torres stepped next to Ash and grabbed hold of his left arm.

Ash swung free of the deputy's grip and stumbled backwards. He yelled, "You are not pinning this on me!" In one swift motion he scooped Darla into his arms and took another step back.

"Ash, we need to talk this through." Mike inched toward him with the cuffs in hand.

"I ain't got nothin' to say to you."

"Take your pick," Mike said. "We can talk about the sawed branch that crashed into the greenhouse or the vandalism at the school. And we searched your house."

Ash shook his head, turned, with Darla in his arms, and ran into the grove. Mike and Deputy Torres took off after him. Tori and RJ exchanged a glance and ran after Mike and the deputy.

Pushing through the dead orange trees, Tori kept up with RJ and shuffled past him as they came out the other side. She stopped at the driveway. Ash's truck was backing up, spitting gravel. Mike and the deputy scrambled to their squad cars. Tori shot over to the sheriff's car, opened the passenger door, and jumped in.

"You're not coming," Mike yelled at her as he turned the ignition.

She slammed the door shut and buckled her seatbelt. "Drive."

He flipped on the lights and siren and pulled out of the driveway. Tori looked out the back window. The deputy's squad car followed.

Turning onto Clay Pit Road, Mike accelerated, speeding down the two-lane road after Ash's truck. The black Chevy looked a solid eighty, ninety yards ahead.

Tori turned to Mike. His face looked flush, a blue vein protruded from his neck. "Your blood pressure is going up."

"I'm fine," he said through clenched teeth.

"No, you're not." She could see the green number on the speedometer. They were going sixty-five. Seventy. Seventy-five. "You need to slow down."

Mike didn't answer. Ahead, an old pickup truck pulling out of a farmhouse driveway swerved onto the shoulder to avoid hitting them. Tori gasped and grabbed the dashboard.

Ash's truck passed a mail truck. Mike came up on it fast. The speedometer needle dropped. Sixty-five. Sixty. Fifty-five. The sirens blared. He honked. The mail truck didn't move over. Cussing, he crossed into the oncoming traffic lane and sped ahead of the mail truck. Veering to the right, he sped up.

The black Chevy was even farther down the road, approaching the train tracks. Tori heard a train whistle.

"You've got to slow down." She glanced at the speedometer. Seventy-five. Eighty. Eighty-five.

"Pete Alexander, 2,198 strikeouts, 2.56 ERA." Mike gripped the steering wheel. The squad car sped up. "Bob Gibson, 3,117 strikeouts, 2.91 ERA."

In front of them, Ash's truck jumped the railroad tracks as the lights on the crossing gates lit up. Bells clanged.

"Slow down. Now," Tori screamed, her voice strained.

The train whistle grew louder.

She looked at Mike, at the approaching gate arms and flashing lights, back at Mike. "We're not going to make it."

"Eddie Plank, 2,246 strikeouts, 2.35 ERA," Mike muttered, and gunned the squad car toward the crossing. The gate arms were dropping. "Bob Feller, 2,581 strikeouts, 3.25 ERA."

She saw the train now. Racing toward them.

The bells rang faster. Lights flashed.

They rumbled over the tracks and the gate arms dropped. One struck the back of the squad car. She let out a breath as the train rushed past, behind them. The sheer speed rocked the car.

Mike sped forward, catching up to Ash's truck.

"You okay?" he asked, without taking his eyes off the road. The clanging bells faded behind them.

Tori stared straight ahead, eyes wide, mouth open. She didn't answer. Both hands gripped the dashboard.

In the distance they spotted the bridge over Twin Lakes. Ash's Chevy raced toward it. Mike came up on his tailgate.

She glanced at Mike and the speedometer. Seventy. Seventy-five. Eighty. "He's headed for the bridge," she said.

He nodded. Their speed increased.

She couldn't take her eyes off the numbers. Eighty-five. Ninety. She looked back at the bridge. "Ash is gonna turn."

He nodded, accelerating even more. "Clayton Kershaw, 2,275 strikeouts, 2.39 ERA."

"Ash isn't slowing down." Now Tori didn't dare look at the speedometer. They were coming to the bridge. "He's got Darla in there."

A green sedan was crossing the bridge, slowing at the stop sign.

Ash's truck turned.

The sedan rolled to a stop.

The large truck tires screeched. Brakes smoked.

Bouncing up on the bridge entrance, the truck snagged the sedan's bumper, spinning the little car into the street.

Ash lost control and the truck hit the railing, recoiling into the air. Balanced on two wheels, it teetered for a second and dropped onto its side. An earsplitting crash of metal twisting on pavement echoed across the lake.

Tori screamed.

The sheriff's car screeched to a sideways stop, blocking the narrow bridge.

Tori snapped around to see the truck's doors pop open. Ash climbed out, carrying Darla in his arms. He staggered, his head bleeding, and he set Darla on the ground. He fell, motionless, beside her.

Mike was out of the squad car just as fast. Tori ran behind him.

She approached Ash and Darla. Embracing the little girl, she checked her arms and legs. There was a cut on her face. Other than that, she looked okay.

Behind her, Mike dragged Ash to his feet and frisked him. He placed handcuffs around Ash's wrists.

Tori stood and took Darla's hand. The little girl gripped her fingers, looking up at her with wide eyes. Tori gave her a feeble smile. Turning, she squinted as the deputy's squad car approached, blue lights flashing, sirens blaring. It stopped at the bridge entrance.

Behind it, a caravan of cars—Winnie's station wagon, the pastor's church bus, the mayor's Cadillac, and the others from Brooke's front yard—parked, and the passengers got out. They crowded around the deputy at the bridge entrance.

Tori watched Mike position Ash face down on the pavement with his hands behind his back. She couldn't tell how bad he was hurt, but blood gushed from his head. Somewhere in the distance, the approaching wail of an ambulance grew louder, and Tori held Darla tight in her arms, waiting for it to arrive.

CHAPTER TWENTY-EIGHT

CONS_QU_NC_S

Tori let out a long breath. It was done. Now she could go home and sleep, which was the only thing in the world she wanted. They'd picked up the Jeep from the mechanic's shop, and RJ cranked up Justin Timberlake as they headed out of Elroy Springs. She glanced at him behind the steering wheel and turned up the AC. The afternoon was going to be a scorcher. If he could do seventy all the way back, they might get home by three thirty. Hopefully, there wouldn't be any speed traps to worry about.

RJ sped along Clay Pit Road. As they came to the narrow bridge stretched over the lake, neither felt a need to speak. Tori stared out the window. Yellow tape stretched across the gap in the railing where Ash's truck had slammed into it. Orange cones remained in front of the bent and twisted metal.

While clearing his throat, RJ turned down the music. "We did a good job," he said. "We followed up on leads. Investigated clues. Learned a few life lessons. Found bravery. Vanquished evil."

"We don't have anything to brag about," she said, and stared out the window, watching the sun glint off the water between the metal bridge rails. "Ash didn't murder Brooke."

RJ glanced at her. As they crossed the bridge and exited onto the mainland, they passed the billboard advertising Sneaky Pete's.

He snapped his fingers and pointed at it. "I still want to try that gator tail."

Tori shifted in her seat. "I think we should just get out of here."

He brought the Jeep to a crawl and paused at the fork. Turn left and they'd head back to the interstate. Right would take them to Frostproof.

He looked over at her. "It's the best in the county, you know."

She remained cool, frowning. "Drop it."

"We still gotta eat."

"I said drop it."

Half an hour later, Tori and RJ sat at a table in Sneaky Pete's, overlooking the lake. They were the only customers in the bar and grill. Mounted bass and fishing equipment decorated the walls. A large bulletin board near the cash register overflowed with dozens of photographs pinned onto it.

After a couple of minutes, a friendly waitress chewing a large wad of gum approached the table, and Tori smiled at her.

"I know we're a little late for lunch," Tori said.

"It's all good." The girl set menus on the table. "It'll get busy soon with the dinner crowd."

RJ grinned at the server. "So, how's the gator tail?"

"Best in the county." The server smacked her gum and winked at him. "You want me to put in an order for you?"

Tori opened the menu and set it down in front of her. "So, I heard there was quite a commotion here a few weeks ago."

RJ kicked her shin under the table. "ixNay on the ookeBray's urdermay investigationyay"

The server looked at RJ then at Tori, puzzled. "What do you mean?"

Tori shifted in her chair, moving her leg away from RJ's strike zone. "I heard there was a husband who caught his wife on a date with another man. They got into a fight and tore up the restaurant."

RJ put his head in his hands and sighed.

The server's mouth twitched with amusement. "Oh, that. I think that's a little bit of an exaggeration."

"There wasn't a gunfight?" Tori asked.

"A gunfight?" The server laughed. "Oh, nothing that crazy. There was a woman waiting for someone and her husband showed up and started yelling at her. It happened right over there." She pointed to a booth in the back of the restaurant.

Tori turned to follow the server's direction. The booth looked private enough. It could disappear in a crowded restaurant. Did Ash catch Brooke there? And who was she with? She looked back at the server. "What was he yelling at her about?"

"Oh, my stars, he was ranting and carrying on. Accusing her of being unfaithful and meeting a boyfriend."

"Was she?"

The server considered the question for a moment. "She was waiting for someone. She said she was. But whoever he was, he never showed. He probably saw her husband here and ducked out real quick."

RJ perked up and craned his neck to look at the empty booth in the back. "So, Brooke had some secret rendezvous," he said.

"I guess." The server winked at RJ and smiled, clearly finding this tidbit of juicy gossip titillating. "Her husband thought so. He was demanding to know who. She wouldn't say, and he exploded. He got so angry that the law was called and carted him away."

Tori stared at the booth, imagining the events in her head.

Finally, the server took their order. Ten minutes later, a salad with grilled chicken, burger, fries, and a large basket of breaded gator tail arrived, along with the dinner crowd, as predicted.

RJ picked up a crunchy strip of gator tail and popped it into his mouth. He shut his eyes and made a low moaning sound, as if it was the best he'd ever had. Tori picked at her salad. She kept looking at the booth across the room.

In a low tone, she said, "Something doesn't make sense here."

RJ grabbed another strip. "I don't like the sound of that."

"I'm serious. Something is off."

"Don't go there." He put down his fork. "A lot of things don't make sense. Why are pizza boxes square? Why do we press harder on the remote when the batteries are dying? Why do cartoon characters wear the same clothes in every episode?"

A smirk tipped the corners of her mouth. She couldn't ignore that cynical inner voice. "The sheriff showed up here to break up the fight. The sheriff, right?"

"Yeah. So?"

"Why would the sheriff of Elroy Springs come all the way out here, to Frostproof? Why wouldn't the local police have come out?"

"I don't know. He was in the area?"

"Bingo." She snapped her finger for added effect. "He was in the area—as in, he was the mystery man Brooke was meeting."

RJ's expression stilled and grew serious. "You're playing Hangman again."

She wasn't sure she heard him. "What?"

"You know, the word game."

"I know what it is. What's your point?"

"My point is, you're out of letters. Your little stick figure is dead and hanging. But you're still guessing. The game's over. You lost."

"No, there's still one letter left." She leaned across the table, speaking fast as her mind organized the details. "Brooke was meeting with the sheriff—or was going to, then Ash showed up. When the sheriff got here, he broke up the argument."

RJ picked up another strip of gator tail and spoke as he chewed. "Even if that were true, what does it have to do with Brooke's murder? It doesn't change anything."

"The principal wasn't having an affair with Brooke. He was sneaking around with Zoe. So, Brooke wasn't rendezvousing with the principal, she was waiting for the sheriff."

"Still, Ash knew she was steppin' out with *someone* and killed her for it," RJ said. "Whether it was the principal or the sheriff or her mailman is irrelevant. Ash still murdered her." He shook his head and got up from the table. He headed for the cash register.

Tori watched him pull his wallet from his back pocket and hand the cashier a twenty. Turning, she looked back at the booth where Brooke had been sitting. Tori could almost see Brooke sitting there, waiting.

Dismissing it, she got up and headed for the ladies' room. Inside, she leaned across a sink with antiquated fixtures, toward her reflection, to refresh her coral lipstick. Her cell phone rang. She glanced at the unknown number and answered it.

"You've left town?" came a familiar voice over the line.

"Zoe?" Tori's voice echoed off the tiles in the small room. "What do you want?"

"I'm sorry for the ruse and I know I should've said something sooner but put yourself in my position."

"It doesn't matter."

"Yes, it does." Zoe's sounded weak, almost frightened. "And Principal Quinn is right. It was too dark for us to see what happened at the water tower."

"You pointed the finger at Ash." Tori's voice grew louder, angrier. "You said you witnessed him murder his wife."

"I was wrong."

Tori couldn't believe what she was hearing. "Ash is in jail because of you. Darla has lost both her parents because of you.".

"You're right. And I believed that last night, but I found something yesterday while RJ and I were in his house. I didn't think about it at the time, but then I realized it today."

"You realized what?"

"It wasn't Ash who was there that night at the water tower, it was someone else." Zoe's voice trembled.

"Who?" Tori held her breath.

The bathroom door banged open. About to protest the interruption, Tori looked up from the sink to see, not a woman, but RJ. He shut the door.

"What are you waiting for, Christmas?" he said. "We gotta get on the road."

Her eyes met his in the mirror and she mouthed the word "Zoe." Tori turned her attention to the phone. "So, who murdered Brooke?"

"I-I c-can't say. ... Not here. Not over the phone."

"Did you go to the sheriff?"

"I can't go to Sheriff Bennett."

"Why not?"

"Look, I need to show you something. Once you see it, you'll understand."

Tori glanced at her reflection in the mirror. Her lips puckered with annoyance. "I'm not playing this game any-more."

"I'm serious."

"What is it you have to show me?"

"I can't show you over the phone."

RJ approached her. He held her gaze in the mirror above the sink. "C'mon, we gotta go."

She turned away from him and spoke into the phone. "Why not?"

"I need to show you ... in person ... at the Martin house."

"What?"

"I can't talk over the phone about it." Zoe sounded panicked and her words rushed out with a flood of emotion. "Just meet me there. You'll see."

"We've already left town. We're on our way back to Tampa."

"Turn around. Please."

A woman opened the restroom door. She looked confused to see RJ and Tori by the sinks. RJ waved her inside as Tori turned away from them to concentrate.

"Where are you?" she said into her phone.

"I'm at the Martin house. Waiting."

"Okay. I'll be there."

The surprised woman slipped into a stall and shut the door.

Tori said, "Hang tight, Zoe. I'll be back there as soon as I can." She hung up and looked at RJ. "We have to go back."

He raised his hands. "Oh no, we don't. We'll lose our jobs."

"This is too important." She rushed past him and out of the ladies' room. She headed for the Jeep. Moments later, he raced out the restaurant behind her. She ran faster.

Getting to the Jeep first, Tori opened the driver's side door and hopped behind the wheel. She yelled at him to climb in.

He opened the driver's-side door.

"The Fourth of July is in a day away, and we have to cover the boat show," he said, motioning for her to relinquish the seat. "We can't go back."

"Ash is in jail for a murder he didn't commit." Tori pulled the handle, but RJ held tight. She struggled to close the door, speaking through clenched teeth. "We owe it … to him … to uncover … the truth."

"We owe it … to ourselves … to keep our jobs." RJ pulled on the door handle, straining. "Pittman will … fire us … if we're not … on site … tomorrow morning … to cover … the boat show."

"This is … bigger … than … our jobs." She gripped the door with both hands. She fought to close it; he fought to keep it open.

"Simone Adams … is already … covering all this… Let it … go." He pulled harder and the door whipped toward him.

She pulled it back toward her, almost getting it to close. "She's moving … in the wrong … direction."

"What … are you … going … to … do?" He gripped the door handle with both hands now, prying it open. "Interview Zoe … Put your own … report together … Pittman will … never … air it."

"Then … I'll … write … a … book." Their tug-of-war took its toll and she lost her hold. The door swung open, flipping her out of the Jeep and onto the pavement. The sudden release flung RJ backwards like a snapped rubber band and he tumbled, landing on his butt. Looking over at him lying on the concrete, she raised herself to her hands and knees. She breathed heavily as she spoke. "I'll write a book. You said I would make a good true crime author. This is it. This is the opportunity."

"Life doesn't work that way."

RJ sat up and got to his feet. He dusted off his backside before stretching a hand toward Tori. She took it and he helped her to her feet.

"Why not?" She looked down at her dirty knees and then at the dirt and gravel on her palms. She rubbed her hands together while saying, "We need to go after what we want. Stop settling. You said that. Remember?" She shot him a side glance. He was inspecting the Jeep door and she wasn't sure if he was even listening. She caught her breath, and a surprising confidence filled her voice as she said, "If you want to be this great paranormal investigator and YouTube star, then let's do it."

He straightened and shot her a long, thoughtful stare, as if her words had resonated with some inner ambition locked away in his heart. His eyes brightened and he opened his mouth, and then closed it. Shaking his head, he told her, "Maybe that could happen in some perfect world where there's no global warming, teachers make as much as NBA players, and radio stations never play Mariah Carey," he said. "But unfortunately, that's not the world we live in."

Tori leaned toward him, balling her right fist and planting it with a smack in her left hand. "It's now or never. Ash needs us. Darla needs us. The truth needs us."

"You're out of letters, Tori. Don't you get it?" He let out a defeated laugh and stepped back. Turning away from her, he ran his hands through his hair and flipped back around. "Don't you get it? You're out of letters. The game's over."

Tori chewed her bottom lip, shaking her head. "No, it's not."

He pointed at the lake behind the restaurant, in the

general direction of Elroy Springs, and said, almost under his breath, "If you go back there, I'm not going with you."

She paused. Her hands dropped to her sides. "What?"

"I'm not going with you," he repeated, a little louder, with more strength behind his words. "You're throwing your career away. I can't do that."

Tori released a long breath. She turned toward the Jeep and walked around the back bumper. "You're right. And I can't ask you to do that. I'll call a ride. I'll hitchhike if I have to."

"Tori—" He followed her around the Jeep.

"RJ, I have to do this." She opened the passenger door and gripped the handle. She paused, and then turned to him. "Have I ever told you about the book, *Made Up for Murder*?"

"No, and don't even go there." RJ raised his arms in self-defense. "I don't want to hear about how another true crime book compares to everything going on here."

"Okay. ... Okay. Then let's talk about *The X-Files*."

"Oh, don't you bring *The X-Files* into this, either."

She leaned against the side of the Jeep, next to the open door. "Remember that episode where the toddler is killed by some evil entity, and everyone thinks it's the superstitious, old-world witch of a grandmother who conjured it up?"

He raised an eyebrow in amused contempt. "And your point?"

"The old witch of a grandma was the obvious suspect, but everyone was wrong. She was conjuring up a protection spell and was trying to protect the family. It was the spirit of the kid's twin brother who murdered the toddler." She paused, watching his expression. She looked for some hint of understanding. When she saw none, she continued. "Everybody is wrong here too. Ash is being blamed, but he didn't do it."

"Or maybe," RJ said, "it's like *Her Last Breath* and the husband staged a suicide to cover up an accidental murder. But at the end of the book, he still murdered his wife."

Unblinking, Tori considered his point.

She stepped toward him and hugged him. His arms encircled her, one hand on the small of her back. She buried her face against his chest. When she released him, she stepped away and fished her suitcase from the backseat and her black sleeveless dress hanging from the roll bar.

"Just so you know," he said, his voice a little hoarse with emotion, "you're throwing your career away."

Tori blinked her watering eyes and, holding her luggage handle with two hands, the black dress draped over like some kind of empty body bag, said, "What career? I'm a joke there."

"You're throwing everything away. You're throwing me away." RJ smiled sadly and shook his head to fight away tears. "And you know what the real kicker is? I can't figure out if you're scorned and want to get even or if you're desperate for Mike's attention. Either way, you're hung up on him."

Tori bit her lower lip. "I don't know what to tell you. This isn't about the sheriff—"

"Mike—" RJ said.

"It's about clearing Ash's name. It's about exposing the truth."

"I know." He touched her cheek.

He leaned down, kissed her hard, gave her a wink, and walked around the front of the Jeep. He hopped into the driver's seat and started the engine. Stunned, Tori watched the taillights blaze red when he reached the end of the parking lot. Turning left, he stuck his arm out the open window and waved. Then he was gone.

Tori looked away. She didn't want him to leave, but she couldn't think of that now. She had more pressing matters at hand. Zoe was waiting.

Ash was waiting.

Mike was waiting.

Tori watched the woman from the ladies' room come out of the restaurant and head for a parked semi. Smiling, Tori approached the woman and asked if she was headed toward Elroy Springs.

CHAPTER TWENTY-NINE

DARKES_ NIGH_

The semi dropped Tori off at the Martin house. As it drove away, her eyes searched the woods and the dead, gray orange trees. The water tower stood like a skyscraper on the horizon. A yellow VW Bug sat parked in the drive beside Brooke's lonely minivan.

The house stood dark. "MURDERER," spray-painted in angry red letters, splashed across the front door. Egg yolk coated the windows and stained the front porch. The bench swing to her left hung motionless. She found the front door unlocked and it creaked open.

The entry hall was dark despite the late afternoon light spilling through the wide windows. A heavy silence blanketed the interior.

"Zoe?" she called out. Her voice echoed, but no one answered.

Everything around her seemed wrong, as if she could feel someone hiding in the shadows, watching her. She stepped into the entry hall and shut the door behind her. The broken vase and dead lilies lay scattered near the narrow table at her side. The heavy emotion of the argument that took place here still lingered. Was that movement in the living room ahead? Or were her eyes playing tricks on her? She turned on a light and called for Zoe again.

The dining room to the right felt muted, hollow. An empty table in the center of the room looked off, as though something—even a bowl of plastic fruit—should've been there to create the illusion of warmth. The whole effect made Tori shiver, compounding the unnatural silence surrounding her.

Stepping cautiously, she walked into the kitchen. Her footsteps sounded like a funeral drum beat on the tile flooring. Finding it empty, she returned to the dining room, passing the marred wall where shattered glass and liquor had stained the drywall. She moved through the front hall and entered the darkened living room. She flipped on another light and looked around. The room was empty. The couch and recliner sat bare in front of the dark large-screen television. Ash's hunting rifles no longer hung on the wall, but the racks were still there.

"Zoe?" Tori called out, softer than before, as if she could feel someone hidden beyond a corner, watching her every move.

A faint plop hit the floor and she whipped around to see what had made the sound. She saw nothing. She took another step forward. A small puddle pooled on the hard wood. She bent down and touched the water. Another drip hit her shoulder. She lifted her head. A circular spot darkened the ceiling. Another drop of water fell from the stain and landed in the puddle at her feet.

"Zoe," she said under her breath, and headed back into the entry hall. She made her way up the staircase, her tennis shoes squeaking. Upstairs, on the second-floor landing, she flipped on the lights. All the bedroom doors were shut. Ash and Brooke's bedroom, to her left, would've been directly over the living room. The water had to be coming from the master bath.

Opening the door, she entered the bedroom. The door to the bathroom was closed and lined in light. She opened it.

Water pooled on the tile floor. The bath faucet was running, spilling water over the edge. A clothed body lay face down in the water, the black hair floating on the surface, a tattooed arm slung over the side.

"Zoe!" Tori rushed to the tub and pulled her from the water. Her body flipped over the edge and flopped onto the floor. Tori checked for a pulse and placed her ear close to Zoe's mouth. Rising, Tori placed her hands on Zoe's chest and pushed several times, and then listened for breathing again. Nothing. She pressed down on Zoe's chest several more times. Zoe coughed and stirred.

Tori let out a breath and fell backwards. The flooded floor drenched the seat of her pants and legs. Looking up, she noticed a message scrawled in red lipstick on the vanity mirror: *Forgive me. I can't live without him.*

She looked down at Zoe. Lying face up, she still gurgled water from her mouth.

Tori turned to the tub. She turned off the faucet and noticed something shiny at the bottom of the tub. She reached into the water and grasped it. Her fingers touched a ring and she pulled it out of the water, holding it close to her face.

A gold wedding band.

Was this what Zoe wanted to show her?

The bathroom door slammed shut, and Tori recoiled from the tub, startled. Something fell against the outside of the door with a hard thud. She got to her feet and rushed to it. The handle turned, but the door wouldn't budge. She was struggling with it when the piercing scream of a smoke detector stopped her heart. She banged on the door and ran to the window. It wouldn't open.

She looked back at Zoe, who was lying crumpled on the floor in a pool of water.

They were trapped. The smell of smoke filled her nostrils.

Tori looked around, thinking. She pulled the metal toilet paper holder from the side of the cabinet and hit it against the door. She hammered and smashed a hole in the wood. Fitting an arm through it, she felt around the other side. Her fingers grazed the back of a chair. Pressed beneath the handle, it blocked the door. She slipped her arm out of the hole and looked through it. A yellowish-orange light flickered in the bedroom. She pushed her arm through the hole and pressed against the back of the chair. It wouldn't move. She pushed harder. The chair wobbled. She screamed, forcing all her strength through the one arm. The chair fell forward. The door jolted free.

She pulled her arm from the door and turned. Zoe had not moved. Tori leaned down and lifted the girl to her feet. Together, they stumbled through the bedroom. The hallway erupted in flames. Smoke stung Tori's eyes, burned her nostrils. They moved toward the staircase while flames reached for them.

She held her breath. Holding Zoe's arm, she pulled her back into the bedroom and slammed the door shut. She ripped the comforter from the bed and dragged it into the bathroom. After drenching it in the tub, she wrapped it around herself. Returning to the bedroom, she found Zoe and pulled her under the protective cover.

They stepped back into the hallway. Smoke filled the area. They headed for the staircase and made their way downstairs. She felt the heat through the thick fabric. They made it to the front door and out to the porch.

Zoe fell onto the gravel driveway. Her eyes still shut, she whispered, "Darla."

Tori looked at her. "What?"

"Darla," she said again. "Inside."

Tori looked back at the house. She heard screams from the second story. Then several loud bangs. Darla was in the window, banging on the glass.

Covered in the sopping comforter, Tori hurried into the house. Fire consumed the entire upstairs landing. Darla's screams rang out over the crackle of the flames. Wrapping the comforter tighter over her shoulders, Tori rushed up the staircase.

The fire had not yet reached Darla's room. Tori pushed on the door. It wouldn't budge. She kicked it. Forced it open. Rushed into the bedroom. She hugged Darla and pulled her under the comforter.

Tori used her foot to slam the door shut behind her, shielding them from the crackling heat on the other side.

"Lie down on the floor," she said. "Stay as low as you can."

They dropped to the worn carpet. It felt warm against her arms as she crawled to the window. Tori pressed against the glass, struggled to raise it. They could crawl out onto the roof and over the front porch. The window wouldn't open. Was it locked? Smoke filled the room—and her lungs.

She picked up the rocking horse and smashed it against the glass. The wooden horse splintered into two pieces, cracking the glass. She held the rocker by a single blade and hit the window pane again, harder. The wood broke apart in her hand.

A deafening crash roared around them. Darla screamed. Tori turned as the bedroom door along with a section of the wall fell. The roof over the stairway caved in, dumping an avalanche of white and orange embers into the burning hallway. The heat became unbearable.

Tori held Darla as a figure appeared in the bedroom window. The glass shattered. A hand reached into the room.

Tori looked into Mike's face. Flames reflected in his eyes.

She scooped Darla up in one swift motion and lifted her toward the window, into Mike's arms. He carried her through the window frame and disappeared. Tori looked back. The heat suffocated her.

A roaring blaze surged across the ceiling into the bedroom. Beneath a boiling sea of flames, the gray plush elephant lay on the floor, as if calling to her. The edges of its ears were seared. She ran to it. Bent down. Grasped it.

Coughing, she fell to her knees. Crawling, about to pass out, she reached for the window. Two strong hands gripped her arms and lifted her to her feet. "Sheriff?"

"Mike." He breathed into her ear. "It's Mike."

In the light of the burning room, she saw his boldly handsome face looking down on her as she lost consciousness.

CHAPTER THIRTY

B_FOR_ I WAK_

Tuesday, July 3

Tori opened her eyes and looked around. She blinked, trying to focus, before wincing. Her head pounded.

Mike stood over her, at the edge of the bed, and his voice startled her. "Good morning, Sleeping Beauty." He took hold of her hand. "How you feel?"

She rubbed her temples. "I think I'm okay. ... Where am I?"

"You're at the hospital," he said. "You inhaled a lot of smoke."

All the events of the past night came rushing back. Zoe's body floating in the bathtub. The fire at the Martin house. Darla. Mike's hand reaching out toward her before she lost consciousness. She looked into his eyes. "You were there. You pulled me out of the fire." She struggled to sit up. Her head still felt foggy and she shook it, hoping to clear out the cobwebs.

He placed a hand on her shoulder, pushing her back against the soft pillow. "You need to take it easy," he said. "You want the nurse?"

She sat up and looked around the room. "Darla?"

"She's okay. She's in the children's ward."

"How'd she get there? At the house, I mean." Tori's voice cracked a little, her throat dry and itchy. "How does she keep getting back to her home? Who's taking her there?"

"I don't know." Mike leaned against the bed. "But don't worry about that now."

She stared at him for a moment. "Zoe?" she asked.

"She's in the ICU. She took a heavy dose of painkillers."

Tori shut her eyes and said, "They were both drugged, and someone set the house on fire." When she opened them, she stared at the white sheets on the bed. "Right is left. Up is down. Marvel is DC. Cats are dogs," she said under her breath.

Mike's brows drew together. "Come again?"

She looked up and forced a smile. "Nothing. Just something RJ said once."

"What were you doing there?"

"Zoe called me." Tori looked him square in the eyes. "She wanted to talk."

"She called you?"

"To talk about Ash. But when I found her ...." Her voice trailed off.

After a moment of silence, Mike placed a palm flat on top of the sheets next to her legs and leaned forward. "Do you have any idea what she wanted to tell you?"

He was close enough she could feel his hot breath on her cheek. "No," she said without looking at him.

"Well, then ... I'm glad you're okay." He didn't move, remaining close to her, his breath coming and going. "It looks like she attempted suicide."

"No. She didn't."

"Deputy Torres found a note she typed in her computer this morning."

"Deputy Torres?" She turned away without waiting for a reply. "Did he find a message scrawled on the bathroom mirror at the Martin house too? Zoe didn't write either."

"We're looking into it." He straightened his back and folded his arms across his chest. "She was embarrassed about the whole psychic thing and saying she was communicating with Brooke. She felt humiliated, and her relationship with the school principal was exposed."

"Where's the principal now?"

"He's in jail waiting for a bail hearing." His stern expression relaxed, and he gave her a quick smile. "I don't know about you, but I'm ready to put this whole thing behind me and move on."

"It's not even close to being over." Tori faced him again. Her voice rose as she spoke. "Zoe wanted to talk about Ash. She said she had proof he didn't murder Brooke. She had evidence."

"Zoe is a troubled teenager. She's unbalanced."

Tori thought about Sneaky Pete's and booth in the back. Was he meeting Brooke there? She wanted to know what they had going on, but she couldn't muster the courage to ask. The timing wasn't right. She felt too vulnerable. Too weak now to be confrontational. Instead, she asked, "Why do you keep doing that? You keep blocking me."

"I don't know what you mean."

"Sure, you don't." She pushed herself past him and wobbled out of the bed. Her body ached from lying in one position too long and her legs felt rubbery, as though they might collapse at any moment.

"What're you doing?" He grabbed her arm and held her steady. "You need to rest."

"I need to check on Darla." She placed a hand on the edge of the bed as he released her.

Mike stood in front of her, towering over her. "She's fine. There's nothing you can do for her right now."

"If you're not going to do anything, then I will." She stepped toward a white dresser across the room. Her clothes were folded on top of it, along with a worn paperback book. The cover read *Her Last Breath*, by Priscilla Prescott. She picked it up and turned to Mike.

He nodded. "I found a copy at the used bookstore downtown and read through it."

"And?"

"You were right. This whole mess with Brooke and Ash is very similar."

"I was wrong." Tori put down the book and picked up her clothes. They smelled of smoke. But what choice did she have? She needed to get out of here.

Holding her jeans, she felt something in the pocket. Her hand slipped into it and pulled out the gold wedding band. She held it in her palm. Looking back at Mike, she slipped the ring back into the pocket and said, "Excuse me. I need to change."

Mike said he'd wait for her in the hall. She changed clothes and left her hospital room. The long hallway was busy and crowded. She looked around and went to the nurses' station.

A heavyset woman behind the counter looked at her and said, "What are you doing up?"

"Where's the children's ward?"

"You need to get back to bed." The nurse came out from behind the counter.

Mike stepped beside her and placed a hand on her shoulder. "It's okay," he said. "She's with me."

The nurse shook her head. "Okay, sheriff. But she needs her rest."

Tori followed Mike to the elevators and the children's ward, two floors up. They found Darla in a room, sitting in bed, coloring. Leonard napped in a chair in the corner, and Veronica greeted them when they entered the room.

"How's she doing?" Tori asked.

"Better," Veronica said. "But the doctor wants to hold her for another day to be sure."

Tori approached the bed. She brushed a strand of hair from Darla's forehead. The little girl didn't respond.

When Tori left the room, Mike followed her down the hallway.

"Someone keeps taking her back to that house. Why?" she asked as they returned to the elevator.

"Don't worry about it," he said. "We're looking into it."

Tori stepped into the elevator. Mike stood beside her. When the doors shut, and they were finally alone, she glanced at him. It was now or never. She needed to know. Clearing her throat, she said, "We—RJ and I—stopped at Sneaky Pete's on the way out of town yesterday. I talked to the waitress and she told me about the fight you had to break up."

Mike chuckled. "This again?"

"No, listen. I want to know why they called you?"

"Ash was out of control. He was fighting with Brooke."

She detected a hint of censure in his tone, but that didn't stop her. She spoke slow for emphasis and so there would be no misunderstanding. "Why would a bar in Frostproof call the sheriff of Elroy Springs to break up a bar fight?"

He stared at her, saying nothing.

She continued as the elevator came to a stop. "What were you doing there? Were you supposed to meet Brooke?"

When the doors opened, a male voice called out Tori's name. Startled, she turned and stared at the white-haired, square-shouldered man standing in the hallway.

"Tori?" he said again. "Hey, you're Tori Younger, aren't you?"

She stepped out of the elevator. Then the realization struck her—the slim build, the shock of white hair, she'd seen this man in a photograph in Winnie's living room: Howard Daniels.

"He made it home last night," Winnie said, stepping beside him. A Band-Aid covered the cut above her eye now, but it didn't look too bad. She hugged Tori and gushed, "Thank God you're okay."

Tori looked over at Mike. Their conversation wasn't over, but there was little she could say in front of Winnie and Howard. She embraced Winnie, and then extended a hand toward Howard. "Pleased to meet you," she said.

He was not traditionally handsome, but he displayed an aura of unspoken self-assurance that contributed to his sales numbers and that a girl like Winnie might find appealing. He wore a dark blue sports jacket and tie, and a shock of white, slicked-back hair topped his large head.

"Tori Younger," he said, shaking her hand. He slipped her a business card. "I've heard a lot about you."

"I've heard a lot about you too." She read the card in her hand. *Howard T. Daniels, Senior Sales Professional, Mercer Brock Pharmaceuticals.* Glancing at his left hand still extended toward her, she noticed he wasn't wearing a wedding band.

The ring in her pocket pressed against her thigh.

She looked back at him. "I'm sorry you missed Brooke's funeral."

"Brooke was a fine woman." He nodded and looked down, a shadow of regret crossing his face. Affection and sympathy mingled in his tone. "She introduced Winne and me, you know."

"I heard," Tori said, looking back at the elevator. The doors had shut without Mike joining them. He'd left without saying 'goodbye.'

Winnie touched her shoulder, grabbing her attention. "Let's see about checking you out of here," she said. "You're coming home with us."

Tori rode in the station wagon's backseat, with the worn copy of *Her Last Breath* resting in her lap. Winnie sat up front next to Howard and picked at the Band-Aid above her eye. She never said a word as he drove and told them all about the ins and outs of pharmaceutical sales.

When they pulled up to the house, Tori could hear the barking all the way in the driveway. Four dogs—the cocker spaniel, the pug, the Chihuahua, and the Jack Russell terrier—greeted them in the kitchen when they entered through the back door. The pets were jumping and barking, and a snorting pot-bellied pig rubbed its head against Tori's leg.

"A pig? Seriously?" Tori asked, setting her purse on the table next to the boxes of plastic apples and bags of Tootsie Rolls and Jolly Ranchers.

"Her name is Bacon." Winnie bent over, greeting the pig. "The Dugans are leaving town for the holiday and will be back on Sunday."

Bacon looked up at Tori and snorted.

"Seriously?" Tori said again. "A pig?"

"They're like dogs." Winnie bent over and scratched Bacon on top its head, between the ears. "They make great pets."

She left the kitchen and went into the dining room, with the dogs leaping and barking at her legs. The pot-bellied pig trotted behind them.

Tori took a shower to wash the stench of smoke off her body and changed into some fresh clothes.

Winnie had baked chicken with broccoli for Howard, and heated a bowl of tomato soup for Tori, who wanted to eat light. Apologizing, Winnie served it on the crowded kitchen table, among the boxes of plastic apples. Tori made room for her steaming bowl, and Winnie opened a bag of Tootsie Rolls. A thunderstorm roared outside as they ate, and the four dogs and pig cowered under the table. The cocker spaniel maneuvered between Tori's legs and the pug sat on her feet.

Thunder crashed and lightning brightened the window with a brilliant flash. Unfazed, Winnie unwrapped a Tootsie Roll and was about to pop it into her mouth, when Howard slapped it out of her hand.

"Calories, calories, calories," he said in a mocking tone. Grabbing the bags from the table, he got up and carried them to the counter. Thunder boomed, rattling the windows, and the cocker spaniel jumped into Tori's lap. The Jack Russell howled.

Howard turned to glare at them. "And what's with all these dogs? We runnin' a kennel now?"

He picked up a dog food bowl in his right hand and the bottle of valerian root oil in his left. Tori noticed his ringless finger again.

Later that night, long after the storm had passed and left rising humidity in its wake, Tori retired to the guest bedroom upstairs. She dialed RJ, but he didn't answer. Frustrated, she climbed into bed.

The worn paperback of *Her Last Breath* lay were she'd discarded it on the nightstand. She picked it up. Of all the books Mike could've read, why'd he choose this one? She tossed it back onto the nightstand, next to the gold wedding band.

She picked up the wedding ring and thought about Howard. Had Winnie noticed? Could this be his ring? Was this what Zoe wanted to show her?

Tori's cell phone dinged, seizing her attention. She looked at the message. It was from Mike.

"We need to talk."

She texted him back, typing, "You ready to tell me what you were doing at Sneaky Petes?" The response returned a minute later.

"Unfinished business. Meet me at your old lake house."

Tori took Winnie's runabout and headed north on the lake. As she approached her old house, she found Mike standing on the dock.

"So, what's this unfinished business?" she asked, tying the boat to a thick post.

He approached and gave her a hand. His fingers were cool and smooth as they touched hers. "Thanks for meeting me. Let's go onshore."

She stepped onto the dock and let go of his hand. She kept her face noncommittal; if he wanted forgiveness, let him work a little harder for it. "And?"

"And …." He looked away. She followed his gaze to the boathouse above them. Beyond it, the rope hanging from the tree over the lake swayed gently in the wind. He noticed it too. "Sometimes I think about James Dean and the planetarium. I've never really been some place. You know what I mean?"

She considered it a second, and said, "You played in the minors. You traveled all over the country."

"Till they let me go. Damn heart." His breath came and went in no particular rhythm. "But I never left this place. Not really."

"And now you're having regrets?"

"And now I'm having regrets." He seemed to be waiting for her to comment, and when she didn't, he muttered to himself, "I guess it's funny how life works out."

"Sheriff." Tori cleared her throat and touched his arm. "Are you going to tell me what you were doing ay Sneaky Pete's?"

He paused, as if considering how to answer her question. "Are you going to tell me what you were doing at the Martin house?"

She smiled. She could play the game. "I was meeting Zoe. She called me and asked me to meet her there."

"And did she sound suicidal when you spoke to her?"

"No, but she said she wanted to show me something. She didn't say what, but I found a gold wedding band there, in the Martin house. I think it's her evidence."

"A wedding band?"

Tori nodded and removed it from her pocket. She handed it to him. "I think it belongs to Winnie's husband. I noticed he isn't wearing one."

He took it, studied it for a moment, and handed it back to her. "Or it's Ash's. He isn't wearing a wedding ring, either."

"But why would Zoe want to show me Ash's wedding ring?"

"Because Ash killed Brooke," he said. "He told me he took his ring off his finger and threw it at her the night she died. They fought and he was ready to leave her."

"No, there's something we're missing." She gripped the ring in her fist and shot him a penetrating glare. "Your turn. What were you doing at Sneaky Pete's?"

He stared at her unblinking, his eyes boring into her. His voice hardened. "You know what I was doing there. Ash was out of control. I had to break up—"

"Let me put it another way. Why were you seeing Brooke in secret?"

"That's crazy."

"Why would a bar in Frostproof call the sheriff in Elroy Springs to break up a bar fight? You were there because Brooke was waiting for you. Only, Ash showed up first."

"No!" He turned away from her.

She gripped his arm, forcing him to look at her. "Why did you call me here if you're not going to tell me the truth. You obviously want to. So, tell me. What happened that night?"

"You're right," he shot back, and took a deep breath. "Okay, you're right. Brooke and I were talking. But it's not what you think."

"You were seeing her."

"No, we weren't seeing each other."

"Then why were you meeting? Why were you sneaking around?'

"To talk! Just talk."

"About what?"

"About Darla." He looked down at the grass and back at her. "I'm her father."

His words stopped her cold. They stared at each other across a sudden ringing silence.

"Wh-at?" The word caught in her throat.

"I'm Darla's father." His eyes had turned red and watery. "Brooke wanted to tell Ash the truth. And tell Darla. That's what we were meeting about."

Tori's mouth dropped open. He was Darla's father? No. How? Why? She struggled with it. Her stomach was tight. The tension in her jaw returned. "All this time, you've been lying to me? And to the people of this town?"

"It's not what you think." His breath came out in a desperate rasp. "Brooke and I made a mistake once. It just happened. We weren't carrying on an affair for the last five years."

Five years. Five long, tumultuous years wondering why he'd left and why he didn't love her. And all that time, Brooke had known exactly what was going on. It couldn't be true. It was a joke. A mistake. An error.

Tori exhaled, still trying to wrap her head around this. "Brooke was a married woman. How do you know Darla is not Ash's child?"

"Because ..."—Mike turned to the lake— "Ash was in rehab. You and I were having problems before the wedding. Brooke and I got to talking one night, and it happened."

"Wait. Before our wedding?" Tori paced the ground in front of him. She stopped and said, "You left me because of Brooke?"

An arrested expression clouded his face as he spoke. He struggled to get this out. "Brooke told me she was pregnant.

She didn't want to leave Ash and wanted to raise the baby as his. It hit me hard and I ran away."

"You should've told me. We could've worked through this together."

"I didn't know what to do. I was confused. I panicked."

"You took our honeymoon tickets and ran. You took off to Cancun and met … met … What's her face there." Tori crossed her arms and waited.

Perspiration beaded on Mike's forehead. His face flushed, and she knew what that meant.

He shut his eyes and took a deep breath. "Sandy Koufax, 2,396 strikeouts, 2.76 ERA. Steve Carlton, 4,136 strikeouts," he mumbled, and lifted his left arm. His right hand gripped his left wrist, holding two fingers over his pulse.

"How you feeling?" Tori asked, knowing how utterly useless she was right now. "I think there's a bottle of water in the boat."

He stopped the recitation and opened his eyes. "I'm okay. It's passing."

"How bad is it?" she asked.

He looked away a moment, and back at her. "Look, Charlotte doesn't know about Darla and can't ever know about what happened between Brooke and me. She'll take the twins and leave me. The scandal will cost me my job."

"That's not what's important right now. You need to get your health under control. This job's too stressful. I was joking before about being a librarian, but—"

"It's not the job, it's the secrets," he said. "You can't keep that bottled up, or it'll eat you up inside."

* * * *

Wednesday, July 4

Tori woke early the next morning to voices carrying into her room from outside. Looking out the window, she found Winnie and Howard in front of the barn. Tori dressed and, within a few minutes, walked out the backdoor to see them.

The station wagon was backed into the barn, parked in front of the float. Howard leaned down, fixing the trailer to the hitch below the station wagon's rear bumper. Tori noticed his left hand again and his naked ring finger.

"Morning," she said, standing over him. His white head popped up over the bumper.

"You slept late," he said, fiddling with the red, white, and black brake light lines.

"Yesterday was a long day," she said. "Where's Winnie?"

"In the kitchen, I suppose." He never looked up.

She watched his hands attaching the wires. "You mind if I ask you a question?" She leaned down against the rear bumper, so she was level with his head.

He glanced at her and nodded and continued working.

One corner of her mouth twisted upwards. "Where's your wedding ring?"

He stopped and lifted his head. "My wedding ring?"

"I noticed you're not wearing it."

He raised his left hand. A pale tan line encircled his ring finger. "I lost it," he said. "In my hotel in Atlanta. The cleaning lady will contact me if they find it."

Tori felt the ring hidden in her pocket, brushing a hand across the lump it made in her jeans. Could this be his ring? And if so, why did Zoe have it? What was it doing at the Martin house? Or was Mike right and the ring belonged to Ash?

"Please don't tell Winnie," he said. "I don't think she's noticed yet."

"Don't tell Winnie what?" Winnie said, entering the barn with a steaming coffee mug. She handed the mug to Tori, and then took a step back and frowned. A fresh Band-Aid covered the cut above her eye. "You look terrible. How'd you sleep?"

Tori cupped the mug with both hands. "I slept fine. It's just going to take a couple of days to recuperate. How's your eye?"

"Could've been worse, all things considered." Winnie laughed and turned to her husband. "What is it you're not supposed to tell me?"

Howard stood and wiped his hands on his overalls. "There's a brake light out. I've got to replace it."

Tori leaned toward Winnie and whispered in her ear. "We need to talk. I need to tell you something."

"Is everything okay?"

"Yes, it's just ...." She looked at Howard.

Winnie hesitated, and looked at her husband too. She asked him to give them a minute, and he begrudgingly obliged.

"I'll go find that brake light," he said.

Winnie yelled to him and told him to stop.

He halted and turned around, smiling. "Yes, dear?"

"The hotel in Atlanta called," she said. "They found your wedding band and are over-nighting it to you."

His smile vanished and he shook his head. Turning around, he headed for the house.

When they were alone, Tori touched Winnie's arm and led her past the float, deeper into the barn. "I need to talk to you about your brother."

"What is it? You're scaring me."

Tori leaned against the parade float. She thought of Darla. The fights between Brooke and Ash. Brooke's murder. Mike's secret.

Winnie placed a hand on Tori's shoulder. "What's going on with my brother?"

Tori said, "Mike told me something. Five years ago, before our wedding—"

"Let the fairy tale begin!" Charlotte sang out, interrupting them when she entered the barn. Dressed as Snow White, in a blue-and-yellow princess gown, she carried a box of red plastic apples. The twins stood on either side of her, dressed as Snow White's dwarves. "Don't we just look adorable?"

Tori looked from Winnie, to Charlotte and the twins. "You look great," she said. "I still don't get the connection to the Fourth of July, but you look great."

Charlotte squealed and raised a hand to her forehead, as if some traumatic memory resurfaced and caught her by surprise. "Oh, dear. You gave us quite a scare." She put down the apples and rushed to Tori, hugging her. "What happened?"

"I'm not even sure anymore," Tori said, returning the hug.

When Charlotte broke the embrace, she looked around the barn. "Where's your boyfriend, RJ?"

"He left, went back to Tampa."

"Oh, you poor soul. He left you?" Charlotte hugged her again. "Now, don't you worry. I can drive you back to Tampa if you need."

Tori shot Winnie an annoyed grin. "It's all good."

"I don't mind." Charlotte took Tori's arm, and they strolled toward the front of the barn. "Besides, the shop will be closed for the Fourth and for repairs to the greenhouse. I can drive you back tomorrow."

"I don't think I'm going back."

"What?" Charlotte said and stopped.

Tori halted alongside her. "I don't have a job to go back to. RJ isn't speaking to me. I'm not sure I even want to go back."

"Are you staying here?" Charlotte looked flustered. "What are you going to do?"

"I don't know yet. All I know is that today is the Fourth and I have a parade and fireworks to watch and I don't have to worry about it until the fifth."

Charlotte chuckled and waved at the twins. "We could dress you up like a dwarf if you want to join us on the float."

"No, thanks. I'll watch from the sidelines."

"Whatever you feel up to. We'll chat later." Charlotte released her hand and herded the twins away from the float.

Howard passed them as they left the barn. He grabbed Tori's arm and said, "Did you talk to Winnie?"

He stared at her for several seconds, and Tori wondered if he knew more than he was letting on.

"You seem upset. I hope everything is copesetic," he said.

"It's fine." She broke free of his grip. "Thank you for asking."

They maintained eye contact for several seconds without speaking. Turning, she ran after Charlotte, into the house.

That afternoon, Tori sat on the curb along Main Street, among the hundreds of people downtown ready to watch a variety of floats and organizations cruise down the parade route. She waved a small American flag to join in the festivities. To be honest, it was the last thing on earth she felt like doing right then.

The Elroy Springs High School band got things going with a rendition of "Yankee Doodle Dandy." They marched along near the courthouse, up one side of the street, and around the roundabout where the town founder's statue stood, and then back down the other side of the street. A green John Deere tractor followed them, and Tori watched it pull the first float along.

Edison Beyer joined Tori at the curb. She looked over at him. The Canon camera swung from his neck.

"Where's your float?" she asked.

"I'm a 'catch the beads' kinda guy," he said. He raised the camera to his face and snapped a picture. Putting the camera down, he turned and grinned at Tori. "Not a 'throw them from a moving vehicle' kinda guy."

"Good for you." Tori looked away and admired the floats coming down the street.

Mayor Winslow followed next. But instead of having a traditional float or donning a sports car with his name on its side, he drove a road grader with signs reading: SMOOTHER ROADS AHEAD, indicating he'd address the many potholes if reelected.

"So," Edison said, "I hear you're not going back to Tampa."

"Doesn't look like it."

"You want your old job back at the *Gazette*?" he asked as the mayor's float went by.

"Really?" She hadn't thought that far ahead. In fact, she hadn't thought of anything but Darla, since Mike made his revelation the previous night.

The high school cheerleaders and the color guard followed the mayor, dancing in sync and twirling large American flags. The veterans had the first real float, with red, white, and blue streamers and a giant eagle. Next, the Rotary club rolled by with a giant Statue of Liberty, followed by a float with the members of the PTA—dedicated to Brooke Martin.

Tori saw Winnie's float, and nudged Edison. She pointed at Mike, who looked charming in blue tights, a puffy shirt, and satin cape. Charlotte, as Snow White, and their kids, as the dwarves, stood beside him, each with a hand around a heavy horizontal rope for stability. Winnie wore a gray robe and a pointed, black witch's hat that covered the bandage on her forehead. She threw plastic apples from the float and handed a couple to the twins to throw too. The children who caught the apples opened them, letting the Tootsie Rolls and Jolly Ranchers spill out.

The parade rolled on for another hour, until the heat of the day brought with it rolling rain clouds. As expected, midafternoon showers interrupted the festivities, but all rested assured that the bar-b-ques and sparklers would resume in the evening.

Shortly after dark, Tori returned to Winnie's house. Fireworks in the distance sounded like the rumble of faraway thunder. She looked at the sky. Brilliant, glittering lights exploded above the trees and came showering down over the lake. More fireworks launched with a loud wheeze and lit the night with dazzling flashes of reds, blues, and silvery whites.

She watched the show for a few seconds, and then entered the house through the back door, expecting four welcoming dogs and a pot-bellied pig to accost her. She flipped on the kitchen light, surprised by the quiet. No pets were in sight.

Stepping into the living room, she found the pug snoring in the corner. The Jack Russell terrier and the Chihuahua lay spread out on the couch. Curled up on the lazy chair by the TV, the cocker spaniel lifted a groggy head as if to give Tori a disinterested nod before slipping back to sleep. Outside, fireworks boomed, but didn't disturb the animals.

Tori stepped upstairs and into the spare bedroom. Bacon lay on the rug in the center of the room, just as dead to the world as the dogs downstairs. It snorted with a low grunt that caused waves to ripple down its white, jello-ey belly. She chuckled at the sight.

Grabbing her clothes from the closet, she packed her bags and carried them downstairs. She stepped over the snoring pug and sat at the kitchen table. A scheduled Uber driver would take her to the car rental agency. She could rent another car to drive back to Tampa. Then what? She didn't know.

A box of red plastic apples sat on the table in front of her. It must've been forgotten, left behind when Winnie and Charlotte rushed out of the house earlier that morning in a whirlwind of costumes and props. She stared at the apples a second, thinking about the fairy-tale castle float and the parade. It had been a fun afternoon, and the fireworks show was still going on. Independence Day cannon fire now pierced the night. She wished she could stay.

But she didn't have time to think about that. The Uber driver would be there soon.

Getting up from the table, she listened to the soft snores of the pug compete with the distant explosions of fireworks. The bag of Kibbles sat in its usual place on the counter. Beside it was the small bottle of valerian root oil. She picked it up.

The pug's snoring stopped for a moment and then turned into a gurgled cough. Could dogs develop sleep apnea? She put down the bottle and looked at the box of apples, bright red and bustling with temptation—filled with Tootsie Rolls and an assortment of Jolly Ranchers. She picked one up and opened the top. A cherry Jolly Rancher sat inside it. She looked back at the bottle of valerian root.

"Poison apples," she whispered. She glanced at the empty key hook by the door. Brooke's keys with the brass capital *B* hanging below the ring had disappeared a couple of days ago. Now Winnie's were gone too. Howard probably had them. Tori considered the apple in her hand. "Poison apples."

She dropped it into the box, grabbed her cell phone, and dialed the hospital.

"Yes," she said when the switchboard operator answered, "I'm checking on Darla Martin. Can you connect me to her room?"

"I'm sorry. Darla Martin has checked out."

"Checked out? Who checked her out?"

"Sheriff Bennett," the woman said. "About an hour ago."

"Sheriff Bennett?" Tori ended the call. Knocking the box of apples off the table, scattering them across the floor, she rushed out the back door.

CHAPTER THIRTY-ONE

WHAT_V_R I AM, YOU MAD_ M_

Tori took Winnie's runabout across the lake, watching the southern sky as a volley of sparkling white flares shot skyward with high-pitched whistles. The lights exploded in an intense shower of red, blue, and silver-white streamers that flew wide apart and faded like drops of hot water on a griddle. A muffled cheer rang out from crowds on either side of the lake.

Bringing the boat to the shore, she hopped out and headed for the remains of the Martin house.

At the front, Tori expected to find a vehicle parked beside Brooke's minivan. Though there was none, Tori knew Darla was here, somewhere inside that house. The cinder block and siding remained, but the windows and doors had burned out. Tori stepped onto the porch and pulled two flimsy strips of yellow police tape from the door frame. She peered into the gaping hole where the front door had been and wrinkled her nose against the stench.

Darla had been brought here again. Tori knew it. She could feel it.

She faced the ruined room. Light filtered through the caved-in roof, illuminating the blackened walls. Charred wires and frayed chunks of insulation dangled from the ceiling. Puddles of pasty black soot pooled in the corners. Melted furniture, electronics, and photos littered the floor, along with solid masses of unidentifiable things the fire hadn't digested.

Tori stepped inside. Her foot slid on the slick floor planks, covered with a muddy film of wet ashes. Careful to avoid the puddles and keep her clothes from brushing against the walls, she made her way through the entry hall.

One of Darla's drawings had somehow survived and lay on the dining room table. The edges of the paper were burnt, but the drawing itself—the black sky, the water tower, her mother's stick figure body—remained. Something, some flash of motion, caught Tori's attention and she put the drawing down.

She peered out the window opening. Her eyes searched the woods. She returned to the porch.

From there she could see the water tower. Its rusty tank and rotted pillars stood like a sentry watching over the house. The weathered letters: "BROOKE WILL YOU MARRY ME?" had almost faded away. Or perhaps, it was too dark to see them. The structure was thrown into an abrupt silhouette when a rocket shot up and exploded over the lake. The faint clamor of a faraway crowd burst into a roar of approval.

She noticed movement again. In the dead orange grove. Something or someone was running. Tori moved closer to the edge of the porch. Darla must be out there.

And she knew who was with the child.

They were headed for the tower.

Tori raced into the yard and into the dark grove. Whipping through brush and limbs, she plowed through the trees, ignoring the scrapes and scratches to her arms. A branch cut her cheek. She swatted at it, wiping the blood away with the back of her arm. Picking up speed, she willed her legs to move faster and made it to the edge of the grove. The crickets stopped, and the woods around her turned still.

For a second, she could have sworn she saw Brooke out there ... standing in the clearing, flowing white, glowing, and looking up.

Tori raised her head. The dirty white, brownish-red structure loomed high above her. A loud thud echoed in it. Followed by another ... movement within the drum. When she looked back, Brooke had vanished ... if she was even there in the first place.

Tori ran into the clearing and paced around the legs of the tower. Finding the rotten ladder, she paused. The banging above grew louder. She had no choice.

Taking a deep breath, she climbed the ladder. She didn't look down. Focusing on the top, she forced herself to climb. The wood splintered in her hands, but she kept moving upwards.

At the top, she maneuvered off the ladder and onto the narrow platform around the drum. She shuffled across the ledge area, running a hand along the rough, orangey metal railing. Pausing, she listened. There *was* rustling inside.

That narrow opening, barely large enough for her to squeeze through, waited for her like she remembered. Kneeling, she peered inside. A flashlight would've helped. However, she could sense movement within the blackness ... slight movement near the beams of moonlight shining through the rusted holes in the ceiling.

Squeezing through the opening, she entered the drum. Her foot sloshed in the muddy puddles and she noticed something shiny in the shallow water. It sparkled in the weak light, and she bent to pick it up. Her fingers grasped a thin chain and she lifted a large pewter *B* from the dirty water. Several keys dangled from the ring, jingling—Brooke's spare house keys and the minivan key.

Something moved in the shadows along the curved wall across from Tori, and she turned her head toward it. A black mass huddled by the floor, something solid, something breathing. A child. Darla.

Tori splashed toward her and dropped to her knees. She touched Darla's cheek. Their eyes locked, communicating without words. Darla's lip trembled, a thick rope hung from the girl's neck. Tori gasped and reached for it, was about to remove it when she felt a pinch on her neck.

Stepping back, she swung around. "What the—?"

A shadow whipped behind her. Moonlight glinted off the syringe in the figure's hand. When she stepped from the shadows, the pale light hit her face.

"I had a feeling you'd show up," Tori said. "You can stop with the theatrics, Carla."

"It's Charlotte." She dropped the syringe and dusted dirt from her blue-and-yellow gown. Moonlight glinted off her Snow White tiara. "And weren't you expecting my husband?"

"I was expecting Brooke's murderer."

"I would sit down, if I was you." She lifted her dress with two hands and traipsed through the puddle, the back edge of her hem skimming the top of the muddy water. "You've been drugged with a high dose of valerian root. I grow it at the flower shop."

Tori raised a hand and stumbled backwards. She placed her other arm around Darla. "Why are you doing this?"

Charlotte's voice echoed in the dank drum. "Because I'm will not allow anything or anyone to come between Michael and me."

Tori felt lightheaded. "What do you mean?" she said. "Who's coming between you and … and your husband?"

"First, Brooke, with the news about my Michael being that, that bastard child's real daddy." Charlotte's head turned toward Darla, who hid behind Tori. Charlotte smiled, mocking the little girl. "Now, now child. You already knew that, didn't you? Your mommy was making plans."

"You think Brooke and Mike were making plans to leave you?"

"No," she said. Her eyes enlarged and mouth opened wide with horror, as if the thought never even occurred to her. "I think Brooke had plans. She wanted my husband." She hesitated, and then added, "Michael loves me and only me."

"I don't know what went on between Brooke and Mike." Tori raised a hand but couldn't hold it steady. "You need to take it up with him. Darla has nothing to do with this."

"She has everything to do with this!" Charlotte stomped a foot, splashing muddy water, and lunged at the girl.

Darla screamed and moved farther behind Tori's leg.

"The greenhouse," Tori said, inching toward the opening with Darla cowering behind her. Her head spun and she struggled to keep it clear. "You cut that branch. You tried to kill Darla."

"But Winnie whisked her out in the nick of time." Charlotte stepped with Tori, keeping an eye on Darla. "If there was any justice in this world, that glass shard would've cut out her eye."

"And you..." Tori stumbled, stretched a hand against the curved wall, and fell to the muddy floor. "You kept bringing Darla here, to the water tower?"

"I was hoping she would fall. A clean, quick accident. And when that didn't work, I tried to burn her alive." Charlotte laughed and pointed at Darla. "She made me into this. Don't you get it? She and her slutty mother made me into this. I'm not a violent person. I don't hurt people. But... but whatever I am now, they made me."

"You tore the note ...." Tori fought to get the words out. "From Ash's letter. You tore the note."

"And you," Charlotte said, leaning to speak into Tori's face, "don't you play innocent in all this, little Miss Stick-Your-Nose-Where-It-Doesn't-Belong."

Tori forced herself up onto her arms and knees. Darla stood beside her, trying to help.

Charlotte moved closer. "Miss Nosy-Nose," Charlotte said, spitting the words. "I know you're still in love with my husband. I know you have designs on him. You turned me into this as well. You're just as guilty as they are. You have as much blood on your hands as they do."

"You're cra—" Tori struggled to speak. "Crazy."

"Am I?" Charlotte brought her index finger to her mouth as if she was pondering the thought. "Is it crazy to keep your family together? Is it crazy to keep immoral, soulless women away from your husband?" She stood at arm's length from Tori and Darla and placed her hands on her hips. "I will not let anything tear my family apart."

With a flash of the blue-and-yellow gown, Charlotte grabbed Darla by the hair. As the little girl screamed, Charlotte dragged her to the opening in the wall and hauled her through it.

Tori struggled to follow. Crawling, she fought the blackness from swallowing her and willed herself to keep moving.

She scooted to the edge of the tank. Forcing herself through the narrow, rusty opening, she dropped onto the catwalk. The night was brighter outside than in the drum, and her eyes blurred. Maybe it was the over-dose of valerian root in her system. She raised a hand to shield them, when a rope looped around her neck.

A noise came out of Tori's throat as her hands grasped the rope. It tightened, cutting off her air supply.

She gasped. Struggled for a breath. Heard Charlotte rant.

"You will not tear my family apart!" Charlotte's voice echoed in the night as a volley of fireworks exploded like thunder over the lake.

She forced Tori to her feet, pulling her by the rope to the edge of the catwalk. Tori struggled, but unconsciousness was overtaking her. She felt as if she was watching herself being pushed toward the ledge, leaning over it, while Charlotte tied one end of the rope to the upper railing. Then, like a dream, she felt a strong push. Flipped end over heel. Then, weightlessness.

Light. Airy. Weightless.

She was falling … falling … falling. Seconds felt like an eternity and everything around her—the night sky, the wind, the ground—moved in slow motion. And for a brief second, she saw her again. Brooke. Standing on the ground in flowing white, looking up.

A painful constriction yanked Tori's neck. Violently. Midflight.

The noose tightened. Pinched. Bit. Erupted her senses. Her throat burned. Gravity pulled her body. The rope dug deep beneath her chin. Cutting off airflow. Heat rose in her face. Her chest ached. Painful, gripping pressure.

The drug no longer had any effect. And in that second, she knew she was hanging to death.

Her legs flailed. Arms thrashed. Fingers scratched at the fibers of the rope. She fought for breath.

Struggled.

Gasped.

Kicked.

Wheezed.

Spit.

Then something solid. Firm.

It gripped her arm. A hand. She fought against it. Panic overtook over. Kicking. Flailing. An arm embraced her waist and pulled her sideways, toward the metal framework. The rope loosened around her throat.

Air rushed into her lungs.

She inhaled.

She gulped deep breaths, panicked breaths, and turned to find Mike's blue eyes staring back at her. He had an arm wrapped around her, clutching her to him.

"Are you okay?" His voice seemed out of sync with his lips. She wondered if she was dreaming.

She tried to answer but couldn't speak. Her throat burned. She managed a weak nod.

He smiled again and lifted the rope from around her neck. The hard rope scraped her chin. It was almost off when a heeled foot from above connected with Mike's jaw. His head snapped back. Tori opened her mouth to protest when she felt her body swing, pushed by the momentum of Mike's backwards fall. Again, the rope constricted around her throat and she felt herself hanging.

Her eyes bulged.

His arm swung out toward her. He reached forward. Grabbed her again. Pulled her close. With one hand, he loosened the rope gripping her throat. With the other, he grabbed the edge of Charlotte's dress. She kicked at him and screamed obscenities. He held her in place.

Tori tried to scream but could barely gasp as she felt herself falling backwards, about to swing out over the ledge. She wouldn't be able to survive another strangulation. She knew that.

He released Charlotte and grabbed a firm hold of Tori. He removed the rope from around her throat as she clung to the metal framework. Above them, Charlotte screamed again and climbed upwards. He climbed after her.

Tori gulped a breath. Shut her eyes for a second and hoisted herself up. Only a heartbeat behind, she watched, helpless.

Mike grasped Charlotte's leg. She kicked him in the face. His nose erupted with blood. He reached for her again but lost his grip. She climbed to the upper platform. Mike came up right behind her.

Tori scrambled upwards too. She made it to the catwalk and raised her head.

Darla ran, making her way around the drum. She wasn't fast enough. Charlotte grabbed hold of the girl, just as Mike stepped over the railing and onto the platform.

"Get away from me." Charlotte wrapped her arms around Darla. "You come any closer and I will toss her over the railing."

He raised a free hand, surrendering. "I won't come any closer. Just don't hurt her."

"It's not fair." Tears streamed down Charlotte's cheeks. "I just want my family. That's all. I want my family."

"No one is taking your family away from you."

"How can we be a family when this … this abomination is out there? This reminder?" Charlotte pulled on Darla's hair. "This child will always be pulling on my husband, taking him away from us. We have our own children. They need their daddy."

"I'm not leaving you or the twins. Our family is fine."

"No one will ever take you away from us. From me." She grabbed Darla by the shoulders and yanked her toward the railing. She tried to force Darla over, but the girl clung to the upper railing. Charlotte knelt and spit in Darla's face. "You will not take my husband away from me!"

She lifted Darla till her feet came off the platform grid. Her body leaned over the railing.

"Do you understand?" Charlotte pushed her till the child's upper body folded over the railing.

Darla let out a scream.

Charlotte screamed louder: "You will not take him away from me!"

Mike approached them as Tori's hand reached up from below. Grabbing Charlotte's ankle, she yanked hard.

Charlotte gasped and slipped. One leg stumbled off the platform as her face cracked against the lower railing. Her body went limp, her gown blowing in the wind. Darla tumbled forward, crying. Mike reached for her and grasped her shorts.

The railing broke. Darla and Mike tumbled. Charlotte gasped. Tori wheezed. Mike held Darla with one arm and gripped the iron framework with his free hand. She struggled to move toward him. Could she reach them in time?

"Hold on," her voice squeaked. The words gushed from her sore throat. "I'm coming."

Mike looked at her. His hand was slipping.

"Hol—" She couldn't get the words out as she inched across the railing. She stretched out a hand.

He lost his grip. His free hand slipped. With one last glance he flashed a quick smile at Tori, and he and Darla dropped.

Air raced out of her throat, without sound. She watched them fall. He held Darla in his arms. Protecting her. Holding her up with both hands.

And when his body slammed into the ground, it cushioned her fall.

Tori couldn't speak. She watched Darla, startled, the wind knocked out of her, slowly climb on her hands and knees, on top of his broken body.

CHAPTER THIRTY-TWO

_NE F_R THE R_AD

One month later ...

The wind blew against Tori as she walked toward Brooke's grave site. Winnie and Howard stood next to the headstone. Darla knelt beside the dirt mound. She held a white peace lily in her hand and laid it on the ground over her mother. Ash lifted the little girl into his arms as Tori approached.

Winnie waved and smiled. The cut above her eye had faded into a pale, pinkish line on her forehead. "How you holding up?" she asked.

Tori shuddered. "Better than I look." She self-consciously raised a hand to her neck, her fingertips grazing her own pale, pinkish line, a remembrance of the noose digging deep into her throat.

"Never be ashamed of a scar," Howard said as he extended a hand to Tori then glanced at Winnie. "It simply means you were stronger than whatever tried to kill you."

"Thank you." Tori nodded and removed her hand. "Maybe I can cover it with some makeup or something."

Winnie took his hand and kissed his cheek. Tori looked past them to find Ash and Darla on the other side of the headstone. The little girl laid her head on her father's shoulder.

"I guess she can rest in peace now," Tori said as she came up beside him. She wrapped her arms around them both.

Ash returned the hug best he could and whispered in Tori's ear. "I'm sorry for everything that happened."

Tori nodded and turned to Darla. She placed a hand on the girl's back. "Your mother was an amazing. We'll never forget her."

Darla remained unresponsive, her head still on her father's shoulder.

"She loved you very much," Tori added, then released them. She looked up at Ash. "She loved you both."

"We'll miss them both." Winnie called to them. She held an urn with her brother's ashes. "So, where do we lay him down to rest?"

"On a pitcher's mound," Howard said with a chuckle.

That made Ash laugh too. "I think he'd like that." he said.

Winnie patted his shoulder, still holding the urn in her other arm. "Mike had a good life."

"He saved my life," Tori said. "I guess I owe him."

She took the urn from Winnie's hand and turned to Ash. "Are you two headed out?"

"We're staying with my parents in Michigan for a while," he said, pointing toward the entry gates. His truck and the U-Haul sat parked along the curb.

Winne turned toward the parking lot, then back at Ash. "Are you coming back?"

"Probably. Maybe." Ash set Darla down and took her hand, He led her away from her mother's grave.

"We'll miss you," Winnie yelled. "Stay in touch!"

"Wait," Tori called out, and ran to him. She dug into her pocket and pulled out the wedding band she'd found in his house. She placed it in his palm and closed his fingers around it.

"I think this belongs to you," she said, squeezing his hand in hers. She kissed his cheek.

He smiled and hugged her one last time. Finally, he turned and helped Darla into the U-Haul truck. Then he swung into the driver's side and started the engine. As the U-Haul backed away, Winnie came up beside Tori and draped an arm around her shoulder.

"So, what happened to Charlotte?" Winnie asked. "I

haven't even spoken to my sister-in-law since ... well, since everything happened."

"From what I understand, she's locked up somewhere." The urn felt heavy in Tori's arms. "How are the kids taking it?"

"I haven't told them yet."

"Oh," Tori said. She turned to face the headstone.

"Howard and I," Winnie said, gesturing to her husband still standing next to Brooke's headstone, "we're applying for custody of the twins."

Tori refused to look at her and didn't respond. They stood in silence for several moments.

* * * *

In a white locked room with six folding tables and chairs, Charlotte stood among the patients and made her way to the painted block wall. Gazing out a narrow rectangular window with outside bars, she hit the pane with her fists.

"Michael!" she screamed. "Where are you, Michael, darling? Where are you?"

Her raised voice caused two men, who'd been catatonically sitting at a folding table, to scream with her. Another woman with wildly uncombed white hair fell to her knees, folded her arms over her head, and sobbed. A young-ish, toothless woman, leaning forward on a walker, giggled and clapped at the attendants in white as they rushed into the room and approached Charlotte.

"Michael!" she screamed, banging on the glass.

The two men came up beside her and took hold of her arms. One of them injected her upper left arm as the other leaned her body back toward him.

Charlotte's screaming faded as her heart slowed and her breathing calmed. She moved away from the window with the two men. With hazy eyes, she glanced to the one on her right, the shorter, cuter of the two men. She grinned.

"My husband is coming," she said.

The attendants said nothing and led her to a folding

table. Sitting on the metal chair, she looked up at the man, staring into his kind eyes.

"We have twins," she said. "You want to see pictures of them?"

* * * *

Tori left Elroy Springs and took Route 103 / Clay Pit Road along the lake. The potholes shook her Camry, wreaking havoc with the alignment. She passed the bridge, noticing the repaired railing. Its shiny new metal strips hinted at the damage Ash's truck had caused, which seemed like a million years ago. She rolled over the bumpy railroad tracks. The crossing arm still bore scuff marks and one long crack where it had struck the back of Mike's squad car. She continued along the two-lane highway until coming to a dusty drive with a mailbox marked YOUNGER. She turned left and drove downhill, through dense woods, toward the water. After a few hundred yards, she came around a sharp bend and had to brake hard. The drive dissolved into the lake.

She sat, bemused by the way life works out sometimes, thinking it must be fate's idea of irony. To her right, just beyond yards of overgrown bushes and trees, sat her old house.

She rolled forward and stopped beside a white patrol car. Sheriff Torres was waiting on the front porch, holding the FORECLOSURE sign and post.

"Looks like you pulled that right out of the ground," she yelled to him as she approached the front steps.

"Single-handedly." He waved the sign, flinging dirt from the post. "I wanted to welcome you home."

"Home. I like the sound of that." Tori shook her head. Yes, it had to be fate's idea of irony. "I cleaned out my apartment in Tampa and my furniture was delivered last week."

"I saw." He looked back at the front door, and over at her. "How's the new job?"

"The *Elroy Springs Gazette*? It'll tide me over until I

finish my book."

"Your book about us?" he asked. "About Brooke?"

Tori looked away. She focused on her home's exterior. "It needs a lot of work."

"If you need a hand ...."

"Thank you," she said, stepping onto the porch and opening the front door. "You coming inside?"

"I gotta get back to the station." He tapped the gold badge on his chest. With a tip of his hat, he headed to the rear of his patrol car. Opening the trunk, he laid the sign inside it. Pausing, he turned to Tori. "Hells bells, Tori ... it's good to have you back."

She watched him drive away, and then stepped into the house.

Boxes of books, all her biographies, encyclopedias, self-help, and that enormous collections of true crime, cluttered every free space of floor. Mismatched bookcases leaned against the walls, their empty shelves waiting to be filled. Her sofa and coffee table stretched haphazardly in the center of the dining room, still sitting where the movers had left them. Above the fireplace, the picture of Mike as a teenager, wearing his baseball uniform and holding a trophy, rested on the mantle. She picked it up and stared at it for several seconds and set it back down. She stepped into the kitchen and opened a bottle of wine.

Returning to the den, she sat in the corner and propped her feet up on a box. Her laptop fit comfortably on her lap and she typed the first word ... then the second. Her hands skimmed across the keyboard as though the ideas in her head were pouring out through her fingertips. Whole paragraphs appeared on the lightened screen—of their own volition.

On Saturday evening, June 23rd, Brooke Martin, mother, wife, teacher, and friend, was found hanging from the old water tower on her property.

Tori wrote long into the night, with no awareness of time passing. The screen kept on filling up with words. She stopped typing when she heard music coming from outside. A soft glow lit the boathouse by the dock.

Getting up, she opened the slider and stepped onto the back porch. Justin Timberlake's "Can't Stop the Feeling" blared in the dark, coming from the lake. She ran across the yard, to the dock, and climbed the steps to the boathouse. The music was coming from above, and she scrambled up the side to the roof. She looked over the edge.

Sitting there among cartons of Chinese food and a purple iPod, RJ turned his head and grinned. "I got you chicken lo mein and sweet 'n' sour chicken." He held up a six-pack of beer. "And Coronas."

Tori opened her mouth. "What—what are you doing here?"

"I quit the show."

"You what? You're not a cameraman?"

"I've still got my camera." He twisted the cap off a bottle and held it out to her. "And my YouTube channel has over five thousand subs. You know what that means?"

"You're a paranormal investigator?" She remained on the edge of the roof.

"Well, I got a case." He set down the bottle and grabbed a carton of lo mein. "You remember Bobby Greene?"

"Of course. How's his family? How're his friends holding up?"

"Looks like April is communicating with Bobby, from the great beyond." He pointed to his equipment bag lying below them on the deck. "She got EVPs from the kid. Bobby's father was about to blow the whistle on some illegal dumping of phosphates into Tampa Bay, and it's all there."

"You mean—"

"I mean, we've got some digging to do. We've got some dirty dealings to expose." He twisted the noodles around the plastic fork and scooped them into his mouth. He continued talking with his mouth full. "This is going to be huge. And maybe not just *An Unreasonable Woman* huge, but *Silent Spring* huge."

Tori smiled. Climbing onto the roof, she rushed to him and wrapped her arms around his neck, kissing him square on the lips with more passion than she ever dared.

ABOUT THE AUTHOR

JC Gatlin lives in Tampa, Florida and wrote a monthly column in New Tampa Style Magazine. He has written three
indie mystery novels set in Florida and is a member of the
Florida Writer's Association.

Made in the USA
Lexington, KY
02 December 2019